BAKER, LIAR, CON MAN, THIEF

ESCAPING THE LAW ONE IDENTITY AT A TIME

DJ ADLER

WILDBLUE
PRESS

WildBluePress.com

BAKER, LIAR, CON MAN, THIEF published by:
WILDBLUE PRESS
P.O. Box 102440
Denver, Colorado 80250

WILDBLUE PRESS is registered at the U.S. Patent and Trademark Offices.

ISBN 978-1-960332-77-6 Trade Paperback
ISBN 978-978-1-960332-78-3 eBook
ISBN 978-1-960332-76-9 Hardback

Cover design © 2024 WildBlue Press. All rights reserved.

Interior Formatting and Cover Design by Elijah Toten, www.totencreative.com

BAKER, LIAR, CON MAN, THIEF

DEDICATION

This book took over twenty years to write and serves as a time capsule for everyone involved in that time of our lives.

I first want to dedicate this book to my beloved mother, Sunny. She helped me remember much of what happened to us, and she read about half of the chapters before she passed on during the COVID-19 pandemic. I miss her every day.

I next want to express profound thanks to Michelle and Ilene. They remember the incidents in this book and took the time to read, edit, and reread every chapter from the beginning. Their encouragement has been invaluable.

I also want to thank my editor and true believer, Eve Porinchak. Her editing has been a masterclass in writing, and her experience and optimism helped drive this book to completion.

Finally, to David and Joey. They were taken before their times and are missed by all.

DISCLAIMER

This story is based on real events and people, but certain liberties have been taken with the dialogue, names, some characters, and some facts for storytelling.

The criminal activity depicted in this story is real unless any statute of limitations hasn't run out. In that case, everything is fictitious, and this story shouldn't be construed as an admission or confession to any criminal wrongdoing.

PROLOGUE

Summer of 1982

THE bus is hotter than a habanero. Inside it must be at least ten degrees hotter than the outside temperature of ninety-plus. The humidity clings to the skin like a bad habit and forms beads of sweat on the heads and faces of the passengers, drenching their clothes and stinging their eyes. Body odor and feral testosterone give the air a rancid bite.

The bus is equipped with perpetually locked, non-tinted windows. The inadequate air conditioner wheezes a pathetic Freon-induced trickle of cold air to cool a cabin filled with federal prisoners, all wearing the same orange jumpsuits accessorized with chains connecting their ankles, wrists, and waist. As a result, each prisoner can only raise their arms a couple of inches higher than their navels—which is why they can't blot the sweat from their heads or faces.

David Adler sits three rows back next to the window. At first, he enjoyed watching the world pass by, having spent the previous year in a federal jail cell awaiting trial. But after the first day, it becomes a painful reminder of the world he won't see for the next five years.

The bus travels with no discernable pattern to every federal hell-hole prison east of Missouri. It started at the Chicago Metropolitan Correctional Center and stopped for days in Terre Haute, Marion, Leavenworth, and Lewisburg. Now, it's heading to Atlanta. At each stop, the prisoners get to spend quality time with some of the most deranged and evil badasses in the prison system.

Thank the Lord they aren't allowed any personal property, because most of them would have been shaken down on the first day—hell, make that the first hour—of the first stop.

This stretch of the ride is twelve hours non-stop, and all David can think of as they pass into Kentucky is how badly he needs to take a piss. There are no rest breaks on this bus trip to hell, and heaven help the prisoner who pisses himself and gets up with a dark orange wet spot on the crotch of his jumpsuit going into the general population of another high-security prison.

David tries not to think about the pain in his bladder by remembering what brought him here in the first place. After hearing dozens of inmates talk about how they were innocent, were entrapped, were victims of unjust laws or, at the very least, victims of an unjust judicial system, he knows that his circumstance is the consequence of his own decisions. He has no excuses but curses himself for his mistakes.

Before his arrest, David, still a teenager, was wanted in Florida, Louisiana, Arizona, California, Texas, Nevada, New Jersey, Wisconsin, and Illinois by the FBI, the Secret Service, and, oh yes… by organized crime families. But he wasn't alone. His partner in crime was his mother and together, they were the most sought-after con artists you never heard of… until now.

PART I: HOLLYWOOD, FLORIDA

CHAPTER 1

Ft. Lauderdale, Florida, 1973

DAVID answers the ringing desk phone. It's unusual for the phone to ring after business hours at HPC Finance. Before he can speak his usual "HPC Finance, may I help you?" he hears a deep, sinister male voice:

"I see you." The voice is breathy, like someone trying to impersonate the Un-cola Man in those Seven-Up commercials. "I can see you right there at your desk through the scope of my hunting rifle. You gonna die tonight, and you only have yourself to blame."

HPC's branch office where David works is in a strip shopping mall, as are most small consumer loan companies. It isn't hard to believe that someone could see David behind his desk when it's ten feet in front of a large pane of storefront glass. It's night, and the bright fluorescent lights are blazing. David and the office are lit up like a stadium on game day against the dark parking lot.

David sits at his desk on the other end of the phone connection. If he's disturbed by the call, he doesn't show it. He knows who is on the other end of the line, even with the absurd attempt to disguise the voice. Sure, it's a bit extreme, but it isn't the first threat he has suffered since becoming a branch representative, which is a fancy word for collection agent, at HPC Finance.

David rolls his eyes and cradles the phone between his shoulder and cheek. He reaches into a hanging file folder to his left and removes a file labeled *Devon Green*. He immediately notes the date and begins his shorthand. Notations on accounts are absolute necessities, as hammered home by the office manager who coined the clever mantra, "If the note ain't writ then the collection's shit."

David writes the first entry. *DC*, which means "debtor called." This is a badge of success for locating deadbeat debtors.

"Yeah, well, don't you think it would be easier to simply bring in your payment rather than commit a homicide? Besides, if you were going to kill me, you wouldn't have called first. I recognize your voice… Reverend. Just bring me twenty-five dollars by five p.m. tomorrow and I'll take your name off the call list for another month."

The phone clicks off.

Lester Jones, the assistant manager, leans back in his chair in the adjoining cubical. His extra fifty pounds almost make the chair tip over. "Was that Reverend Devon Green? Did he agree to pay? I'd love to cross him off the list. We're just a couple of thousand dollars from making our monthly break."

Lester is a collection lifer. He's built like a fire hydrant. He regularly wears short-sleeved, button-down shirts with waist buttons that strain against his pot belly. Once he bragged about having ten pairs of the same eggshell-colored pants so that he didn't have to think too much when he got dressed. He wears a crew cut for the same reason: low maintenance. He makes a career collecting money from people who are the least able to pay—and he relishes the perceived sport of it.

Before the federal government passed laws to protect debtors from overly enthusiastic (and in Lester's case, sadistic) bill collectors, it was pretty much the Wild West in the collection game. Lester loves to harass the deadbeats. He calls them every hour around the clock. He uses every racist slur in his hillbilly lexicon. He threatens spouses and children. He loves it when the debtors yell, plead, and threaten. But what he really loves is when they cry and beg. All of this is to get the deadbeats angry enough to come into the office with enough of a payment to allow Lester to cross them off the list for a month.

Lester knows that once a debtor enters the office, no matter how angry they were before they get there, they'll pay at least the minimum amount owed. To David, it's an unexplained phenomenon how so many people pushed to the brink of homicidal rage will come into the office and timidly bring money as if they're supplicating the gods. Every payment is an affirmation to Lester not only that he's good at his job, but that he's a better man than all the deadbeats who dare challenge his ability to collect.

"It was the reverend," says David. "Reverend" is an honorarium that Devin Green received from a Baptist church on the mean side of Commercial Boulevard. Lots of debtors have nicknames inside the office. Devin Green was always called "Reverend," not as a sign of respect but ironically, as if he lacked the character to deserve the name.

"Sadly, the reverend hung up before committing to a payment." David marks the file *CD* for "client disconnected" as opposed to the coveted *P2P* for "promise to pay." "He said he had me in the crosshairs of a hunting rifle."

Lester laughs. "Where the hell would he get the money to buy a hunting rifle? I thought he was completely broke. Fuckin' liar. I suppose we'll have to set him up for a chase." "Chase" is what Lester calls it when he goes into the field and personally confronts the deadbeats.

Lester continues, "Soften him up a little first, though. Put him on tonight's call list."

David reluctantly adds the file to a stack of others in his cheap plastic briefcase. "Sure, Les," he replies sarcastically. "What's one more wake-up call?"

That night, David groggily wakes up to a trilling that comes from the clock radio he set before he dozed off. He gets off the rack and looks at the clock. Two a.m. He reaches into his briefcase and removes all the files that he took from the office.

He slowly drags himself into the kitchen where the phone is. Not only is he still fighting to stay awake, but he also dreads what he knows he has to do. Unlike Lester, David doesn't have the same appreciation for harassment. Nevertheless, he needs the job. He places the phone in front of him, next to the file folders. He sighs heavily, mentally prolonging the task ahead.

Wake-up calls are one of the worst parts of his job. He gets up and searches a cluttered junk drawer for a pen. No ink. He goes back to the drawer and settles for a dull pencil. He takes a steak knife out of another drawer and whittles the pencil to a serviceable point. Then he sits back down, picks out a file, and begins to dial. He starts with Reverend Devon Green.

The phone rings. A sleepy child answers. "Hello?"

"Hello," David says, "Is Reverend Green in?"

"No, sir," the child answers in a pitiful drone.

"Is the reverend your daddy?"

"Yes, sir."

"And he's not there?" David asks incredulously.

A pause. There is an absence of sound, as if someone is holding their hand over the phone. It's a sound that David knows well from many late nights of harassing phone calls.

The child's voice returns. "No, sir."

"Is your momma there?"

"No, sir."

"Is there any adult there?"

"No, sir."

Frustrated, David takes a long pause. Then he decides to bait the child. "Tell me, is your daddy truly a reverend?"

"Yes, sir."

"And does he preach the Good Book on Sunday?"

"Yes, sir."

"And are you proud of your daddy?"

"Yes, sir." The boy's voice perks up with pride.

"Tell me then, how your daddy can stand up and preach the Good Book on Sunday and then have his baby lie to me like a sinner on Monday?"

David hears the phone drop. In the background, he can hear the child calling, "Daddy!"

The phone gets picked up. "This is Reverend Green. I'll bring in a twenty-five-dollar payment tomorrow. Now stop calling me at this God-forsaken time."

He hangs up the phone, and David marks the file *P2P* with tomorrow's date. He gets no satisfaction in the notation, and he silently regrets what kind of person the job has turned him into.

He suddenly feels a gentle hand on his shoulder that nevertheless makes him jump. His mother, Sunny Rossi, gives David a hug from behind. "Hi, honey. Can I get you anything?"

David shakes his head groggily while he caresses his mother's hand. "No. Thanks, Mom. I'll be headed back to bed soon. Just have a few more calls to make."

"You work too hard, you know. Remember, you've got to be up at eight in the morning. Try to get some more sleep. Okay?"

"Sure, Mom. As soon as I make these calls."

His mother goes back to bed and, half-asleep, David makes ten similar calls with varying results. Barely able to keep his eyes open, he carries the files back to his bedroom. Saying that David's room looks like it was hit by a tornado gives tornadoes too much credit for neatness. Every surface area, including his unmade bed, is covered in junk and trash. He cascades the files onto his cluttered nightstand and flops into his disheveled bed.

As he drifts off, David considers his nineteen-year-old life already a failure. He works long hours on a fixed wage, and he makes a living by bringing misery into other people's lives. He feels like a third wheel living with his mother and her new husband, Sal Rossi, who is obsessively tidy and as structured as a blueprint. But David consoles himself in his final moments of consciousness because...

He has a plan.

CHAPTER 2

SAL Rossi gazes out at the restaurant dining area of the Abacus Steak House. He has only been a server there for a few months and already he despises the joint. The tips are good, but that's not because the diners are particularly good tippers. The food is cheap, and the portions are more than adequate, so the joint is always packed. Sal is responsible for such a maze of tables that he feels like a circus juggler. It's a lot of work, but more diners means more tips.

The owner is Dick Greenwood. Tall, middle-aged, with graying hair that makes him look more distinguished than old. He's never seen in public without his signature Brooks Brothers suit—today a navy single-breasted—white shirt, and a humorless tie.

Dick and his wife orchestrate the crowds like roadies on a Rolling Stones tour. After so many years, they know exactly how they want everything done from the menu preparation to the service at the front of the house. They know most of their guests personally, and they usher them to tables from the long lines at the door with precision, even when some guests approach Dick with requests for their special table.

Sal is a favorite with the ladies, which makes him a favorite of Dick's. Despite having to wear a mustard-colored uniform with stains from various entrees, Sal is a striking Italian man with muscles that ripple like waves on the Atlantic. He's in his early thirties, with a full head of dark hair, walnut skin, and deep, penetrating brown eyes that partner with a smile both playful and vaguely dangerous. He's as charming as Satan and as confident and playful as a game show host.

But that playful smile turns dark as Sal sees two customers—a couple—saunter into the dining area. A good Catholic boy, he recites a silent Hail Mary and crosses himself to seal the deal that they won't end up at his station. But if Jesus hears his silent prayer, he cedes it to the lord of the dining room, Dick, who ignores it as he sits the couple at Sal's best table.

Sal remembers the woman. A week before, despite Dick's best efforts, she'd sat alone at one of his tables until closing. She didn't want to go home. Sal had noticed the bruising on her face and the tears on her cheeks that she tried to discreetly blot with a white cloth napkin, which became the color of her foundation and eye makeup, revealing her welts and bruises. If Sal wasn't married, he would have suggested that she stay with him rather than go home to be used as one of those new popular aggression relief punching bags. Now here she was back to eat with her insignificant other.

Even if the guy weren't a cowardly asshole, this is the type of guy Sal instinctively hates. He struts in like he's going to knife someone. He wears a white suit, black shirt, and white tie like a wannabe gangster. Sal has known real gangsters most of his life and this *finocchio* wouldn't even get in the door. Even the guy's shoes are black and white. He's tall and thin and vaguely effeminate. He drips condescension as he takes the table like he's ready to play blackjack instead of ordering dinner.

Sal hates men who hit women and wants so badly to take off his skinny tie, slowly come behind this guy while he's choosing between steak and fish, loop the tie around his neck, and tighten the knot until he chokes to death. But

Sal needs his job and is trying to control the temper that has always seemed to get him into trouble.

Sal approaches the table with a pitcher and pours out water into the glasses. He grits his teeth and barely manages the shadow of his normal smile. "Hello… sir," he says to the asshole, although he hates to use the word "sir." It always seems to stick in his throat, especially now. "Can I tell you about today's specials?"

Although a little thin for his taste, the woman has very attractive, long blond hair and a face that belongs on a magazine cover (now that the bruising is gone). She's wearing a sexy red blouse with a plunging neckline that offers a promise of cleavage but doesn't deliver because of her athletic body. She buries her pretty face in the menu without looking up. That implies to Sal she's afraid he might say something to her date about their previous encounter.

The asshole studies the menu through reading glasses perched precariously on the end of his aquiline nose. He holds his hand out, palm facing toward Sal in a gesture of *shut up and wait until I tell you to leave.* Sal uncomfortably waits. Then the guy snatches the menu away from his date and abruptly tosses both menus toward Sal. He motions Sal to pick them up. "We'll both have the four-dollar, ninety-nine-cent steak dinner. Salads and baked potatoes."

Sal takes out a pen and pad and writes this down.

"Water will be fine. And listen to me, boy. She will have her steak medium. She's not picky. But I don't want my steak medium, and I don't want my steak rare. I want it right in between that. Do you understand me, boy?"

"Yes… sir." Sal's grip tightens on the pen. "You want your steak medium rare."

"Exactly. So, don't fuck it up." The asshole dismisses Sal with a wave and turns to talk to his date.

The kitchen at the Abacus is a cavernous affair. The foremost area is an oversized grill arranged in a semi-circle with a counter in front for service from the grill to the wait staff. Three cooks work on the grill, mostly cooking steaks. Spatulas ring off the metal grates like a chorus of metallic crickets.

The head cook is named Samson, which is appropriate because he's huge. He resembles a black Telly Savalas, which is also ironic because he constantly sucks a lollypop just like Telly Savalas in that cop show.

Samson resides in a Dade County ghetto with his wife and daughter. Although he exchanged high school for juvie in his junior year, Samson is determined to become the best fry cook in the state of Florida and eventually own his own restaurant. Samson and Sal, who also grew up poor, often share their breaks. Samson tells Sal about the ghetto, and Sal tells Samson about growing up Italian, which Samson finds fascinating.

Now Sal approaches Samson and puts the check on the carousel for service. "Man, I don't think that I'm going to be here much longer."

"Come on now, m'man. What is it this time?"

"I got this douche out there. He wants a steak that's not medium, and not rare, but right in between."

Samson gives a great belly laugh. "You know we only make 'em three ways: rare, medium, well done, and burnt."

"That's four ways."

"Yeah, whatever."

Samson slides two sirloin steaks from a tray onto the grill to accompany the rest of the meat in various stages of doneness. He dings his spatula off the grate, and it twirls around his fingers like a cowboy's six-shooter. "Don't worry. I'll take care of it."

Sal leaves and services other tables. When he gets the order for the asshole and his date, he brings it to their table as quickly as possible and tries to get away just as quickly.

He doesn't make it.

"Boy!" The asshole shouts at Sal even though he's only a couple of feet from the table. "Come here, boy!"

Sal turns around, grinding his teeth so loudly he can hear them in his head. "Is there a problem... sir?"

"Damn right, there's a problem. Does this steak look medium to you... boy?"

Sal bites his lip. Hard. It takes him a full five seconds to respond. "Would you like me to take it back... sir?"

"Damn right, I want you to take it back and cook it the way I ordered it! You got that, boy?"

"I got it." The "sir" is now gone—a bad sign.

Sal takes the plate back to Samson. He loosens his tie on the way into the kitchen. His hand trembles with barely concealed anger as he sets the asshole's plate on the service area next to the grill. "I'm really trying," he mutters as much to himself as to Samson.

"What is it, m'man?" Samson scoops away the plate.

Sal's voice is slow and measured. "The douche says that the steak isn't done enough."

Samson grabs the steak off the plate with a hand so calloused it's fireproof. He throws the steak back on the grill and watches as flames erupt around the meat. He waits no more than five seconds before he rescues the steak from the flames with the same practiced bare hand and throws it back on its other side for another five seconds. Then he grabs the steak up and drops it gently back onto the plate. "There you go. Take that back to the douche." He laughs.

Back in the dining room, Sal places the plate in front of the asshole and hustles again to get away from the table.

Before he's out of earshot, he hears, "Hey, dummy!"

Sal freezes. Then he slowly turns. Sal's temper is like falling off a cliff. It's like that scene in the first Billy Jack movie, where Billy Jack calmly and quietly takes shit until he snaps and breaks the tyrant's jaw with a reverse crescent kick. Sal doesn't know karate. He doesn't need to. He just goes berserk.

"Are you talking to me?" Sal walks slowly back to the table, a wicked and not playful smile on his face.

"Yeah, I'm talking to you, dummy. Does this steak look medium rare to you?"

Sal bends over the plate and places his hand under it with mock deference. Without warning, he picks up the plate and shoves it onto the asshole's chest hard enough that the asshole and his chair fall backward onto the floor with a thud like a fender bender. The asshole's medium-rare steak is a messy tag on his white linen jacket. His face is red, and he shakes visibly as he tries to get off the floor. Sal pushes him back down with his foot.

"Yeah, maybe that steak isn't medium-rare." Sal whips off his jacket. "Now, you want to see a real medium-rare steak, you come outside, and I'll show you a medium-rare steak!" His jacket lands next to the asshole on the floor.

Dick Greenwood breaks in between them like a prize fight referee. He turns his back on Sal, blocking him, and helps the asshole to his feet. Dick looks to the date still sitting at the table, barely stifling a satisfactory laugh. "Are you all right?"

She nods, smiling. "The steak is delicious."

"Sal," Dick asks, barely looking over his shoulder at him, "did you just quit?"

"Yeah, damn right I quit. But I want his ass outside!" Sal storms out the front door, where a valet is parking cars. "Hey, Juan. You know the douche dressed in black and white that came in here about a half hour ago?"

Juan thinks about it for a few seconds. "Not sure."

"He was with a hot blonde, about five feet six inches, straight blond hair, red top."

"Oh, yeah. I know the one you're talking about."

"Can you do me a solid? Where did you park his car?"

Juan points. "Around the corner. Can't miss it. Red Shelby Cobra."

Sal walks around the corner. He thinks, *Cool car for such a douchebag.* When he gets to the car, he sits on the hood and waits.

An hour passes according to Sal's Timex self-winding watch, which always seems to run ten minutes slow, and Sal wonders why the douche didn't call the cops—although he felt his actions were justified. Sal always feels justified when he's incensed. But now the adrenaline is gone, and he realizes that his job is gone and with it, the consequences of his temper don't seem to justify the satisfaction.

Sal wonders if he should go back into the restaurant and look for the guy, or apologize to Dick, or maybe just go home. No. He's still too pissed off to just go home or apologize. Besides, he doesn't believe in apologies. *After all, apologies never fix anything.* He'll wait.

But he doesn't wait much longer before Sal sees Samson striding down the street toward him in his chef's uniform, wearing his trademark smirk and sucking his lollypop.

"Man, you are one crazy fuckin' honky."

"Damn right. Where is he? I've got his car right here."

Sampson shakes his head. "Yeah, I know you do, but you might as well go home. He's gone."

Sal slides off the car hood. Another rush of adrenaline. "No, don't tell me that. How could he get out without his car? Without my seeing him?"

"Look. You got your revenge. That dude was so scared that he took that fine-ass white lady through the kitchen and into the alley and called a taxi. The dude had not an ounce of courage. You don't get more embarrassed than that. Go home, m'man. There ain't nothing left here."

Sal looks back and contemplates keying the car, breaking the windshield, or slicing the tires. But looking at the gorgeous red coupe with the black racing stripes on the hood and the side scoops, he says to himself, *Nah. It would be a crime to hurt something this beautiful.*

Then, as Sampson goes back to work and Sal can't return, the full weight of his actions strikes him like a bare-knuckle punch from George Foreman. *How am I going to break the news to my wife that my temper cost me another job?*

CHAPTER 3

MOST people know Hollywood as the quirky, star-studded city in Los Angeles, California. But between Miami and Ft. Lauderdale, Florida, there is another Hollywood. It isn't known for movie stars or an abundance of uber-luxury cars. It's just a normal working-class city with a population of over one hundred twenty-one thousand.

On Sterling Road, a main street in Hollywood, is Romano's Bakery. It's one of those businesses that every local knows and enjoys. Romano Bakery's specialties are high-gluten bread, beautifully decorated cakes, and assorted Italian pastries. Nobody in Hollywood would plan a wedding or a major party without considering Romano's Bakery for at least the cake. After ten years in operation, Romano's has been quietly put up for sale.

David plans to take over Romano's Bakery. But if he knew that his plan would succeed and where it would all lead, he would have simply burned the place to the ground.

But now he has an appointment with Joey Romano. Joey is a semi-lecherous, short Italian man with a horseshoe-shaped receding hairline of black hair, sapphire blue eyes, and a snowman body. He's a master baker, as were his father and his grandfather. He knows hard work. Every day, Joey comes to the bakery at three in the morning to supervise the proofing, baking, and decorating. He's proud of the store, but the long hours for so many years have made him arthritic. At seventy years of age, he's ready to retire.

Joey greets David before he even enters the store. David recognizes Joey from the white chef's suit and the hat right off a label for Chef Boyardee beefaroni, of which David has consumed so much he practically belches with an Italian accent.

"Joey Romano? Hi, I'm David Adler."

Joey looks conspicuously up and down at David, eyes shifting like an elevator. "You're David Adler? You're so young. I expected to see a full-grown man."

David hasn't yet seen his twentieth birthday.

David extends his hand even though Joey doesn't offer his right way. After two awkward beats, Joey finally takes David's hand and shakes.

David says, "Don't let the age fool you."

"How did you find out we're selling?" Joey asks.

"The *Hollywood Herald* classifieds said that a prominent bakery in Hollywood with six-figure annual sales was for sale. I took a shot. This was the only bakery that fit the description."

"But you didn't contact the business broker?"

David hesitates. He doesn't know how his answer will be received. "I figured that I might get a better deal if you didn't have to pay a fee."

Joey erupts with a broad smile. He puts his flabby arm around David's shoulder. "Ah, you're a real big-time businessman for one so young. Huh? Come on, big-time businessman. Let me show you around."

They go inside, and Joey gestures around the front of the store. Gleaming floor display cases highlight different flavored cannoli, rum babas, tiramisu, various cakes, and fruit tarts. The wall display is filled with various loaves of Italian bread, French bread, white bread, and rye bread, and highlights Romano's famous high-gluten bread. One case has decorated cake displays. There is a small table with a cash register and chair.

Customers grab numbers from a dispenser and line up at the register for baked goods. A very pretty Latina girl whom David estimates as a junior in high school, with short-cropped dark hair, wears a black tee-shirt with *Romano's Bakery* written on the front. She works at the counter and the register with quiet efficiency. When Joey enters, she gazes at him with a look somewhere between adoration and admiration.

Joey asks David, "Are you a baker?"

"No. But my stepfather is," David lies.

"Really? What's his name?"

"Rossi. Sal Rossi."

"Italian. Good! Very good! Let me show you the kitchen. But first…" Joey looks at the young girl. He gestures to a high shelf filled with bread. "Honey, do me a favor and bring a couple of those French breads toward the front."

Joey elbows David and motions him to watch as the girl gets a small step ladder and, facing the wall, climbs up a couple of steps while reaching upward for the bread. Joey not so subtly motions to her ass.

"Man, what a caboose," he whispers to David. "Nothing I can do about it. But you? Maybe." Joey smirks and jabs David with his elbow. David turns his head as if Joey has suddenly developed halitosis.

Joey notices David's irritation and says, "Let's go to the kitchen."

As they step through a door at the back of the room into the kitchen, David says to Joey, "Believe me when I tell you that teenage girls are very overrated. I should know, I'm right out of high school myself."

Joey waves David off dismissively.

Once they enter the room, David realizes the kitchen is deceptively large. Floured counters line one wall with stations for large mixers, a commercial oven, bread proofers, cake decorating stations, and various racks holding just-finished bread and pastries.

"I have over sixty thousand dollars in equipment and additions. Do you see these mixers? They would cost over six thousand apiece if you bought them new." Joey walks over to the oven. "And this baby? This would cost you between ten and fifteen large."

Behind one station is a door for the restroom and another door that leads to a small office. Joey motions David into the office.

Joey sits at his desk in the office and gestures to David to have a seat. "So, big-time businessman, what are you prepared to offer me for my carb kingdom?"

David thinks this is a trick question. The classified ad had the price at forty thousand dollars. "Aren't you asking forty thousand?"

"That depends. Are you offering me cash?"

David has total savings of five hundred dollars. "No. I was hoping for terms."

"Twenty thousand down, and I'll hold paper on the other twenty. But we need to close this quickly. I have other buyers, and we're still haggling on price." Joey hesitates, then adds, "But we're close."

"I'll need some time to get the down payment together. If I give you a good-faith payment of five hundred dollars, would you hold it for me?"

Joey laughs. The laugh feels more like an insult than mirth. "That's not much money."

"I'm only looking for... ninety days?"

Joey considers the offer. Then he stands up from his chair. David watches Joey's belly overlap the table. "Maybe you're not such a big businessman after all. I won't sell to anyone but you for, say, thirty days. But I'll continue to show the place."

David thinks about this for a few seconds. "How about we split the difference at sixty days?"

Joey's face becomes grim. "How about fifteen days?"

David is momentarily confused by Joey's counteroffer. Then he gets the tactic. "Okay, thirty days. I'll be around tomorrow with a cashier's check."

David and Joey shake on the deal. As David gets up, he asks Joey, "By the way, where do you do your banking?"

"American Bank of Hollywood. Right down the road. We've had our accounts with them since the beginning. See Greg Anderson if you need a reference."

"Also, can I get a list of all this equipment and the furnishings?"

"You can pick that up along with financial statements when I get the check tomorrow."

Joey sees David out, and they shake hands again at the door. "Your stepfather better be a hell of a baker. He has some big shoes to fill here."

The American Bank of Hollywood is a local bank that prides itself on close relations with all of its customers—particularly its commercial customers. David hopes that the bank will lend him the money to purchase the bakery so that they don't lose the business account to another bank. The day after David brings Joey the five-hundred-dollar check and picks up the documents, he makes an appointment to visit Greg Anderson the following day.

* * *

When the bank opens at eight-thirty a.m., David is at the door waiting to get in. He spent all night preparing what he considers adequate financial projections for the bakery's first year under his management. After calling in late for work, he has the first appointment of the day with Greg Anderson, who it turns out is the vice president for commercial loans.

Greg is an ambitious bank officer who worked his way up from the teller position and considers himself a partner to small businesses in Hollywood. He wants to make a difference in the burgeoning community, and he's currently short of his loan portfolio projections. David is correct in that Greg doesn't want to lose the Romano's Bakery account.

David walks into Greg's office with enough contagious energy and optimism to power a small city. He takes out two binders labeled *Romano's Bakery* and sets one in front of Greg. "Mr. Anderson, if you look at the financial projections for the bakery, I think that you'll agree there will be plenty of money to repay a twenty-thousand-dollar loan within three years."

As Greg Anderson looks at the typed documents, David continues. "The owner wants forty thousand dollars to purchase the business and will take half of that down. If your bank can lend me the twenty thousand dollars for the down payment, these numbers show that repayment with interest is virtually guaranteed." He doesn't sit back. He leans forward, as if trying to will the favorable material directly into Greg's mind.

Greg can do his own review. He leans back in his chair to distance himself from David's hyperbole. He carefully looks at the binder. After a few minutes, he casually tells David, "There is no collateral for the loan. As far as I can tell, you have virtually no marketable assets." He sets his binder down on the desk between them. "Who will run the business? Who has experience baking?"

David says, "We can hire a baker—"

Greg cuts David off in mid-sentence. "You can't manage a bakery, especially one as reputable as Romano's, without knowing how to bake." He sits silently, waiting for David to answer.

David's optimism starts to falter. The pen in his hand starts to tremble. He somewhat meekly asks, "Can't the collateral be the equipment and fixtures of the bakery? They're worth at least sixty thousand dollars."

Greg shakes his head. "David, I don't know what the market value of the equipment is and neither do you. Also, do you know how hard it is to sell restaurant types of equipment in case of liquidation? You get pennies on the dollar. I'd love to help you, but the bank must be protected."

David picks up his binder.

"If you come up with answers to these questions, come back to me. But right now, the answer is no. Or at least, not now."

David thanks Greg and leaves the bank feeling deflated. He has less than four weeks to convince the bank that they should lend him the money, and he has no clue how to do that.

CHAPTER 4

WOLFIE'S Delicatessen is a favorite and famous spot for meeting and eating in Miami Beach. It's open 24/7/365, and it hosts its share of celebrities, sports figures, students, politicians, radio personalities, and anyone else who wants good food, huge portions, and friendly service.

And the best and friendliest service at Wolfie's comes from David's mother, Sunny. Most women, even the least seductive, are beautiful in one way or another. Maybe it's a smile, a curve, or a look. Sunny is, literally, the whole package. She's a drop-dead and resurrected gorgeous blonde with flawless skin, arctic blue eyes, and a body like springtime in the tropics.

Even sexpot connoisseur Hugh Hefner personally recruited Sunny to be a Playboy bunny at his Chicago club. Sunny politely declined Hugh's and many similar offers as she was already managing a different club called the Dolphin in the Chicago suburbs, where she was known as the Blonde Bombshell and brought in huge crowds.

That was ten years ago. Now she's in her late thirties, and somehow her beauty has been tempered with a charisma and grace that holds men—and some women—spellbound. Her name, Sunny, more than matches her disposition. Few diner challenges ever phase her—if the men keep their hands off her ass.

Sunny is witty and smart, but she knows that true intelligence is the ability to make other people feel like they're smarter. She knows how to discreetly talk to everyone in her orbit. She's supportive of and befriended by all, and their friendships grow deeper each year that she works here.

Sunny takes a break and sits at a booth with her husband, Sal. Even though two bench seats are facing each other at the table, Sal always insists that Sunny sit next to him.

"How else am I going to reach out to caress those pretty legs?" he would say at first. Now the seating arrangement is simply an intimate habit. Sal sheepishly smiles at Sunny. "Honey, we've been married for almost a year."

Sal stops and takes a pickle out of the relish jar—the relish jar is Wolfie's trademark. He dabs off the extra brine and puts it on his bread plate. "Don't you think it's time for David to find his own place? He's an adult. Almost twenty. When I was twenty, I was working two jobs, living on my own, and getting more ass than a toilet seat."

Sunny's eyes dart away, and she slides from Sal. "Look, I understand how you feel. I do. And you know that I love you and the fact that you took me and my son as a package deal. Let's have this conversation again when we're home. Before David gets home, we should have some time."

"Fine. I just think that an almost twenty-year-old should be out on his own. Not living with his mother." Sal just wants the intimacy of living alone with Sunny. Having David there is getting in the way of Sal's groove.

Sunny leaves to service her station. "We'll talk later, okay?"

David loves his mother like he loves life. Like the North Star to ancient sailors, Sunny has always guided him through life's challenges with the comfort and caring of, well, a devoted mother.

Sunny was a single mother raising David and his sister, Ava, during the sixties. She divorced their father when David was seven. She could have married a doctor, a pilot, an executive, or a movie star. She could have even become a movie star herself if she was willing to audition on the casting couch. Even a priest wanted to give up his vows to be with her.

But Sunny was, before anything, committed to her children, and she didn't trust any man to share that devotion. And career opportunities for single mothers in the sixties were as rare as finding a ticket to the Academy Awards stuck in a car windshield. So, money was always tight, and Sunny and her children moved around more often than the Ringling Bros. and Barnum & Bailey Circus.

Despite the chaos in the lives of Sunny and her children, Sunny did everything in her power to make her children feel comfortable, even fortunate. Faith in Sunny was the bedrock on which David and Ava cemented their young lives.

When Ava left home and David graduated high school, Sunny thought that it was finally, finally, time to move on. And in the age-old man/woman cliché, she married Sal, the bad boy with a heart, after dating him for just a few short months.

A few minutes after Sunny leaves, David shows up unexpectedly and slides into the booth across from Sal. "Hey, dude," he says to Sal as he grabs a menu.

Five minutes later, Sunny comes by. "Hi, guys! How are my favorite men?"

"Starving!" David says. "Have you eaten, Sal?"

"Well, I had a pickle." Sal turns to Sunny. "Could you fix me a corned beef sandwich?"

"Same here," David says while grabbing a pickle for himself out of the relish jar.

"No problem. I'll get the sandwiches and join you in a few minutes."

Sal and David sit awkwardly for a few minutes in silence. Pickle juice drips onto the table in front of David, and Sal snarls and blots it up with his napkin. "C'mon, man, can't you clean up after yourself?"

David just shrugs.

Finally, Sal says, "You want some coffee?"

"No thanks," David says. "You know I don't drink coffee or tea."

Sal grimaces. "No coffee, tea, alcohol, or cigarettes. Have you ever tried pot?"

"Never."

Sal shakes his head disapprovingly. "What the hell are you saving yourself for? Have you ever even tried a drink? Maybe just a beer?"

"Nope. Not my thing. But now that you mention it, an egg cream sounds pretty good right now."

David gets up and walks to his mother. A few minutes later, she brings him a chocolate egg cream in a large soda glass with a straw. He strips the paper from the straw and dunks it into the drink.

Sal watches as David sucks the drink up through the straw. "David, why do you need a straw? Are you twelve?"

David rolls his eyes. Sal seems to always have a critique. "Why's that a problem?"

Sal takes his water glass. "Here. If I drink straight from the glass"—he picks up his water glass and takes a drink, tipping the lip of the glass into his mouth—"two things happen. First, I look more like a man taking a drink. I don't look like I'm sucking on a long, thin *cazzo*. Second, you quench your thirst better by drinking like a man. Third, your drink will last longer."

David takes the straw out of his drink. He dabs it on his napkin and sets it aside. Then he takes a drink the way Sal suggests. He narrows his blue eyes and arches his eyebrows. In mock surrender, he says, "You know, you're right. I'll change my fairy ways. But I have reservations that you look at a straw and think it's a dick."

Sal grimaces. "You should loosen up. Get a little freaky. At your age, you should get into a little trouble. If you could look up 'tight ass' in the dictionary, your picture would be there."

David puts the straw back into his glass in protest. "Here. Consider this my rebellion. Sal, all I want is to find a way to make money. At least enough so my mom can stop waiting tables, I can get my own place, and we can be a remotely dysfunctional family. I want to make enough money so I don't have to worry about money. I'm not interested in wasting my time getting freaky, getting into trouble, or being a nonconformist. I went through twelve years of school without so much as a detention, and I don't intend to turn maverick now."

Sal takes a pen out of his pocket and draws a square on one of the paper placemats. "You need to think outside of the box."

David looks at the box and chuckles sarcastically. "Sal, that isn't a box. It's square. A box is a cube."

Sal doesn't miss a beat. "You're making my point. You like to play the angles. A square has only four angles. If you think three-dimensionally, you'll realize that a cube, or a box, has an infinite number of angles."

"So, you actually mean, think inside the box. Just outside the square."

Sal angrily balls up the placemat. "I mean you're a smart kid. Just put that smartass brain of yours to good use."

Before David can reply, Sunny returns to the table with corned beef sandwiches. She sits down next to Sal.

Sal speaks first in a whisper, head hanging low. "Honey, I'm sorry. I lost my job again. But it wasn't my fault."

Sunny shifts in her seat to face him. "It's okay, honey. I'm sorry to hear that. What happened?"

Sal tells the story of the battered woman and the guy she came in with. His explanation is light on details about losing his temper and dumping the guy on the floor and gives her only the gist of what happened before Dick fired him.

Sunny gives Sal a forgiving smile and puts her hand on his shoulder. "Are you all right? Did anyone call the police?"

"No," Sal says, "at least not that I know about. I'm just worried. We need the money."

"I know. But I always say that money and things can be replaced. People can't."

David gives his own bad news. "I'm struggling on the bakery deal."

Sal says, "Yeah, that's what you said about the meat market, the restaurant, and a dozen other businesses. Look, if you manage to get a business going, I'll run it. I don't even care what it is. All you'll have to do is sit back and collect your share of the profits."

"What do you know about baking?" David asks.

"What's to know? I'll learn whatever I need to know. I'll hire a baker and be their boss and their apprentice at the same time. See? Problem solved—"

"You know what?" Sunny interrupts. "We have a terrific baker here named Ray. He makes all the pastries Wolfie's sells, and people love them. Let me see if he can join us."

She leaves and a few minutes later, she returns with Ray Dakati. Ray is a tall, thin, good-looking Jamaican. David guesses he's in his late thirties. His smile is genuine, and his voice lilts with accent. He's dressed in a white chef's suit and hat. David notices the similarity between Ray's outfit and the one Joey wore. He takes that as a good sign.

Ray sits down. His soft gaze and broad smile make clear he likes Sunny at least as much as everyone else at Wolfie's does.

"Ray, this is my son, David, and my husband, Sal."

Handshakes all around.

"We have a proposition for you. My son is going to buy a bakery in Hollywood that we would all manage. I would like you to manage the baking part of it."

David interrupts. "Do you know how to make bread as well as pastries?"

"Of course." Ray grabs a basket of rolls and sliced bread from another table. "You don't think the cheapskates here would pay even wholesale for this, do you?"

What Sunny doesn't know is that Ray is already unhappy with his job. The white manager of the restaurant has far less experience than Ray, but privately treats Ray like he's an idiot. Also, he constantly tells jokes about Blacks, Pollacks, and Italians. The only group he avoids are Jews—because the owners of Wolfie's are Jewish.

A couple of days ago, he came into the kitchen and said, "Hey, Ray! You like being called Black or Colored?"

"I like being called Ray," he answered. "But how about this? If I'm Colored, that would make you clear, right?"

Unphased as if he didn't even hear Ray's answer, the manager continued, "Well, let's see. You've got James Brown, Vida Blue, Slappy White, and Al Green. I'd say that makes you Colored." He started laughing like he was ready to perform standup at one of the Miami Beach hotel lounges.

Ray sheepishly smiled. When the manager left the kitchen, Ray approached the lead cook. "Hey, do me a favor and let me know when you've prepared his lunch. Will you? I have something special to add."

"So, sure," Ray says to David. "I can bake bread, I can decorate cakes, and you know that everyone loves Ray's pastries."

Sal says, "We'll double your salary if you make the move."

Sunny puts out a hand to indicate that Sal should stop talking. "Ray, we can't do that right away. But you'll have full creative power, which I know is important to you. And you know that I'll be more than fair to you. You can count on a future with unlimited potential with us, including equity in the business. Can we count you in?"

Ray reflects on the offer for a moment. "I'll consider it when we can work out the money."

David responds, "Ray, can you give me a resume of the places where you've worked as a baker and your contact information? Can I use that information while I try to pull the deal together?"

"Sure. What do I have to lose? Have whoever you want." Ray turns to Sunny and gives a barely perceptible wink. "Anything for Sunny." He gets up and gestures to Sunny. "All right, break's over. Time to get back to it."

Sunny gets up. "All right, guys, I'll see you at home. I have tables to take care of."

Now that he has a legitimate baker, David mentally checks off one of the bank's objections to getting the bakery loan. Now, he thinks, *All I need is to convince the bank, or someone else, that there is collateral for the loan. And I have less than three weeks to do it.*

CHAPTER 5

"YOUR ad said that you specialize in commercial loans. I gave you this package a week ago and… Yes, I know it takes time, but you assured me that you knew the right investors to get this done. It's an established business. Sixty thousand dollars in equipment for collateral. I only have another week before my option to purchase is over, and I lose the deal. Fine… Fine. Okay, thanks." David hangs up the phone. "For nothing," he says under his breath.

Sunny hears the conversation. "How bad is it?"

David finishes tying a half Windsor knot in the black tie he usually wears to work. "It's not good. Even with Ray on board, I need collateral like real estate or marketable securities. No one will simply lend money on the bakery equipment. I've contacted relatives, friends, and everyone advertising that they 'Fund all commercial projects. Nothing too big or small.' "

"Kind of funny when you work for a loan company."

"Believe me, the irony isn't lost on me. Speaking of which, it's back to work. I'm beginning to hate my life." David kisses his mother on the cheek as he rushes out the door, leaving a trail that Sunny cleans up.

When David arrives at the office, he sees Lester's fat face waiting at the door.

Lester checks his Timex watch to verify that David is there on time and motions for David to come with him to the room behind the office. "Come on. It's time you learned how to chase the deadbeats."

There's a well-worn table and chair. Lester sits down at the table in front of a stack of attorney letters. David stands behind him, looking over his shoulder.

"These are collection letters pre-signed by our attorney that imply serious legal action to the debtor." Lester picks one up, carefully folds it, and stuffs it into an envelope. "The trick is to make the letters look official. Like they're coming directly from a courthouse. We place the letter into an envelope marked *Broward County Collection Department* with this office address." David notes that the envelope is of very high quality with a Broward County watermark. He's amazed at what can be done by printing with the illusion of officialdom.

"Next—and this is my own little touch—I seal the envelope with a gold seal." Lester takes a brilliant gold, star-shaped sticker and applies it to the back of the envelope. "Then I use this stamp to emboss the seal."

The stamp is a heavy desk type into which Lester places the envelope with the gold star over the round embossing plate. Lester pushes down the handle and when the envelope is removed, there is a raised impression of *Broward County Court of Collections* over the foil gold star. He does the same to the rest of the envelopes.

Lester takes all the adorned envelopes and carefully writes the names and addresses of the debtors to whom he plans to deliver them. He escorts David to his car, and the two leave the office for the field. The field, as Lester calls it, is the most impoverished neighborhood in Broward County.

Lester is giddy. "I love this part of the job. The first thing is to serve the deadbeats with the letters." He hands the envelopes to David. "They don't know you, so you're the one who's gonna do it. Simply go to the door and whoever answers, give them their letter and say, 'You've been served.' That's it. Don't answer any questions. Don't wait around. Just give it to them, say, 'You've been served,' and go. Got it?"

"Yeah," David says. "Are you sure this is safe? Is it even legal? You're making people believe that they're being sued or in some criminal trouble."

"What the fuck, dude, you're a collector, ain'tcha? You do what's necessary. Besides, these Jigs don't want a white man hanging around their house. They're too chicken shit to do anything."

When they get to the first house, David does what he's told. He walks up to the door and knocks. A little girl of about six years old answers.

David says, "Is your mommy or daddy home?"

The little girl runs and gets her mother who comes to the door.

"Can I help you?" the mother asks.

David hands her the letter. "You've been served."

The woman looks at the gold seal on the back of the envelope and starts to tremble. "What is this?" she asks David.

As Lester instructed, David turns and walks away.

"Please!" the woman calls after him. "What is this about? Tell me!"

When David returns to the car, he tells Lester, "I'm sorry. I can't do that again."

Lester smirks. "You'll learn to do it if you want to keep your job. Let's move on. I have lots more to show you."

Lester drives past homes that are falling apart and empty lots stretching out like dunes interspersed with liquor stores and an occasional Seven-Eleven. As they drive, he lectures David. "When people make loans with us, they're told to list their furniture and personal property. Do you know why? Because if you read the fine print, everything on the list becomes collateral for the loan. Nobody knows that until it's too late!"

Lester is so excited he bounces in his seat and leers menacingly at the road. He turns the car down a gravel street near one of the dilapidated houses and gets out of the car. David follows him down a walkway to a house that looks as fragile as a Jenga tower. If it's possible, David thinks, *The air has the smell of despair*.

Lester continues the lecture as they walk. "We go to somebody's house because they've turned their phone off and they aren't responding to notices."

David thinks, *The way we harass them over the phone it's a wonder that any of their phones are connected.*

"Chasing a deadbeat is expensive, so we only chase deadbeats that have sufficient balances. Do you know how many of these Jigs don't pay their bills but drive Cadillacs? Don't get me started. And don't go feeling sorry for them. When we go out, we need to get results."

Lester signals David to stand back about twenty feet as he goes to the door. He doesn't knock on the door politely. His knock is intrusive and abrupt. It's the kind of knock a cop would use before he busts down the door.

The door tentatively opens. It's a Black man about five feet ten inches wearing shorts, a white wife-beater tee-shirt, and a look of embarrassed defeat when he sees Lester. "Look, man, I ain't got the money. I lost my job two weeks ago, and we barely makin' it as it is."

Two kids are behind him crying.

Lester shows the father the list of furniture that he inadvertently pledged as collateral. "You see this list?" He pokes the document with a fat finger. "This your signature?"

"Yeah, I signed that."

Lester looks at the list and points to a dining room set. "Do you have this set? And you'd better say 'yes,' because it's a crime to get rid of our property without our permission."

The man shakes like fragile leaves in a storm. He's trembling from the inside out. Lester carries himself with authority, and this guy wants no hint of trouble.

"Yes, sir, Mr. Lester, we got it."

Lester says, "Good. I will take one of the chairs. Bring them all out."

Lester still holds the frame of authority and for a long moment, he and the man stare at each other. Then the man goes into the house and comes back with two chairs, one in each hand.

Lester smirks with derision. "Give me the one in your left hand."

The man complies.

Lester takes the chair and places it in the center of the man's yard. Then he goes back to his car, gets a gallon of gasoline out of the trunk, pours it on the chair, takes out the Zippo lighter that he uses to light his skinny cigars, and lights the chair up.

David can't believe what he's seeing. He grabs Lester by the arm and spins him around. "No way! That's enough." He hears the children crying. The father is visibly humiliated.

Lester shakes off David's grip. "Don't you tell me how to do my job." He turns to the father. "I'll be back next week. Either have the payment for me or another chair."

The man looks on the verge of breaking down. His eyes fill with tears that don't quite spill onto his cheeks. He trembles with embarrassment at the fire in his yard.

"Just hold on." He disappears into the house and comes out with two twenty-dollar bills. "Will this square us away for the month?"

"Yeah," Lester says, snatching the bills. "Do you want a receipt?"

"Sure. Then please leave."

Back in the car, Lester turns to David. "And that's how it's done."

David wants to throw up.

The next day, David shows up to work early. He's ready to quit without notice. He prides himself on his integrity, and he cannot imagine why he would continue to be involved with this cruel company and the malevolent people who work here no matter how much he needs the money.

After going out into the field with Lester, he just feels dirty. He knows that his future cannot be tormenting people who made the mistake of borrowing money from HPC Finance.

At the end of the business day, after the cash has been balanced, David agrees to stay and close the office for the manager. Alone at his desk, he starts to compose a resignation letter.

There's a knock on the door. A tall man in an expensive suit excitedly wants to get in. David points to the clock to let the customer know that the office is closed, but the customer persists. Finally, he opens the door. "Hello, can I help you?"

"Yes, please. I need to get my payment logged in tonight before it's late, and I must be at an estate auction in an hour."

"Sure. I'll help you." David goes to the cashier's area to find a receipt. "Can I get your name?"

"It's Perry Meyer."

David looks through the customer cards and finds the one he needs. He notices on the front of the card that Perry Meyer's occupation is listed as auctioneer. "I'm curious. What kind of things do you sell at auction?"

"Just about anything. Estate sales, commercial equipment, and fixtures."

"Really?" David's interest perks up. "Like, do you sell bakery equipment?"

Perry is annoyed because he doesn't have time for small talk. Regardless, he hurriedly answers. "We auction commercial food service equipment all the time for restaurants that go out of business."

"Can you predict what you would get for the equipment at an auction?"

Perry looks at his watch. He doesn't want to be rude because David did open the door after closing. But still… "Well, we can set a bottom amount to bid on the equipment, called a reserve. We could arrange not to sell the equipment below that amount."

"Do you also appraise stuff before the auction?"

"Sure." Perry again anxiously looks at his watch. "We do it all the time. Please, I must go." He reaches into his pocket, pulls out a card, and gives it to David. "The name's Perry." Then he realizes that he has just told David his name twice. "Sorry, you know that already. I guess I'm just in a hurry."

He holds out his hand, and David shakes it. "Call me tomorrow, and we'll talk."

Rather than resigning, David calls in sick for work the next day. He calls Perry and offers to buy him lunch at a restaurant near the bakery. Perry agrees and after lunch, they visit the bakery. Joey Romano recognizes David and invites them both into the kitchen.

As they walk around, Perry inspects the equipment and writes notes on a clipboard.

"Perry, what I need from you is an appraisal of the equipment." David explains about the loan and that he wants to use the equipment as collateral.

Perry says, "Let's take a walk."

When they're outside, David follows Perry up and down the strip shopping mall.

Perry lights a cigarette. "Do you mind if I smoke? You've got huge balls, kid. You want to buy this place without any money of your own?"

"I don't have a choice. The money I have wouldn't even buy a hand mixer."

"Okay, I'll tell you what I can do for you. I can get you a policy. An insurance policy to guarantee that if this equipment is sold at one of my auctions, the equipment will generate cash of at least twenty thousand dollars based on my appraisal. Guaranteed. It's called an appraisal guarantee policy backed by an A-rated insurance company out of Missoula, Montana."

David struggles to comprehend what Perry is telling him. "Are you saying that I can go to the bank with a guarantee on the value of the collateral? That they can use the equipment as collateral for the loan without risk?" In his head, he has checked off the remaining objection that Greg Anderson had. Ray, the consummate baker, could run the bakery, and the equipment could be used for collateral without risk to the bank. It seems impossible.

"It is exactly what you're looking for. However, the cost of the insurance policy and my fee for the formal appraisal will be a thousand dollars."

"Please do it. I'll find the money. Just please hurry. My option to purchase is nearly over." David gives Perry the equipment list.

Two days later, David signs over his entire next eight-hundred-dollar monthly paycheck. "I know it's not everything, but it almost covers what I owe you. Can I give you the rest in a couple of weeks?"

Perry takes the endorsed check and quickly slips it into his pocket. He hands a file folder to David with his appraisal of each piece of equipment and a policy from an official-looking insurance company in Missoula, Montana that guarantees if the equipment is liquidated for less than the appraised amount, they will cover the difference.

"Sure, kid. I trust you to make up the difference. Best of luck with the bank."

With two days left on his option, David returns to Greg, dressed to impress in a black suit, blue-and-silver rep tie, and a new loan proposal. "Mr. Anderson, you gave me two reasons that you wouldn't make the loan for the bakery. The first was that I'm not a baker. I get that."

David lays down an eight-by-ten photo of Ray and his resume. "I present to you Ray Dakati, head baker for Wolfie's restaurant in Miami Beach."

"I'm familiar with Wolfie's restaurant. How will Mr. Dakati be involved in the bakery?"

"He'll be fully in charge of the bakery production. He has agreed to an initial two-year contract after we close."

Greg reads the resume and looks impressed.

"Your other concern was the collateral for the loan. You told me that you couldn't use the bakery equipment as collateral because the value of restaurant equipment was negligible." David lays a copy of the appraisal and the insurance policy on Greg's desk next to Ray's photo and resume. "I've solved that problem. With this policy, if you're forced to liquidate the equipment to pay a default on the loan, simply contact Perry Meyer, a well-known liquidator and auctioneer." He hands Greg Perry's card. "He'll handle the liquidation of the equipment on your behalf. If he doesn't raise enough to cover the loan, then the insurance policy will cover the difference." He slides the insurance policy across the desk toward Greg.

Greg reads the policy with interest. "It's not exactly a AAA-rated insurance company."

"It's an A-rated company. More protection than you probably have on most of your portfolio. And I give you my word that all banking from Romano's will remain with American Bank of Hollywood."

"You've certainly given me a lot to think about."

"I need a commitment by tomorrow."

"Fortunately for you, our loan committee meets tonight. I'll give you an answer by tomorrow at the end of business."

The next day at noon, while sitting at his desk at HPC Finance, David gets a call from Sunny. "David, I just got a call from a Mr. Greg Anderson at the bank. You need to call him right away."

David calls Greg back right away.

"David?"

"Yes. Tell me great news."

"Your loan is approved. Congratulations."

David is struck silent for several seconds.

"David?"

"Yes. Thank you so much."

"I spoke to Joey Romano. He'll close with you as soon as his attorney is available. A check will be ready for him right after closing. You can have the closing here at the bank in our conference room."

David joyously pumps his arms but forces his voice to keep calm. "Okay. Thank you, Mr. Anderson." He hangs up the phone, finds a box in the back of the office, and immediately starts packing his personal property.

Lester looks at David as if he's having a seizure. "What's going on?"

David looks over at Lester. "Oh. I forgot to send you a sympathy card for your loss."

"What are you talking about?" Lester waddles over to David, confused.

"Simple. I quit, you racist piece of crap."

David walks out of HPC Finance for the last time thinking that all his problems are behind him. He has no idea how wrong he is.

CHAPTER 6

DAVID took a big swing to get Romano's Bakery. But here's the thing every little league baseball player knows: it doesn't matter how big the swing is if you don't connect with the ball.

David thought that owning Romano's Bakery was the answer to, well, everything. He expected money, prestige, and respect. Romano's Bakery had been a fixture in Hollywood, Florida for over a decade. It had regular devoted customers. It was the go-to bakery to cater for weddings and other events. In short, it was a money machine. But just two months after taking over the business, the customers stopped coming, and the profits dried up like so much biscotti.

It turns out that, unless you happen to have a uranium mine or property next to Spring Perrier, business requires more skill than just making good pastries. Neither David, Sal, nor Sunny have skills in accounting, marketing, or the management of a small business. They took over the business without enough capital or a real growth plan.

Sal manages the kitchen with Ray. Sunny works the front of the store. David spends time making deliveries and cleaning. But aside from an unlimited supply of bread and pastries, none of them have money to live on. All the money from the bakery goes into the expenses needed to run the place and with every week, it seems like there is less and less money to cover even that.

But for David, it's about more than money. It's about utter humiliation. It's about the collapse of his reputation, which, at his age, has barely evolved. Once the collector, David is now the deadbeat being harassed for payments. No, he's worse than a deadbeat because he controls a once successful business and is fucking it up. He has no excuse but his own inadequacy. His humiliation peaks when the calls come from Greg Anderson at the bank.

"David, please. I went out on a limb for you. I want this to work out, but you must start making payments on the loan."

Greg comes to the bakery, and David hides in a back office rather than face him.

But even those low points seem like winning an Olympic gold medal compared to the time when Sal doesn't have enough money to pay Ray. Ray asks Sal for his check, and Sal's face clouds over before his temper detonates.

"What the fuck do you want me to do, Ray? Pull the money out of my ass?"

Ray hates conflict and tries to reasonably explain to Sal that he expects to be paid. "Look, Sal, you and Sunny made promises to me. How am I supposed to live without a check?"

"The same way I'm living!" Sal snarls. "You think I'm getting money from this fuckin' place? Do you want to be paid? Fine. How about you sleep with my wife? That's what you really want, isn't it, you nigger?" He violently throws metal tools at the kitchen walls, breaking half of them.

Normally cool and centered, David snaps when he hears the argument. He sprints into the kitchen red with rage. "Sal, what the hell are you doing? Ray is right to want his money. We've got to make this happen, and you have to back... the fuck... off!"

David rarely swears, and his use of "fuck" surprises Sal.

In response, Sal storms out of the kitchen. Ray stands crestfallen for a full minute and then he slowly walks outside, takes a used box out of the trash, comes back into the kitchen, and packs up his baking tools. He walks over to David on his way to the front door, puts his left hand on David's shoulder, and with sincere empathy shakes David's other hand with his right hand.

David has no idea what he can say to smooth things over. He feels the tears welling in his eyes.

There are tears in Ray's eyes too. "David, I just can't do this anymore. As bad as it was at Wolfie's, it was nothing compared to this."

Ray takes a last look around at the kitchen, leaves, and never returns.

David thinks with the deepest regret, *If not for Ray we never would have even gotten in the door. He doesn't deserve this.*

There is a special sorrow to losing your dream. When they took over the bakery, David, Sal, and Sunny felt like they'd won the sweepstakes, and everyone called David a genius for making it all happen. He had instant respect from family, friends, and total strangers. But as the money unravels, so does his respect, including his self-respect. David's life is now a termite-infested treehouse ready to collapse.

Shortly after Ray leaves, David commits what he later calls his original sin. He makes the daily bank deposits for the bakery. He notices in one of the deposits a two-hundred-dollar check from an out-of-state bank that Sunny accepted from a customer for a wedding cake and assorted pastries.

After David makes the deposit, he discovers on the deposit receipt that, although the bank can't know when the checks will clear, the bank clears for cash all two hundred dollars of the out-of-state check. He knows it's possible the check could bounce like a fatso on a trampoline, so he watches the returns. Two weeks later, the check bounces, and the bank takes back the two hundred dollars from the bakery checking account.

David wonders, *Is there a limit to the amount that the bank will clear on a check? Does the bank even know who is writing the check?* It's not an easy choice for him to make, but the line between right and wrong seems very dotted and faint when one is faced with public and private humiliation and bankruptcy. He writes a check from his personal bank account for eight hundred dollars—the amount needed for the next week's supplies. He tells no one.

David knows that his check won't clear. He holds it in his wallet as long as he can until Sal complains that they'll have to close the door if they can't come up with the money for supplies.

"What am I supposed to do?" Sal says. "Put my shit in the display cases?"

David deposits the check with the daily sales. It clears immediately. He tells Sal, "We have the supply money. Go ahead and order."

Crisis averted—for a few days.

Before the bank discovers that the eight-hundred-dollar check has the value of dirt, David deposits another personal check for fifteen hundred dollars that the bank also immediately clears. Since the account isn't overdrawn, the bank simply returns the first bounced eight-hundred-dollar check to the bakery. David recovers the check and destroys it.

And the original sin blossoms into a web of money and maleficence. The money becomes a salve to David's guilty conscience and eases the pressure of running the business. A month after purposely depositing the first bad check, David calls a meeting with Sunny and Sal after closing. They pull up chairs in the cramped office. David sits behind the desk. Now that the bakery expenses are under control, even Sal seems calm and rational.

"Guys," David says, "I just want to tell you what's going on. Our sales haven't been better; I've been padding the sales with bad checks out of my own account."

Sal speaks first. His face is contorted with disbelief. He stalks like a cat in a cage. "Okay, but what happens when the checks bounce?"

"It seems that the bank just returns the check if the account isn't overdrawn. I keep depositing checks in larger amounts to keep that from happening."

Sunny is pensive. She gets up and leans on the desk facing David, her face nurturing but concerned. "We can't keep that up forever. It will catch up with us. Is it against the law? It must be against the law. If the bakery is still losing money, we must come up with a plan. Free money just… isn't."

Sal says, "Why would it be illegal? The bank is clearing the checks. It's on them."

David considers this. "I'm writing the checks to myself. Who's going to press charges? Mom's right. What's important is that we use this opportunity to bring the bakery back to profitability. Let's use this time to make enough money to dig out of the hole."

If David killed someone and left the body in the back seat of his locked car, Sunny would ask how a dead guy could somehow accidentally make his way into his locked car. She doesn't just trust David; she now has Messiah-like faith in him.

Sunny plops back down on the chair. She addresses David but makes it clear that she's addressing Sal too. "Whatever you think is right, honey. After all, you got us this place. I know that we'll eventually fix these problems too. Just let us know what you need."

The float continues. As the personal checks get larger and larger, David deposits a check for fifteen thousand dollars to cover a fourteen-thousand-dollar pending overdraft. The teller takes the check and starts to run the deposit. Then she stops and glances questionably toward David. She leans over and shows the check to another teller. She apologizes to David that the account for Romano's Bakery is closed.

"Sir, would you mind waiting here for a moment?"

The teller walks toward the desks at the other side of the room where the bank officers, including Greg Anderson, sit.

Panic grips David like a fist clutching his gut. Suddenly, he feels like he's suffocating. He doesn't wait. He nervously leaves the bank and fast walks to his car, trying not to attract attention. He pulls out of his parking place and toward the exit. He doesn't know where he'll go after that, but it doesn't matter because David is surrounded by police before he gets within thirty feet of the exit. He feels his stomach turn as if he jumped out of a plane, and the chute failed to open.

David is corralled by police cars in front and back. His fear is like a boa constrictor around his heart. He's helpless, and he feels a black hole swallowing life as he knows it. Detective Spencer of the Hollywood Police Department gets out of one of the unmarked police cars and approaches David's door. Spencer sports a buzz cut and a scowl. His polyester suit looks like it was bought off the rack at Sears. His arm pulls back on his jacket. His hand is on his sidearm.

David can't breathe.

"Get out of the car and keep your hands where I can see them."

Twenty years old with no record of any trouble, much less criminal activity, David feels like his life has just ended.

He does as he's told. Spencer applies handcuffs and brings him back into the bank where Greg Anderson is waiting. Greg doesn't say anything. He shakes hands with Detective Spencer, who orders David to sit down on one of three chairs outside of Greg's office. It's like an open cage at the zoo. Bank employees and customers can't help looking at David sitting handcuffed in the chair. The embarrassment is crushing.

Time freezes, and he watches through the window of Greg's office. Police come in and out. David can't tell if Greg and the detectives are in his office for fifteen minutes or hours. His right leg convulses nervously up and down like the bass foot of a drummer in a hard rock band. Other bank officers go in and out of the office while David sits impotently in the chair, not knowing what will happen next. He expects jail. But why isn't he already there?

Detective Spencer storms out of Greg's office. His initial scowl has given way to angry raving, and his pale face is now dotted with pink blotches. He's pissed. He roughly grabs David by the armpit and yanks him out of the chair. Then he directs David into Greg's office and shuts the door.

Greg sits at his desk accompanied by two other unknown men standing at the back of the room. David supposes by their suits and rep ties that they work at the bank.

Greg addresses David in an unperturbed yet firm voice. "David, you just tried to deposit a fifteen-thousand-dollar check into your account. You're the maker of the check, and you know that the account has insufficient funds."

David nods yes. He feels like he has a fever.

"Have you heard of check-kiting?" Greg continues.

"No."

Detective Spencer speaks up. "It's a felony. And we have you so busted."

David cannot even look up to meet anyone's gaze.

"For our own reasons," Greg continues, "we're not going to press charges. We'll increase your loan amount to cover the bank's loss, and you'll pay it all." His tone leaves no room for argument. This is more of a prophecy than a threat. "Furthermore, your banking privileges have been canceled. You'll have to find another bank to do business with."

"I understand."

Spencer is enraged. He screams at the bank officers, "I hope you know that I think this is bullshit. I don't even think this is your decision to make!"

David makes a mental note to himself. *When you're guilty, an angry cop is a good cop.* Those words will later kick him in the balls.

Greg is like a tightrope walker, delicately balancing between the bank's legal position and what is best for the bank with the local police. "I understand, Detective, and I thank you for your cooperation." He turns to David. "We've prepared revised loan documents."

The detective removes the handcuffs from David.

Greg hands David the new loan documents. "Sign the papers and you can leave. And David?"

David looks up at Greg while he signs the papers without reading them.

"I'd better never see you in this bank again."

"Believe me, Mr. Anderson, you won't. Thank you, sir."

The detective glowers at David. "Oh, one more thing. If I find you so much as littering, I will lock you up so tight you'll wish your mother didn't have any kids that lived."

CHAPTER 7

THE arrest at the bank is a turning point for David. His shame eats at him like a hungry beast. Even with Sunny's attempts at comfort, he feels as though he has fallen from any grace he might have previously enjoyed. Any pride he had at his success with the bakery fades into silence like a forgotten melody.

The good news is that now the bakery seems to be making a small profit. Even with Ray gone, Sal continues the production with recipes provided by the original owner and Ray. The money that David brought in by check kiting helps to ease the backlog of invoices. No one is getting rich, but they're beginning to understand the business.

Sunny finds new commercial customers by offering wholesale desserts that restaurants can offer their diners at triple what they pay for them. She offers cannoli shells that can be filled with different flavors of ricotta cheese in the restaurant kitchen before they're served, which makes the margin for everyone even higher.

One of those businesses is Rainbow Diner. Rainbow is in a small but busy strip mall in Fort Lauderdale. It's an upscale sandwich shop that a lot of spring breakers go to because they send hot, bikini-clad babes to the beaches with special flyers.

Broward County Building and Zoning ordered an increase in the mall's parking spaces. To comply, the owner of the mall contracted a construction crew to install additional signage and mark the asphalt. Several holes have been blasted into the asphalt to install the signs which at present sit on the truck.

"Where the hell is Stan?" the contractor asks his laborer. "We're on the clock, and the concrete mix is in his truck."

The laborer knows he isn't expected to know the answer. They've waited for Stan for the better part of an hour. Regardless, he feels obligated to answer the rhetorical question. "I couldn't tell you what that redneck is up to. I only know that we're late for lunch."

The laborer has been pacing around for a half hour griping about his empty belly. "Jesus, there's a restaurant right here. Let me run in and get us something to eat."

"But we got to finish this up, like now. Besides, I can't afford for this to go into overtime."

"Look, I'm starving. How about I just duck into this diner and get us sandwiches? You wait here and watch the site. If Stan comes, send him in, and I'll come right out."

The contractor reaches into his pocket and pulls out a five. "Get me a ham sandwich with lettuce, tomato, and mayo. And hurry back. I got to take a leak."

The laborer goes into the diner but within a few minutes, his boss's urge to piss is stronger. It feels like a drumbeat in his bladder. The contractor thinks, *Shit, I'll only be gone for a minute. Besides, they're only eight-inch holes. What can happen the minute that I'm gone?*

Sunny is inside Rainbow Diner delivering pastries on large metal trays wrapped in plastic. On her way out, the manager of the diner meets her at the door.

"Sunny, would you mind taking back some of the old pastry trays on your way out?"

"No problem." Sunny gathers a half dozen trays, three under each arm. She struggles to hold onto them as she leaves the diner and... steps right into one of the unguarded holes.

Sunny drops the trays. Her foot goes into the hole, but she doesn't twist her ankle. She simply steps down with her right foot into the hole. She expects solid ground and instead, her foot hits nothing but air until it reaches the rocky bottom of the hole. Even though her leg and ankle feel fine, her whole body is jarred. She thinks she's fine when she gets to the van. By the time she returns to the bakery, she's sore but not in terrible pain. As time passes, the pain becomes volcanic.

By that evening, Sunny's lower back feels like someone is holding a blow torch inside it as she stands at the register to count the cash. The pain increases exponentially with every minute. She quickly goes from needing to sit down to not being able to get out of the chair. The pain now travels from her lower back, down her legs, and even into her feet.

She calls out for help and Sal, already heading to the storefront from the kitchen, picks up his pace and rushes over to her. "What is it? What's wrong?"

Sunny is sitting on the chair behind the register. She holds her body unnaturally, as if she were a debilitated mime trying to fit into an imaginary space too small for her frame. Her face is contorted with pain.

"I stepped in a hole on the last delivery. I didn't think it would be this bad."

Sal tries to lift her from the chair.

"No! Please stop!" she cries. Her body spasms with even more pain.

David calls an ambulance and with great care, the EMTs manage to lay Sunny onto a stretcher. They take her vitals and transport her to the Hollywood Medical Center emergency room. Sal rides with Sunny in the ambulance, and David locks up and follows in the car.

By the time David reaches the hospital and parks, Sunny is in x-ray. When they bring her back to the emergency room, she's on a morphine drip for the pain. The pain and drugs make her confused to the point of delirium. When

David arrives, she's riding a morphine wave so potent that reality melts away and leaves her adrift in a sea of illusion.

The doctor enters the room. David would guess he's maybe thirty. He wears the mandatory blue scrubs, a rubber stethoscope, and a severe look on his face. He gives David as much acknowledgment as he would a chair. He heads straight to Sal.

"The x-rays show that your wife has sustained an extensive rupture in both her fifth and sixth lumbar vertebrae. She needs surgery as soon as it can be scheduled. There is a new technology called magnetic resonance imaging, which should be done prior to surgery."

"Of course," Sal tells him. "Whatever she needs. Please just take care of her. I know what kind of pain she's in. I have back problems myself. Doctors have told me that I need surgery, but it's never been as bad as what she's going through."

The doctor continues, "She'll be admitted as soon as a bed becomes available. Someone will be down to take her up."

About an hour later, nurses roll Sunny, babbling in a morphine fugue, out of the emergency room. David and Sal take a different elevator and find their way to her hospital room. David is struck dumb with grief. Sal paces and punches concrete walls.

A few minutes later, a woman as thin as a paper clip with sharp facial features and silver hair walks into the room. She carries a clipboard and wears a meticulous beige business suit with chunky amber jewelry that looks out of place among the medical uniforms and scrubs. "Hello, I'm from Admissions. I need to take the patient's information."

Sal rolls his eyes dismissively and vaguely waves his hand toward Sunny. "Well, she certainly isn't in a position to give you anything right now."

"I'm sorry. Are you her husband? Maybe you can come down to my office and give me what I need."

Sal erupts. "Seriously?! While I'm sitting here watching my wife out of her head with pain? You think I should leave here because you need some information? Get real!"

David rolls his eyes at Sal's reaction. His face is a mask of anguish. But he manages to center himself emotionally, get up, and put his hand out to the woman, who cordially shakes it. "Hi. I'm her son. I'll come downstairs with you. I'm sure I can supply whatever information you need."

They take the elevator to the lobby and walk down the hall to an office that reminds David of his HPC offices. Lots of desks in small cubes. The woman motions David to a chair in front of a desk cluttered with files.

The woman takes her own rolling swivel chair behind the desk, puts on a pair of cheater glasses that formerly dangled from a chain around her neck, and begins. "Name and address."David tells her.

"Date of birth."

"April twenty-fifth, nineteen forty-one."

David knows the answers to all the personal questions she asks of him.

"Does your mother have insurance?"

"No. None of us have insurance."

"Where does she work?"

"We own a bakery."

"And you don't offer insurance?"

"No. It's a small operation."

"Was this a job-related injury?"

"Yeah. She got hurt on a delivery."

"Great. Who is your Workmen's Compensation carrier?"

"I don't think we have one."

The woman takes off her glasses and peers at David. "You realize that your mother needs surgery. Without it she might never walk. She'll be crippled. You don't want that for your mother, do you?"

David feels like he has been shot with a high caliber bullet as he imagines the heart-breaking tableau of his mother confined to a wheelchair. "No, of course not."

"And do you know it's illegal not to carry Workmen's Compensation insurance?"

"No, I didn't."

"She needs to be admitted, and that isn't cheap. We'll need a down payment of at least five thousand dollars to continue her treatment."

David knows that, despite the bakery doing better, they don't have anywhere near that much money sitting around. He starts to consider things that he could sell. Nothing comes to mind. He's filled with dread and silently hates the heartless bitch sitting across from him.

The bitch adds, "You can write a check, or we can take cash or credit card."

David takes out his personal checkbook and writes a check for five thousand dollars on the closed account. The woman gives him a receipt.

She also gives him a piece of paper labeled *Insurance Claim Form.* "If you find that your mother does have insurance, just have her fill out this form, sign it, and get it back to me."

David takes the form, folds it into quarters, and puts it into his jacket pocket. "Sure. Thanks."

He goes back upstairs to his mother's room and says a silent prayer that she'll get the back surgery before the check bounces.

CHAPTER 8

THE United Airlines flight leaves a little late from Newark, New Jersey with a planned destination to Los Angeles, California. It holds eighty-five passengers, two pilots, and four flight crew. One passenger is about to forever change the lives of everyone on board.

Floyd McDonald sits in the aisle of an otherwise empty row toward the front of coach. He's dressed in disco chic with a silk designer shirt under a black blazer jacket. His long, black hair looks like he used a little too much mousse before styling it. Before Floyd takes his seat, he stuffs several small canvas bags into the overhead compartment.

Floyd is young-middle age. He appears to be in his late thirties with the build of an athlete. Maybe a swimmer. He's tall and quiet and struggles with leg room. But other than that, he's as calm as death.

After the plane is in the air and levels off, after the curtain to first class is drawn, and right before the beverage carts are to be pushed down the aisles, Floyd reaches into the pocket of his jacket and produces a hand grenade. He's subtle. There are no flourishes or rantings. It comes out suddenly, like a magic trick. One second his hand is empty, and the next... voila.

As the stewardess walks toward Floyd, he catches her attention.

"What is our ETA into Los Angeles?" Floyd glances down at the grenade and the stewardess's eyes follow his.

Though startled, she's very professional. She notices that the grenade has no pin, and that Floyd is holding the handles together. She knows that there is a crisis but, to her credit, she shows no outward signs of alarm other than the slight quiver in her voice. She manages to stammer out, "I-I b-believe the ETA is 9:03 p.m. Pacific time."

"Thank you. Please check back with me."

She leaves and calmly makes her way past first class to the cabin and informs the captain of the situation. She gives the captain Floyd's seat number.

The captain is also an experienced professional. He's in his forties with short-cropped brown hair. He wears a short-sleeved white United Airlines stock shirt with epaulets and a pocket protector holding two Bic pens and a mechanical pencil. He tells the stewardess, "Wait here. Let me check this out for myself."

When the captain approaches Floyd, he's met with the grenade in Floyd's left hand and a 38-special held in the right hand. Both weapons are held subtly and discretely away from the prying eyes of other passengers.

Floyd says nothing to the captain. His piercing black eyes are predatory. He has a wry grin, as if he's the cat mastermind of a canary caper. Floyd says nothing but locks eyes with a withering look that says, *Don't fuck around here*. With the gun hand he reaches into his jacket breast pocket and gives the captain an envelope with the hand-printed label *HIJACK INSTRUCTIONS* on the front. The captain takes the envelope from Floyd without conversation and walks back to the cabin.

Once in the cabin, the captain opens the envelope. Inside are two typed pages of instructions, a hand grenade pin, and a bullet. The instructions are to land at San Francisco International Airport and park on a specific runway. The instructions also detail how many people are allowed to come near the plane and how those people are to be dressed to ensure they have no weapons. It also advises the distance all ground vehicles need to be from the plane.

After reading the details, the pilot gets to the meat of the demand. One half million dollars in unmarked bills with no sequential serial numbers and four parachutes are to be brought to Floyd upon landing. Once the cash and parachutes are on board, the plane is to be refueled. Once all this happens, the instructions promise the passengers will be released. *Very specific. This guy has given this some thought.* This gives the captain some solace. *At least it's not some suicide attempt or political shit. It's all about the money.*

It's a silk-black night sky as the captain follows the directions and diverts the plane to San Francisco. The passengers are told that the plane is landing there to perform minor mechanical work.

Once the plane lands, Floyd takes control of it. He holds the hand grenade and gun high enough for the passengers to see them. "Everyone stays in their seats." No one moves. "There is a powerful explosive on board besides this grenade. Your cooperation will help you live." Floyd then flashes his cocky smile and adds, "Maybe you can visit San Francisco's famous fish market when this is over. I highly recommend it."

The captain, on the radio, reads the instructions to his supervisors. After remarkably short deliberation, the United officials decide to give in to Floyd's demands for the sake of the passengers' safety.

As one United executive tells the captain, "A half million wouldn't even cover the cost of legal fees if the passengers are hurt or killed."

Two flight bags with a half million dollars in cash and four parachutes are loaded onto the plane. The plane is refueled. No heroic measures are taken to board the plane.

Once Floyd sees that his demands are met, he tells the captain, "Open the exit door closest to the cabin. Have an air step brought for exit, and tell the passengers that they need to get off the plane right now. The flight crew stays."

The captain does as he's told. Stairs are brought to the exit door, and all the passengers file calmly out of the plane. Floyd follows the last of the passengers and closes the door. He then orders the crew into the cockpit area and goes to the rear of the aircraft, where he takes control of the intercom.

"Remember," Floyd reminds the flight crew over the intercom, "there is another explosive device hidden on this plane. Follow my instructions and you'll all live to see your loved ones before this night is over. Don't follow my instructions, and this will be the last flight you ever take." He removes a second grenade pin from his pocket, puts it into the grenade firing mechanism, and places the disarmed grenade into his side jacket pocket. "Captain, take off toward the east eleven point five degrees. Climb to sixteen thousand feet and stay at that altitude with an air speed of two hundred miles per hour." He then adds, "If I see any planes in pursuit, I will detonate the explosive, and nobody will live to tell this story to their grandkids."

Floyd uses his watch to determine how long the plane has been flying. He removes a compass from one of his overhead bags and uses it to confirm the plane's direction. He issues navigational orders to the pilot over the intercom to calibrate their course. Based on the direction and speed they're traveling, Floyd has a pretty good idea of the plane's geographic location. After ninety minutes, he calls over the intercom to the captain. "What's our current position?"

"Utah. About sixty miles southeast of Salt Lake City."

"Remain on course." Floyd takes another bag out of the overhead compartment and opens it. Inside he pulls out a jumpsuit and helmet. He quickly puts those on. He then checks the parachutes that were delivered per his instructions. He reviews the inspection and maintenance records for each one and makes sure that they're properly packed. He selects one and puts it on. He places his clothes and property in the now-empty bag.

He gets back on the intercom. "What's our current position?"

"Approximately fifteen miles southeast of Salt Lake City."

"Bring the altitude to five thousand feet and depressurize the plane." Floyd attaches the bag with his property and the money bags to another parachute. He then attaches a bright red signal light to the outside of the bags.

After the captain depressurizes the plane, Floyd opens the rear door. He opens and releases the parachute on the bag with his money and his property and pushes it out of the plane. Floyd then jumps from the plane into the Utah night sky. No one sees his chute open. After the crew determines that Floyd has indeed jumped, the plane heads to Salt Lake City International Airport.

* * *

Dianne Symmons and Dale Platt arrive at the Salt Lake City Airport less than an hour after the plane lands. Local authorities are holding the pilots and crew in a makeshift command office and are giving them food and beverages. When Dianne and Dale arrive, although their black jackets are emblazoned with "FBI" in large, gold letters, they immediately show their cred packs to the officers at the door.

Dianne introduces them. "Dianne Symmons and Dale Platt. FBI. Is everyone inside?"

"Yes," says one of the airport security officers. "FAA representatives are questioning them now."

Dianne and Dale hustle inside and again show their cred packs to avoid any question of their authority. They cross the room where shaken plane staff drink plastic cups of coffee and recount what happened over and over. They immediately engage with the FAA representative.

The FAA representative points to the stewardess and the captain. "These two actually got a good look at the hijacker."

Dianne's face is sexy but not pretty. Her reddish hair is silky fine and cut short. She wears little makeup, but she has striking features. She has broad shoulders and large breasts and legs that are so long her strides cover twice the ground as her shorter and much older partner. She doesn't smile so much as smirks. She's cocky business.

Even though Dale is the senior partner, Dianne takes the lead. "Good," she tells the FAA representative. "I want each of them in front of a sketch artist within the hour. I also want copies of each witness statement. Where is the plane? I need the stewardess and captain to come with us and show us exactly where this guy was sitting."

An airport security officer escorts Dianne, Dale, and the witnesses to the grounded plane. Dale says very little, but his sunken brown eyes take in every detail. He's in his late forties. He has a bit of a paunch and salt-and-pepper hair trimmed short.

As they're about to board the plane, Dianne holds a hand up to stop them. "Everyone glove up. I don't need any of your fingerprints added to the crime scene."

Dale sighs and raises his eyebrows as he pulls on nylon gloves. He murmurs under his breath, "Like this is my first crime scene." He asks the stewardess, "Can you show us exactly where the hijacker was sitting?"

The now gloved stewardess walks past Dale and Dianne and carefully goes to the row where, a few hours ago, Floyd had been sitting. "Right there." She points to the row of seats. "He sat right in this row on the aisle."

Dianne walks over and stands next to her. "Do you remember anything that he touched?"

The stewardess stares at the seat. "No. Not really."

"Well, was he wearing his seat belt?"

"Yes. He had to wear it for take-off."

Dianne glances around. "Mm-hmm. So, it's a pretty good bet that he handled his own seat belt."

"Yes, ma'am. I'm sure he did."

"Did he use the overhead compartment?"

"Yes! Now that you mention it, he did store some things in there."

"Which one did he use?"

"The one right here." The stewardess points above the seat. "Over his seat."

"Anything else that you can remember that would be helpful?"

"No, not really." The stewardess looks down with a melancholy wag of her head. "I'm sorry."

"It's fine," Dale says. "We appreciate the help. Please go back to meet with the sketch artists."

The FAA representative leaves the plane with the stewardess.

Dale turns to the captain. "Anything else you can tell us?"

"Only that this guy knew what he was doing. He had to have some technical flight training. Other than that, I'm at a loss."

After they return to the command center, Dianne turns to Dale and leans in conspiratorially. "They don't make witnesses like they used to."

"Don't be that way, Dianne. They've all been through so much tonight."

"At least we have a case here that can build our reps." Dianne flashes her patented smirk.

"Only if we solve it and make an arrest," Dale replies.

CHAPTER 9

SUNNY is in her hospital bed recovering from back surgery. It's been two days since she was operated on, and she's feeling pretty good. She's on the phone to David. "Hi, sweetheart. I'm doing fine. Business is good? That's terrific. They say I can probably get discharged in a few days, after they perform some sort of neurological tests."

She's in a sparsely furnished, semi-private hospital room. Typical hospital room fare. Black-and-white tiled floor. There are two hospital beds, each with two chairs for visitors and one of those flimsy tables that roll next to the beds and can fit over them for meals.

On the far wall facing the beds is a thirty-inch color television that the patients operate by remote control from a device attached to their beds. Susan Johnson is in the other bed. Sunny guesses she's in her mid-forties. She has red hair that looks like it belongs to a scarecrow. She's also recovering from back surgery but has only been back for a day. She's in much more pain than Sunny, and the nurses bring her what seems like a never-ending supply of Valium.

Susan impatiently presses the remote control for the television, flicking it forward with her wrist as if the jerking motion will make it work better. "I don't know why this doesn't work. I can't change the freaking channel." She tries slamming the remote control against the railing of her bed.

Sunny says into the phone, "David, let me call you back." She tries her remote control. "Yeah, mine doesn't work either. That's very weird. It was working earlier."

Susan pushes the button for the nurse, but no one comes. She winces in pain as her jerking motions becomes more frantic. "One of my favorite shows is coming on. I don't want to miss the beginning of it."

"I have an idea. Let me change the channel the old-fashioned way." Sunny gets out of bed and walks across the room toward the television. Her eyes are focused upward on the television mounted six feet from the floor. As she reaches up to the channel dial, her leading leg suddenly slips out from under her and she falls backward, her surgically repaired spine taking all her weight.

"What happened?" Susan cries.

"I don't know." Sunny groans, lying on the floor. She struggles to turn over. "I can't get up."

Susan screams out of the door over and over until a nurse finally runs into the room. The nurse gasps when she sees Sunny sprawled out on the tile floor.

"What happened?" the nurse repeats. She sounds an alarm, and the room is quickly flooded with nurses, aides, and a doctor.

"I don't know," Sunny manages to say through cries of pain. "My foot just slipped under me."

It's Susan who first sees it. Her face is more alert with the discovery. "There's a nylon glove. Someone left a nylon glove on the floor. That's what she slipped on!"

One of the nurses quickly scoops up the glove and puts it into her pocket. "I'm so sorry. Can you get back into bed?"

The nurses help Sunny back into the bed and take her vital signs.

The doctor says, "You seem fine for now. Blood pressure is a little high, but that's understandable. Stay in bed! I'll talk to the ortho doctor and see if we need to retake x-rays."

A few minutes ago nearly pain free, Sunny is now in extreme discomfort as she lies back in her hospital bed. She's blissfully unaware of the uproar that her fall has in the hospital administration.

Paul Leonard, the operations manager of the hospital, sits across his desk from the hospital lawyer. In front of him is a file folder labeled *S. Rossi*. He flips through the pages. Leonard is normally very reserved. He's always dressed in dark suits with French cuffs. His monogrammed white shirts are custom tailored. He has a perpetual Florida tan that offsets his silver hair, which is lacquered like a helmet.

Holding a legal pad filled with notes, the attorney says, "I met with the doctor and the nurses who attended Mrs. Rossi. It appears, in my opinion, that we have liability. A nylon glove was dropped by someone in the room, presumably a nurse." He looks down at the notes and runs his finger down the page. "There was an unidentified electrical problem that affected both the television controllers and the nurse call button."

"Damn it. How badly was Ms. Rossi injured?"

"She hasn't been fully re-examined yet."

"Was there negligence on her part? Should she have been walking after back surgery?"

"That will certainly be our argument if we need to make it. But hell, one of the nurses even apologized to her for the glove on the floor."

Leonard face palms. "Are you kidding me?" He loosens his tie.

The attorney continues, "Unfortunately, no. And the patient in bed one saw and heard the whole thing. Maybe we can make a deal to simply cover Ms. Rossi's medical expenses."

"That won't matter to her if she's insured." Leonard picks up the phone and dials zero. "Please get me Admissions." Three rings later, the line is answered.

"Admissions."

"Paul Leonard here. Please give me the account status on Sunny Rossi. Room 502."

There is a short wait. "Sir, nothing has been paid on the account. Ms. Rossi was brought in from Emergency. Someone gave us a bad check for five thousand dollars when she was admitted. Nothing has been paid yet. The check was sent to our Collections Department."

Leonard hangs up the phone. It's a long minute before he resumes the conversation. "What's the criminal punishment for a bad check?"

"Depends on the amount."

"Five thousand dollars."

"I'm sure that would be a felony."

"We can be on the hook for hundreds of thousands of dollars for this shit, and Ms. Rossi didn't even pay for our services. In fact, she gave us a bum check! Unbelievable! But maybe it can work for us. I want her discharged immediately. Don't re-examine her. I don't want to know if she was reinjured. We need to go on the offensive. Make sure that you get someone in the state attorney's office to prosecute on the check. That might give us some leverage if there is a civil suit."

The attorney gives a disapproving look. "That's very aggressive."

"Yeah, but will it work?"

"I don't imagine that it could make things worse. I'll make sure Ms. Rossi is discharged by tomorrow morning. I went to law school with one of the assistant state attorneys for the City of Hollywood. He'll make the check a priority."

CHAPTER 10

DIANNE and Dale, along with Utah State troopers and Salt Lake City Police are at the launching area where they expect the hijacker's parachute landed. They begin their search for either clues, the hijacker himself, or his remains. Two helicopters are commissioned from the Air Force National Guard for aerial support. The Salt Lake City Police captain brings everyone together for brief introductions and instructions.

Everyone gathers to hear details of the search strategy. The helicopter pilots are wearing their headsets and sunglasses. Police eschew their normal uniforms in favor of tee-shirts, denim jeans, and baseball-style caps. They intend to canvass the five-hundred-acre area on foot.

Soon the search captain shouts, "All right! Everyone has their grids! Spread out and move out!"

Dale and Dianne stand with the captain facing the group. Dale wears jeans and a blue tee-shirt with "FBI" printed on the front and back. Dianne wears a black cotton pant suit with her FBI creds on a lanyard.

Once they separate from the captain and the crowd disperses, Dianne complains to Dale, "What a colossal waste of time." She stalks around the grounds chain smoking and kicking dirt. "We're never going to find our guy like this."

"Unless he went splat," Dale answers with a wry grin.

"He didn't go splat. This guy knew what he was doing. No one jumps out of a commercial jet at five thousand feet without knowing what they're doing."

"So where does that leave us? We ran the prints on the seatbelt against the criminal database, and there was nothing."

"Where do you become an expert in sky diving?"

"A jump school—"

Dianne interrupts Dale in mid-sentence. "No, not for this. This is 'Nam shit."

"You would know. It was your war. What branch were you in?"

Dianne lights another lung dart off the one previously in her mouth and smashes the former butt with the heel of her flats. "Army. I wanted to go for Special Forces but... you know."

"Yeah." Dale says, pointing to Dianne's oversized breasts. "Too much on top."

Dianne grimaces and makes a vague gesture toward her crotch. "More like too little on the bottom, if you get my drift."

Dale laughs and glances behind Dianne. "You look like you've got enough ass."

Her impatience is showing. "How about I knock you on your ass, partner?"

Dale rolls his eyes and takes a step back. "Man, broads just don't have a sense of humor anymore."

"Well, this broad thinks it's a riot that you smoke filtered cigarettes. Pussy."

The FBI excluded women from being agents until 1972. Dianne was one of the first female agents just two years after the exclusion was lifted. Although she came in as an army veteran, as a woman she was barely accepted both within the agency and to the public at large. Dale, a senior agent, thought she deserved a chance and took Dianne on as a provisional field agent. He knows she has the goods, if only she didn't have the personality of a chihuahua.

Dianne looks away thoughtfully. "Yeah, I wanted Special Forces, but women weren't allowed anywhere near the combat theater. They tried to put me behind a desk."

Dale stops joking around. His smile disappears. "What do you mean 'tried'?"

"Because I was a woman and typed like the wind, they only considered me for desk duty. What they didn't know was that I had other talents... until I showed them. If we solve this without me having to put my foot up your ass and breaking it off at the ankle, maybe I'll show those talents to you too."

They walk in silence for a few minutes. Annoyed, Dale asks several times, "C'mon. What talents? Are you a black belt? Do you have a photographic memory?"

Dianne dismisses his queries. "Okay, so we can assume this guy's military. We need to run the prints against military records and hope that something comes up. Let's call it in."

"It's a big database," says Dale. "It'll take forever to get results."

Dianne and Dale leave and drive back to the Salt Lake City Airport's makeshift command center. Dale makes the call to check on the prints while Dianne takes another look at the artist sketch from witness accounts. She carries the sketch copy into the room where Dale is on the phone and lays the sketch on the table in front of him. The sketch is a grayscale likeness of a white male with short hair and a triangular face.

"There's something about this guy. I know I've seen him somewhere, but I can't place it."

"Guy like that looks like a lot of people. Maybe some old boyfriend of yours?"

Dianne playfully punches him on the shoulder. "No. It looks like someone we saw recently. But I can't place it."

"So... women's intuition?"

"Fuck you."

"Sorry. You're not my type. Want to get back to the search?"

"No, you go without me. I want to check more on this military theory."

Dale catches a ride back to the search area, and Dianne takes their black Ford Crown Victoria to the local Air Force base. She badges her way through the gate and meets with the sergeant on duty.

He's sitting behind a desk littered with papers and barely looks up when Dianne comes into the office. "How can I help our country's FBI on this fine day, Agent?"

"Isn't it customary to stand when a ranking officer enters the room?"

The sergeant looks up from his desk. "And you are?"

"Second Lieutenant Dianne Symmons."

The sergeant reluctantly stands up, but no salute. "From what unit?"

"Army Special Operations Regiment. Now a civilian."

The sergeant salutes. "I believe once a soldier, always a soldier. All right, what can I do for you, Lieutenant?"

"We're working on this United Airlines hijacking. Have you heard about it?"

"Of course. Guys like DB Cooper. You never caught him, did you?"

"Not my case. This is. I'm thinking this guy is military to make a jump like that. You know any Special Forces types who were around this area and off base?"

"No. And other than testing facilities, this is the only base. But it couldn't be one of our guys."

"And why not?"

"We've been running special drills. No leaves have been given recently and no AWOLs. Besides, I just don't see this being the work of a soldier. At least not an active soldier. Soldiers aren't lone wolves. We work as a team. What I read in the paper, this was done by a loner. It must be a civilian. A trained civilian, but a civilian, nonetheless. Ma'am."

Dianne contemplates this. "A civilian with military training. That leaves two possibilities." She thanks the sergeant for his help and drives back to the airport command center.

CHAPTER 11

LESS than a week after Sunny was discharged from the hospital, she's resting at home. David is working at the bakery register. A young couple comes in and pays for a wedding cake. David goes into the kitchen and with Sal's help carries the cake to the front for them to look at.

"It's perfect!" The bride-to-be beams at the multi-layered cake in red and green with white frosting.

"I love it too," says her fiancé as he teases her by fake putting a finger out to scoop some frosting.

"Don't you dare." She swats his hand away.

"Did you want this delivered?" David asks.

The groom-to-be shakes his head. "No, we have room in the hatch. But could you give us a hand with it?"

"Sure. No problem." David and Sal each take one end of the board under the cake and carry it to the car. They carefully place the cake inside the hatch.

"Hey!" Sal yells at David. "Be careful! Don't touch the frosting on anything."

After the cake is placed in the car and the customer is closing the hatch, just as David is straightening up from placing the cake inside, he hears a voice. "David Adler?"

David turns around to see Detective Spencer with another officer. "Yes?"

Spencer flashes an evil smile. "You're under arrest. Please turn around and place your hands behind your back."

"What? Why?" David does as he's instructed, and the detective attaches handcuffs.

"You have the right to remain silent."

Sal takes a step toward the detective. "Hey. He has the right to know what this is about."

The detective moves toward Sal, closing the gap between them, and glares at him. "It's about you take three steps back or it's about you being arrested for obstruction of justice."

Sal reluctantly steps back.

A small crowd starts to form.

"You know what?" the detective says. "Let's get out of here. We'll Mirandize this asshole back at the station." He walks David to the squad car, opens the back door, and guides his head as he pushes him inside.

Sal asks the other officer, "Where are you taking him?"

"Hollywood Police Station for processing. That's all I can say."

At the station David is fingerprinted, read his rights, and escorted into a small cell with a steel cot bolted to one wall and a steel combination sink and toilet on the opposite wall. The bars are stark and imposing. He fights back tears and asks himself, *How did this happen? Maybe Hollywood Bank changed their mind.* Every minute sitting in the cell seems like a week. Every time he sees a uniformed figure he cries out, "Excuse me! Excuse me! Don't I get a phone call? Why am I here?" Everyone ignores him, which makes him feel more isolated and confused.

Detective Spencer is in his office adjoining a bullpen where police are going in and out. The detective holds court with a few of the uniformed officers. "I'm so glad I caught this case. This kid scored a bakery with nothing. Then he turned around and scammed Hollywood Bank for, like, fifteen large. Then the kid skated because the bank didn't want their name in the paper for how they were scammed."

"Sounds like a real piece of work," replies one of the officers. "Where is this bakery?"

"Romano's on Sterling."

Another officer shakes his head. "Seriously? I know that place. Been there a lot."

"Anyway, now the kid passes paper to a hospital for five large, and they're pressing charges. I'm glad it caught up with him."

Hours pass, and it seems to David like he's been in the cell for a month.

A uniformed police officer finally unlocks the door. "Let's go."

David follows the officer to a room where his hands are handcuffed in front of him to a steel bolt on an immovable table.

A big man in his thirties or early forties wearing a wrinkled beige trench coat, a cheap suit only slightly less wrinkled than the coat, and a tie loosened at the neck sits at a chair opposite him. The man looks across at David with deep brown eyes set below a huge forehead and black hair retreating on his head like a French army. "Are you David Adler?"

"Yes. Who are you?"

"My name is John Foster with Hollywood Bonds. Your parents hired me to post your bond and get you out."

"That's such a relief. So, I can get out of here?" David has no idea how these things work.

"Just sign here." The bondsman gives David three separate documents to sign.

David doesn't even bother to read them. Foster's hands look like his knuckles were broken in a fight or maybe from breaking too many boards in karate class.

Foster, expressionless, collects the papers and tells David, "You should be out in about a half hour." He calls for the officer, who takes David back to his cell.

As Foster predicted, at a half hour to the minute, another uniformed officer comes to David's cell and opens the lock. "Time to go," is all the officer says.

David hustles out of the cell and through two other locked doors to the lobby, where Sunny and Sal are waiting for him.

Sunny lunges at David, arms open to surround him. "Are... are you all right? My poor boy." She starts to cry as her tension releases at seeing David free.

"Yeah, Mom. I'm fine. Just... this has never happened to me before, you know?"

Sal says, "Hey. In my old neighborhood this would be a rite of passage. Like losing your virginity."

"Yeah, well, losing my virginity was a whole lot more fun than this."

Sunny says, "The bondsman gave me the name of a good lawyer. We'll make an appointment first thing in the morning."

As they get to the exit, David stops. "Wait a minute. How did you get me out? Didn't you need security for the bond?"

Sunny's face, usually pallid, turns even a shade paler. She looks around and says in a loud whisper, "We had to put up the bakery."

David stands confused. "But all of that equipment is pledged already on the loan."

Sal says, "Let's just get out of here."

CHAPTER 12

DALE walks into the airport command center.

Dianne sees him approach. "Any luck finding a spattered hijacker?"

"Nah. They've widened the search area."

"Too bad on the one hand. We could have closed the case. On the other hand..."

"She wore a glove," Dale says.

Dianne rolls her eyes. "All the partners I could have gotten, and I wind up working with Henny Youngman's less funny brother. No, on the other hand we still have a chance to solve this ourselves. Build our reps. I went to the Air Force base and talked with the sergeant. He's of the opinion, and I agree, that this is probably not the work of an active soldier. It's someone with a civilian life. That leaves a couple of options. The first is that he's retired military."

Dale interjects, "According to witnesses, this is a guy in his twenties or thirties. Someone with that kind of training would probably not retire that early. We need to find someone who mustered out for some other reason before retirement."

"Good point," Dianne answers. "In fact, that was what I thought of as option number two. Depending on the circumstances of his discharge, that may give us motive. Let's call around and see if we can get a discharge list. I'm thinking ten years back."

Dale looks at the fax machine and muses, "I hope there's enough paper here to keep the fax machine loaded. This will probably be a lot of files."

By the next morning, Dianne and Dale have a blank concrete wall covered with potential suspect pictures. Dianne points to one. "Melvin Hayes. Army Ranger. 75th Regiment. Did two tours in 'Nam. Trained as a jumper."

Dale looks at the file. "Medically discharged due to mental disability. Combat trauma."

"Not a motive. But it's a start. Let's pay Melvin a visit. He lives with his mother in Provo."

The house in Provo can only charitably be called a dump. The only saving grace is that the lot has several acres. But even that doesn't help much as the acreage is acrid and lifeless. Dianne and Dale drive the Crown Vic up a dirt road to the house, leaving a huge dust cloud in their wake.

The windows in the car are closed and both Dale and Dianne are smoking. A cloud of smoke fills the car.

"You think this is our guy?" Dale asks.

"Thirty-five-year-old local with military jumper training and a mental disorder. It beats wasting time looking for a corpse or clues fallen from the sky."

They pull up to the house and knock on the front door. No one answers.

"Car's in the driveway," Dianne says.

Dale says, "I'll go around back."

Dianne peers in different first-floor windows looking for signs of occupancy. Suddenly, she hears the unmistakable *chic-chic* of a shotgun being primed to fire. *The most dangerous sound in the world.* Her hands immediately rise above her head. She says over her shoulder, "I'm with the FBI. I'm a federal agent."

Melvin stands behind her, nudging her with the barrel of the shotgun. He's still in solid military shape although his voice tremors with stress. "Ain't no girl FBI agents. Who are you? What are you doing looking in my windows?"

Dianne starts to turn around.

Melvin puts the shotgun barrel by her head. "Don't fuckin' turn around!" He pats Dianne down and takes her gun. He puts her gun in his own belt. "Move to your left, start walkin', and don't look at me!"

To her left is a small patch of grass and a sturdy but narrow tree with no low branches. Melvin pushes Dianne closer to the tree with the shotgun until Dianne is just a few inches away.

"Now sit down cross-legged with your legs wrapped around the tree!"

Dianne does so with Melvin pressing her shoulders from behind. To her surprise, she finds that she can't get back up. There is no leverage. With all the lower branches of the tree gone, there is nothing to grab on to. Confident that she can't move, Melvin goes inside the house, leaving Dianne vulnerable and cursing in frustration.

Melvin sits the shotgun on a table, goes to the phone, and picks up the receiver. As he dials the phone, he feels a gun muzzle press against his temple.

Dale says, "Don't you move. Don't even blink. Where's the other agent?"

"Wha-wha-what?" Melvin stammers.

"Hands behind your back!" Dale yells. He applies the handcuffs. "Where is the woman that was out front?"

"She's fine." Melvin starts shaking violently with the stress. The shaking grows into a seizure.

Dale lays Melvin onto the floor, secures the shotgun and Dianne's pistol from Melvin's belt, and makes sure that Melvin's breathing isn't obstructed. Then he goes out front to see Dianne stuck to the tree.

Dianne is totally humiliated.

Dale is amused. "Old 'Nam trick when you needed to restrain a prisoner, but you didn't have rope. We used it back in the day too. Let me give you a hand."

He reaches down and pulls Dianne off the tree. After taking a moment to enjoy her discomfort, he tells her, "You know, I'll be damned if having you as my partner is going to be my downfall. I want to retire someday."

Dianne brushes herself off. "Fair warning. You tell anyone about this, you're going to get your ass kicked by a girl."

Dale laughs. "You just got your ass kicked by a tree."

They go back into the house. Melvin has stopped shaking and is now lying on the floor crying.

Dianne says, "Can't be our guy."

"Why not?"

"First of all, someone this unstable couldn't have planned that operation. Second, just look at his face."

Dale now sees Melvin's face clearly for the first time. He sees that Melvin has a large, deforming scar on the right side of his face from his forehead to the middle of his right cheek. His right eye is missing and replaced with an artificial device that looks like it came from a doll factory.

Dale helps Melvin to a chair. "The witnesses would have remembered that. What do we do with him now?"

"I guess we wait until his mother comes home."

As they drive back to the airport Dale says, "So, are you going back to the wall of suspects or are you going to join the search?"

Dianne ponders this for a moment. "I'll probably go back to the wall."

"The problem is, we won't have aerial support for much longer. Those National Guard pilots have to get back to their own lives, you know?"

Dianne turns off the radio. She suddenly looks up and gets a huge smile. "Dale, I do know. In fact, I know exactly where to find the hijacker."

CHAPTER 13

LEX Haller of the law firm of Abraham and Haller is on the phone in his office when David and Sunny are escorted in by his receptionist. He waves his hand in a beckoning motion and then motions toward two leather chairs in front of his desk for them to sit down.

Lex leans forward and authoritatively says into the phone, "I'm sorry, John, no deal. My guy walks with probation, or we go to trial. No, John. You don't have a case. Fruit of the poisonous tree. None of that evidence will be admitted. Talk to your boss, then call me back. I have clients in my office." He lets the handset hover for a moment over the receiver before he drops it, disconnecting the call.

He turns his attention to David and Sunny. "Sorry about that. Nixon's war on drugs should be called the Defense Attorney Full Employment Act. Prosecutors are getting harder on drug mules. It's not as easy to get them to agree that probation is better justice than prison."

Sunny gives Lex the paper with the charges for the five-thousand-dollar check. "I hope you can help us."

Lex looks at the charging sheet. He notes that arraignment is only three days away.

Sunny explains how David used the check to get her admitted to the hospital. She desperately finishes with, "We own Romano's Bakery on Sterling. We can pay your fee. David's never been in trouble before. He has no record."

Lex thinks to himself, *No record, and a sympathetic story. This can be an easy settlement. But an easy settlement doesn't pay the bills or... administrative fees.* He walks to the wall of law books behind him. He goes to the section of books on Florida Criminal Code and selects a volume. He carries the book back to his desk and silently flips through the pages. "The penalty for passing a check of that amount is five years in prison. First time or not, it's entirely possible that when you walk into that arraignment you'll get locked up. If you're convicted, you'll go to Raiford Penitentiary." He gestures to David. "Cons will love a kid like you. Are you a fag, kid? Because you might be after they get done with you."

"I-I'm not..." David manages to stammer out.

"We can't let him go to prison!" Sunny blurts.

"Look. For a case like this, I'll need a minimum ten thousand dollars plus expenses. Cash. I would normally take a check, but... considering." Lex holds up the charging sheet for the bad check. "Bring the cash to me no later than at the arraignment. Otherwise, I won't represent you, and there is a good chance that your bail will be revoked, and it will be a quick downhill slide from there to Raiford."

Sunny and David both know that they don't have that kind of money. Sunny says, "All right, Mr. Haller. We'll see you in court and bring the cash."

They thank him and leave. They walk to the parking lot.

David breaks the silence. "You know we don't have that kind of money, and I can't go back to jail!"

Sunny puts her arms around him. "You won't, honey. We'll figure this out. We always figure these things out."

When they get into the car, David says, "I've got to run. That's the only solution. You guys stay, run the bakery, and just send me money as I need it."

"There's no way on Earth that I would let you become a fugitive by yourself," Sunny says passionately. Tears are streaming down her ivory cheeks. "If you go, we all go.

Besides, if you run there won't be a bakery. We pledged it to the bondsman."

By the time David and Sunny make it back to the bakery, there is no talk of anything but running and what that would entail. They go inside and tell Sal that they need to go out somewhere to talk. An hour later, the three of them are sitting at a table in a nearby Lum's restaurant.

Sal sits silently, with his leg vibrating nervously and uncontrollably as he listens to Sunny explain what happened.

"I don't see any other option. My son and I are leaving. You should come with us." Sunny pauses and puts her hand on Sal's arm. "But I'll understand if you don't feel like you can."

Sal is in a quandary. He thinks, *This is a him-or-me moment.* Meaning that it's her choice between him and David. "Look, you're my wife. David may be your son, but you promised to be by my side. You made vows. I don't want to live with David forever. If I wanted a pet, I would have preferred a Labrador." Sal wishes he could take that back the moment he says it. He presses on. "And what about the bakery? Are we just going to abandon everything we've worked for?"

"Don't you understand?" Sunny says, hiding barely contained anger. "There is no bakery! David leaves, and the bondsman will come and take it away! And you made vows too. You promised to stay with me for better or for worse. Consider this part of the worst!"

Sal considers this. *If we get caught, I haven't done anything wrong. The worst that can happen is David gets caught, and then it will finally just be me and Sunny.*

Sunny persists. "Besides, if it weren't for David's brilliant strategy, we wouldn't have the bakery to begin with."

"Okay," Sal says, "I'm in. But I vote for taking the bakery equipment and selling it."

David finally speaks, "Fine. But we only have three days."

That evening David, a habitual hoarder, sits in his bedroom next to a trash basket. He goes through papers and things that he has collected for years. He looks fondly at pictures and memory-laden souvenirs and weighs whether they're worth taking with him. As he reaches under his bed, he finds the file on Reverend Devon Green from HPC Finance that he dropped during the two a.m. collection call. It seems like that was years ago even though it was only a few months. He opens the file and flips through the pages.

All the reverend's legal documents are in the folder: the note to HPC for the loan, the list of his furniture. As he continues through the documents, David finds a baptismal certificate for Reverend Green. It's a clean white copy with the information business-typed onto the lines of the form. He looks at the fields on the certificate. "Name, Date of Birth, Certificate Number, Name of the Church, Officiated by."

David considers this form for several long minutes. He remembers the adorned collection letters that Lester composed. *I can make this so much better*, he says to himself. *This could be just what we need to hide and start our lives over.*

The next morning, David buys some White Out and carefully covers up all the information related to Devon Green. He then takes the blank form and his White Out to a print shop. He uses a self-copier to copy the blank form. He then carefully goes over any stray lines from the copier with more of the White Out and recopies it until the form is pristine with no stray marks.

He then takes the form to the printer. "What kind of paper do you carry?"

The printer takes out a book of samples.

David flips through them. He stops when he comes on the selection of parchment paper, one that strikes him as particularly churchlike. "Could you make me one hundred copies of this form on this parchment?"

The printer takes the original and within the hour, David has one hundred baptismal certificate blanks that look like they were printed for any Baptist church.

David has had an electric typewriter since eighth grade, a must since he has terrible handwriting. This model has a ball instead of keys. As one types a key, the ball, covered with letters, numbers, and symbols, magically knows the key that was pressed and types the corresponding letter onto the paper. One nice option for those typewriter balls is that they can be swapped for balls with different typefaces.

David goes to a local office supply store and purchases a type ball with a gothic flourish typeface. It's a typewriter equivalent to calligraphy. David loads one of his baptismal certificate blanks into the typewriter and makes up a certificate for a false identity. It includes a completely different name, birthdate, and certificate number. He then scribbles a signature.

The next day, David goes to the Florida Department of Motor Vehicles and presents his certificate. "I need to apply for a driver's license."

"Do you have a birth certificate?"

"No. Sorry. I was born out of state. It was a country hospital, and I don't know if they kept a copy. But I do have a baptismal certificate."

The clerk looks at the certificate with very little concern. "Well, at least you're a good Christian boy." The clerk administers an eye exam and sends David for a driver's test, which he passes easily.

Soon David is having his picture taken for a new driver's license under the name Dominick Caparelli.

Driver's license in hand, David goes to the bakery and meets with Sal and Sunny in the small back office. He pulls out his wallet. "Check this out." He displays the driver's license and hands it to Sal for examination.

"It looks real."

"It *is* real. Let me tell you what happened." David explains how he made the baptismal certificate and converted it into a driver's license.

"We need to get new licenses too," Sunny says.

"That's what I was thinking," David says. "I made baptismal certificates for the two of you with the same last name as mine." He gives them baptismal certificates with the names "Dorothy Caparelli" and "Anthony Caparelli" neatly typed on them.

Sal is perplexed. "Why do we need this? No one's looking for us."

"They will be once we leave," Sunny says impatiently. "Even if we haven't broken the law, they'll search for us so they can get to David. If you don't want to do this, that's fine. Stay here while we go."

Sal thinks about it for several long seconds. He reluctantly takes his fake baptismal certificate from David and puts it in his pocket. Sal looks into Sunny's deep blue eyes and realizes he's not going to stay without her.

"Okay," he says, "but we've got to do this today. We don't have much time since the arraignment is tomorrow. David, watch the bakery while we're gone."

A couple of hours later, Sal and Sunny both have driver's licenses under their new names. When they get back to the bakery, Sal says to David, "Damn, son, that was so much easier than I thought it would be."

The next day is a flurry of packing, arguing—mostly over what stuff will be taken and what will be abandoned—and planning which direction they'll take. David collects all the money and checks from the bakery register and puts up the "Closed" sign. Sal rents a Budget moving truck under his new name.

Everything that they agreed to take is packed from the house, including camping tents and equipment. A little after midnight, the truck pulls up to the bakery entrance. Sal and

David get out and load all the large bakery equipment into the truck while Sunny waits inside the truck cab. Tearfully, David closes and locks the bakery door, and they drive off, never to return to the bakery or even the city of Hollywood, Florida.

As they leave, something snaps in David. He says to himself, *This will be either my worst nightmare or the beginning of something great. Or both.*

CHAPTER 14

THE next morning, there is a full docket in the courtroom of the Honorable Judge Ricardo Diaz. It's arraignment day on his docket, and one criminal defendant after another comes before the judge to ask for bond for crimes ranging from breaking and entering to vehicular homicide. Most of the cases involve narcotics trafficking. The judge has been through the routine so often that he goes through the motions half asleep on the bench.

David Adler's name comes up in the middle of the docket call. The clerk calls his name. "David Adler!" This is followed by silence except for murmurs from the attorneys. "David Adler!" the clerk repeats. Nothing.

The judge says, "Pass," and the clerk puts David Adler's name at the bottom of the list to be called one final time.

The courtroom empties as names are called and decisions are made as to whether defendants will see temporary freedom or await their trial in the Broward County Jail. Finally, the court clerk again calls, "David Adler." The silence is even deeper now as there are fewer attorneys in attendance.

Judge Diaz says, "Does anyone here know where Mr. Adler is?"

Lex Haller and the prosecutor approach the bench.

Mr. Haller speaks first. "Judge, Mr. Adler was going to retain me to represent him today. Can we continue his arraignment until I can speak with him?"

Before the judge can answer, the prosecutor asks the court, "Judge, present in the court is Detective Spencer. He has some insight into Mr. Adler. May he approach?"

The judge motions for Detective Spencer to approach the bench.

"Judge, two things that you should consider: First, although Mr. Adler is only here for one check, I've had previous experience with him. It's my belief that we're dealing with a budding career criminal. I came here to argue that Mr. Adler's bond should be increased or withdrawn. Second, I visited Mr. Adler's place of business before court. Not only is it his place of business, but he owns the business. Your Honor, the bakery that he owns has been cleaned out. In my opinion, it appears that Mr. Adler has fled the jurisdiction. Please issue a warrant so that we can begin a search for him before he gets too far away."

Judge Diaz takes no time in his decision. "So ordered!" He bangs his gavel. "Put out a bench warrant for David Adler."

CHAPTER 15

EARLY in the morning after coming back from Provo, Dale and Dianne sit in the airport command center. Dale is thoughtfully reading their new suspect's file as Dianne looks at the police artist's rendering of the hijacker.

Dianne's smile is between a grin and a sneer. "I told you I recognized this guy."

"If you're right, you got to give the guy credit for the biggest set of stones in the Southwest."

Dianne laughs. "Yeah, you'd need one of those highway truck scales to weigh them."

Dale pages through the file. He picks out sections and reads out loud to himself as much as to Dianne. "He's a pilot, a professional skydiver, and he seems to be having serious financial problems. He fits the profile."

"I know I'm right, but we must be sure. Do you think there's a judge in yet?"

Dale dials the phone. A woman's voice answers. "Judge Levin's chambers."

"This is Dale Johnson with the Federal Bureau of Investigation. We're out of Salt Lake City working on the plane hijacking about a week ago."

"Yes? What can I do for you?"

"We need a search warrant and an order for fingerprints and handwriting samples. Could I speak with His Honor?"

A few minutes later, after a brief explanation, Dale receives a commitment from the Honorable Judge Levin for the orders and the warrant. Dianne and Dale have an assistant US attorney draft the paperwork. They accompany the attorney to Judge Levin's courtroom. The judge is already on the bench when they arrive.

Fifteen minutes after they arrive, the bailiff notifies the judge of their presence; the judge calls a recess and leaves the bench for his chamber. The bailiff escorts Dale, Dianne, and the assistant US attorney to join him. Judge Levin looks over the paperwork and provides the requisite signatures. Dianne and Dale thank the judge and head back to the search site with a full thirty minutes to spare before the helicopters take off for the final sweep of the area.

The helicopter's two rotors engage, and the pilot is getting ready to strap in and put on his headset when Dianne and Dale approach in the Crown Vic.

Dianne says to Dale, "We were looking for retired military, but we forgot the National Guard is basically civilian military. Once that dawned on me, I realized where I'd seen that picture from the police sketch artist." She points to the pilot of the second helicopter. "There he is."

The Crown Vic pulls in tight in front of the helicopter. Dianne motions for the pilot to exit. As the pilot removes his headgear and comes out, Dianne hands the sketch to Dale.

"Am I wrong?" Dianne yells to be heard above the rush of the rotors and engines.

Dale studies the sketch and the pilot and yells back, "No. I don't think so."

Dianne faces the pilot. "Sir, is your name Floyd McDonald?"

The pilot hesitates. "What's this about?"

"Answer the question. Is your name Floyd McDonald?"

The pilot steps closer to Dianne. "It is. So what?"

"Please place your hands behind your back. You are under arrest." She takes out her handcuffs. "You have the right to remain silent."

"Are you kidding me? This is the last chance we'll get to find the hijacker."

Dianne sneers and malevolently chuckles. "I don't think there will be much worry about that." She finishes reading Floyd his rights, and they put him into the car and drive him to the airport command center. "I think we found our hijacker."

"You guys are making a huge mistake!" Floyd repeats.

"You weren't on the hijacked flight?" asks Dale.

"Of course not!" Floyd insists.

Once inside the office, Floyd is handcuffed to a table.

Dale asks Floyd, "Why? Why would you not only stick around but join the search team to find... yourself?"

Floyd is pulling unsuccessfully at the handcuffs and screams at Dale, "I don't know what you're talking about! I'm here with the Air Force National Guard. You've made a huge mistake."

Dianne sits down next to Floyd, invading his personal space. "Floyd, three things are going to happen. First, you're going to give us a sample of your handwriting." She pulls out the court order and lays it in front of Floyd. "Second, you're going to give us your fingerprints." She pulls out the second court order and lays it in front of Floyd. "And third, the Salt Lake City Police are executing a warrant to search your house."

Floyd's expression darkens, and his pallor turns ashen. "I won't give you shit."

Dianne's evil grin broadens, and she leans back in her seat. "We have court orders. You can give us the handwriting and fingerprints with your hands intact or with your fingers broken."

Two large officers bring a fingerprint kit, and Floyd willingly provides fingerprint samples. Dianne hands him a pen and makes Floyd write and print lines of letters and then print several times "HIJACK INSTRUCTIONS" as it was hand printed on the envelope given to the captain.

An hour later, Dale takes a phone call. When he gets off the phone, he walks over to Dianne. "The prints from the hijacker's seat belt are a match for Floyd's." They go back to talk to him.

"I thought you weren't on the plane," Dianne says. "Want to tell me how your fingerprints are on the seatbelt used by the hijacker?"

"I want a lawyer," Floyd says.

About fifteen minutes later, another call comes in.

Dale answers it again. "There is a ninety-two percent probability that Floyd printed the envelope with the hijack instructions. Dianne, we got him!"

The search warrant is executed on Floyd's house. The police find articles of skydiving equipment, an electric typewriter matching the type in the hijacking instruction pages, and $499,970 in cash.

"Damn," Dianne says. "All of that and all he managed to spend was thirty dollars of the half million. I guess crime doesn't pay."

Two days later, Dianne and Dale testify before a federal grand jury that quickly issues an indictment against Floyd. They have a celebratory dinner at a local restaurant with a piano bar. The piano player is singing a soulful rendition of Johnny Mathis's song "Misty."

Dale takes out a cigarette after dinner and pads his pockets. "Dianne, do you have a match?"

Dianne grins sarcastically. "My ass and your face?"

Dale rolls his eyes so hard that even his head goes back. "Not even close to funny." After a few puffs, he says, "So, Dianne, you never did tell me about your... talents. And as far as I can tell, my ass is foot free."

Dianne laughs. "Don't get your hopes up."

"Come on. After all this? What better time? You don't have to be embarrassed."

"I'm not."

"Well, then tell me."

Dianne leans forward. She puts her face close to Dale's and says provocatively, "How about if I show you instead?"

Dale is taken back. He leans away from her.

Dianne laughs out loud. "Don't worry. You couldn't handle that." She goes over to the piano, talks to the piano player, and gives him a five.

He gets up, and she sits down on the piano bench. Her fingers float across the keyboard, and haunting music ensues.

She sings "Misty," the same song that the piano player just finished. But it's different. Her voice lingers on each note with such emotion that everyone stops what they're doing to listen. "Look at me…" She begins the song, and everyone does look at her. When she finishes, there is hardly a dry eye in the house. That's especially true for Dale, who cannot believe his ears.

Dianne finishes to applause that lasts for a full thirty seconds. She gets up and, without fanfare, walks back to her table.

Dale is still clapping. "I had no idea," he pants out. "Not bad for an army grunt."

"Of course, you didn't know." She's totally pompous.

"You should go pro. You could be famous."

"I did, and I was sort of famous. I was on the *Mike Douglas Show*."

"The movie actor?"

"No, you jerk. Not Kirk Douglas. Mike Douglas has a big daytime talk show."

"And then what?"

Dianne thinks back to a time when she wanted nothing more than to be a star. She was sixteen years old when she left home in an old car that she worked odd jobs to pay for and an ID that said she was twenty-one. She made a name for herself performing in nightclubs and bars that she wasn't old enough to even enter. Her talents were completely natural. She took no music lessons. She didn't read music.

She didn't need to. She could play any instrument by ear, but piano was what she preferred.

Dianne played and sang for the drunks, hookers, and players and, eventually, she earned notoriety on the night club circuit. She appeared on local and then national talk shows and there was talk of stardom.

It was Dianne's eighteenth birthday when she appeared in a popular club in New York. After her first set, there was a small party in her honor. Dianne never had a better time in her life. She could feel that her life was about to change—she thought for the better.

Afterward, a man came into her dressing room. More specifically, two men entered. The first was a shorter man, about five foot eight. He had black hair and intense dark eyes. "Miss Symmons," he said in a soft, accented voice while walking uncomfortably close to her. "I enjoyed your set tonight." The two goons were confident and connected and made the hair on Dianne's neck stand up.

"Thank you," Dianne said quietly.

"No, thank you," the shorter man said mockingly. "My name is Vito Pasquale."

The large man stood silently in the background. He looked Asian. He barely fit in his gray dress shirt and blue Armani suit.

Vito then said, "I have a present for you."

Dianne demurred, "That isn't necessary, sir."

"Please, not 'sir.' It's Vito. And I think it is necessary. This is Terry. Say hello, Terry."

The large man spoke for the first time from the back of the room. "Hello."

"Terry, here, is your present. Consider him your bodyguard, or whatever."

Dianne trembled. She looked around for someone, for anyone to come into the room. They were alone. "That isn't necessary."

Vito continued as if Dianne hadn't said a word. "You want to make it in the music industry? Well, it's time that you understood how things really work. You want to work in the right clubs? Get on television? Get your name out? Become a star? Then you must know the right people." He paused for two long beats. "We are the right people."

Dianne knew that these guys were organized crime. She knew who Vito Pasquale was by reputation. She'd heard about this happening to other entertainers, but she thought that she was too small for this kind of trouble.

"And also…" Vito came closer to Dianne and ran his fingers through her fine, silky red hair. "You will want to keep us… happy. Like we'll keep you happy." His hand went from her hair down to her large rack.

Dianne grabbed his hand off her chest and twisted his wrist. Vito winced in pain and pulled back, cradling his wrist.

"Terry, I don't think she understands her options. Please show her."

The big man moved across the room with a speed that defied his size. He gripped Dianne's neck in one large, leathery hand and with the other grabbed a handful of broken glass out of a pocket. The glass didn't even nick his fingers. He held the glass dangerously close to Dianne's face. Dianne saw the glistening sharp edges and tried to move, but Terry held her fast.

Vito shook out his hand and straightened his jacket. "Have you ever had glass ground into your face? Horrible thing. It will scar your face beyond the ability of any plastic surgeon to repair it. You can sing like an angel and play piano like Liberace. But after that, who would watch you? Look, we have your schedule for the next month. Think about it. We'll see you again soon. We own you now. Believe it."

The very next day, Dianne drove to a local recruiter and joined the army. She used her benefits to get a four-year degree in criminology. Then she applied for service in the Federal Bureau of Investigation.

"I met Bob Hope once," she tells Dale as she drags herself out of her thoughts.

"Seriously? How did that happen?"

"I entertained the troops when I was in the army as part of the USO. They made me a second lieutenant."

"Well, that's impressive. It explains a lot. How about a toast?" Dale raises his glass.

Dianne raises hers. "Okay, what are we toasting?"

"Here's to you as good as you are, and here's to me as bad as I am. But as good as you are and as bad as I am, I'm as good as you are. As bad as I am."

Dianne laughs and clinks his glass. "Try saying that when you're three sheets to the wind. How about we just toast to having built our reps and the fast track."

Dale doesn't toast. He considers her words. "You know what, Dianne? You're only as good as your last case. Let's see if our luck can hold out for the next challenge."

Dianne drinks half her drink and holds the glass up. "To you, this is half empty. Right?"

PART II: NEW ORLEANS, LOUISIANA

CHAPTER 16

DETECTIVE Spencer plods through the demolished kitchen of what was Romano's Bakery. He wears an impenetrable green polyester blazer, white open collar shirt, and a scowl that seems to deepen with every piece of broken glass and torn wallboard that he assesses and photographs. He carefully sifts through the debris and looks at every scrap of paper for a clue to David's location.

Suddenly, Spencer holds up his right hand, fingers splayed and covered with what looks like mucus. He bellows to a uniformed officer who follows him like Elvis's posse. "Damn it! What the fuck is this?"

The officer observes Spencer's hand covered in the sticky, milky yellow substance. "I would guess custard, sir. Do you think any of this garbage will give us a clue to where they went? I mean, other than destroying my favorite bakery, it's not like they're the Jesse James gang."

Spencer looks at the officer with disdain before he growls. "Not all bank robberies are at the point of a gun. If you're bored, maybe you'd rather write traffic tickets in the hot sun." Before the officer can respond, Spencer is in the adjacent bathroom washing his hands.

At the front of the store, the manager of the strip mall wades through the garbage and broken glass. He fidgets with a handful of keys, flipping them nervously in his hand as he keeps repeating to himself, "Unbelievable. Just... fuckin' unbelievable."

Suddenly, John Foster bursts in the front door. He's dressed in a green plaid suit that was probably last pressed when President Johnson left office, an indistinguishable button-down shirt hangs partly untucked under his suit, and a crooked tie hangs with the knot loosened at the neck.

The manager looks at Foster's huge shoulders and chest and thinks he would be a great recruit for the Miami Dolphins. "I'm sorry," he says, walking toward the bondsman, holding his hands up in a gesture of *turn around and go back out the door.* "The bakery is closed. You have to go."

"I'm not going anywhere." The annoyed Foster pushes past the manager with one oversized hand as if he were breaking through a defensive line. He enters the destroyed bakery kitchen. Bare pipes stick out where commercial sinks were only a couple of days before. Scrape marks are etched on the floor where heavy equipment was dragged to the door. Foster calls out, "Spencer, you back here?"

Detective Spencer, on the far side of the room, motions for Foster to enter. "What a mess, huh?"

Foster walks around carefully touching walls, picking up debris, and looking for any indication of where David might have gone. "Have you found anything in all of this?"

"No. What are you on the hook for if you can't catch this guy?"

"Twenty large. I can't believe that the jag-off never even made it to the arraignment. Man, I sure didn't see this coming."

"I did. I knew from the beginning that this kid was bad news. I should have booked him when he screwed over American National Bank."

Spencer tells Foster about the check kiting and how Anderson and the other bank officers refused to prosecute.

Foster considers this for a few moments. "You know, after all that, I'll bet that you wouldn't even need a warrant to see the bank records for the bakery. Maybe there's a clue in there."

Spencer smiles. "That's a good idea. I imagine that Greg Anderson has plenty of egg on his face right now. He's out a bundle. He's not going to protect this asshole now that he's a fugitive. If he does, I'll threaten him and his bank with obstruction of justice."

"Can I go with you to talk to him?" Foster asks. "After all, do you care whether I drag him back or you arrest him?"

"Not at all." Spencer smiles wickedly. "Especially if you don't bring him in nicely. The kid deserves a tune up." He turns toward Foster and sticks his index finger into Foster's wrinkled chest. The words barely contain Spencer's rage. "But this is still a police investigation. If you say or do anything that cramps our success, you're on your own. In other words, you can listen but not talk. Capiche?"

"That's all I ask." Foster's face is a wry expression of humility. "Thanks, Detective."

* * *

At the bank, Greg Anderson gathers himself, Detective Spencer, John Foster, and the bank president into a large conference room. The president's blue pinstripe suit is well fitted. It accompanies a red tie and white shirt with no adornment. He appears to be well into retirement age. Today, he appears more fragile than his years. They're seated at a table that could have comfortably seated twice their number. Anderson asks whether anyone wants something to drink. No one accepts.

Before Spencer can start the conversation, to his disbelief, Foster lunges his chair back and leans forward with his massive fists on the table. He turns toward Anderson. "So, does your board of directors know they have morons running this shitty bank?"

Spencer's jaw literally drops open. He barely manages to restrain himself from body slamming Foster and dragging him to the back of his car. Anderson and the bank president immediately spring from their own seats in response to the insults.

Foster continues, "Sit the fuck down. I get it. You took a flyer on this kid and got strung up by the balls. Your loan is shit, including the amount that you extended to cover the amount that he stole from you. I don't know if you've been to the bakery lately, but the collateral—

that I share, by the way—has also been stolen. The dick cleaned the place out, leaving us all fucked. Here's what's going to happen: You're going to open his books like they were the legs of a twenty-dollar whore. Detective Spencer and I are going to do our jobs and find this asshole and bring him back to face justice. And if we get anything less than polite full cooperation from you people, I will personally make sure that this story hits every local media outlet. You'll be known as the business bank that destroys businesses and aids felons."

There is silence for several minutes. Foster relaxes and sits back in his chair. The bank president weaves his fingers through his silver hair. Then he says, "We'll be right back."

He and Anderson leave the room.

When they're gone, Spencer pushes back his chair and turns his whole body toward Foster. "You are an asshole!" He then slowly gets out of his chair, stands behind Foster, and puts his hand on Foster's shoulder. "But I liked it. I liked it a lot."

Ten minutes later, Greg Anderson enters the room with a large file. "Here is everything we have right now. I'll print copies of every check and deposit for the bakery since it was taken over by Mr. Adler. Please let us know if you need anything else." Anderson turns solemnly and walks out of the room. No goodbye or handshake.

Spencer and Foster take the file and leave.

CHAPTER 17

THE Budget truck is as crammed as a sumo wrestler in a Speedo. Not only is the load area filled with so much stuff that there's barely room for air; but Sal, Sunny and David are crammed leg to leg into the cab. The air conditioning bravely tries to cool the ninety-five-plus degrees outside air, but it's a lost cause.

Sal drives up the west coast of Florida without a word of conversation. The tension in the truck is as thick and oppressive as the humid outside air of the Florida summer. That tension is only broken when Florida changes to Alabama.

Sunny is the first to see the *Welcome to Alabama* state sign. "We made it! At least we're finally out of Florida! I thought that state would never end."

With the silence broken, David shifts in his seat where he has been staring out the window. He looks hard at Sunny and Sal. "We have to get rid of this equipment. We have, like, five hundred dollars in cash and another thousand dollars in checks to the bakery. Also, we need to ditch the truck and get a real car under one of our new names."

Sal shakes his sweat-laden head no. Sweat beading on his forehead splashes onto Sunny. She offers him a napkin to wipe his head.

"It's too soon," he says as he blots the napkin, which disintegrates on contact with his moisture. "I want to get out of this rolling sweatbox as much as you do. But we should make sure that we're far enough away from Florida before we do anything."

Sunny nods in agreement. "There's no point in taking chances." She reaches behind her and pulls out a map. She folds it to focus on the Florida border states. "If we continue heading west, Mississippi is the next state. We should reach that soon. Then comes Louisiana."

Sal's eyes brighten as he turns toward Sunny. "How far to New Orleans?"

Sunny studies at the map. She pinches her fingers and moves them around to estimate the miles. "Not far. Maybe two hours."

Sal's mood instantly brightens. "I've always wanted to visit New Orleans. That's where we'll stop."

Three hours later, the Budget truck is rolling down Canal Street, and everyone inside ogles at the beauty of the New Orleans skyline.

Sal doesn't even try to hide his excitement. He says, as much to himself as to Sunny and David, "This is where we're going to rebuild our lives. Maybe all of this happened for a reason." He winces in pain as he twists in the driver's seat. "Let's park somewhere. My back is killing me."

They drive onto Bourbon Street in the French Quarter and park the truck. The air has a lilac fragrance. As they get out to stretch their legs, it feels like they've traveled back in time. Pastel buildings with balconies front streets with people rambling around in and around the street like a modern-day version of Dodge City.

"Do you hear that?" says Sal. "It's the middle of the day and there's jazz in the air." Ignoring his aching back, he gives Sunny a spin, and they start to dance.

David stops to give Sal and Sunny space, and he breaks into a huge smile. He hasn't felt this relaxed since before Spencer took him into custody. "This place looks like a big festival. I can get used to this."

They pass by the Café du Monde and see groups of people in a large outdoor area dining on pastries. The air smells like heaven.

Sunny says, "We have to try this."

They get seated in the outdoor area. Birds are singing, and an occasional brave one flies down between the tables to nibble on a discarded pastry. Everyone looks relaxed and happy. The only food on the menu is beignets, but they look delicious covered in powdered sugar. They each order a plate. Sal and Sunny order coffee. Everything is delicious.

David picks up a beignet and drops half the powdered sugar onto his shirt before the pastry gets to his mouth. "Sal, you're right. This place is fantastic. I feel like this could be our new home."

Sal eats his beignet more carefully and avoids the avalanche of sugar. "First, we need to sell the equipment. Then we need to set up camp. David, see if you can find a Yellow Pages around here."

David goes to the front of the restaurant and finds a pay phone with a Yellow Pages chained to the bottom. He looks up "Restaurant Suppliers" and picks up the phone to call the first listing that looks promising. After he makes the call, he goes back to the table with a smile from ear to ear. "We have an appointment to sell the equipment."

"That was quick," Sunny says after she drains her coffee cup.

"How much?" Sal asks while balancing his last beignet on its way to his mouth.

"We'll find out when we get there. But if there was any doubt that this was the place, the pay phone only took a nickel for the call."

Sunny claps her hands in amazement. "I haven't seen a nickel pay phone since I was a little kid."

The equipment sells for two thousand three hundred dollars. They use the Yellow Pages at the restaurant supplier and find that the closest campground is a KOA in Slidell,

Louisiana. They drive to the campground and set up tents near a wooden bench with a charcoal grill.

Sal's initial excitement at being in New Orleans is short-lived. Now, looking at the eight-by-five-foot tent that is his new home makes it all too real that, even in this paradise, he's living like a fugitive.

He paces around the bench while David and Sunny sit at the bench and look at New Orleans tourist guides. "We have less than three thousand dollars. After we buy a car and ditch the truck, maybe we'll have a grand. We can't get jobs because we have no backgrounds. We can't use our education or work experience." He turns to David and glowers. "What's the plan? Please tell me that we have a plan!"

David doesn't return Sal's gaze. Instead, he looks briefly to his mother and then to the ground. "I don't know yet. We have another thousand dollars in bakery checks. I suppose we can open up an account in our new names and deposit them. That might help."

Sal comes behind David and taps him roughly on the back of the head as he sits next to him on the bench. It was a *get your head out of your ass* tap.

"Hey, you *cappa tosta*. Why don't you just send the bank a postcard, with love, from New Orleans?"

"The checks are from our commercial accounts," David says. "Who will know if we deposit them into a different account? They're just going from the customer's bank into our new bank. They'll bypass Hollywood Bank. I don't see the problem. And as you say, we need the money."

CHAPTER 18

THE next morning, Sal drives to Slidell National Bank with a feeling in his gut that it's a mistake to deposit the bakery checks.

Yet he thinks to himself, *David is right. Who would know where we're banking if it doesn't go through the American Bank of Hollywood?*

Sal walks into the bank lobby and notices how small it is compared to the banks in Florida. He approaches a woman in a conservative, blue flower dress with salt-and-pepper hair and way too much makeup. He guesses that she's in her mid-fifties.

At his approach, she looks up and smiles. "And how may ah help you, sir?" She speaks in a delightful Southern drawl.

"I'd like to open an account."

"Have y'all ever banked with us before?"

"Uh. No. I'm just in from Florida."

She reaches into her desk drawer and hands Sal paperwork to fill out. Sal has to look at his new driver's license to remember all of the details. After he fills out the paperwork and returns it, she asks, "May I see your driver's license?" He nervously gives her the Florida license under the name Anthony Caparelli.

"And how much will you be depositing?"

"One thousand one hundred dollars." He gives her a hundred-dollar bill and the endorsed checks made out to Romano's Bakery in the amount of a thousand dollars.

She studies the checks with a sour expression. "Hmm. These are third party out of town checks. It will be a while before they clear."

"I understand."

"Will there be any other signers on the account?"

Sal considers this carefully. He wants to make it a joint account with Sunny but if something goes wrong, he would rather David suffer the consequences.

"Yes. Could you put my son on the account? His name is Dominick. Dominick Caparelli."

She fills out a signature card and hands it to Sal. "Have him sign and return this card. I'll add his name to the account and to the checks." She hands Sal a book of temporary checks.

"How long will it be before the permanent checks arrive?"

"About a week. Do you want them sent to the home address?"

Sal uses the campground address and isn't sure how the mail works or how long they'll be there. "Can I pick them up here?"

"Of course, you can." She takes the cash and checks to a teller and returns with a deposit receipt. "Anything else I can do for you?"

"No ma'am."

"Well, I hope that you enjoy your stay here in Louisiana."

Sal takes the paperwork and heads back to the truck.

While Sal is making the deposit, Sunny and David have breakfast in a small restaurant adjacent to the campground. David orders bacon and eggs with a Tab. Sunny orders waffles and sausage with her usual coffee. A small television is tuned to a local news station. On the screen is an interview tape of the governor of Louisiana, Edwin Edwards.

One reporter asks, "Governor, what is the biggest challenge that we face today in Louisiana?"

"The biggest challenge currently is to increase tourism. Our economy depends on it, and it is now our primary focus."

Watching the interview, something sparks in David's thoughts.

Sunny watches him pick at his food and stare trancelike at the television. As she drowns her waffles in maple syrup, she looks up at David. "Honey? Are you still with me?"

"A World's Fair!" David screams. He raps his knuckles on the table. "What would fit better in this town than a world's fair?"

Sunny, always supportive, chuckles to herself. "Yes, I can see that. I remember there was a World's Fair in Chicago. But what does that have to do with us?"

David stands up and goes through his pocket for change. "I'm going to tell the governor my idea."

"Seriously? How are you going to do that?"

David ignores Sunny and catches the server's eye. "Can you tell me the capital of Louisiana?"

The server turns and quickly says, with a dismissive smile, "It's Baton Rouge, sweetie."

David goes to the nickel pay phone at the back of the restaurant. It's a chromium device encased in a metal cabinet filled with small holes like a perpendicular metal colander. Sunny leaves their unfinished breakfasts and follows. David dials 411 for information. "Can you give me the phone number for the governor's office in Baton Rouge?" He motions to Sunny for a pen. She pulls a plastic Bic pen out of her purse, hands it to David, and David pulls off the cap and scribbles down the number on a piece of litter rescued from the restaurant floor.

He hands the pen back to Sunny.

She puts the pen back into her purse and shakes her head. "Do you actually think that the governor of Louisiana is going to talk to you from a campground payphone in Slidell?"

David shrugs and cheerfully asks, "How do you know unless you try?" He dials the number and deposits more change.

A female voice answers, "Governor's office, may I help you?"

"Yes, ma'am. I just saw the governor's news interview where he's looking for ideas to improve tourism in Louisiana. I'm just in from Florida, and I have a fantastic idea for him."

"One moment please," the female voice says. The line goes silent on hold for several seconds.

"This is Governor Edwards. How may I help you?"

David is momentarily struck dumb. He gathers himself quickly and says, "Mr. Governor, my name is Dominick Caparelli," invoking his alias. "I'm in from Florida, and I heard your interview for tourism ideas. Have you considered hosting a World's Fair in Louisiana?"

"As a matter of fact, not only have I considered that idea, but only a few people know that I have begun an exploratory committee to look at the feasibility of a World's Fair here in Louisiana. Would you be interested in helping us out?"

"Why I'd be honored to help, Governor." David turns to Sunny and gives her a thumbs up.

"The man in charge of the committee is my budget director, Hyram Goldman. Let me give you his direct number."

The governor gives David the phone number. David mimes writing so that Sunny will give him back the pen. He writes down the number next to the governor's number.

"Thank you for your interest, Dominick. If anything else comes up, feel free to call me back."

David stands holding the receiver of the payphone for several long seconds as he and Sunny stare at each other. Finally, he hangs up the phone.

"I… don't believe what I just witnessed," Sunny says in stunned amazement.

They walk back to their table in silence. David speaks first. "There has to be a way to make some money on this."

"If there is, I know you'll figure it out."

By the time David and Sunny meet Sal, David has called and made an appointment with Hyram Goldman.

Sal listens to the story but isn't impressed. "Are you guys completely insane? We're fugitives! We should be laying low, and you want to play footsie with the fuckin' governor of Louisiana? How do you see this playing out? How will this help us?"

"I don't know yet," David says. "But I do know that this is an opportunity."

The next day, David and Sal purchase a 1969 Chevy Malibu for twelve hundred dollars. David follows in the Malibu as Sal drives the Budget truck back to Florida and to the far end of the first Budget rental lot they find. He leaves the keys in the ignition. Sal then takes the wheel of the Malibu and drives them both back to the campground in Slidell.

The next day, David takes the Malibu to Baton Rouge to meet Hyram Goldman. The government office is barely decorated. It's simply thrown together with functional office furniture. David notices a sterile smell to the building as he steps inside the reception area. A receptionist immediately shows David into a conference room where Hyram stands looking up at a wall map of Louisiana. The map is festooned with various colored push pins.

Hyram is a paunchy, middle-aged man. He's dressed as a Southern Conservative in a sky blue suit with broad lapels that have edges so sharp they could draw blood, a blue bow tie, with a cunning gleam in his eyes. His red hair is coiffed in a style that seems to defy gravity and makes him look like a beardless dwarf.

Seconds later, he practically vaults over the table to shake hands with David. He speaks in a staccato rhythm and leaves no room for interruption.

"Hyram Goldman." Hyram grabs David's hand and quickly pumps it while gesturing with his other hand to sit down. "The governor called and told me that you were interested in joining the World's Fair Committee. Have a seat, my boy. You're younger than I expected. Please. Let me tell you where we are in the process. We have our bid to host the World Fair in the great city of New Orleans. We're in the middle of the proposal to the Bureau of International Expositions."

Hyram makes a wide gesture at the wall map.

"We need to find a location in this area of the city. We're thinking about forty or fifty acres. This can be the shot in the arm that Louisiana needs to increase our tourism dollars. There are several business leaders already on the committee—"

David seizes a moment to interrupt. "So, what are your immediate needs to make this happen?"

"We need a site. We need someplace that we can include in the proposal to the Bureau of International Expositions. As I said, it has to be about forty or fifty acres, in the city proper. We must also be mindful of the costs. Maybe a long-term lease."

David considers this. "I actually may have just the site for you," he lies. "But I don't want to go into details until I've talked to the owner. It's a friend of mine, and I don't know whether there would be interest. It may require some... finessing."

"If you have a lead on something, the governor and I would be very interested. Don't keep us waiting, though. This proposal must come out before another state or country gets their hooks in. Is there anything you need to make this happen?"

David shakes his head no. "I'll get back to you when I've discussed this with my friend."

Hyram extends his hand for another quick shake. David takes his hand and gets up from the chair. Hyram, in a tone that says, *This is just another waste of my time,* says in his same rapid-fire monologue, "That sounds good. Please get back to me on that and share some details of your own background, won't you? We can use the help. But right now, I have to get to other matters. Thanks for coming out."

David leaves the offices, descends the stairs to the parking lot, and slides into the car seat. On the way back to Slidell, he remembers back to his time in collections. He remembers one of Lester's lessons:

"Collectors have to be more than just good at persuading deadbeats to pay." Lester is leading David into the Broward County Florida Assessor's office. "A good collector is also a detective."

Lester continues as they take a seat at a large, dark wooden table surrounded by voluminous, spiral-bound books that look like they were forged on Mount Olympus.

"A lot of deadbeats simply skip, thinking that moving will keep us from being able to do our job. Part of our job is to keep finding them and hounding them wherever they go. That's called skip tracing."

Lester takes a large book labeled *Cross Directory* out of his briefcase. He also puts a box of doughnuts on the table. David reaches out to take one, and Lester swats his hand away.

"They're not for you. Now listen and learn. We have the deadbeat's references. We can call them and, if we're lucky, they will tell us where the deadbeat went. That's good for maybe one post skip contact. After that, the deadbeat tells the references to clam up.

"Second, we don't lend money to unemployed deadbeats. We have job information. Calling the job is very persuasive. No one wants to have their deadbeat dirty laundry aired at work. Unfortunately, one reason that deadbeats become deadbeats is because they lose their job. Having work information can be shit."

"Okay, so how do we find someone who moves? I assume that they don't call HPC and leave a forwarding address."

"It's called 'skip.' Not 'move.' The deadbeat doesn't move; they skip. As in skip out of paying their bills."

David draws a breath. "Okay, so how do we find someone who skips?"

"It depends. Where do deadbeats live?"

"This is a trick question."

"No, it's not. Deadbeats, or at least our deadbeats, live in either a house or an apartment. If they live in an apartment, this is our toolbox." Lester pulls the cross directory between them.

"With this book we can look up the address. If the address is an apartment, we can see all the other tenants of the apartment building whose phones are listed."

"Okay. And then?" David asks, already dreading the answer.

"And then we call the neighbors. Or the landlord. Someone may know where the deadbeat skipped to. Sometimes the deadbeat just stops answering their phone, and we can ask their neighbors to bring them to their phone."

"How humiliating that must be for everyone."

"I know, right?" Lester's voice goes up a full octave with excitement.

"What if they live in a house?"

"That, my apprentice, is why we're here. Every piece of property has a record, and every record is in the County Recorder of Deeds. In Broward County, Florida, it's the County Assessor's office."

Lester takes the box of doughnuts and motions for David to follow. They go to a counter where a young, plain, bookish-looking woman sits reviewing one of the large volumes. She's about twenty pounds overweight. Her dark hair is severely pulled back and fastened so tightly with a clip that it would probably survive a tidal wave.

"Hello, gorgeous," Lester says as they approach the counter.

The woman smiles weakly. "Hello, Lester. What brings you here today?"

"I just wanted to bring you these." Lester produces the box of doughnuts and puts them on the counter.

The clerk breaks into a huge grin as she reaches for the box. "Dixie Cream. My favorite."

"I know. I hope I got the right kinds."

The clerk opens the box and pokes at the contents with a manicured finger.

"These are perfect, Lester. Thank you so much for thinking of me."

"You're welcome, Charlene. I'm just here with a trainee. I wanted to show him the ropes."

Lester turns to David. "Any information you want on any property in Broward County, you see Charlene. You're supposed to have a legal description but if you just give her the address, she'll point you to the right volume, and she'll even help you understand what you're looking at. She's helped me find people more times than I can remember."

The day after they visit Baton Rouge, David and Sunny go to the New Orleans Public Library and scan the Sunday classifieds for acreage in New Orleans. "I don't understand," Sunny says. "Is your plan to negotiate on behalf of the State of Louisiana for one of these pieces of property?"

"That was my original thought. I figured that maybe I could negotiate some sort of finder's fee. But to do that I have to join their committee and come up with a background.

Sal's right. As fugitives, we have to be smarter than that. You know what's weird?"

"Always," Sunny says with a wry smile.

"I've played by the rules my whole life. I worked hard, got good grades, and tried to be a good person. Maybe it was the ruthlessness of the collection work or maybe it was the fact that my whole life right down to my name has been flushed down the crapper. But now I'm ready to embrace an outlaw's life. Maybe it will take us to where we wanted to be in the first place."

Sunny thoughtfully listens to David's confession. "I think something broke in me too when we had to leave Florida. I blame myself for getting hurt in the hospital. Maybe I could have been more careful."

"Don't go there. It wasn't your fault. It was simply how the cards were dealt." David photocopies several classified listings of acreage property for sale in the New Orleans area that Hyram showed him on the wall map.

Collecting the copies, David tells Sunny, "For the next step in this plan, we need to visit the New Orleans Parish Recorder of Deeds. But first, we must make a stop."

As they enter the Recorder's office, David notices several clerks. Sunny notices that the place is dim and smells like wood polish. He finds a clerk who looks lonely and bored. He has Sunny approach him with the box of beignets from Café du Monde that they picked up on their way in.

"Hello. It's getting close to lunch, and we thought you might be hungry," Sunny purrs.

The clerk peers over thick reading glasses. He's as thin as the aged pages that he carefully turns in the oversized binder. His sparse, brown hair gives way to a wide horseshoe hairline. When he sees Sunny look at him with those deep blue eyes and California blond hair, he becomes as nervous as a hormonal teenager on his first date.

"Th-thank you," he stammers, taking the box of beignets.

David comes over and stands beside Sunny. "We were wondering if you could help us. We're looking for locations of vacant parcels in New Orleans. Can you help us identify the current owners of some of them?"

"I suppose. Are you with a title company or a real estate firm?"

"No. We're working on a private project."

"It's rather unusual, but I suppose there is nothing wrong with helping someone find information for their own use."

Sunny flashes a "you are so smart and so helpful" look, and David can see the clerk puffing up with pride.

David hands the clerk some of the classified ads. "I thought we could start with these."

The clerk takes the papers and sets about finding owners for those and other vacant parcels.

David follows him, stopping just before the archives. "We're looking for parcels of forty to fifty acres or more."

"Let me see what I can find."

The clerk brings book after book and shows David where to find the names of the owners. Finally, David looks up. "This parcel is perfect. Forty-eight and a half acres in the area that Hyram indicated. No mortgages listed. Owned by a Miss or Mrs. Dixie Jones."

Sunny stands up impatiently and stretches. "We've spent all day on this. Where is this going?"

David stands silently with his index finger pressed against his lower lip. He motions for Sunny to follow him to a private corner of the room, where he explains the plan to her. Sunny's conspiratorial expression reveals her approval. After they leave the building, David finds a pay phone and calls Hyram.

CHAPTER 19

THE parcel of land is bordered by three well-trafficked streets. There are warehouses in the vicinity. It is mainly flat except for a few trees growing wild toward the rear boundary. In the middle of the property, near the main road, is a sign.

"For Sale by Owner, Forty-Seven + Acres" and a phone number."

Hyram and David stand near the sign looking out over the vast acreage.

Hyram fidgets with his watch waiting impatiently. His porcine face is petulant as he paces.

"Are you sure this gal is interested in taking a haircut on the value of this parcel? The State has a budget and, as good as this parcel is, we can't exceed it. Also, we can't agree to the purchase until our proposal is cleared."

"I get it," David says as he turns toward the road in anticipation.

"It's the proverbial chicken and egg. You need the location for the proposal, but you can't make the purchase until the proposal is accepted and the budget is released."

Suddenly, a rented black Chevy Camaro glides up to the curb. As Hyram and David wait in anticipation, the driver's door opens, and Sunny steps out of the car dressed in a silky flowered shirt, jeans with a turquoise belt buckle, and just the right amount of silver turquoise jewelry to match. Sunny is always attractive but when she tries, she's stunning.

"Hello. I'm Dixie Jones," she drawls. "David here tells me that you want to buy my property for a World's Fair?"

Hyram looks at Sunny a little too long before he steps up and extends his hand.

"Hyram Goldman. A pleasure to meet you. I'm told that you want five hundred thousand for the parcel. That's pretty rich, even for the State of Louisiana."

Sunny is all business with a feminine softness. She beams a smile at Hyram like a silver laser reaching for the heavens. "Well, it *is* prime property in an ideal location. As Will Rogers once said, 'They ain't makin' any more of the stuff.'"

Everyone chuckles. Sunny saunters to Hyram and loops her arm through his. The gesture makes Sunny appear vulnerable and available. Her words ooze Southern charm. "Are you prepared to make me an offer?"

Hyram doesn't remove Sunny's arm. His face grows serious. "Depending on the engineering studies and subject to committee approval, we can go as high as three hundred sixty-five thousand dollars. Or, alternatively, a long-term lease deal."

Sunny pouts for several seconds.

"I'm sorry, but that is way under market value for the property." She unhooks her arm. They stand silently for several minutes, considering the impasse in price.

David breaks the silence. "Dixie, can I talk to you for a minute?" He takes Sunny by the arm and escorts her about fifteen feet away from Hyram, who can see them talking conspiratorially.

When they return to Hyram, Sunny says, "David informs me that there might be some tax advantages to leasing the property to the State."

Hyram smiles. "Indeed there are, little lady. What kind of lease are we talking?"

"Let's say ten years with an option to renew for as long as you need. Option to purchase at four hundred thousand dollars."

Hyram flinches in pleasure at those terms. A grin smears his bloated face. "Perfect! I don't see how the committee can reject those terms. That assures us the property will be available for the fair and allow us to maintain the site afterward."

Sunny turns to look out over the property. When she turns back, she says, "The only problem that I have is, you want me to take it off the market until your committee can make the commitment. I'm not comfortable with that."

David turns to Hyram. "Can you simply take an option on the property? We'll put the terms right in the contract."

Hyram strokes his hairless chin as he considers this.

"I don't see why not. It solves all our problems and puts the terms right out there. It also gives our lawyers and engineers a chance to do their due diligence."

"Good," David responds. "Let's say an even ten thousand dollars to hold the property. I think that the State of Louisiana can afford that, don't you?"

"I'm sure that won't be a problem. I'll have our lawyers draw up the contract."

Sunny says, "I have to go out of town, so we'll need to sign the option agreement by the end of the week. David will have my itinerary until I get back. You can reach me through him."

Three days later, a call comes into the answering service that David previously retained for a contact phone number. He calls the answering service from pay phones several times a day for messages.

A female voice answers. After he identifies himself, she says, "Mr. Caparelli, you have one new message from Hyram Goldman. He says that the contract is ready. Please call him to make signing arrangements."

Thanking the service, David immediately calls back Hyram from the pay phone. After a short delay from Hyram's receptionist, David is put right through.

"David? It's Hyram. We're all ready for Miss Jones to come in and sign the option contract."

David says, "I know it's not a workday, but can we meet on Saturday? Dixie said that she wouldn't mind taking a road trip to Baton Rouge for the meeting."

"Why, that would be splendid! Save me the miles going back to New Orleans. Can you make it at, say, eleven a.m.?"

"The time should work. I'll coordinate it with Dixie. But there is something that she insisted on."

"What is that?" Hyram asks dubiously, thinking that there is some deal buster coming.

"Dixie insists that the ten-thousand-dollar check be certified. I told her that I didn't expect that to be a problem. Was I correct?"

"You're as right as the good Lord made little green apples," Hyram says, kind of butchering the Bobby Goldsboro song. "We'll plan to see you and Dixie Saturday at eleven."

David walks from the pay phone back to the campground.

Sal and Sunny chorus, "Well? Did you hear from Hyram?"

"We pick up the check Saturday morning."

Cheers, hugs, and jumping all around as they all celebrate.

Finally, Sal demurs. "I'm nervous. What if it's a trap? Is there any way that they know she's not Dixie Jones or that our goal was the ten thousand all along?"

"That's why I made it on a Saturday. They'll have started their weekend. Nothing will be investigated until at least the next week."

Sal places an arm around Sunny. "I wish I found that more reassuring."

David says, "Mom, if you can stay cool, the ten grand is as good as ours."

Sunny looks at Sal and gives him a soft embrace. "Hey, I'm so cool that those fools in Baton Rouge will have a brain freeze when we're done."

Sunny then turns to David. "What if they stop the check?"

"Not a chance. A certified check is guaranteed by the bank. It can't be stopped no matter what."

CHAPTER 20

DAVID and Sunny arrive at the Louisiana State Capitol building in Baton Rouge at ten forty-five a.m., a little earlier than the appointed time. When they climb the stairs and step into Hyram's office, David notices that the building no longer has a sterile odor. It has been replaced by the scent of freshly baked cookies.

The receptionist is all smiles as they enter the office lobby. She immediately gets up from behind her desk and drawls, "You're early. That's wonderful! Please follow me to the conference room."

The conference table is filled with a variety of foods. There are three types of homemade cookies, chips and onion dip, a tray of melon, and a bowl of crawfish floating with pieces of corn on the cob in some unidentified liquid. There are various bottles of liquor and some cold bottles of soft drinks.

Hyram stands at the back of the room holding court with two middle-aged men wearing pastel-colored polo shirts and khaki slacks and a woman in her mid-twenties wearing a yellow sun dress and holding a cup of some dark-colored liquor.

Upon seeing David and Sunny, Hyram immediately waves and comes toward them with his visitors towed along in his wake. He puts a friendly arm over David's shoulder and takes Sunny's hand. "You're early. Good to see you. Allow me to introduce Clifford, Aiden, and last, but never least, Scarlett. No relation to *Gone With The Wind.* They're all members of the World's Fair Committee, and they want to meet the fine lady who made our plans come true."

Clifford and Aiden shake hands with David and Sunny. Scarlett raises her hand slightly in a gesture of greeting. She puts her drink down. "It means so much to us that you can lease us your land. Now we can get our proposal in before someone else tries to one-up us for the fair."

Neither Sunny nor David expected a celebration. Sunny is shaken by the outpouring of gratitude but tries not to show it. With trepidation, she answers, "This will work out for all of us, I'm sure."

Hyram approaches Sunny with a bowl of crawfish. "Dixie, can I get you something to drink or eat? We have some delicious crawfish."

The crawfish look like a bowl of red bugs. Their black eyes bulge at Sunny out of the bowl. Sunny suddenly feels an involuntary urge to throw up, but she knows that a Louisiana girl would never get sick from a bowl of crawfish.

David steps between Sunny and the bowl of bugs. "I think that what Dixie needs is a drink."

Sunny stops her gag reflex. "Sure. Bourbon neat, if you have it." Her drink of choice is Canadian Club, but she thinks bourbon would be more appropriate.

Hyram laughs from down in his belly. "A woman after my own heart." He gets her a glass with a generous splash of bourbon.

Even though the offer wasn't made to him, David says, "I'll just have some Coke." He turns to Sunny, pulls her arm slightly, and says loudly enough to be overheard, "Dixie, don't forget that we must pick up your daughter for dinner. It's at least a four-hour drive back to New Orleans."

Sunny turns to Hyram and gulps her bourbon. "Dominick's right. While I appreciate all of this, I didn't expect to spend that much time here. Do you have the contract ready?"

"Of course, I do, Dixie." Hyram escorts David and Sunny into an office. "Please have a seat. I'll be right back with the documents all approved by our council."

As soon as the door closes, Sunny turns to David. Between the crawfish and the pressure, her trembling lips are contorted into a fearful grimace. "I'm never doing this again. I feel horrible. They threw a party to thank us for ripping them off. Come to think of it, maybe this is all a trap. They might be getting the police right now!"

"Mom, no one throws a party for a thief. What happened to Miss Brain Freeze? Besides, we're in all the way now..."

Hyram and the receptionist stride back into the room with a manila folder filled with paper. Hyram takes out a ten-page contract and a check. He slides the contract over to Sunny. "There you go, Dixie. All the terms that we discussed."

David takes the contract from Sunny and pretends to read it. *It doesn't matter if this thing says that we give up our first-born kids and our eye teeth. The only document that matters here is the certified check.*

After a couple of minutes, David slides the contract over to Sunny, who says, "Dominick, since when did you become my lawyer? Look, Hyram, I've always believed that if a man can't be trusted with a handshake, then a contract doesn't mean anything either." She extends her hand, and Hyram gives it a firm shake. Sunny signs the contract and slides it back to Hyram.

Hyram turns to the receptionist. "Honey, can you notarize this for me?"

"Certainly," the receptionist says. "I'm sorry, Miss Jones. Could I see some identification?"

And here is the point where it might all go wrong. Sunny reaches into her purse and takes out a wallet. She removes the Louisiana driver's license that she picked up a week earlier with another baptismal certificate.

The receptionist takes the license from Sunny and the contract from Hyram. She flips to the signature page and writes down the driver's license number. She then pushes a stamp onto the page. Under the stamp she affixes her own signature and date. "Here you go, Miss Jones." She returns the driver's license and gives the notarized contract back to Hyram.

Following the notary ceremony, Hyram slides the check over to Sunny.

Sunny quickly takes the check, folds it in half, and makes it disappear into her purse.

Hyram then signs the contract and leaves the room for a few minutes with the receptionist.

Sunny looks nervously at David, who says softly, "We wouldn't have this check if they knew the truth."

Hyram comes in and hands Sunny a copy of the contract. He shakes Sunny's hand again and attempts to put his arm around her shoulder. Sunny suddenly stands up, which shakes Hyram's arm off. She reaches out her hand to shake Hyram's. "A pleasure doing business with you. Like I said, if you need me just call David here. He has my itinerary and will be able to reach me while I'm out of town."

Hyram stands up also and speaks in his staccato voice. "When you get back into town, let's plan lunch with the governor. I'm sure he'd love to meet you. He's a great guy. It has been an honor to meet you, Dixie. Be careful in your travels. Also, thank you, Dominick. I hope to see you at the next committee meeting."

"Thank you, Hyram. I can't wait to meet the governor." Sunny heads toward the door with David right behind.

As they pass into the lobby, Sunny waves and says loudly, "Pleasure to meet y'all."

* * *

When they return to the campground, they find Sal sitting on the bench next to their tents. Sunny and David join him on the bench and take turns telling Sal everything that happened. They're still in the grip of adrenaline.

Sunny suddenly stares out at the horizon. "I just feel like crap. We might have screwed up their chances at the World's Fair."

Sal follows her gaze. "These guys are going to be fuckin' furious when they find out what happened."

Everyone is silent for a full minute. Finally, Sunny stands up and breaks the silence. "Okay, so we're going to live an outlaw's life. That's fine. Heaven knows that being straight didn't get us what we deserved. But from this moment on, we must be very careful. We also need to have rules of engagement so that we don't feel like crap afterward."

David says, "I think it goes without saying that we have to stay loyal to each other no matter what."

"Agreed," Sal says.

Sunny looks with disdain at the tents. "We need to get out of the campground. We can at least rent a couple of apartments now."

David laughs. "Right. You guys will finally have a place of your own. Also, I know it's a weird rule, but we need to listen to our guts. If something doesn't feel right, we back out even if we don't know why."

Sal touches Sunny's shoulder. "Okay, but we also need to distinguish between real instinct and just fear. I was scared shitless today while you were gone, but it turned out all right."

Sunny turns to face both Sal and David. "And we should always choose our targets carefully. We never want to hurt any individuals or small mom-and-pop businesses. We'll stick with large businesses and government."

Sal and David nod in agreement.

David takes out his license. "Now we need to reassess our identities. My identity as Dominick is burned because that's how Hyram knows me. Mom, you need to get a bank account and cash the check under Dixie Jones. Once you pull the cash, of course, you must burn Dixie."

Sunny shakes her head. "I think that we should burn all of our identities and start fresh." David and Sal nod yes in unison.

On Monday, Sunny opens a checking account under the name Dixie Jones at a small bank in New Orleans. The certified check is held by the bank for only twenty-four hours before the cash is cleared. Sunny withdraws ninety-nine hundred dollars the next day, leaving the account open.

David, Sunny, and Sal get new driver's licenses under the names Brian Baker, Susan Baker, and Sam Baker using the address of an apartment that David found in Metairie, a tiny suburb of New Orleans. They enjoy the irony of taking names after their bakery business in Hollywood. They leave the campground and lease two of the Metairie apartments under the Baker identities.

Flush with the World's Fair cash they shop for furniture, clothes, jewelry, food, and booze (for Sal and Sunny) to replace what they abandoned in Florida. One item that catches David's eye is at a pawn shop on Canal Street. It's a pair of standard nickel-plated handcuffs complete with handcuff keys.

David asks the pawn broker, "Are these genuine police handcuffs?"

"It's what every cop in Louisiana uses. Even use them in prisons."

David stares at the handcuffs for a long moment. After he purchases them, Sal mocks him. "What are you going to do with those? That's got to be bad luck or something."

"No. You don't understand," David answers. "You've never had to be in these." He removes the handcuff keys and throws away the actual handcuffs. Then he takes a piece of nylon thread and loops the keys through his belt loop so that the keys hang a few inches into his pants below his waistband. "I never want to be without this protection again."

Having binged on consumer goods, David, Sunny, and Sal celebrate at the French Quarter with a delicious dinner of jambalaya and poor boy sandwiches before they split up. Sunny and Sal listen to jazz by Dizzy Gillespie at his club on Bourbon Street.

Newly empowered by his independence, David simply goes to explore and maybe get laid. In the back of his mind, he realizes that whatever remains of their ten grand won't last forever. He'll have to come up with a new plan to keep the money flowing in.

CHAPTER 21

THE first call that Sunny makes when their new phone is installed is to her daughter Ava, David's sister. Ava is a couple of years younger than David. She lives in Phoenix, Arizona.

After five rings, Ava picks up the wall phone in her small kitchen. Two pots are boiling on the electric burners of her oven. "Mom? I'm so glad to hear your voice. I've been trying to reach you for weeks, and all your phone numbers are disconnected. Hold on a second." She opens the oven, puts in a roast, and sets a timer.

A man slouches on the couch in the next room watching a game. "Honey, bring me another beer, will you?"

Ava takes a beer out of the refrigerator while cradling the phone and stirring a pot. "What happened? How is the bakery?"

"Gone. Things have been complicated."

Ava tries to bring the beer into the other room, but the cord is too short. She motions to her husband, Chris, to come and get it. "Where are you living now?"

"I'd rather not say. We're all doing fine, though."

Chris looks quickly at Ava with a pained expression that shows he isn't to be interrupted. He holds up his hands and makes a "bring them here" motion. Ava tries again to talk to Sunny while stretching the cord. "Is David still with you?"

Sunny cradles the phone a little closer to her face. "Sort of. He has his own place now. Are you all right?"

"Hold on." Ava lets the phone drop to the floor and runs the beer over to Chris. Sunny hears a clunk and several moments of silence.

Sunny's face darkens. "Hello? Are you still there?"

Ava recovers the phone and retreats to a corner of the kitchen. "Mom, I'm having a baby."

In amazement, Sunny holds the phone on her lap for a few seconds and then returns it to her ear. "That's… that's wonderful!"

Ava sobs into the phone. "I need my mom. There's no one to help me. There's no one I can talk to about this."

Sunny puts her hand on the phone mouthpiece and holds it away. A tear escapes her left eye. She gets back on. "What about Chris?"

"He's not my mother. And… I don't think he wants me to keep it." Ava sobs uncontrollably. "Please, Mom, I need you."

Sunny stifles a sob. Tears roll from her eyes with abandon. "Just hang in there. I'll be there soon." She hangs up and sends Sal to get David from his apartment.

When they're together, Sunny tells Sal and David about her phone conversation with Ava.

David paces nervously. Sal waits, deep in thought. Finally, Sal interrupts his own reverie. "No question. We'll go to Arizona. Fortunately, we have enough money to fly over there."

David nods in agreement. Other than his mother, he has always considered Ava the most loving and kind person he knows. Growing up no one ever had a bad thing to say about her. Like Sunny, perhaps because of Sunny, all her life she dreamed of being not just a wife and mother; but the best wife and mother that the world had ever seen. To that end she left home, married at a very young age, and never looked back. "We do have enough money, but it's limited. Sal, you get the plane tickets with a check from the Slidell bank. I can cash out the Slidell account after you're in the air before the check to the airline clears."

Sunny hugs Sal and looks at David through moist eyes. "Thank you."

Sal Breaks Sunny's embrace. "The other question is whether we're going to visit or whether we need to move there. I don't know if a quick trip will help her." Sunny and David shake their heads. Sal continues, "I think that we should move there. At least temporarily until she's stable. So, one-way tickets."

David goes to the refrigerator and grabs a can of Coke. He pulls off the tab from the top and takes a drink. "In that case, you guys should go, and I'll stay here to take care of our stuff. You get us places to live there, and I'll get everything packed up in a trailer and drive our stuff out to meet you."

Sal goes to a drawer where the remaining cash is hidden. "We'll buy a couple hundred dollars in traveler's checks and take the rest of the cash."

David looks down uncomfortably at the proposed arrangement.

Sal continues, "You keep a couple of hundred dollars too. Once you clean out the Slidell account, you should have plenty of cash to get what you need and meet us in Phoenix."

David stares impassively. "It makes sense. All right. Make your plane reservations and I'll head to Slidell tomorrow once you're gone."

David takes three of the permanent checks from the Slidell account. Sal signs one and David puts them all in his wallet.

The next day, after driving Sunny and Sal to the airport, David drives to Slidell to close out the account. He bypasses the woman Sal opened the account with and takes a check to the teller. The teller is a friendly young girl with plain, black-frame glasses that complement her pretty face.

David presents the check with a friendly smile. "Hello."

The teller takes the check. "Do you have ID?"

David gives her his Dominick Caparelli driver's license. "Of course."

The teller accepts the driver's license and writes the number on the check. She takes the cash out of her drawer. Before she counts it, she stops for a long moment as she looks at something to her right. "Sir, would you wait here for just a moment?" She walks away from the counter.

David feels electric needles in his spine. He has a flashback to the bank in Hollywood where he first met Detective Spencer. As casually as he can, while the teller is distracted, he pretends that he left something important in his car. He leaves the bank, gets into his car, and drives off. The electricity doesn't leave him. He starts to sweat. His hands on the steering wheel tremble.

Not even a minute later does he notice an unmarked car following him. It matches him turn for turn, but it doesn't put on cop lights. David looks into the rearview mirror so often that he loses his sense of direction. He's both chased and lost. His body is a cocktail of urgency and fear. On a winding road, he accelerates and pulls ahead of the car following him. He then pulls into the private parking lot of a large bar. He hopes his pursuer won't notice. The parking lot ends at the shore of a swamp that surrounds Slidell. A pier extends into the slimy water. The odors of fungus and battery acid permeate the air.

David stops and lunges out of his car. He heads toward the pier and hides behind some large crates. In the distance, he sees the pursuing car enter the parking lot and pull behind his car, blocking it. He sees a large man with a sidearm step out of the pursuing car. He sees the man's face as he peers into his car windows. John Foster—the bail bondsman from Hollywood, Florida who is now a bounty hunter. Foster turns and walks toward David but doesn't notice him behind the crates yet. David sees Foster's approach as he would his impending doom. His heart beats so hard he thinks his chest will burst. He has only one move and makes the dreadful decision to wade out into the swamp away from the pier and go under.

Foster searches in and around every crate on the pier. He looks out into the water, but it's dark now, and David is careful to make no ripples. Eventually, Foster returns to the Slidell bank and enters the office of the vice president, where he has been on and off for a week waiting for activity on the account.

"I was right," he tells the vice president. "When the bank in Hollywood saw activity on the bakery account, they directed me here to where the checks were deposited. Your teller did the right thing when she flagged the transaction."

"And what happened, Mr. Foster? Did you catch your fugitive?"

Foster sits back in the plastic chair in front of the desk and looks in the direction of the pier. "No. I think he went into the water to avoid capture. I may need some help to find him when he surfaces."

The vice president takes out a Kool cigarette and taps it on his desk before he puts it between his lips and lights it. "Mr. Foster? There ain't no need to search the swamp. There ain't enough men to search it anyway. It's a small sheriff's office. But more importantly, if your man went into that swamp, he ain't comin' out. That swamp is teemin' with gators, snakes, and skeeters that will take enough blood to require a transfusion. I'm sorry, but I would bet biscuits to bacon that your boy is gator chow by now."

CHAPTER 22

DAVID trudges waste deep in mud. He's surrounded by trees, vines, and plants that he can't begin to identify. The sky fades from dusk to black. His mouth tastes metallic, like he just sucked on a mouthful of pennies. The moisture from the swamp mixes with his fear and rage, and he feels like a soaked, dirty dishcloth. He notices that, about fifty yards to his right, is a well-trafficked road. He stays clear of the road but keeps it in sight as he slowly lurches forward. Each step gets him sucked deeper into the muck like it's quicksand.

After thirty minutes, the swamp sucks off David's shoes and socks. Mosquitos the size of golf balls whine in every direction. It helps that the dark turns David's surroundings to shadow. He can only focus a few feet in front of him on the water. Wet plants sting his skin as he passes. He hears sounds. Unknown things rustle around him. Insects buzz as they try to taste his wet skin. He feels crushed by the humidity and smell of decay. His hands reach out for purchase through this foreign world like he's trying to read braille. All he can do is put one foot in front of the other. Just one… step… at… a… time.

An hour goes by, but to David it feels like he has been in this swampy purgatory for a week. He starts to give up. He's exhausted, and he just knows this swamp will be his wet grave. He loses hope and starts to give in to the inevitable. He's sad but also relieved that his ordeal is over. Suddenly, through the dense foliage, he sees a familiar bright neon sign. *KOA*.

With new hope, he pushes himself harder until, shoeless, exhausted, and covered with mud, he drags himself out of the slime and muck at the edge of the campground.

David knows where the campground public shower is and that is the first place he goes. He showers and washes his muddy clothes in the shower as best he can. Wet and barefoot, he goes to a pay phone and calls a taxi to pick him up.

The apartment building in Metairie where David now lives is a three-story building with about thirty units. It's of newer construction and has a U-shaped driveway from the main road. As the taxi approaches the driveway, David sees three police cars parked near the entrance. Their lights flash and officers are standing at the entrance.

That can't be a coincidence. He leans forward to the driver. "It's your lucky day. Instead of this address, can you take me to the French Quarter?"

The driver doesn't even take the full "U" of the driveway. He backs out and inconspicuously heads in the opposite direction toward New Orleans.

When they arrive in the French Quarter, David breaks a hundred-dollar bill to pay and tip the driver. His wallet, remarkably, protected its contents from the swamp water. His clothes are reasonably dry now, but they're as crumpled as old parchment. Aside from the cash, in his wallet are his ID for both Baker and Caparelli and two remaining Caparelli checks.

David finds his way to a shoe store and uses one check to purchase socks and a pair of four-inch platform boots. He then goes to a funky clothing store and purchases with cash a white jumpsuit with a rhinestone belt buckle and a matching white "pimp" hat sporting a colorful feather. He goes to a payphone and calls his sister's number from memory. "Ava? It's David. Has Mom arrived there yet?"

Ava gives the phone to Sunny. Sal takes the extension and David fills them in on the events of the past few hours.

Sal excitedly states the obvious. "You have to get out of there."

"Great advice, Mr. No Duh. The question is how. It's a cinch that there are people looking for me at the airport, bus terminals, and so on. Anyway, I have less than fifty dollars in cash."

Sunny interjects, "We can rent a car, drive back, and pick you up."

David thinks about that but rejects the idea. "First, there is no way you two are coming back here. Second, it's too slow. But you're on the right track. See if Ava will fly into New Orleans one way and rent a car. She can pick me up in the French Quarter, and we'll drive to the airport in Jackson, Mississippi."

Sunny gets off the phone for a couple of minutes. David hears muted conversation in the background as she explains to Ava. Then the phone is picked back up. "Ava will be there with Chris. Where can they call you when they get into town?"

"I'll call you back and let you know where to pick me up."

Sunny takes a sharp breath. "I'm afraid the police are going to see you. Get off of the street."

"Don't worry. I will. I'm in disguise. Sort of."

They hang up, and David thinks back to the night right after he had dinner with Sal and his mother in the French Quarter. After dinner, he'd looked for a place to find some girls. As he walked through partying crowds holding Hurricane drinks and dancing in the street, he came upon a club on Bourbon Street called The Red Parrot.

The storefront was irresistible. The building had two levels and the wall of the second level had two windows. Inside the windows were swings, and riding those swings were gorgeous girls. As they swung toward the windows only their long shapely legs would arc through, completely revealed by the short dresses they wore. Occasionally, one of the girls would grab the window jamb and pull herself out to entice passing guys into the club.

David knows this is simply an enticement to get guys into the bar and buy drinks. To these girls, most of the guys are simply marks to fleece for their bosses. But David has a plan.

After he walks in and secures a seat at the bar, he orders a Perrier with a twist of lime. An attractive girl with long, red hair streaked in blond steps out of the window and comes over to him. She invades his personal space and pulls the stool next to him very close. She smiles and touches his shoulder. "I saw you outside. What's your name?"

David's jumpsuit is so tight you could practically tell his religion. In a voice as effeminate as he can muster, he says, "The name's Brian." He turns as if just noticing the girl. "Oh, my, aren't you just the cutest little thing? If I wasn't gay, I would so take you home with me tonight."

Flame's smile has a hint of shyness. "Wow! I didn't expect that! They call me Flame." She leans in conspiratorially. "But my real name is Debbie. What do you think of my outfit?"

Flame is wearing a midriff red shirt with The Red Parrot embroidered in white and a very short black skirt with red-and-black garter and fishnet stockings.

"Hmm." David looks her up and down, then twirls his finger, indicating for her to do a little spin. "It's... all right," he says dismissively. "I always prefer to leave a little bit more to the imagination."

She hits him on the shoulder. David grabs himself in mock pain and whines, "Oh! You're so violent. Are you this physical with all your boyfriends?"

She motions the bartender to pour her a short amber drink. She downs it and leans with her back against the bar. "That depends on how they behave."

"Well, I never behave. Besides, touching this fine body"—he runs his hands over himself—"isn't cheap. It'll cost you."

She touches him on his chest. Then she touches his legs.

"Stop that!" he squeals. "Unless you're planning to run up a tab."

Flame laughs at that and leans toward him. "Maybe I will. You're not like other guys here."

David turns away and sips his sparkling water. "I should hope not. Maybe I'll take you home with me after all."

"Maybe I'll let you."

Flame introduces David to her friends at the club who are all very happy to meet a customer they think won't take advantage of them. After the shift ends, Flame takes David to her apartment. There are moving boxes strewn about. Plastic and paper dishes and silverware litter the counters and tables along with general filth. David feels right at home. Flame takes him by the wrist and drags him into the bedroom.

Her walls are draped in a parachute rescued from some action picture that was shot in New Orleans. The light blue parachute is ballooned over the walls and ceilings of her bedroom like some vampire boudoir. The overhead light has a red bulb that, when filtered through the parachute, bathes the room in an eerie violet glow. The king bed has red satin sheets and a silk comforter sporting odd geometric shapes.

David walks into the bedroom and is immediately mesmerized. Flame slowly unzips his jumpsuit.

David smiles. "Maybe I'd better check your credit with the tab that you're running up."

Flame pushes him hard onto the bed and follows herself. "Don't bother. I never pay my bills."

He peels off her shirt, then finishes taking off his jumpsuit. He reaches behind Flame and effortlessly unhooks her bra. Flame takes off her panties, leaving on her skirt. "I know that you like to use your imagination," she teases.

They kiss, and David pulls her hair just enough to enhance the experience. He caresses her in places that she expects, but he also finds parts of her body that she didn't know could be aroused. He gets behind her and licks the small of her back. Then, slowly, he licks her inner thighs. When he's ready to lift her skirt, she has already pulled it off and sent it flying into the parachute.

After they make love, she says, "Wait a minute. I thought you were gay!"

He gives her a wicked smile. "I guess I just hadn't met a girl like you before."

Flame likes that and melts into his arms. He feels her soft, warm, satisfying skin and he nuzzles her soft, long, flaming red hair.

He thinks, *Whoever said "crime doesn't pay" was working the wrong angle.*

David uses Flame's phone to call Ava and finds out that they expect to arrive the next evening. He falls asleep with Flame in her satin bed. In the morning, Flame makes scrambled eggs, bacon, coffee, and orange juice. As they leave, she gives David her home number.

That evening, David buys Flame a poor boy sandwich—a rustic roll filled with sautéed shrimp, lettuce, tomato, pickle, mayonnaise, and a tangy creole mustard. They go back to The Red Parrot and hang out while waiting for his sister and Chris to arrive. The girls pay for his soft drinks and even let him use their office phone.

When Ava and her husband arrive at The Red Parrot, she doesn't recognize him. He rushes over and gives her a big hug.

"You look like a pimp. You look… great!"

Chris shakes David's hand. He can barely take his eyes off the girls, and he admires how they seem to fawn over David. David excuses himself and goes over to Flame, who is getting ready to mount the window swing.

"Flame, I have to go."

She gets off the swing and hugs David passionately. "Will you be back?" she asks, holding him expectantly.

He holds Flame's face and kisses her reassuringly. "Maybe. I have your number. I'll be in touch." But that is the last time David sees Flame or returns to New Orleans.

PART III - PHOENIX, ARIZONA

CHAPTER 23

DAVID fills in details with Chris and Ava about the bakery, his legal problems, and his close call in Louisiana. Then his eyelids start to close. He stretches out on the back bench seat of the rented late model Buick Regal and falls asleep. For three hours, he resembles a corpse stretched out with his feathered pimp hat that shields his face from the sun pouring in through the car windows. He finally wakes up about fifteen minutes from the Jackson Municipal Airport in Mississippi to Chris screaming at Ava.

"Jesus H. Christ! Shut up already, will you?"

At first, it seems like part of a bad dream as David stirs from slumber. He opens his eyes and bolts upright in his seat.

Ava looks back. Tears pool in her eyes. "Hey, brother. Did you sleep well?"

"Yeah. Is everything all right? I thought I heard yelling."

Chris turns slightly back toward him for a moment, a guilt-ridden smile on his lips. "No, bro, everything's cool. We'll be at the airport in a few minutes."

David sits up alert, leaving the pimp hat behind and stretching the kinks out of his back. His spine gives a satisfying crack as he slowly twists his torso left and right and looks around. "I can't thank you guys enough for bailing me out back there. Man, I appreciate it."

Chris looks at David in the rearview mirror. Ava covertly dries her eyes and turns completely in her seat. She extends her left hand over the seat back for David to take.

Chris says, "No problem at all. We're family. That's what we do."

David smiles and takes Ava's hand. "I'll take care of the plane tickets when we get to the airport."

Ava says, "We couldn't reserve anything because we didn't know when we'd be here."

Chris looks at her as if she's addled. "He knows that."

At the airport there is no luggage to check. David uses his last Dominick Caparelli check to pay for three first-class tickets to Sky Harbor Airport in Phoenix. The sections on each side of the aisle have two deep leather seats, and David arranges for Chris and Ava to sit together, Ava at the window and Chris on the aisle, with himself across the aisle from them.

Chris takes his and Ava's tickets from David. "Wow, first class! I've never flown first class before!"

David looks for a spare pocket on his jumpsuit to put his ticket. He gives up and zips it into his chest. "Yeah. That makes two of us."

Ava takes David's hand. "That makes three of us."

Chris's jaw tightens at her little joke, and he fixes his eyes on her like Alex Trebek when a Jeopardy contestant blows a softball question.

They walk casually to the gate. They have no bags. As they wait for their flight, David watches a small courtesy television. One commercial in particular catches his eye. A couple on vacation at some sort of beach resort talk about having an expensive dinner while a thief breaks into their car and steals their purse and wallet. The thief cackles gleefully as he finds a wad of cash inside and stuffs it into his pocket.

Karl Malden appears holding an American Express Traveler's Check. In his deep voice, he warns, "Don't let this happen to you. American Express Traveler's Checks. If they're lost or stolen, you can get them back immediately at over sixty thousand locations. Don't leave home without them."

Once settled on the flight, Ava says very little. All Chris can talk to David about across the aisle are the "smoking hot girls" at The Red Parrot and how they were all into David.

"How did you do that? They acted like you had a twelve-inch cock."

David offers a polite smile. "I assure you I don't."

Chris tilts his head for more information. "Come on. Tell me your secret."

"Sure. I convinced them that I was gay."

"No, seriously."

"I am being serious."

Chris turns his back completely to Ava. "But then why would they want to fuck you?"

David leans back and closes his eyes. "Believe me, Chris, if a girl wants to have sex with you that won't stop them."

Chris shakes his head. "I don't think I could ever do that."

David reaches across the aisle, puts his hand on Chris's leg, and squeezes. "Well, fortunately you don't have to. You're a happily married man."

He sits up and looks across Chris at Ava. "By the way, congratulations on the baby. Have you picked out names?"

"If it's a girl, we're thinking Ida. If it's a boy, we're partial to David."

"Really? I'm so flattered."

Ava laughs. "Don't be. It's also Chris's grandfather's name."

Chris is conspicuously silent as they talk about the baby.

The flight attendant rolls a cart down the aisle with a gleaming silver covered tray. She lifts off the cover to reveal a perfectly cooked prime rib roast. "Would you like some prime rib for lunch?"

Chris stares at the crusted delicacy and notices that there is also a heaping bowl of impossibly fluffy, buttered mashed potatoes and vegetables. His mouth waters as he pulls his tray down. "Yes. Please."

The flight attendant prepares a plate for Chris. "Can I get you something to drink?"

"What do you have?"

The flight attendant smiles. "Pretty much anything you want."

Chris makes room on his tray. "Scotch and soda?"

"No problem." She turns to Ava. "Can I get you something to drink?"

"Just water, please."

Chris's head snaps to his right to face Ava. "Seriously? Just water?"

Ava offers a fading smile. "The baby."

"Christ, you can have something more than water."

"It's all I want for now."

David touches the flight attendant's back to get her attention. "I'll have a Perrier. Maybe my sister will have one too. It's still water—just better."

Ava says, "Okay. I'll try a Perrier water."

Chris seethes silently while he cuts into his roast.

When they arrive at Ava's apartment, Sunny hugs David like a human boa constrictor. Sal waits until she's done and gives him a hug of his own. Tears in her eyes, Sunny waits her turn and hugs David again. "I was sure we'd lost you."

David nods. "I thought I was going to die in a Louisiana swamp. What a horrible way to go."

As if for the first time, Sal notices David's outfit, the now very wrinkled and stained white jumpsuit. "Even in the French Quarter, you aren't going to blend in in that."

"I thought it would be good reverse psychology. No one trying to lay low would dress this conspicuously. It was like hiding in plain sight."

After David settles in, he, Sal, and Sunny take a walk around Chris and Ava's apartment complex. The weather is gorgeous. It's warm and sunny with a slight refreshing breeze. The sky is an unnatural clear blue.

The apartments in the complex are clean, low-rent setups. The buildings are beige, three-story nondescript structures covering several acres. Lawns of sand and desert rock are dotted with the occasional cactus. In front of the buildings is a small, paved road that leads to a larger road with a diagonal car park.

As they tour the grounds, Sunny says, "We should move in here. We came here to be close to Ava."

Sal frowns and gets right to the point. "I'm guessing we've lost everything from New Orleans. Is that right?"

David keeps silently walking.

Sal stops walking to get his attention. "David? Is that right? Did we lose everything again?"

David turns back to look at Sal and manages to force a smile. "We still have our health."

Sal storms off ahead about ten feet. He turns around and yells back at David and Sunny. The artery throbs in his neck, and his dark eyes narrow. "We're back where we started. Right? A few thousand dollars and no place to live. I don't get you guys. How can you be so casual about this? How can you be so fuckin'—"?

David does a playful spin. "Centered? For my mother, it's in her DNA not to panic. For me, it's because I have a plan. I agree that we need to get an apartment here. We have more money than we had when we got to New Orleans. Let's make it a two-bedroom unit to start."

CHAPTER 24

DIANNE Symmons sits at a desk completely covered with piles of newspaper clippings, maps, legal pads scribbled with obscure notes, and an ash tray overflowing with lipstick-stained cigarette buts. Her cube is bordered by ugly gray cloth dividers on which she has used multi-colored push pins to affix over a hundred Post-it-sized pieces of paper.

Bruce Aaron, executive assistant director, approaches the chaos that is Dianne's work area. He's a tall, good-looking fifty-something executive with a perfectly groomed full head of salt-and-pepper hair that looks like he stepped out of an old guys' hair mousse commercial. He wears an impeccable blue suit, white shirt, and conservative rep tie that practically screams bureaucrat. His glasses sport conservative black frames. He's thin. Maybe he would weigh a hundred and sixty pounds, but only if his pocket carried five dollars in pennies. "You know, Dianne, this is the FBI. We have a standard to maintain. Do me a favor, will you? Stand up for a second."

Dianne doesn't respond at first except to lock eyes with Bruce in an "are you fuckin' serious?" stare. When Bruce patiently waits, she reluctantly pushes her chair back and gets to her feet. "Okay, Slim. What is it?"

Bruce motions with his open palms toward the entire room. "Just look around. What do you see?"

Dianne looks past the borders of her cubicle. Every other cubical in the honeycombed cavernous room is pristine. Desks are clear except for the paperwork being actively used by their analysts. Nothing is affixed to the cube walls except for an occasional discrete calendar or picture.

"One of these things is not like the others," Bruce hoarsely sings to the *Sesame Street* tune.

Dianne picks up the tune in her exquisite alto voice. "One of these things doesn't belong." She sheepishly smiles.

Bruce frowns. He isn't amused. "Seriously, Dianne. You have got to get organized."

"I am organized." She quickly sits back down.

"Okay, prove it. Where are you at on the Macintyre case from three months ago?"

Without taking her eyes off Bruce, she reaches behind her into a stack of paper on the corner of her desk. She pulls out two sheets of paper from the middle of the stack and holds them up to read. "Alex Macintyre and his girlfriend robbed eight banks in Wisconsin and Illinois. I tracked them down from a parking ticket on his getaway car." Without losing focus on the first page, Dianne extends her hand to Bruce, which holds the second page with a copy of the ticket. "After confirming that the address on the ticket was indeed his address, I requested special agents to pick him up there. No one has gotten back to me yet on status." Dianne pauses a beat. A satisfied sneer forms at the edges of her smile. "It could be that the field agents need better organization."

Bruce shakes his head in amazement. "You are such a smart ass. But excellent work on that. You know, if you ever got organized for real, you'd be dangerous."

"Then be thankful I've got a governor." She gestures to the cluttered desk.

Bruce barely stifles a chuckle. "Speaking of governor…" He smiles at his pun before handing Dianne a manila envelope labeled *World Fair Con*. "I have a new case for you. The governor of the beautiful state of Louisiana has personally asked us to find some con artists that scammed the State out of ten grand. They haven't a clue where to find them. It's a con team of one young man and a slightly older woman. No pictures yet."

Dianne starts to read the file. She visibly grows more interested with each page.

Bruce picks up a brown-stained paper coffee cup on the corner of Dianne's desk and shakes his head as he drops it into a trash can. "I don't have to tell you how important it is that we bring these people to justice. The support of our states' governments is vital to our mission. We want to show the governor of Louisiana that we take his complaint seriously. Please put this on the top of your considerable 'calendar of thrills.' Any resources that you need, just let me know."

"Well, one resource that will help is if you get off my ass about spending time cleaning. Since when is intra-state fraud a federal crime?"

Bruce pushes his glasses up on the bridge of his nose. "He used a phone to effectuate the fraud. That's wire fraud."

Dianne looks up from the papers and squints at Bruce. "That's a thing? I've heard of mail fraud."

"Pretty much the same crime. One uses federal mails, the other uses federal wire communications."

Dianne continues reading the file. Her left hand waves Bruce away.

Bruce smiles and leaves. He says over his shoulder, "Just want you to be the best you can be."

Dianne raises a middle finger salute. She scans the pages of the file again and calls the number for Hyram Goldman.

His receptionist answers.

"This is Dianne Symmons with the Federal Bureau of Investigation. May I speak with Mr. Goldman?"

"One moment please."

"This is Hyram Goldman."

"Mr. Goldman, Dianne Symmons with the Federal Bureau of Investigation. I've just received the file on the fraudulent theft of money by—"

"Dominick Caparelli and a swindler we know as Dixie Jones," Hyram interjects.

Dianne writes Hyram's number on a new piece of paper and sticks it on her cluttered cube wall. "Can you tell me first-hand what happened?"

Hyram closes the door to his office. His face turns apple red as he recalls Dixie and Dominick. A moment later, he takes a measured deep breath and explains to Dianne what happened.

"When we sent our engineers over the next week, the real Dixie Jones was at the site. She had no idea what we were talking about or whom we made a deal with. That's when we knew we were dealing with a team of con artists of the first order."

"How did the fake Dixie convince you that she was the owner?"

"First of all, they were very convincing. But she also showed my assistant a Louisiana driver's license."

"Hmm. Do you happen to have the number of that license?"

Hyram presses the intercom button. "Hold on a minute." The line hisses on hold, then comes back. He thumbs through a file on his desk and retrieves the contract. "Yes. I have it right here." He gives Dianne the license number that his assistant wrote on the contract near the notarized signature.

Dianne scribbles the number onto another note and puts it under Hyram's number on the cluttered partition. "Thank you, sir. I'll be in touch when I have something."

She contacts the Louisiana Department of Motor Vehicles, and they fax a copy of the license with Sunny's picture. Dianne notices a copy of the cashed certified check from the State of Louisiana in the file and calls the bank where it was deposited. The address used on the Dixie Jones license and the bank account leads to a campground in Slidell, Louisiana. Dianne calls Slidell's chief of police.

"I know those names. Had a bounty hunter looking for the kid. I'm surprised that the FBI is getting involved with a Florida paperhanger."

Dianne makes another note. Already her desk is getting littered with more pieces of paper. "I'm looking into a fraud on the State of Louisiana."

The chief goes to a file cabinet and thumbs through to a file. He takes it out and opens it onto his desk. "Don't know anything about that. Dominick Caparelli is wanted in Florida. He disappeared into the swamp about a week ago, I haven't heard anything since. I doubt if he ever made it out of the swamp alive."

Dianne frowns. "Have you found any remains to verify that?"

"No, but if the gators got him, it's not likely there would be anything left. You might also want to talk to a John Foster in Hollywood, Florida." He gives her the number.

She writes the phone number on the back of a piece of scratch paper. When she calls Foster, he explains about David Adler, the bakery, the check kiting, the bad check, and his parents, Sal and Sunny, who posted bond and then fled with him.

Dianne reflects on this new information as she studies the grainy black-and-white fax photo of Sunny. She rips off a sheet of legal paper and puts down three names: *Dominick Caparelli, Sunny Rossi,* and *Sal (Salvatore?) Rossi.*

Under those names she begins writing aliases: *David Adler, Dixie Jones.* The pen pauses over the page. She writes a question mark under the known aliases and under Sal. Then she writes, *Uses identities like a bank robber uses a gun.*

CHAPTER 25

AS David, Sal, and Sunny walk to the office of Ava's apartment building, David asks,

"Do we have a way to get around?"

Sunny shuffles toward Sal, who puts his arm around her. "We're renting Ava's Honda. Fifty dollars a week. We still drive her wherever she needs to go."

David gives a subtle nod. "That's good. I'm sure she can use the cash."

The apartment manager's office is more of a reception area than an office. It has a sofa, comfortable chairs, and two desks of which only one is occupied. The occupant is a pretty girl whom David estimates to be somewhere between eighteen and twenty-one.

She's waspy attractive with angled features and straight, blond hair that stops right past her smallish breasts. She wears an orange jumper and red shoes that fight for attention with her purple knee-high socks and flowered blouse. She welcomes the three into the office with a nasal voice. "Hello, I'm Megan. Like, what can I do for you?"

Sal answers. "We'd like to rent a two-bedroom unit."

She takes a pen and rental application form out of her desk. "Sure. Have you, you know, like, rented with us before?"

Sal sits down in front of the desk. "No, but our daughter is already one of your tenants."

Megan starts to write on the form. "How rad. Like, what's her name?"

Sunny and David look at each other, barely stifling laughter. "Ava and Chris Brady. They live at thirty-one, unit three zero one."

Megan scribbles on the form. "Totally. Like, we have a two-bedroom in the same building. You know? It's like, on the first floor."

Sal leans forward. His face is relaxed, and his movements resemble someone trying to touch a deer without frightening it. "What is the rent?"

Megan sits up like she's giving a speech. "Like three hundred, one-month advance and one-month security deposit. You know?"

"Like three hundred? Or three hundred?"

Megan looks at Sal with puzzlement. "Three hundred." She produces a month-to-month lease and gives Sal the rental application. "We can, like, waive the waiting period because, you know, you have relatives already here."

Sal signs the lease and signs six one-hundred-dollar traveler's checks.

Megan collects the checks like a small deck of cards. She counts them, pads them together, and puts them in a locked desk drawer that she opens and re-locks. "Like, awesome! Welcome to our place in the sun!"

She goes to a gray metal box hanging on a wall behind her desk and runs her finger through several slots until she comes to the one for the selected unit. She retrieves those keys and hands them to Sal. "There should be, like, you know, three sets of keys. One for, like, each of you."

Sal, David, and Sunny leave the office, barely making it before Sunny says in her best Megan imitation. "Like, welcome to our place in the sun."

David laughs and follows. "It's totally tubular!"

Sal laughs despite his obvious frustration. "What an airhead!"

They move into the apartment, and no one is happy with the arrangement. Especially Sal. He's constantly surly at having to live with David again. He follows David around, picking up his detritus with a side of constant criticism.

After New Orleans, David feels emotionally under water. He wants—no, he needs—to break through with another plan. It takes weeks. He spends that time locked in his room, only going out to visit a local art supply store and to pick up fast food.

The art supply store is both David's muse and his toolbox. He'd always thought of art as the pictures hanging in office buildings and museums. He never considered that the same source of materials for masterpieces and shlock paintings would be the source of materials to forge identities and more.

He discovers transfer letters in every size and font. He discovers Exacto knives and stamps that can be custom cut. He buys several books on printing and art, and he devours them. He learns about different inks, paper stock, printing, and layout. He learns how to use cameras for something other than vacation memories.

David works alone in secret behind his locked door as he operates with the accuracy of a surgeon. Hanging on a blank wall opposite his bed is a large, white poster board with an intricate design that appears to be an inflated North Dakota driver's license; at least so far as David imagines an official North Dakota driver's license would look. The board covers a huge swath of the wall.

But the license is incomplete. There is a blank blue background where the picture should be. The actual name, license number, and personal information are also blank.

David labors at a table next to his bed with cuts of poster board, large, press-on black letters, numbers, and characters. In front of him in a neat stack are completed strips of poster board the same color as the hanging oversized license. Each piece of board has different pieces of information that he can affix to the license with double stick tape. With that information attached, the oversized board can become an "official" driver's license in as many identities as he wants.

David goes to a local library and, from an encyclopedia, finds a picture of the State seal for North Dakota. He orders a twenty-four-inch stamp of the seal from a local stamp maker. When the stamp arrives, he uses a plate of red ink and a roller to ink the stamp and carefully presses it onto the center of the poster board. He then attaches the strips of information over the stamped image. It looks as official as if it came right from the North Dakota Secretary of State.

Finally, David purchases a Polaroid camera and a tripod. He calls a meeting with Sal and Sunny in the living room. "I know that we're strapped for cash, but I have a plan. We still have traveler's checks. Right?"

Sunny and Sal nod in unison.

David waits for effect. "What if the checks were lost?"

Sunny suddenly flashes on David's plan. "We would get a refund for the lost checks. That's the point of traveler's checks."

David touches his nose as he points to Sunny. "And we would still have the checks that we reported stolen. We can use those just like cash."

Sal continues the thought. "Right. When we purchased the checks, we got receipts for each of them. If we pretend to lose them, we still have the receipts to get them replaced. So, we double our money."

David snaps his fingers and points at Sal. "Exactly. We need to step up our game. We can keep getting driver's licenses using baptismal certificates, but that's limited for what I want to do with the traveler's checks."

David takes Sal and Sunny into his bedroom for the first time since he started his project. The first thing Sal sees is a room strewn with scrap paper and discarded fast food wrappers. "What the hell, David! You live like an animal.

This is a living area, not a dumpster. It's amazing that this place doesn't have roaches by now."

Then, on the wall, Sunny and Sal notice the replica North Dakota driver's license the size of a thirty-six-inch by forty-eight-inch poster board. Sal and Sunny are thoroughly confused.

Sal says, "That'll never fit in my wallet."

David chuckles. "We'll see."

He loads the Polaroid Swinger camera with color Polaroid film. He positions the camera on the tripod in front of the poster board and adjusts the focus. He picks up one of the strips of poster board on the table. It has the name *Alex Jones* in large block letters. He uses double-sided tape to place the strip on the poster board next to where it says *Full Name.* David then places strips with the remaining information in place on the board. "Sal, stand under the board with your head in the blue section."

David positions both Sal and then the camera so that only the poster board license with Sal's face fills the frame. He focuses and snaps the picture.

The photo comes out looking exactly like a driver's license. David deftly trims the photo, and, with a glue stick, he attaches it to a thick white paper backing and trims it again. "All we need to do now is bring it somewhere to be laminated."

Sal and Sunny look at the finished product. They agree that it looks genuine.

Sunny holds it to a light. "Why North Dakota?"

"I wanted a state far enough away that no one would recognize the design. Also, I wanted a state that most people wouldn't consider sophisticated or ask questions about."

In the next several hours, David, Sunny, and Sal each have twenty different North Dakota driver's licenses in twenty different names and addresses. Even Sal is excited about the plan.

David stacks the fake licenses. "How much money do we have left?"

Sunny checks her purse. "We have about five hundred dollars."

They travel to a local printer that allows customers to do their own laminating. David runs the fake licenses through the laminator. There are ten per page. He uses a paper cutter to evenly trim them apart.

Phony licenses in hand, they travel to the closest bank in Phoenix. David purchases five hundred dollars in traveler's checks using one of his North Dakota licenses. The traveler's checks come with a register log that the purchaser is supposed to keep as a record of the spent checks.

The bank teller advises David, "Make sure that you keep the register separate from the checks. If the checks are lost or stolen, you'll need the register to get them replaced."

The next day, David returns to the bank. The logical part of his mind tells him that he's safe. After all, he's the "victim" reporting that his traveler's checks were lost. Sal and Sunny enter the bank lobby separately after David and take posts next to the deposit receipts. They watch for any signs that, somehow, a teller or a bank officer knows what is happening.

David stops halfway between the entrance and the teller counter. He sucks up his fear because he has been stung twice in bank lobbies. He looks carefully at the three women servicing customers. One of the women appears to be in her thirties. She's dressed in a blue pantsuit with smallish hoop earrings. He estimates the second as much older. She has short, dark brown hair, and she wears a very conservative brown dress. Reading glasses dangle from a chain around her neck over her breasts.

The third teller is much younger. David thinks that she's barely out of high school, or maybe in her senior year. She's pretty, with auburn hair tied up in a ponytail. He walks to her window even though her line has an extra customer.

He creates an embarrassed expression as he approaches the teller counter with his check register. "I feel so stupid. I had my traveler's checks last night at dinner. When I wanted one to pay the bill, they were gone. I couldn't believe it. It's a good thing my girlfriend had some cash, or I'd be washing dishes right now."

The teller smiles sheepishly at David. "I'm so sorry to hear that. Did you keep the register separate from the checks?"

David hands her the register.

The teller retrieves a document and hands it to David. "Hang onto that. You'll need it to fill out this form."

David fills out the form and presents it with the register and his North Dakota license. The teller looks at the license for several seconds. She turns it over and examines the blank backing.

David nervously tries to start a conversation. He leans forward toward the teller. "Have you worked here long?"

She still looks carefully at the driver's license. "No. I'm studying banking at the University of Arizona and… You're from North Dakota?"

"I am."

The teller gathers the documents along with the license. "Quite a change for you. Can you excuse me a moment?" She looks again at the blank back of the license. She walks to the end of the counter and consults silently with the oldest teller, who puts on her reading glasses and reviews each of the documents.

David tries to act cool. He leans against the counter and looks around. He feels his hands tremble uncontrollably. He wants to take off, but he knows that would be his worst move. His nerves are like ice water as conflicting thoughts enter and leave his brain.

When the teller returns, she asks David. "Do you want cash or more traveler's checks?"

David silently exhales as he relaxes. He didn't realize that he was holding his breath. He takes cash. Now that the tension is over, he realizes that it was easy. It was too easy.

He drives to Tucson with Sunny and Sal and makes several purchases with the "stolen" traveler's checks. No merchant ever questions their authenticity or providence. They really are as good as cash. No ID required. At the end of the day, they collect nine hundred dollars and change.

On the way back to Phoenix, David sits satisfied in the back seat. "The experiment was a complete success. We doubled our cash, and no one seriously questioned the driver's license."

Sal looks at David through the rearview mirror. "I'm sorry that I lost faith. It's just, you know, it was so hard leaving Florida and then having to leave New Orleans."

Sunny turns and puts her hand on Sal's shoulder. "When we make enough money, it won't matter. We'll live anywhere you want."

Sal shakes his head. *Anywhere, as long as it's just the two of us... alone.*

Using the nine hundred dollars, the next day and the day after that and the day after that the pattern is followed by David, Sunny, and Sal with their various driver's licenses. The identifications are as disposable as toilet paper. They use one once and destroy it. The money increases exponentially. Nine hundred dollars becomes two thousand dollars, which becomes four thousand dollars, and so on. They use different banks and spend the traveler's checks elsewhere in the state. Within a week, they've accumulated fifteen thousand dollars in cash.

CHAPTER 26

THE next week, they're car shopping. With all the time they're spending on the traveler's check gambit, as they call it, they don't want to leave Ava without her car. And besides, she no longer needs to rent the car to them. They explain to her what they're doing, and she reluctantly approves. They give her secret cash and buy anything she needs.

Sal contacts a moving and storage company in Metairie, Louisiana and pays cash to have their personal belongings moved into storage in Phoenix. He watches the storage locker at a distance for two days before he pronounces it safe to rent a trailer and get their things.

The extra furniture and personal stuff only make the small apartment more crowded, and David's space looks like a hoarder warehouse sale. Sal stalks around the apartment like a cat in a cage. "Let's move out of here. I can't stand living like this."

David pokes the cat. "Can't do it. You signed a lease."

Sal turns and glares at David. "So?"

David's smile is broad and sarcastic. It's a "gotcha" smile. "So, you wouldn't want to break the law, would you?"

Sal snarls. "You're a total asshole. You know that?"

Not long after that exchange, they have their weekly dinner with Ava and Chris. Ava shows up. Chris is conspicuously absent.

"I'm sorry," says Ava, wearing a muted smile that says, *Please don't ask me any questions.* Unfortunately for Ava, her subdued smile is accompanied by a purple bruise on the side of her face that the Maybelline concealer doesn't quite hide. Sal notices it first. He's struck dumb and paralyzed with anger.

Sunny quickly picks up on Sal's body language. Now Sal has his fist in his mouth and is biting his knuckle so hard that she sees a rivulet of blood. She sees Ava's face. "Ava. Please sit down."

Ava obediently sits, like she's been given a hypnotic command.

Sal and David stand off to the side while Sunny holds Ava. In a patient and understanding voice, Sunny says, "Please, baby, tell me what happened."

"It's my fault," Ava says between sobs. "I've been so absorbed with the baby."

Sunny holds her tighter. "You should be. It's a huge deal."

Ava pulls out of the embrace. "But Chris is worried. I should be more understanding. And then you guys suddenly have so much money. I just think he's a little jealous. I made him mad. I didn't mean to. He threw a large book at me. I don't think he meant to hit me with it. It… just happened. Then he yelled at me to go live with my rich parents and left."

Ava cries into Sunny's shoulder for a long minute. Sunny is calm on the outside for Ava's sake but inside, she feels a burning rage.

Sal finally approaches. His voice is calm and as steady as a sniper. "Honey, do you keep a gun in the house?"

"Yes. In the bedroom. Top drawer of Chris's dresser under his socks."

He puts a gentle hand on Ava's shoulder. "Is it loaded?"

Ava sniffles. Sunny gives her a tissue. "I think so."

"I don't think it's a good idea for you to have a loaded gun in your place with all of these... tensions. Let me get your keys so I can bring it over here."

Ava gives Sal her keys, and he goes to her apartment. Sunny and David stay and support Ava in her grief.

Sunny sets the table. "Let's have dinner. Then I think you should spend the night. We have a very comfortable pull-out sofa."

Ava nods and dries her tears. "I'd like that. I don't know when Chris will be back, and I don't want to be alone."

* * *

Sal sits like a wraith on a love seat in the living room of Chris and Ava's dark apartment. His mind seethes as each minute passes, while he recalls over and over Ava's swollen face and how her jealous piece of shit husband made it about his current good fortune. Sal finds the 22-caliber revolver right where Ava said it would be. It's loaded. The gun is now in the small of Sal's back, secure in his waistband.

It's midnight when Chris returns home. He reeks of lower shelf booze. He stumbles into the darkened apartment near the kitchen and by reflex turns on the kitchen light. He doesn't see Sal twenty-five feet away in the still dark living room. He doesn't see Sal until, in a voice as calm and still as snowfall, Sal murmurs, "Good evening, Chris."

Chris jumps back in shock and grabs his chest. The shock sobers him up instantly. "Jesus! What are you doing here? You scared the shit out of me."

Sal slowly gets off the miniature sofa, a cat pacing toward its prey. His expression reeks of insanity. "This is your time, Chris."

Chris recovers from his initial shock, puts his keys in a bowl, and takes off his Members Only jacket to hang it up on a hook near the door. "My time?"

Sal works his way between Chris and the door without a scintilla of change in his expression. "This is your time, Chris," he repeats.

Chris backs away from Sal, his hands raised defensively in front as Sal closes in. "What time? What the hell are you talking about?"

Sal steps in and throws a right hook to Chris's ear so hard that Chris feels like his eardrum explodes. He covers his head with his arms as he turns away. Sal follows like a shadow. "It's your time, Chris. What did you do to Ava? To our daughter?"

Chris moves his arms and looks at Sal. "It was an accident. I didn't mean to hurt her."

Sal backhands Chris across the other side of his face. Chris drops to his knees. "You didn't mean to hurt her. Right?" Sal kicks Chris in the ribs. "What? It was just you losing your temper?" Kick. "Well, let me tell you something about tempers." Kick. "I have the King Kong of tempers." Kick. "So, whose fault is it that I kick your ass?" He kicks Chris on the ass.

Sal kneels next to Chris and with his left hand pulls his head back with his dirty, long, black hair. With his right hand, Sal draws the gun out of his pants. He loses the safety and holds the gun under Chris's chin.

Chris's eyes silently scream in terror when he realizes that Sal has his gun and that he might die. "Please…"

Sal presses the gun barrel hard against Chris's chin. He takes a controlled deep breath. "Shut the fuck up.

"I see that you favor a 22-caliber. You know, some people call this a woman's gun. Not a lot of kick. But me, I kind of like a smaller caliber weapon. You know why?"

Chris doesn't answer. Sal hits him lightly on the side of his head with the gun butt. "I asked you a question."

Chris sniffles. "No. I don't know why."

"Because the bullet doesn't have enough juice to exit the body. It just keeps traveling through your guts, tearing shit up until its momentum passes. It's a very slow and painful way to die." Sal puts the gun barrel to Chris's chest. "Now, you're going to make me do something that I've never done before."

Chris shakes uncontrollably. "Please. Please."

"You're going to make me pull a gun on someone.... and not kill them."

Chris pisses his pants. Sal gets up, leaving Chris a puddle of gelatin and urine sobbing on the floor.

"You're the father of my grandson and the husband of my daughter. That's the only reason you're alive right now. Ava need not ever know what happened here tonight. Do I have to say what will happen if you ever mistreat her or your son again?"

Chris hangs his head. Tears leak onto the carpet. "No."

"Damn right, no. Clean yourself up. Ava will be back in the morning."

Sal walks over to the upright refrigerator and freezer. He finds a bag of frozen vegetables. He looks through their drawers until he finds a spade that he has seen Ava use to till the soil on her potted plants. He tosses the frozen vegetables to Chris.

"Here. Put this on your head and face. It'll help with the swelling."

Sal keeps the gun, turns, and walks out the door.

Chris stays on the floor for several minutes. When he finally gets up, he puts the frozen vegetables on his swollen cheek. He trudges into the bedroom and sits on his bed staring at the nightstand. He stays that way for twenty minutes, in unmoving, deep meditation.

Finally, Chris ends his meditation. He picks up the phone on the nightstand and dials 911.

Before Sal goes back to his apartment, he gets in his car and takes the I-10 west. As expected, it isn't long before he hits a large area of undeveloped desert. He takes an exit that looks promising and when he feels sufficiently isolated, he pulls over and uses the spade to make a trench in the loose soil. He drops the gun in the trench and buries it, packing the sand and soil hard with his shoe. Only then does he go back to the apartment.

CHAPTER 27

SAL doesn't get back to the apartment until after three in the morning. Sunny is asleep and so he silently climbs into bed without disturbing her. She wakes up at nine thirty in the morning to a loud knock on their front door. It's more of a pound than a knock; an urgent and intrusive pounding that leaves little doubt that entry is imminent.

"Maricopa Sheriff! Open the door!"

Sunny comes to the only conclusion she can. She believes that they're being busted for the traveler's checks or for the Louisiana World's Fair or for helping David jump bond, or for all of the above. She starts scooping their identifications into a convenient purse. In the panicked rush, she forgets that her clean Arizona driver's license is also in the purse.

Sal knows exactly why the cops are at the door. He quickly slides into a pair of green work pants and a plain black tee-shirt. "They're here for me," he tells Sunny in a barely audible monotone.

Startled at the admission, Sunny spins toward him in surprise. "What? Why?"

"Open this door now!" A shouted command comes from the other side of the door.

Sal opens the door.

Two sheriff's deputies in tan uniforms carrying sidearms and handcuffs pour into the apartment. One officer's sidearm is drawn and he sticks it in Sal's face. They immediately take charge of the room. Sergeant Richard Osborne follows. His hair is snow white. So are his long eyelashes that frame steel blue eyes under gold, wire-frame glasses. His shoulder holster holds a 44-magnum revolver. On his thick, brown leather belt, a silver badge and a brown leather case with handcuffs surround a belt buckle the size of the top of a soda can emblazoned with a steer and the name "Dick" in gold embossed letters. "Salvatore Rossi, you are under arrest. Turn around and place your hands behind your back."

Sunny is in shock but recovers quickly. "What is this about? What did he do?" She moves toward Osborne, trying to get between him and Sal.

Osbourne puts a hand on his sidearm. "Not another step. Who are you?"

"I'm his wife."

Osbourne's eyes narrow. "Let me see ID."

Sunny glances at the purse on the nearby table. In less than a second, she considers her options. *They'll never buy any excuse I come up with for not having ID. If I can simply get to my purse and rummage through it like some kind of ditzy blonde, I may be able to pull out the right ID before they can see all the rest.* "Let me get my purse."

Sunny moves a little too quickly toward the purse. Big mistake. A deputy cuts her off. "Don't you fuckin' take another step."

Sunny looks back to see Osborne's gun out of the holster and pointed at her head.

Osborne points to a far wall. "Stand over there." He moves to the table and opens the purse. He pours all the IDs out onto the table and whistles softly. A broad smile appears on his face. "Well, looksee here! We got us some bad guys! Well, Miss Whoever the Hell You Are, turn around and put your hands behind your back too. Looks like you get to ride with your husband, or whatever the hell you two are."

* * *

David is saved by his literal love of burgers. When he was a young boy growing up in the suburbs of Chicago, Sunny and David's father would take him to Tops Department Store every weekend. There he and Ava would wander into the toy department, and Sunny would help them pick out the perfect toy to take home. But first, David's father would stop at his favorite restaurant, Tops Big Boy Burger.

Tops Big Boy had everything that young David could ever want in a restaurant. It had fresh ice cream sodas. It had friendly servers who treated young David like an adult. It even had its own free comic books right there in a rack up front for the taking.

And it had the best burgers David had ever tasted. Before the Big Mac, the Big Boy burger was the undisputed double decker burger of choice. David grew to love that Thousand Island Big Boy sauce and the taste and texture of a bun, American cheese, and double beef patties that anchored all the weekend feelings of love, family, and security with every bite.

Florida didn't have Big Boy restaurants. But in Phoenix, there was a Big Boy restaurant a scant two-block walk from Ava's apartment complex. Once he had extra cash, David spent every morning at the Big Boy restaurant to have a burger—all right, two burgers—fries, and a strawberry ice cream soda to plan his next nefarious day.

So, David isn't at the apartment when the Maricopa County sheriff arrives and arrests Sal and Sunny. As David walks back to Ava's apartment complex, he notices two things—neither of which is good news. First, there are four police cars in front of the apartment office with their rooftop bubblers going. Second, Ava is in her Honda parked along the intake road, waiting for a satiated David to come strolling back.

David slips into Ava's front passenger seat next to his sobbing sibling, who is now shaking like it's ten below zero even though the temperature is in the mid-eighties. Tears stream down her cheeks and snot trickles from her nostrils.

"Th-th-the police," Ava stammers. "Mom and Sal. They've been arrested. It's my fault."

Although seated, the ground seems to drop out from David's feet. He lowers his head and grabs the bridge of his nose with his thumb and forefinger. "Where did they take them?"

"The officer said, after they were processed, they would be in the Maricopa County Jail."

David waves to the road behind them. "All right, drive. Let's get out of here and find a payphone."

Ava drives David back to the Big Boy restaurant, where David gets five dollars' worth of dimes and quarters from the cashier and bogarts one of their three pay phones. He hands the handset to Ava. "Call the Maricopa County sheriff. See if you can find out what the charges are and what their bond is."

Ava sobs into a Big Boy napkin that she took from a table service. "I know why they took Sal. He attacked Chris last night after we went to bed. I've never seen Chris so scared and angry. Sal did it because of me. Because of the bruise on my face."

"Sis, don't go there. This isn't your fault. What about Mom?"

"I don't know. They just took them both."

David puts a comforting hand on Ava's shoulder. "All right. Let's focus on getting them out. Call and find out if there are bonds for either of them."

Ava gets the number of the Maricopa County Sheriff from Information and makes the call. In a voice as sweet and innocent as the host of a children's show, she gets as much information as possible. "All they'll tell me is that Sal is charged with assault with a deadly weapon. His bond is twenty-five thousand dollars."

"Nothing on Mom?"

"Not yet."

Under the pay phone, David has the Yellow Pages open to "Bail Bonds." He desperately calls one after the other.

Each of them says in turn, "We can post bond on your stepfather, but we won't be able to do anything for your mother until she's charged. You'll need collateral and ten percent of the bond, twenty-five hundred dollars, to bond out your stepfather."

David writes on a scrap of paper. "What kind of collateral?"

"Most people use their house or other real estate, but anything of value will do."

Finally, one bondsman, sensing the desperation in David's voice, gives David the key to the Maricopa County Jail.

"You know, if you have real estate collateral but not cash, you can simply pledge the real estate right with the sheriff's office. They'll accept it as a bond directly without me. There's a specific form…"

In his excitement, David hangs up without warning. He and Ava drive to the sheriff's office and ask for the form suggested by the bondsman. After he gets it, David leaves, gets a newspaper, and has Ava drop him off at the Maricopa County Recorder of Deeds.

CHAPTER 28

THE cell is all steel and concrete and every inch, including the bars, is painted in a pale yellow that reminds Sal of infected mucus. The cell length is small enough to cross in three small steps and half as wide. It's lit by stabbing fluorescent light bulbs positioned outside the bars on the ceiling of a catwalk where guards cross by and verify that prisoners aren't hanging themselves—or each other.

To say that Sal has obsessive compulsive disorder is to say a male peacock is understated. He stands at the door to the cell and recalls another time in his life when he felt this helpless and out of control.

* * *

He was just ten years old. His father had always been a hard man. A Sicilian construction worker with no education after grade school, he spent the Depression years making a living by hammering six-inch steel spikes into railroad ties with a sledgehammer twelve hours a day. He was the physically strongest and emotionally coldest man Sal has ever known.

Sal's mother was his father's opposite; a warm, friendly woman who loved to cook and loved to eat and had the plumpness to prove it. Sal adored his mother and feared his father.

In this memory, Sal recalls his mother making a big pot of lima beans for dinner. As he sat with his mother and father at the dinner table, Sal picked at the beans after eating the rest of his food. His father noticed that he wasn't eating and became surly.

"Hey, dummy, why you no eat your vegetables? They're good for you."

"I can't, Dad. They make my stomach hurt. I think I want to vomit."

His father turned to his mother. "If lima beans make him sick, get rid of them! I don't want to see another lima bean at this table."

But Sal's mother had received the beans at a bargain, and she'd made a huge pot. She thought maybe Sal was just being picky and might feel differently later. Instead of throwing them out, she kept them for a few days and served them with another dinner.

His father didn't notice the lima beans on his plate until he saw Sal skewing a single bean on his fork and trying to force it into his mouth. Then his father erupted. "Lima beans! Lima beans?! I told you that I never wanted to see lima beans on this table again!"

His chair flew to the wall as he sprang up and tore to the refrigerator to find the large bowl half filled with lima beans. He carried the bowl to the table and smashed it on the tabletop. Lima beans exploded all over the table and poured out onto the floor. He took off his belt and wound it around his huge fist so that a length of leather with the buckle was exposed. He cracked the buckle on the tabletop and held it up menacingly to Sal's mother. "You like lima beans so much? You eat them! You eat every one of them!"

Without feeling it, he cracked the buckle against his other huge, calloused hand. Sal's mother was terrified. She started to pick up the lima beans from the floor to throw them away.

"Oh, now you going to waste food? I said to eat every one of them."

Sal cried out in despair and fear for his mother. "Daddy, please, look. I'll eat the lima beans." He shoved a forkful into his mouth and began to chew. Then he gagged as he tried to swallow.

Sal's mother became quiet and complacent. Her face a visage of acceptance, she collected the lima beans from the floor and table. She put them onto an empty dinner plate and then added the beans from Sal's plate and his father's.

Sal pleaded with his father, "Please, Dad. Please don't make her do this."

"Every last one." He watched intently and malevolently as Sal's mother slowly consumed each and every bean, forcing the last few spoons between coughing and gagging on the bile that rose in her throat.

Only then did Sal's father become calm. He put his belt back on his pants and got up. His lips curled up in a satisfied smile as he turned to Sal's mother. "Now clean up this mess. And don't you dare vomit on my clean floor. Sal, you want to go out for ice cream?"

Sal ran sobbing from the room. Sal's father shrugged and went out to the local tavern.

* * *

Now Sal is pushed by two guards into the cell. As he enters, he silently aches for the apartment with Sunny and David. There are already three prisoners in the tiny space made barely habitable by four metal bunks bolted to the bars, two on each side of the narrow cell just large enough to hold a prone man. Four men locked in a cage 24/7. On the far end of the cell is a metal toilet with what looks like a tiny steel sink on its back instead of a toilet tank all bolted into the concrete wall.

On the toilet, one of the prisoners is taking a shit while at the same time eating an apple—a thin white dude with a shaved head and hideous prison tats. On his neck, under his left ear, is a swastika tattoo. Sal recognizes him with disgust as a skinhead. He looks no older than eighteen, maybe nineteen. Sal looks incredulously at him as the cell door snaps locked behind him.

The skinhead on the pot notices Sal's stare. "You got a problem?"

Sal never breaks eye contact. After a long moment, he speaks in a tone reserved for old gym teachers conscripted into teaching middle school health. "You ever hear of dysentery?"

The skinhead sneers at Sal. He takes another bite of the apple. "You ever hear of shutting the fuck up?"

One of the prisoners on his top bunk shifts his weight and sits up, feet dangling over the prisoner below him. To Sal he appears to be Mexican, but he could be from Puerto Rico or Cuba. He's short with a boxer's body, rope muscles on his arms and shoulders, and cut, six-pack abs. He has short, receding black hair, a close-cropped black beard and mustache, and piercing black eyes that lack even a flicker of kindness. He takes in the new arrival and turns to the skinhead. "You ever hear of a mercy flush, *pendejo*?"

The skinhead, struck silent at the intervention, reaches behind him, gets toilet paper, wipes, and flushes the toilet. He doesn't bother to wash his hands. Apple still in hand, he climbs onto the right-hand bottom bunk.

Sal grimaces at the thought of the skinhead still eating the apple. He moves toward the only unmade bunk, right above the skinhead.

He considers the boxer the alpha of this debased group. Sal isn't afraid of a beef. Not from these guys, that's for sure. But he looks at the toilet, used by four men, a mere eighteen inches from where he sleeps. He smells the fear and sweat from the other three prisoners. Their only personal space resides in the mattressed metal slab that they occupy all the time. Sal can't help but see the stains and trash that shares the space with them. He looks around the cell and at the catwalk with renewed fear. "When do we take a shower?"

The skinhead flashes a half sneer at Sal. "Whenever the fuck they want us to take one."

Sal isn't afraid of a beef, but he *is* terrified that he will have to spend days, weeks, or months in this filth. Sal believes in hell, and this is a close approximation.

A guard comes by the cell and places a disposable razor on the bar of the door. "Here's your weekly razor."

Sal climbs down and takes the razor from the bar. When he turns back toward the cell, the other prisoners stare intently at him.

The boxer breaks the silence. "What do you think you're doing?"

Sal turns and holds up the disposable Bic razor by the handle. "Taking my razor."

The boxer slides off his bunk and extends his hand for the razor. "Ey, *maricon*, you think you're at the Hilton? You think you get room service here?"

The other prisoners carry the taunt. Especially the skinhead. "Yeah, dude, you put in your wake-up call? Want your dinner menu?"

Sal starts to lose it. "Fuck you!"

The boxer smiles, showing empathy for Sal. "The razor is for all of us."

"All four of us? For a week?"

The boxer's kind smile turns malevolent, and he takes the razor from Sal. "Welcome to Maricopa County Jail." He places the razor on a shelf above the toilet.

Sal shakes his head in disbelief and settles onto his bunk, smoothing the sheets and blanket underneath him. He already misses Sunny and David, even David's messes. He's afraid he might never see any of them again.

The boxer returns to his own bunk, sits up, and looks across the cell at Sal. "Hope you don't get too long a sentence, mano."

My graduation picture. A year before
the collection agent job.

Sunny and Sal – 1973 shortly after their wedding.

New Orleans World's Fair. The fair didn't open
until 1984. It cost the State of Louisiana $5 million.
The fair lost money and their checks bounced
like Superballs before it became insolvent.

Hamburger Hamlet. One of my favorite burger joints
where I planned my con games and recognized
Christian from the Equitable Building.

Equitable Building on Hollywood and Vine

The Sands Hotel and Casino Las
Vegas. Our first casino heist.

Big Boy Restaurant where I introduced
Chris to their signature burger and where
she gave me a Saint Dismas medal.

Apartment building where I lived
with Tina and her children.

The parking lot where the FBI agent found the Playboy
Club chip in my car and where I was ultimately arrested.

My wife Tina about 1981.

Another photo of Tina around 1980 – 1981.

In Times Square with the Naked Cowboy after retirement from law. I used to write briefs and he used to wear them.

CHAPTER 29

THE same cell setup awaits Sunny as she walks through the catwalk on the women's side of the Maricopa County Jail. She carries a bedroll and a small bag containing toothpaste, a toothbrush, and tampons. Unlike Sal, as Sunny approaches her cell, the occupants are downright friendly. With their black-and-white striped uniforms, they look like a degenerate backup group for a punk band called The Thirsty Zebras or something.

A petite Hispanic woman perched on the top left bunk pauses from reading her Bible. "All right. About time we got some new action."

On the left bottom bunk sit two women. One is tall with chestnut hair trimmed short to the bottom of her neck that Sunny thinks she cuts by herself. She's as white as a Jimmy Carter political rally. Very pretty. She's thin but with very large breasts. Sunny thinks she might have been a model in another life.

The other woman is black with short dreads tied so that most of her scalp shows through. She's heavy, but not so fat that she looks weak. Her bulk, in fact, gives her an intimidating quality. The two women sit across from each other, although most of the room on the bunk is taken by the Black woman. Between them is a deck of cards arranged as if they're playing two-person solitaire.

Sunny enters the cell with a cautious smile as the door slams behind her with a reverberating metallic clanking. She sees the three prisoners and the four bunks. "Permission to come aboard?"

No one laughs at her quip.

The woman dealing the cards looks up and smiles. She says with a heavy Texas drawl, "Just pick whichever bunk ain't got no bedroll. Where y'all from?"

"Originally, Chicago. West side. Been living out in Florida for a few years and... traveling since."

The heavy Black woman jumps off the card-strewn bunk. Her body seems to fill the cell. "No shit, homey! I'm Chi-town too." She lumbers over to Sunny and gives her a bear hug. "Hey, you got any smokes?"

"No, sorry. Don't smoke."

"Damn! I need a coffin nail bad! Got any rolling papers?!"

Sunny shrugs. "Sorry."

The woman left on the bottom bunk gathers the cards. "I'm Alice from Dallas." She smiles, giving Sunny time to laugh at her introduction. Sunny chuckles. Alice points to the large Black woman. "This here's Jasmine. And the floor above me is Maria. We call her Preacher."

Preacher puts down her Bible and extends her hand for Sunny to shake. "Tell me, have you found Jesus?"

Sunny looks at the floor and shakes her head. "I'm afraid not. I'm Jewish."

Preacher shrugs and picks up her King James Bible. "Nothing to be ashamed of there. Did you know Jesus was a Jew?"

"I've heard that."

Alice gets up and lifts part of her mattress. "You hungry, honey?"

Sunny sets down her bedroll. "Well, yes. I haven't eaten since breakfast."

"Would you like a grilled cheese?"

Sunny looks quizzically at Alice. "Uh, sure. But..."

Alice reaches behind her pillow and pulls out half a loaf of bread and two slices of American cheese. She makes a sandwich. "Preacher, you got watch."

Preacher sits up and looks over the catwalk. "Clear."

Alice pulls out a dense wad of toilet paper rolled into a cylinder and positions it under the metal frame of her bunk. Jasmine hands her a match and Alice sets it on fire. It burns with surprising efficiency. Using a space in the metal frame, Alice places the sandwich on the frame and moves the flame back and forth to toast the bread. "This here's a TP bomb. Toilet paper is wood, you know. You pack it tight enough and it burns long and even. The other side of the sandwich cooks quicker."

Preacher turns from the catwalk. "She's starting the walk."

Alice toasts the other side, throws the flaming toilet paper in the toilet, and flushes the ashes. Then she hands the gooey sandwich to Sunny, who wraps it in more toilet paper.

Sunny takes a bite. "It's delicious."

Alice smiles.

Preacher turns her back on the catwalk. "Turn away from the catwalk. Someone's coming."

After the guard passes, Sunny finishes the sandwich. "How did you get the bread and cheese?"

Jasmine laughs. "Must be your first bit. Women's cell, we get pretty much what we want within reason. We got the power of pussy. The currency of the BJ. We give them what they want, they take care of us. Food, drugs, whatever. Bitches come in fucked up and get even more fucked up before they leave."

Alice invites Sunny to sit down on her bunk. "Want your fortune read?"

Sunny hesitantly sits beside Alice. "Sure."

Alice deals the cards between them then begins to turn over cards and examines them with interest. "Hmm. You have two men in your life."

Sunny narrows her eyes. "That's very true."

Alice turns over more cards. "They're very close to you emotionally. But one will leave you before long."

Sunny shivers. "What does that mean? Is someone going to... die?"

Alice shrugs and looks into Sunny's eyes. "I just read what the cards say. I don't ask them what they mean. Any other questions?"

Sunny sits back against a wall. "Will I be rich?"

Alice snickers. "Everyone asks that." She deals out more cards and turns them over. "No. You'll make money, but you'll spend it just as fast." She turns up the ace of spades and looks at it gravely and silently.

Sunny sees Alice's frown and finally blurts out, "What? What is it?"

Alice doesn't take her eyes off the ace of spades. "I don't want to say."

Sunny leans forward and points to the card. "Now you have to say. What did you see?"

Alice looks up at Sunny. "You'll have a near death or total death experience soon."

Sunny tilts her head for more information. "So that means I'm getting out? I'd have to get out to be in danger, right?"

Alice shakes her head from side to side. "Y'all will get out and... it's tied to what's going to happen to you." She conspicuously gathers the cards, wraps them with a rubber band, and places them under her thin mattress. She lies down and motions for Sunny to do the same in her own bunk. "They'll bring dinner in a couple of hours. Meantime, y'all might want to set up your bunk."

Dinner consists of a bologna sandwich, coffee, and an apple served on plastic trays from a large, gray metal cart that a trustee pushes down the hall accompanied by a tall female guard. Sunny takes her tray and sets it on her bunk before she carefully boosts herself back up to keep the contents of the tray from spilling onto her bed.

She looks to the cell door where Jasmine stands, looking out at the catwalk. Jasmine's obesity dims the light coming into the cell. "Hey, Miami!" Jasmine calls to the trustee, a Hispanic woman with large hips and small breasts that are swallowed up completely by her baggy, striped prison top.

Miami gives Jasmine a furtive glance and tries to walk away. Jasmine places her face between the bars. She won't be ignored. "Miami! You got any smokes?"

Miami looks at the guard ten feet away and covertly shakes her head. The guard motions Miami to keep the cart moving. Miami looks back at Jasmine. "No. I ain't got no smokes."

Jasmine tries to shake the bars in frustration. The bars don't move. "Any papers?"

Miami glances helplessly at the guard scrutinizing her every move. "Can't. Sorry." She hustles to the next cell, leaving Jasmine frustrated and pissed.

"What the fuck! I gotta get me a smoke!"

Sunny is in her bunk with her legs dangling off the edge. She precariously balances her tray in her lap. She eats with caution and keeps her eyes on Jasmine's frustration. She knows when frustration can turn to anger.

Preacher looks down at Jasmine with an expression of empathy to her addiction. "You know, all needs can be filled by Jesus!" All eyes in the cell roll except for Jasmine's.

"Really, Preacher? You think Jesus can help with my nicotine fix?"

Preacher holds up her bible. "Sure. With Jesus, all things are possible."

Jasmine lowers her head in acceptance of Preacher's words. "Where does it say that in your Good Book?"

Preacher places her tray aside and flips through the pages of her Bible. Her face brightens as she believes she has finally found a potential convert. "Isaiah 53:5. *But he was pierced for our transgressions, he was crushed for our iniquities; the punishment that brought us peace was upon him, and by his wounds we are healed.*"

Jasmine reaches out to Preacher. "Can I see that passage?"

Preacher hands the Bible to Jasmine, who takes it, opens it, turns away, and proceeds to tear a page out of it. Preacher leaps out of her bunk like a feral cat and lands on Jasmine's back. Jasmine easily shrugs Preacher off, and she falls backward on her ass. Jasmine tosses the Bible back onto Preacher's bunk.

Sunny expected something like this to happen. She pulls her legs onto her bunk. She puts the tray to the side. She glances desperately at the compressed cell space and feels foolish for her brief respite of comfort with women who, just a few minutes before, made her feel welcome.

"Bitch, keep the damn book!" Jasmine snarls at Preacher even as she deftly pours tobacco onto the torn page and rolls the paper into a makeshift cigarette. As Jasmine rolls the page, she pretends to read. "And the Lord helps those that help themselves."

Preacher springs up from her prone position at Jasmine's feet. "That's not even in the Bible."

Sunny says casually, "Yeah, I think it was Ben Franklin."

Jasmine puts the tobacco-laden Biblical page in her mouth and lights it up. "I don't give a fuck who said it." She tokes deeply. "I just care that I feel the Holy Spirit with this fine tobacco."

With that, Preacher's rage sparks again, and she lunges for Jasmine. Her fists thrash at Jasmine like a meth head in a mosh pit. "I'll kill you, bitch!"

Jasmine tries to restrain Preacher with her bulk, but Preacher's rage transcends her physical limitations. She bites, she pushes, and she slaps. And one of the slaps sends the flaming Bible page fluttering out of Jasmine's mouth and onto the sheet of Alice's bunk.

Combustion requires three things to occur: an initial ignition source, such as a flaming page from the Bible; fuel, such as Alice's cheap cotton sheet; and an oxidant, aka oxygen. The sheet immediately bursts into flame and sends Alice to the other side of the small cell, except for her desperate reach back to retrieve her cards from the flames.

When the flames run out of fuel from the sheet, they find an even better source in the toilet paper bombs that Alice premade for her makeshift grill. The combustion point of those TP bombs is just enough to start the cheap foam rubber mattress on fire, and the toxic plastic fumes quickly fill the cell and cascade into the catwalk.

There is no escape. The small cell offers no refuge from the heat, and the fumes quickly begin to overcome all four of the women, who stand grasping the bars and screaming desperately into the catwalk.

Sunny is frozen in terror. She pulls the pillow near her face to blunt the bitter smoke. She's grateful to be on the second level away from the flames. Then she has an adrenaline-fueled epiphany. She jumps off her bunk with her blanket. Running on instinct, she instantly douses her blanket in water from the toilet. Like a possessed demon, she turns and screams, "Get on the ground!"

All three women drop to the cement floor at Sunny's command. Human balls of pain and fear, their faces turn to face the catwalk for air. Sunny holds the wet blanket like Batman spreads his cape and drops down to join them, the wet blanket covering most of their bodies. The water in the blanket sizzles with the heat, but it protects the women from the flames.

It takes the guards a full long minute to respond after women from every cell on the block cry out for their help. When the guards get to the cell, the women are pulled off the floor and escorted to a holding cell at the end of the block. Two guards with fire extinguishers contain the blaze, but the cell is a lost cause.

Sunny and her cellmates sit locked in the holding cell, choking on the remnants of smoke. Preacher kneels in the corner as she thanks Jesus for her life. Jasmine stands transfixed, looking out at the smoke-filled catwalk. The prisoners from other cells scream obscenities at the guards and yell for doctors and lawyers.

Sunny sits with Alice, both struck dumb with shock. When the shock ends, a single tear escapes Sunny's right eye. "We could've died. Right there. In a concrete prison cell. I don't get it. Why? What's the point?"

Alice looks thoughtfully at Sunny. She reaches into her pocket and retrieves the only non-living thing that survived the fire. Without looking at the deck, Alice cuts the cards and holds the chosen card for Sunny to see. "It's just the ace of spades."

CHAPTER 30

THE Maricopa County Sheriff's Compound includes the jail and a tacky adjoining administrative building where bond is posted and into which prisoners are released. On Saturday afternoon, David is waiting in the lobby for Sal.

David waited an extra day for Saturday to make sure that no one could call the Recorder of Deeds from the jail. He used the classified ads to find a residential property with more than enough equity to cover Sal's bond. Using one of his old blank baptismal certificates, he convinced the Department of Motor Vehicles to issue him a license under the name of the property owner. He went to the Recorder of Deeds and got a copy of the warranty deed and documents to show clear title. Now David presents the duty officer in charge of bonds with his driver's license, the bond application, and the property documents that he signed over to secure Sal's bond.

David waits for Sal to come through the heavy metal door that separates the lobby area from the jail.

Sal strides toward David with his arms open and his eyes focused past him on the exit. After a long, uncharacteristic hug, Sal points his thumb at the exit.

As they head out, Sal asks. "Where's your mother?"

David frowns and looks back at the building. "She's still in there."

Sal pulls angrily away from David. They pass through the door to a drizzly, cloud-laden sky. Sal turns and clutches David's arm. "You should have gotten her out and left me."

David looks up at the rain and says to the sky. "No. You don't understand. They haven't set a bond for her. They haven't charged her with anything yet."

Sal shakes his head in disbelief. "We need to get her a lawyer."

* * *

"Let her go."

Arizona Assistant State Attorney Chris Miller sits at one end of a cheap conference room table festooned with mismatched chairs. Miller is young, maybe two years out of law school, where he graduated at the top of his class. He commutes to work in a Honda and plays *Dungeons and Dragons*. He's also in charge of the local investigations into Sunny and Sal.

Across from Miller sits Lieutenant Osborne. Osborne's pale face is red with anger across his cheeks and forehead. He can't believe that Miller, whom Osborne swears still has teenage acne, is going to pull the plug on his bust. He leans forward just a couple of inches from Miller's face. "Fuck you. I mean, respectfully, fuck you!"

"What do you expect me to charge her with? Having too many names? You've done your diligence. Not one bad check. Not one complaint. No record on any of her names."

Osbourne shakes with fury. "She's some kind of fuckin' con artist."

Miller sits back and puts space between himself and Osbourne. "Fine. What's her con? Tell me."

"I don't know yet, but we'll figure it out."

"And how did you get the incriminating identifications? Did you have a search warrant?

Osbourne's eyes narrow into a sinister "don't fuck with me" stare. "Exigent circumstances. We thought she had a weapon."

Miller shakes his head. "It's weak. We have no crime. We have no probable cause. Her husband kicked the shit out of a guy who was abusing his daughter. As far as I'm concerned, the victim had it coming."

"He had a gun. Assault with a deadly weapon."

"Mm-hmm. Did you find a gun? Was there evidence of a gun discharge?"

"No, but that doesn't mean—"

"I'd probably cut him a sweet deal before he even saw a judge. But you had to drag his wife into it. Do you even know what their real names are?"

"Nothing came up on either of their fingerprints."

"Cut her loose."

"No."

"All right, let me drop the other shoe right on your ass. The wife almost died last night. In the jail managed by our esteemed sheriff."

Detective Osborne's mouth drops open, and his slate-gray eyes stare intently between long, white eyelashes at Miller.

"There was a fire in her cell. Apparently, it was started by her cellmates over some argument. She saved their lives. I don't give a flying fuck what you think she did. At best she might become a local hero and martyr. At worst she sues the State, Maricopa County, and every damn one of you for negligence. *Cut her loose!*"

They sit staring at each other for a very long and silent minute.

Osbourne drums his fingers on the flimsy table. "She's planning something. I know it."

"So, keep an eye on her. Watch her like she's in the Zapruder film. I don't care. Just open the cell and let her go. Do it now."

"Fine. I just hope that this doesn't splash shit on both of us. And by that, I mean on me."

CHAPTER 31

DAVID and Sal go through their apartment with the care of a shopping spree winner clearing the grocery store shelves. David is tearing apart his wallboard and putting all the identifications into a burn bag. Sal is shoving their belongings into random boxes acquired from several grocery and liquor stores.

Sal puts his sweaty face into the sink and drinks large gulps of water from the sink faucet. "I am *not* going back there."

David walks over and puts an assuring hand on Sal's shoulder. "We need to get out of here before Monday. Who knows how long it will take them to figure out that the security for your bond is a forgery?"

Sal pulls his wet face out of the sink and shakes like a dog in from the rain. "I know. Keep tossing and packing."

They put the boxes with all their and Sunny's possessions into a trailer attached to the back of their car. David wants to leave the apartment strewn with trash, but Sal insists on working long into the night to keep the apartment in the same shape that it was when they moved in. "There's no reason to make more enemies than we already have. We're breaking our lease. We don't have to fuck the place up before we go."

At seven the next morning, the phone rings. Sal and David have been asleep for maybe two hours. David trudges, half asleep, to the phone. "Hello?"

Sunny coos into the phone. "Where are you?"

"Where are you?"

"I'm in the lobby of the administration building waiting for you."

David gets as close to Sal as the cord will allow and waves his arms to get his attention. "What happened? How did you get out? Never mind. We're on our way."

David and Sal are dressed and on their way in ten minutes. Twenty minutes later, they arrive at the Maricopa County Jail Compound. Sunny is waiting for them in the lobby.

Sal rushes over to her and takes her hands in his. "What happened? How did you get out?"

Sunny hugs Sal and David quickly and motions to the exit door. "I don't know. I don't care. Let's just get out of here."

David drives them all to the Big Boy near their apartment, where they agree to have breakfast and talk about plans.

Sal sees it first. "We're being followed."

On impulse, Sunny turns to look behind her. "Are you sure?"

Sal checks again in his side view mirror. "Blue Crown Vic. Been tailing us since we got off of the freeway."

David confirms it in his rearview. "If it's the cops, there's nothing we can do. Let's just have breakfast and see where things go."

They pull into the Big Boy parking lot. The Crown Vic keeps driving. Sunny calls Ava and asks her to meet them for breakfast.

Sunny holds her menu but stares out the window. "Maybe it was our imagination."

Sal shakes his head. His eyes are set in a worried stare. "Crackers to Krugerrands it's not."

They sit conspiratorially at the booth. Everyone shares their version of events. Most of the focus is on Sunny and her story of the fortune teller, the fire, and how she saved her cellmates.

David soon takes the conversation to the matters at hand. "We should be out of here by tomorrow. I vote we head west. California."

Sunny laughs. "Swimmin' pools. Movie stars. It worked for the Beverly Hillbillies."

Sal doesn't laugh. "What do we do when we get there?"

Sunny looks at David "How much money do we have left?"

David checks the cash and the remaining traveler's checks. "Maybe ten grand."

Sunny starts to look for breakfast on the menu. "More than we've had before. Let's play it by ear. We'll head out there, get a place or places, and take a vacation before we make our next move."

Ava walks in and sits next to David.

Sunny casts a worried look her way. "Hey, you all right?"

"Yeah, I'm fine. Chris has been, well, cautious since Sal scared the crap out of him."

They all order breakfast except for David, who orders two Big Boy burgers.

Sal looks at him with a wicked sneer. "Burgers? For breakfast? Your stomach must be cast iron or something."

"Who knows when I'll be able to get more Big Boys? Gotta get them while I can."

Sunny turns to Ava. "We're going to California. Probably Los Angeles. We'll keep in touch, but we can't let you know where we'll be."

Ava squeezes David's hand. It isn't an affectionate squeeze. It's fear. "I understand. Is there anything I can do?"

Sunny leans over to Sal. They whisper back and forth. Then she turns to David. "Give Ava three thousand dollars."

David immediately gives Ava the money.

Sunny and David exchange a private look with tears filling their eyes. Sunny blots with a napkin. "We can always make more money, but you need to have something of your own to hold onto. We don't know what your future will be like with Chris, but until we get back, we want to make sure that you aren't out on the street while we're gone."

Now tears well up in Ava's eyes. "I don't know what to say."

"Don't say anything. Just take care of yourself and little David."

"I will. I promise."

David pays the check and leaves a generous tip. Ava drives back to her apartment in her Honda. David, Sal, and Sunny get into their car with the trailer and stop for gas and a road map of the western states. Sal takes the wheel, and they turn and head toward the California state line. Less than five minutes later, Sal slams his hand on the dash. It makes Sunny gasp. "It's back. The blue Crown Vic."

Sunny turns completely in her seat. "What do we do?"

David doesn't even bother to look. "Keep driving. Stay to the speed limit. They haven't stopped us yet for a reason."

Detective Osborne is on the radio in the Grand Vic. "Get me ASA Miller."

After several minutes, a voice comes back.

"Miller here."

Osbourne presses the call button to respond. "I did what you suggested. We staked out the wife. Her husband and another guy picked her up at the jail. I think they spotted me right before they pulled into a restaurant. I went around the block and the car was still in the lot. Can't miss it; it's pulling a trailer. I'm sure they're planning to jump bond. They're heading toward the California State line."

"Can you give them a police escort?"

"What? The husband is jumping bond!"

"So? The judge will issue a warrant for his arrest, but no one will extradite him. Meanwhile, whatever they're planning, let it be California's problem. And with any luck, they'll be locked up in California and won't even think about filing a lawsuit here. Give them a police escort. Make sure they pass the California State line."

Osborne radios for two marked cars to accompany him. Without lights or sirens, the three cars stay immediately behind the trailer. Occasionally, they stop traffic at intersections to allow Sal to drive through without stopping.

Sal chuckles to himself. "You ever see those old westerns? We're being ridden out of town on a rail." He grimaces. "My back is killing me, but I don't want to stop."

The pursuit takes them to the California State line. As soon as the car and trailer cross, the police escort peels off like an air force maneuver and heads back into Arizona.

David is already working on his next plan.

PART IV: HOLLYWOOD, CALIFORNIA

CHAPTER 32

DAVID loves burgers like a child loves the playground. He now finds himself at a new favorite burger joint.

Hamburger Hamlet is on Sunset Boulevard in Hollywood and the burgers are thick, juicy, and irresistible to David. It's part of a chain of restaurants popular among Hollywood celebrities and locals alike. It was founded in 1950 by actor Harry Lewis and his wife Marilyn, who wanted to create a place where actors could hang out and enjoy gourmet burgers with exotic toppings. Actors come there to this day from wannabes to A-list celebrities. The first Hamburger Hamlet charged thirty-five cents for a burger; now they're about a five-spot apiece. But to David, no price is too large for a good burger.

David frequents the place three times a week while trying to put together the right plan. It's not easy to get a table, but he's a regular and a good tipper and will occasionally give the hostess a five-dollar handshake, so he usually gets to cut the line—just not before the celebrities or tycoons.

He and Sunny run games and make decent money, just not buy a Mercedes and move to Beverly Hills money. David thinks of literally hundreds of scams, but he has standards. He tries not to repeat the same game too many times. The risk/return on the game must be adequate. It can't hurt individuals. It should be original and clever. He tries to think around the corner because he knows that the fortune fountain won't last forever. And if he's honest with himself,

Los Angeles with its luxury cars, star-studded parties, competitive—make that cutthroat—culture, has made him a bit greedy.

* * *

When they got to California it was unanimous that they were going to settle in or near Los Angeles. Hollywood was the place where anything was possible. As they cruised down Sunset Boulevard for the first time, they saw a sprawling mansion. On what looked like a fencepost in the vast front lawn hung a simple sign: "For Sale by Owner."

Sunny's jaw nearly unhinged when she saw that. "Are you freaking kidding me? That's got to be a million-dollar home. For sale by owner? I love this town already."

The first thing they did was choose new names. David created new baptismal certificates, and they got driver's licenses under the names Sally and Vincent Marino for Sunny and Sal and Robert Marino for himself.

Sal still wants a normal life with Sunny. He wants to take his and Sunny's share of the money and go back to serving tables. Sunny and David want to push for a bigger score. The one thing that David can't provide is false social security numbers that would pass muster with Uncle Sammy.

However, like it or not, well-hidden or not, they remain fugitives. That is, until they can make enough money to buy their way out of their cumulative problems. Their desperate minds create the illusion that enough money will solve any problem. They… just… need… enough… money.

They stay at the Tropicana Motel in wild West Hollywood, a three-story, sun-bleached stucco resort dotted with palm trees and white terraces that runs the length of the building. They take the winding road down to see the classic Hollywood landmarks that they hear so much about.

It's there that David negotiates a solution to simultaneously make Sal happy and work out his next game.

As they marvel at the Walk of Fame in Hollywood, trying to find their favorite stars like every other lame tourist, they find themselves at the corner of Hollywood and Vine. The Capitol Records building looms large with its record turntable rooftop.

David shields his eyes from the fierce California sun as he looks up at the buildings. "Isn't this the famous spot where stars were discovered?"

Sunny's eyes follow David's gaze and fall on the iconic Hollywood corner street sign. "Of course, it is. Hollywood and Vine."

David can tell that she's thrilled to be in the Bermuda Triangle of stardom.

Sunny points across Hollywood Boulevard. "Lana Turner was discovered right across the street in that diner."

Not to be outdone, Sal follows up with, "And I think Marilyn Monroe was discovered right around here."

They're in front of the Equitable Building. Built in 1929, at the height of the Great Depression, it's an iconic landmark due to its location. It houses various businesses and professional offices.

David says, "Why don't you two have lunch across the street and see if you get discovered?" Then he realizes the double meaning of his remark. "I mean, discovered in a good way. Not 'caught' discovered. I'll be right back."

When Sunny and Sal go to lunch, David ducks into the Equitable Building, looks at the lobby directory, and finds the building manager's office.

The office hums with a seductive tension, and at its center sits an Amazonian blonde office manager. Her black, tailored power suit evokes complete confidence and yet, somehow, makes her approachable.

As David enters the office and lays eyes on her, he's filled with a mixture of trepidation and desire. "Do you have any vacancies?"

"That depends. What do you plan to do, and how much space do you need?" She only half smiles at David. It's a crescent of a smile at only the corners of her lips.

David doesn't smile back. He's all business. "I plan to produce soon-to-be-famous independent films. And all I need is a desk and a chair."

The manager takes him to an office that is literally the size of a medium walk-in closet. It hosts a desk, a small executive chair behind the desk, and two small chairs for visitors. She looks dismissively at David. "This is the smallest space we have available. I assume it's probably too small for your office."

David sizes the space up. The game is already forming in his mind. "No, this should work. What do you want for this… cozy space?"

"We're looking for one hundred fifty a month. One month in advance and one fifty security deposit."

"Come on. This place is so small there's barely enough room for breathable air. Tell you what. I'll give you seventy-five dollars for the next six months on a month-to-month lease. If it works out, I'll give you a hundred dollars a month with a hundred-dollar security deposit and a one-year lease."

The manager sits down in the executive chair and puts her elbows on the desk. "I'll go along with everything except the security deposit, which has to be paid up front."

David holds out his hand. "Deal. Give me the keys, and I'll give you the cash."

He follows the manager back to her office. After a quick signature, he has the keys to the office. He closes on the office before Sunny and Sal finish their entree.

David takes the booth opposite Sunny and Sal and holds up the keys. "I have a plan."

Both Sunny and Sal stop eating and lean toward David in unison.

"We have an office across the street. Sal, it's risky to get a job under your fake name. Even as a server, they'll run your social security number. But you want to do something on your own to make a living. I get that. I think we can make that happen."

Sal motions the server for another cup of coffee. "I like what I'm hearing."

David leans back prone in the booth. "According to the directory, there are over a hundred businesses in that building. I suggest that we purchase a cart, a coffee maker or two, some pastries, doughnuts, and maybe some dairy. The cost will be negligible, especially if we purchase the equipment used. Then you can make delivery runs through the building. For lunch, you can sell prepackaged sandwiches."

Sal's brow starts to furrow as he considers this. "Don't we need some sort of a license to do that?"

"Don't know, and frankly, don't care. We'll purchase from licensed bakeries and restaurants, wrap everything in plastic, and make coffee in the office. If we get shut down, it won't matter. You'll certainly have made more money than the cost of the rent and equipment."

Sunny presses the idea. "This may be just what you need." She puts her arm around Sal's shoulder and whispers conspiratorially, "You can make your own money aside from what we've done illegally. Isn't that what you want?"

Sal takes a long pause, weighing what could go wrong. "Well, yeah. That would be nice."

David finally sits up in the booth and snags a dinner roll. "Besides, I already have the office. Let's go check it out."

They pay the check and walk back across Hollywood Boulevard to the office.

Sal isn't impressed. "It's cramped. I've seen sardine cans with more room."

David walks around the small space. "How much room do you need? We'll take out the extra chairs, and you should have enough room to park the cart. We'll bring the food in every day. There's a kitchen where you can get water for coffee. Dude, it's what we can afford on a month-to-month basis. Make money, and we can get a larger office if you need it. But for now"—he sniffs the air—"it smells like opportunity."

The next day, they find a used catering cart at a restaurant supply store. They rent a commercial coffee maker. They find a bakery that agrees to sell wholesale pastries and doughnuts. Just forty-eight hours after David rented the office, Sal is in a paper hat and apron, pushing the cart through the Equitable Building halls selling food, coffee, milk, and canned soft drinks.

But David doesn't share with Sal his ulterior motives for the office. After Sal begins his first delivery run, David takes Sunny aside. "Look, Mom. You know how moody Sal can be, so I didn't want to tell him my other reason for the office. The lease is for movie productions. We're on the most famous corner in the most famous movie town in the world. I'm thinking we can make some calls and get profitable deals producing fictitious movies and TV shows all over the country."

Sunny frowns and crinkles her nose like someone farted. "What about Sal?"

David shrugs. "Give him a choice. I'm betting that he'd rather stay here and work on his new business."

She doesn't give him a choice. He stays.

Through his clandestine experiences, David has developed the belief that the bigger the bureaucracy, the bigger the opportunity. He has developed a sixth sense for bureaucratic weaknesses and arguably, the biggest bureaucracy in the country is Ma Bell.

Ma Bell is better known simply as "the phone company." Owned by AT&T before its breakup, it runs the Bell system and has a virtual monopoly on long distance calls everywhere in the United States. And those calls are expensive. Many a business has been forced into involuntary bankruptcy simply because they couldn't pay their phone bill.

If you have a business, you need a phone—and a listing in the phone book. If you have a phone number and a listing in the phone book, you have a business, even if your office consists simply of a desk and a chair. Legitimacy is assumed. Even if you don't have the phone number listed in the phone book, a short time after your phone number is approved, it can be invoked simply by calling the ubiquitous 411 or, as it's more commonly referred to, Information.

David reasons that the phone company can't stop people from using duplicate names for their phone service. It would be way too complicated. If two names are the same, or too similar, the 411 operator will ask, "Which listing do you want?" and give you the different addresses. The challenge for David is to make the name and address similar enough to a big production company that a reasonable person would assume that it's the same business.

David has the address: Hollywood and Vine. The business's name? Warner Productions.

After the phone is installed and a message machine is attached to take calls, David and Sunny take lunch while Sal is making deliveries.

David looks at a small side salad like it contains a bug condiment. "Why would anyone give you a side salad when you order a burger platter? It's like a place holder before you get the real meal."

Sunny smiles as she pours French dressing on her own salad. "It's California."

David pushes the salad to the side. "You ever been to Las Vegas?"

Sunny lights up. "I've always wanted to."

David leans forward and raises his eyebrows. "Let's pick a hotel and talk movie deal to one of the hotels there."

"We don't know anything about movie making. Do you think we can pull it off?"

The server sets down the entrees and takes the salad dishes. "From what I hear, for every good or great movie made here, there are a hundred that barely make it onto the silver screen. I'm guessing that we can run a bluff, get money for a budget shortfall, and complain that it couldn't be made for whatever reason. We walk away with some cash and have some fun."

Sunny digs into her chicken breast. "David, if anyone can pull this off, it's you."

David chows down on his burger. "No, Mom, if anyone can pull this off, it's us."

CHAPTER 33

THE next day, Sunny studies a map of the United States. "Why Las Vegas? We can do this anywhere."

"Well, it's not far from Los Angeles." David points to the distance on the map. "It's supposed to be a blast, and as a famous bank robber once said, 'It's where the money is.'"

The first thing David needs is a movie script or treatment. Fortunately, finding a movie treatment on Hollywood Boulevard is easier than finding water in a monsoon. He lets it drop at some local bars and eateries that he's looking for a movie to produce. In less than a week, wannabe screenwriters, filmmakers, and various movie and television wheeler-dealers are attracted to David like he has his own gravity.

David selects a movie treatment featuring a guitarist who finds a legendary set of precious silver strings that unlock the world of music. The hero travels to Las Vegas (David's touch) where he goes from obscurity to stardom before his fortunes turn and he learns humility before the climactic ending where he understands what is truly important in life. It's perfect to showcase Las Vegas, the entertainment capital of the world.

David calls the Dunes Hotel, the Flamingo Hotel, and the Riviera Hotel. With each hotel, he has a variation on the same conversation.

"Can I speak to your department of Public Relations?"

"Of course, sir."

"This is Jack Greene from Warner Productions." David feels like a nice Jewish name makes sense. "We're considering using your hotel for a movie location."

"We would love to discuss the project with you. How will our property be featured?"

"Very prominently. If selected, it will be the backdrop for every indoor scene."

Every hotel wants to discuss it further. But the Riviera Hotel bites hard.

"We're very interested in this project. If you want to come out to discuss it, we'll completely comp your trip. Transportation, food, a suite, and a line of credit if you're a gambler."

Jackpot. Viva Las Vegas.

Sunny and David choose to drive to Las Vegas for the meeting. They want to make sure that they have their own transportation in case they need to make a hasty getaway.

They've prepped for the meeting like studying for college finals in a required class. They made copies of and studied the treatment. They poured through books on making movies—who knew how many books on moviemaking there would be in the Hollywood library?—and they quizzed each other on movie jargon. Sunny purchased a camera because, well, a producer of motion pictures should take pictures.

But the truth is, they didn't have to bother. When the management of the Riviera decided to do the project, David and Sunny only had to ride the tidal wave of the hotel's desire to be part of the movie. And the answer to every difficult question is, "It's up to the director."

Sunny and David drive up Interstate 15 to Las Vegas the night before their scheduled meeting.

As they approach, Sunny's eyes widen like full moons. There is absolutely nothing like your first time seeing Las Vegas lit up at night. As they approach and drive through the strip, they're as mesmerized by the spectacle as children seeing fireworks for the first time.

They pull up to the Riviera lobby entrance. The bellman meets them and takes their bags. From the moment they enter the hotel, they're transfixed. The casino is everywhere. The cacophony of noise and pervasive cigarette smoke are sensory overload. They make their way to the front desk and, when they give their fake names, backed with California licenses secured with another of David's baptismal certificates, there is a sudden aura of reverence from everyone in their presence.

After she checks them in, the eager desk clerk, a pretty girl in her twenties with a broad smile, practically trips over herself as she comes around the desk to shake hands and give them keys to their suite. "Please, let me show you to your room and make sure that you're comfortable."

Sunny and David might as well be A-list celebrities as they follow the desk clerk to the elevator. Heads turn, and whispers of excitement fill the air even beyond the electric atmosphere of the hotel and casino. The bellhop with their bags and the night manager accompany them like an entourage. The night manager invites them to have breakfast at the World's Fare Buffet in the morning and tells them that they're special guests at the long-running show *Splash* with premiere seating near the hotel manager with, of course, all meals and refreshments comped by the hotel.

David and Sunny share a private smile when they hear that the buffet is named World's Fare. Sunny whispers, "It must be fate."

The next day, Sunny and David enjoy a late breakfast at the World's Fare Buffet. Their names have been left at the cashier as VIPs. David even notices the little "VIP" printed next to their names. It's the biggest buffet that either of them has ever seen.

The room is divided into islands of different culinary indulgences. Every type of breakfast or lunch food is represented. Sunny has been to a smorgasbord before, but this is easily five times that modest effort. She and David are in a state of gastronomic euphoria.

David looks up from his second dessert plate. "I told you this would be a blast."

Sunny seems uneasy. "Yeah, but it's too much. You know? I keep waiting for the bomb to go off."

Just then, a man and a woman approach the table. It's as if the server specifically notified them when David and Sunny finished breakfast. The woman is maybe twenty-five, petite and very formal. Her black hair is in a severe style, and she wears oversized tortoise shell glasses that give her face the look of a librarian who could turn into a sexpot if she let her hair down.

The man is the Riviera manager who is biting on the Hollywood hook like a bonefish. He's a tall, fit, and very clean-cut gentleman. No facial hair. He's approaching fifty but looks maybe twenty years younger without a wrinkle on his face. "You must be Jack and Doris Greene from Warner." He shakes their hands like they're on a used car lot, and he has a sales quota to meet. "I'm Benjamin Jensen. We spoke on the phone."

Benjamin and his assistant pull up a seat next to David and Sunny. Girl, boy, girl, boy.

Benjamin gently shakes Sunny's hand. "So, how was your brunch?"

David smiles broadly. "To paraphrase Groucho Marx, it was the most fun we've had without laughing." Everyone laughs out loud.

Benjamin signals for a server. "So, tell us about the movie."

Sunny is prepared. She distributes copies of the treatment from her bag with notes conspicuously made in the margins. "I think this movie is made for Las Vegas—as you can see by our notes. It has everything that this town is known for. A roller coaster of success and failure and redemption. Music. Romance—"

The assistant moves her index finger forward from her pursed lips to interrupt. "What about gambling? How will it be used to motivate our guests to gamble?"

Benjamin gives her a stern look. He silences his assistant with a glance; Benjamin's glances command quite a bit of deference.

Sunny nimbly continues. "It's okay, Benjamin, I'm glad to answer that. As I understand it, the whole point of the buffets"—she sweeps her hand around the room—"the entertainment—in fact, all the trappings of every hotel on the strip—are to get people into the endless casinos to try their luck. If this movie is successful, millions of people will see the Riviera Hotel—if we agree to use the Riviera—as the place where dreams can come true. Many will want to stay here to see if that applies to their dreams also."

Benjamin and his assistant say nothing. Their nods affirm approval. The assistant turns to David. "Speaking of gambling, have you or Doris played at the tables yet?"

David gives his best angelic expression. "No, we just did a few slots."

"You each have a credit line of ten thousand dollars. Just give your names to any cashier, and they'll let you sign for chips."

The assistant reaches into her briefcase and removes a piece of paper the size of an unfolded cocktail napkin. David looks at the paper. It's a credit application. Name, address, occupation, bank name, bank address, average balance.

She hands it to David. "In case you want to increase your credit line, simply fill this out and give it to any cashier."

At HPC Finance, David saw credit applications for twenty-five-hundred-dollar personal loans that were a landscape of questions seeking personal references, credit references, and employment going back to high school. This is nothing.

Benjamin stands. His assistant follows.

The server comes to the table, and Benjamin dismisses her. "What do you need from us at this point?"

Sunny stands. "We just need to walk around, take some pictures, get the feel of the place."

Benjamin starts to leave and then turns back toward the table. "Will the filming affect the business operation?"

"It's up to the director. But we'll make sure that it's a positive experience." Sunny smiles sheepishly yet also with a hint of playfulness. Very Marilyn Monroe.

Benjamin waves to the cashier and gives her a sign to make sure there is no charge. "We hope you'll choose the Riviera for this project. Let me know if there's anything I can do to answer any questions or help with any roadblocks you may encounter. Also, you're invited as my guests to the Riviera show *Splash*. It's very good. The first show is at seven. Simply let the maître d' know who you are, and they'll set you up at my table. Great seats. I'm afraid that I can't make it, but you two enjoy yourselves."

The assistant smiles seductively at David as she gets ready to leave. "If there's anything at all that I can do to help, let me know." She hands him a Riviera business card. "This is my direct line. Call anytime with any questions or requests."

Sunny and David return to their suite. As the adrenaline rush subsides, they collapse on the furniture.

"Mom, you were absolutely stellar!"

Sunny visibly exhales. "I think we're in. We can do no wrong at this point. It just feels too easy. You know?"

David takes a Coke from the minibar. "Does your gut tell you to pull out?"

"No, not yet. It's just overwhelming. You know?"

"I'm thinking we buy some bathing suits and hit the pool to give us perspective."

After the pool, they go back to the suite, change out of their swimsuits, and head down to the casino. They give their names to the cashier and, just as the assistant promised, the cashier asks how much they want in chips.

Sunny turns to David. "What do you think?

David raises his shoulders in indifference. "We have ten grand apiece. I suggest we start with seventy-five hundred."

"I agree. As some advice column says, we want to leave something behind for Miss Manners."

David laughs. "Yeah. That column was Miss Manners."

They take the chips, gamble, and lose about five hundred dollars apiece. They cash the rest of the chips out and put fourteen grand cash into their room safe. Feeling great, they get dressed for the evening, David in a red blazer, black dress shirt with no tie, and black dress pants. Sunny wears a black silk blouse with a plunging neckline tucked into jeans, bedazzled with dice showing seven and cards showing blackjack. They take some pictures, have dinner at the steakhouse, and take the long walk through the casino to the Versailles Theater, excited for the show.

* * *

Splash is a combination of swimmers, divers, and dancers all perfectly choreographed. It's a spectacle with advanced lighting, many costume changes, and phenomenal stage design. The theater is massive, and Sunny and David are seated perfectly to view the anticipated show at a table for six.

After they're served drinks, Sunny has a seven and seven. David has a virgin pina colada. He goes back through the theater to find the men's room in the lobby.

That's when Lady Luck fucks them hard.

Sunny hears a man's voice. The timber and tone are familiar, if not the man behind it.

"Sunny! Son of a bitch! The Blonde Bombshell! Is that really you?"

Sunny's knuckles go white as she grasps the table, turning her head to see who is calling her real name.

A balding, cigar-chomping, middle-aged man with a tight-fitting black nylon dress shirt, no less than four front buttons open, and a face with a nose that looks like it has seen more breaks than a heavyweight boxer, sits in the seat that David vacated. He puts a meaty arm around Sunny's shoulders as he pulls his face next to hers. Cigar smoke oozes from his nose and mouth and mingles with his bourbon breath.

His conversation is rapid fire staccato. "It's me. Sammy D from the Dolphin. I haven't seen you in a coon's age. Where've you been keeping yourself? No, wait. Are you here to show that Mormon fuck Benjamin how to run a club the right way?"

Sunny is struck dumb. Now she recognizes him—and with the recognition comes dread. She and David are originally from the Chicago area where Sunny managed a nightclub in the sixties in the northern suburbs called the Dolphin Lounge. She went from being a cocktail waitress to being the main draw for the club. She knew how to bring the party. Celebrities like Jack Brickhouse, Frank Sinatra, and Dan Blocker rubbed elbows with locals and... quite a few of the Chicago outfit.

Sammy D is among the latter. And Sunny knows. She knows that she can't pretend to be anyone else. She knows that this is a moment that could spell the literal end for her—and, no, no. David. *Keep it together. Figure it out. Maybe he'll walk away with no one the wiser.* "Sammy D. Of course, I remember you. What brings you to Vegas?"

"Las Vegas. Saying just Vegas is for tourists."

Sunny picks up her drink with a barely trembling hand. "Las Vegas."

"Let's just say that we have a vested interest in this place." Sammy D gives a sly wink. "Wait till you see the show. What is it the kids say? It'll blow your mind."

He crushes out his stogie in the ash tray in front of Sunny. The foul smoke seems to purposely funnel toward her. He repeats, "What brings you to Las Vegas?"

"I'm on vacation with my son."

"Little Davey's here? I remember him. You'd bring him around during the day sometimes. A husky boy, as I recall. So, you ever get married?"

"Yeah. I—"

The server steps in with another seven and seven and a second virgin pina colada. "I'm sorry, Miss Greene, there is a two-drink minimum. Still no charge, but we must bring the second drink as we can't serve during the entertainment. Enjoy the show."

Okay, Sammy D doesn't exactly pay annual dues to Mensa. But he has enough sense to read these tea leaves, and a storm starts brewing behind his lizard-like brown eyes. He turns menacingly toward Sunny.

"Miss Greene. Miss Doris Greene? I heard about VIP Jack and Doris Greene from Hollywood. You're running some sort of scam, aren't you?" Sammy D doesn't wait for an answer. He doesn't expect one. His features become as cold as a Chicago tombstone. Then the storm bursts within him. "You dumb fuckin' bitch! Sunny, I love you, but you are one dumb fuckin' broad! I'd drink a gallon of your piss just to see where it came from, but"—he picks up Sunny's second drink and downs it—"what am I going to do with you? These guys will put both you and your son in a hole in the desert and no... one... will... know. And I might be the one to fuckin' do it!"

The blood drains from Sunny's face. She begins shaking like the temperature has dropped forty degrees in an instant. She's trapped in the moment like a ship in a bottle. She gives Sammy D a pleading look. "Please." Tears on a housefire.

Sammy D leans back in David's chair. He runs his intense eyes over Sunny like a predator taking its time with prey that knows it's doomed. Or maybe like a scientist observing an intriguing specimen. It's a full minute before he speaks.

"For old times' sake, I'm going to forget I ran into you tonight. You and your son, get the fuck out. Now. Do not pass go, or the only thing you're going to collect is a bullet to the brain. Capisce?"

"Capisce." Sunny jumps out of her seat. "Thank you, Sammy. We're out of here now."

Sunny takes the stairs two at a time out of the theater and finds David in the lobby just leaving the men's room. She grabs him by the arm. "Come on! We go. Now!"

David is confused, but he trusts his mother—especially when she uses that urgent tone of voice. They briskly walk but don't run to the suite, grab the cash from the safe, slam everything into their suitcases, and force them locked so that they look pregnant once they're closed. They drag everything straight to the valet and order the car. No check out. Less than twenty-four hours after they arrived as honored guests at the Riviera, they're on the way down Interstate 15 back to Los Angeles.

Sunny tells David about Sammy D as they drive through the dark desert night. The car's gas tank is full, but they're personally running on fumes. They don't stop until they reach Los Angeles.

When Sunny sees Sal, she knows she must tell him about the danger, but it's the last thing she wants to do.

Sal wakes up to Sunny opening the front door. "I didn't expect you this early. How did it go?"

Sunny drops her bag in the living room. "Good. And bad." She tells Sal about how they were treated like royalty. How they cleared fourteen grand. And then, she tells him about Sammy D.

Sal seethes. "You fucked with the mob?"

"Not on purpose. We thought we were dealing with a large, legitimate business."

Sal's olive face goes red with fury. "It's your son. It's David. It's always David. That's it! We're done with this shit."

Sunny says nothing. She knows that arguing is futile when Sal is this angry. Besides, she knows that the worst is yet to come for Sal. "I think we have to give up the office."

"No! I've worked my ass off on that business."

"It's the only connection to Las Vegas. Can you say that you'll feel safe there now?"

Sal looks down at the carpet and snarls. "I'm beginning to hate your son."

CHAPTER 34

SO now, David is sitting in a booth at Hamburger Hamlet, steeped in burger meditation and playing out in his head what new game to run. After Las Vegas, tensions with Sal seem to be even tighter than usual. For Sunny, although shaken by her close call with Sammy D, there are fourteen thousand reasons for her to feel that Las Vegas was successful. And in her heart, she knows the Las Vegas adventure was exactly what David said it would be: a real blast.

David is lost in thought when he realizes he hasn't ordered yet. He looks around, thinking, *Service is taking longer than a Zeppelin song.* But as he looks for his server, he sees someone he instantly recognizes. His eyes widen as if he's unwrapping a long-awaited present, and multiple thoughts flood his head.

That's Freddy Prinze! I love Chico and the Man. *He's got to be so cool. We're about the same age. I've got to meet him.* David searches vainly through his pockets for a pen and something to autograph.

Just then the server comes to his table. "I'm sorry it took me so long to get here. I'm kind of new, and it's busier than usual."

David stops padding his pockets for a pen. "That's okay. Do you have a piece of paper and a pen I can borrow?"

The server may not be the most seasoned, but she looks over at Freddy Prinze and knows what David has in mind. She leans conspiratorially toward David. "Sir, please don't do what you're considering. You plan to go to Freddie Prinze's table while he's enjoying lunch and ask him for an autograph. Right?"

David frowns with indignation. "Yeah, why?"

"If you appreciate him, and he seems to be a great guy, you'll let him enjoy his meal in peace. It's bad form to bother celebrities. Leave that to tourists who don't know better."

David may be a con man, but he tries not to be a putz. He recognizes that she's probably right and, with one last glance toward Freddy Prinze's table, he turns to his menu to order. As he places his order, he suddenly takes a second look at the server.

She's tall with an athletic yet feminine body draped in a form-fitting uniform that accentuates her curves. She reminds David of a huntress. Her flowing blond hair cascades over her shoulders and seems to glow under the fluorescent light. Every motion is deliberate. Every step is purposeful, as if she were a predator stalking prey in a jungle of tables. She half smiles at David, revealing a crescent of a smile at only the corners of her lips.

"I know you!" David says.

She rolls her eyes and shakes her head. "I don't think so."

"You were the building manager at the Equitable Building."

Her half smile expands to just short of a full grin. "That's right... you're the... producer of some kind. You rented the smallest office I've ever seen, and then you hired someone to serve coffee and doughnuts." She laughs out loud at the memory. "Very clever. All the other tenants enjoyed the service. Especially the hunk you hired to push the cart."

David doesn't feel the need to tell her that the hunk is his stepfather.

"Your name's... Crystal, right?"

"Close. It's Christian. You can call me Chris."

David smiles smugly. "Isn't Christian a boy's name?"

Chris narrows her eyes. She enjoys this game. "Usually, but not this time."

David sits back in his chair and looks away from her. "Hmm. I was going to ask you out, but well, you have a boy's name. So, I don't know."

Chris laughs out loud. "What makes you think I would even want to date you?"

David tilts his head innocently. "Whoa. Slow down, Christian. Who said anything about a date? You're kind of pushy for someone I hardly know who has a boy's name."

Chris hits David playfully on the shoulder. "You're kind of funny. I like that." She takes out a blank check from her pad and writes her phone number on the back. "I get off at four. Now, I have to go back to this job all of you pay me for."

David leaves a generous tip, tears a piece of the blank check, and writes down his California name (Robert). He calls her that evening.

Later that night, David meets Chris for drinks at the Starwood Nightclub in West Hollywood. It's Chris's suggestion and from the time David enters, he feels as conspicuous as a spotlight in a sea of darkness. The Starwood is one of the first Hollywood nightclubs to feature punk rock, including the Germs, X, and the Go-Gos. The crowd is a seething mass of denim and leather rebellion punctuated with more safety pins than a dry cleaner and more ink than the local taggers use on the graffiti walls outside.

David, with less facial hair than a baby's bottom, wears a blazer, khakis, and a mock turtleneck. His hair is a clean-cut pompadour. His look makes Jimmy Dean look like David Bowie. The crowd is a sea of ripped clothing, studded leather jackets, spikey fluorescent hair, and so many piercings that David wishes he brought a metal detector.

And there at her own table, talking to a cocktail waitress who looks like a hardware store display, sits Chris looking like, well, like a rock goddess. Tight leather jacket and pants, band tee-shirt, and hair tipped with neon pink and green. She's sexy as hell.

David approaches the table. "You could've warned me."

Chris smirks. "That I'm not a member of the Young Republican Club?"

"That we were meeting at the circus." He regrets the words as soon as they leave his mouth.

Chris glares at him. "Hey, if you don't like the place, don't let the door hit you on the dick on your way out."

"I think the expression is 'don't let the door hit you in the ass.'"

"Yeah, but with your attitude, I think you're all dick."

David puts up his hands in surrender. "Okay. Please. Let me start over." He stares admiringly at her outfit. "It's amazing. I came that close"—he holds his hands about six inches apart—"to wearing that same outfit tonight."

Chris laughs. "Oh, you did, did you?"

"No, not really, but I might have worn my rhinestone jumpsuit."

"Cool. Ziggy Stardust?"

"Actually, more like Elvis Presley."

"Interesting. I like Elvis Presley. I used to be a big fan."

The cocktail waitress comes to the table, and David orders a Perrier water with a twist of lime. Chris notices as she downs her own shot of cheap tequila.

"You aren't drinking?"

"No. I don't drink."

"Rehab?"

David laughs. "Yeah, I'm twenty-one years sober."

The glass of Perrier comes. David picks it up and squeezes the lime into the water, then drops in the peel. He takes the straw out of the glass, drops it on the table, and drinks over the rim. "I'm told that real men don't drink through straws."

"Remind me never to buy you a milkshake." They both laugh. David likes her. "So why did you leave Equitable?"

"The usual. Rich fucks who think that their rent also entitles them to a lease on my tits. So now I'm a waitress at the Hamlet, and I work part time in Admissions at Cedars of Lebanon Hospital. It pays the bills, but not much more."

David thinks back to Florida and the hospital admissions bitch who got him to write the five-thousand-dollar check that started him down this purgatory. Patterns fall into place like colored glass in a kaleidoscope. "Yeah, tell me about what you do at the hospital."

Chris takes a drink while focused on the band. "I check in patients, get their histories, find out what their symptoms are for the doctors, and I find out who carries their medical insurance so we can make a claim."

David turns to face Chris. "And what if they don't have insurance?"

"We still have to treat them. Hippocratic oath and all that. But we discharge them as soon as we can. Sometimes I feel so sorry for people who don't have coverage."

David shakes his head. Total focus. "And what if they do have insurance?"

"Then we keep them as long as possible. We get a claim form from the insurer and process the payment. Why the interest?"

David turns away from Chris. "Just curious."

Three songs into the next set, Chris and David are making out. By the end of the set, David thinks he might enjoy punk rock.

Chris whispers in David's ear, "You know, nothing is going to happen tonight."

David whispers back. "Are you sure? I did have a lease at Equitable."

Chris quickly moves away from David and examines his face for signs that he's serious. She knows by his expression that his remark is completely tongue in his own cheek. She gives him another playful punch on the shoulder. "I ought to kick your ass for that remark." The set ends, and the crowd thins out. Chris looks into David's eyes. "So, what do you think?"

"They're not Elvis, but… yeah, I can get used to it. But it's too loud in here to have a decent conversation, and I want to get to know you better. You ever hear of a busman's holiday?"

Chris purses her lips and narrows her eyes. "No."

"It's when you take someone to enjoy the thing that they work at all day. You're a waitress, so let me take you to lunch where you can be waited on. Are you off tomorrow?"

"As a matter of fact, yes."

"Great. There's a restaurant on Sunset Boulevard that looks cool. Give me your address, and I'll pick you up at noon. Besides, I might have a proposition for you, one new rebel to my guru rebel."

Chris writes her address on the back of a wet cocktail napkin. David pays the tab, gets up, and starts to leave. Chris walks him to the door, where they share a soulful kiss.

David can barely pull away. He wipes his lips.

Chris looks hurt. "Are you wiping off my kiss?"

He laughs. "Naw. Just rubbing it in. I like you, and I want to get to know you better. But more than that, I think we're going to find an amazing opportunity with each other."

Chris gives David a half smile. "When you put it like that, how can I stay away?"

CHAPTER 35

THE next day, David is in a frenzy as he goes through his cluttered closet and finally finds the jacket he wore when he brought Sunny to the Hollywood Medical Center after her back injury. He goes through the pockets and finds what he's looking for: the claim insurance form that the Admissions bitch gave him to fill out if he ever discovered that his mother had insurance coverage.

David doesn't just review the form; he studies it like he expects a pop quiz later. As he reads it, the form morphs in his mind from a clinical administrative document into a treasure map. His excitement builds as he envisions how the system that turned him into a wanted fugitive can maybe, just maybe, be one of the most lucrative cons yet. He can't wait to talk to the rest of his team.

Sunny and Sal come over fifteen minutes after David's call. Sal is still sulking like a storm cloud. David motions Sunny and Sal to have a seat on the sofa. He lays it out as he stands in the middle of the room like a professor giving a lecture. "I've thought about a lot of insurance scams. Auto accident. Slip and fall in a grocery or department store. Property liability. You know what's wrong with each of them?"

Sal looks past David. He appears to not care about the answer. Sunny is on the edge of her seat waiting for the answer like a marathon runner within sight of the finish line. She raises her eyebrows expectantly.

David lets the pause rest for five full seconds. "Adjusters. In each case, the insurance company has a department that gets intimately involved when a claim is filed. That team argues the amount of the liability, the facts of how the liability occurred, and anything else to show that the insurance company shouldn't have to pay."

He looks to each of them for acknowledgment. Finding none, he goes on. "Insurance companies are basically gamblers. They bet on something not happening and give odds to the bettors. Bet you live to see seventy. How much? Well, say forty dollars a month. They even have handicappers called actuaries to handicap their bets." He pauses again for effect.

Sal gets off the couch and stares out of the window. Sunny doesn't move.

"But what happens if they lose their bet? Does the insurance company cheerfully pay what they agreed to like a gentleman or lady? No. They do everything possible to welch on their bet... except in one case."

Sunny's eyes open wide. She leans forward, her elbows on her knees. "What is that?"

"Medical coverage. Doctors and hospitals are so confident they'll get paid by the insurance companies they pay money up front. Doctors, medicine, and equipment are purchased by the hospital before they see a dime from insurance payments. To stay with the gambling metaphor, hospitals bet in advance that the insurance companies will pay off. If we'd had coverage, the Florida hospital would have taken Mom in and treated her without any concern about our ability to pay. Without any concern that the insurance company would cough up the money."

Sal turns from the window and stares shaking his head at Sunny. He turns to David and smiles without amusement. His eyes are sinister. "David, please make a point. Or don't. I really don't care. I am so through with this."

David slides the claim form from a counter like a blackjack dealer and passes it to Sunny, who reads it and gives it to Sal. "There are no guardrails on medical insurance. Look at the form. You choose to assign the benefits directly to the hospital. It asks whether there is any other insurance coverage, which indicates to me that they don't know unless you tell them."

Sal hands the form back to Sunny impatiently. "So, you assign the coverage to the hospital. How does that get you any money?"

David drops the hammer. "What if you have more than one insurance policy? What if the insurance companies have no clue how many claims you're filing? Maybe you assign one check to the hospital and keep the rest of the checks."

Sal and Sunny say nothing.

"How much is a typical hospital bill? I had to bounce a five-thousand-dollar check to get Mom into the Florida hospital. Let's use that. Five thousand dollars times five policies. Twenty-five thousand dollars. Pay the hospital, you still have twenty thousand dollars. And that's a conservative estimate. I've seen hospital bills over ten thousand dollars easily."

Sunny gets up from the couch and for a full thirty seconds paces the room holding the bridge of her nose. She picks up the claim form again and rereads it. "Won't the insurance companies know that you're getting multiple policies?"

"If they did, the form wouldn't need to ask the question. Besides, they're competitors. How would they know? They just want to sell policies."

Sal flops down on a chair. "The hospital would tell them."

David tells them about his date with Chris the night before. "I'm going to make her a business proposition later today. If she agrees, the hospital won't know how many claims are filed. We can get and make copies of the hospital bills for each insurer, sit back, and collect the checks. Each one for the medical bills minus the deductible."

Sunny sits back down on the couch. She motions for Sal to join her. "How many policies are you thinking about?"

"I counted about fifteen health insurance providers in the Los Angeles Yellow Pages. I suggest we start with five. Maybe Mutual of Omaha for one…"

Sal chuckles, finally warming to the idea. "I don't know why, but I've always hated that freak Euell Gibbons from… What was it called? Oh yeah, *Wild Kingdom*. Made me hate Mutual of Omaha for sponsoring it. Who can make a meal of tree bark anyway?"

Sunny makes a face like she hit a pothole at fifty miles per hour. "Wait a minute. Who is going to get sick? Who goes to the hospital?"

David's narrow eyes become slits as he makes eye contact with both Sunny and Sal. His voice is steady and confident, leaving no room for doubt. "I'll be the one to go into the hospital. We'll stage a mugging near the hospital where Chris works, and I'll go in through Emergency. We'll get an ambulance bill, an emergency room bill, and when I'm admitted, all the other charges that hospitals are so good at. I'll stay as long as I can."

Everyone is silent. "Any questions?"

Sunny turns to Sal. "It could work."

Sal says nothing, but he stops brooding. Sal is tough as leather and subscribes to the philosophy that snitches get stitches. But if he could see what was coming around the corner, he would have called the police and turned everyone in.

CHAPTER 36

DAVID picks up Chris and takes her to his other favorite burger joint in Los Angeles, away from Hollywood. They pull into the parking lot behind the building. Chris knows where she is and doesn't even want to leave the car. David exits the car and goes to the passenger side to open her door. Chris doesn't move. Her face looks like she swallowed a bug.

David pulls the door open. "Come on."

Chris shakes her head side to side. "You're kidding, right?"

"What's the matter? Don't you trust me?"

"I thought you were going to take me someplace with class."

David laughs and gives Chris a hand out of the car. "Class is overrated. Come on, it's iconic." Chris finally takes his hand and exits the car.

Circling the building, Chris sees the iconic Big Boy statue and rolls her eyes like a bored teenager. "Seriously? This is your busman's holiday?"

David leads her to the front door. "I guarantee that someone will serve you. Have you ever been here before?"

"I don't know. Maybe once when I was eight. I thought we would go to someplace more, well, upscale."

"Like you would expect with the rich Equitable tenants? I'd rather not be that try hard."

Chris doesn't respond to David as he holds the front door open for her. She just sort of drags herself through. David tells the hostess he needs a booth for two, and she brings them right in and drops the menus on the table. David motions for Chris to slide in first, then he slides into the same booth after her. He scoops up the menus and slides them out of Chris's reach. "Don't worry about the menus. I'll order for us."

Chris turns her nose up and sniffs. "Well, aren't we confident?"

David responds with a self-satisfied smirk. "Don't worry, what I order you will change your life."

David orders two Big Boy burger meals. He has Coke and Chris has Diet Coke. They each order ranch dressing for their salads.

Chris is dressed in a tight, short-sleeved red shirt that hugs her ample breasts. She wears a white scarf stylishly tied around her neck and a short, red-and-white striped skirt. She's sexy, but not provocative. It's a far cry from the punk club costume. She also wears dark aviator sunglasses that she leaves on even though they're inside. Very starlet incognito.

Chris's facial expression can only charitably be called defiant. "You're pretty sure of yourself for someone who's as exciting as a vanilla shake, aren't you?"

Now David sniffs. "Always. And you have no idea what I do for kicks."

The burgers come with fries and a salad. Chris isn't impressed. "It's a Big Mac."

"Yeah, like a Cadillac is just a Chevy. Try it."

Chris picks up the burger. It's bigger than a Big Mac. She takes a bite. She decides… that it changes her life. "I hate to admit it, but…" Another bite. "This is good."

"Right?"

Halfway through the meal, David gets down to business. "Everyone in this town is striving for something. What's your story?"

Chris doesn't answer right away. "I'm from Los Angeles. I don't have a story. I live in the moment." She puddles ketchup on her plate, snags a couple of fries, dips them, and pops them in her mouth. "Do you have a story?"

David isn't eating. He senses the pressure of convincing Chris to help him with his plans to scam the medical insurance companies. He plays to her self-avowed rebel nature. "I'm about making money off the grid. I'm about taking money from the establishment and using that money to fund the things that will make me happy."

Now Chris stops eating. "That's vague. Are you a bank robber? A dope dealer? No, you're too straight for dope."

David takes his first bite of burger. "Let's just say that we are each rebels in our own ways. You work in Admissions at Cedars of Lebanon, right?"

Chris's forehead furrows. "Yeah. Why?"

Now David knows that he's committed to making the proposition. He forces his hands not to fidget. His leg not to shake. "If you agree, someone will come into the hospital through Emergency. Later, several claim forms will be given to you for the same claim. Sign them all. Keep one for the hospital and give the rest to my representative. We'll do the rest."

Chris snags a couple more ketchup-puddled fries. "That's it?"

David calms down. She didn't tell him to go to hell. "Pretty much. I don't expect any inquiries, but if there are, just say that you aren't aware of any other policies than the insurer calling."

Chris thoughtfully sips her Diet Coke straw. "How much money are we talking about?"

"I expect to clear more than forty grand. I can give you five thousand minimum and twenty-five percent of anything over."

Chris dips her straw in the drink and covers the top to trap some cola. She absently pulls the straw out of the glass and releases the cola back into the glass. "I'm risking my job. I think forty percent is a better number."

David slides away from Chris in the booth and touches her straw-laden hand. "How much do you make in a year? I'm guessing not much more than five grand."

"Okay. Thirty-five percent."

"Thirty percent."

Chris drops the straw and extends her hand to shake. "Deal. How will I know when and who the poor schmuck is from the emergency room?"

David shakes Chris's hand. "My father used to tell me if you want something done right, do it yourself. You'll know the name when it comes across your desk. Just let me know when you're on shift."

Chris writes her schedule on the back of a placemat and slides it to David. He folds it and puts it into his pocket. They finish their burgers and fries. David skips the salad. The server drops the check, and David scoops it up. Then he moves closer to Chris and whispers, "What happened to you?"

Chris snaps her head toward David but says nothing. After a few seconds, she looks up. "What do you mean?"

"You're wearing dark sunglasses. The fluorescents here aren't that bright. I could be wrong, but I don't think so."

Chris takes off the glasses. Her right eye is blackened. There is evidence that she tried, unsuccessfully, to cover it up with some sort of concealer. "It's not what you think."

David knows he's nobody's guardian angel, but he can't help himself. "Look, deal or not, I really like you. Can I help you in some way?"

Chris is several years older than David. Her back straightens up and she half smiles, half sneers as she looks over the sunglasses at David. "Okay." She examines David like he's the dessert menu. "Are you a top or a bottom?"

David's mouth opens in confusion. "What?"

"Are you a top or a bottom?"

"You're describing a jar of pickles."

Chris laughs out loud. "In sex, are you a top or a bottom?"

David likes the fact that sex is on the table. "I'm good either way. On the top or on the bottom."

"You may be the straightest, most naïve dude I've ever been out with. I may need to check your license to make sure you're legal." Chris motions David to slide out of the booth, and she follows him. David pays the check, and they head to his car. He opens her door. Before she goes in, she softly kisses him on the cheek and gently says in his ear, "When we get back to my place, I want you to come inside."

* * *

David is excited. That they say nothing on the way to Chris's apartment excites him even more. When they arrive, Chris lets herself out of the car and walks directly to her front door. David dutifully follows.

The apartment is simple, yet very tasteful with sparse modern furnishings and soft hues in the living/dining room that evoke coastal living. Even though Chris doesn't live on the ocean, her floor-to-ceiling window allows for a fair, but partially obstructed, view of the beach.

Chris's smile is halfway between seductive and predatory. "Make yourself comfortable."

David makes himself comfortable.

Chris pours herself some orange juice with a generous splash of vodka. "Can I offer you something to drink?"

"No. I'm fine." David shudders involuntarily. With everything he has been through, how can he be nervous in the apartment of this beautiful woman?

Chris walks through a door that David just knows is her bedroom. She crooks her finger for him to follow. He follows. She says in a danger-laden voice, " 'Come with me, said the spider to the fly.' "

The room is large. There is a four-post king-size bed with a wrought-iron canopy. Chris flips a switch, and the room is bathed in ultraviolet light. The sheets and linens glow purple in the incandescence. On the walls are neon pictures of imperious women in various poses. Chris opens a closet, and on the inside of the closet door is revealed an assortment of leather and metal collars, chains, handcuffs, and gags. David's first impression is that these are the accoutrements of Chris's punk lifestyle. He's half right.

Chris motions to a high-back chair on a wall facing the bed. David sits down in the chair and Chris sits on the side of the bed. "Have you ever heard of S&M? Bondage and domination?"

David shrugs.

Chris touches David's leg. "Okay, I like rough sex. Where one partner dominates the other."

She reaches under the bed and pulls out a chest. The hasp lacks a lock, and she opens it easily. She reaches inside and removes a whip and what looks like a riding crop. "One partner dominates the other." She holds the business end of the whip. "The partner dominating is the top. The one being dominated is the bottom. Which do you prefer?"

David is sure that he's experiencing his own episode of the *Twilight Zone*. He nervously laughs. "Well, I guess I'd rather be the whipper than the whippee."

When he sees that Chris isn't amused, David gets serious. He touches Chris on the arm and looks into her eyes. "Chris, there is no way. No way that I can hurt you like that."

Chris grabs and pulls David's hair. "That's good because I'm more of a top. The other night, I tried to be a bottom and that's how I wound up with this." She lets go of David's hair and puts her hand on her sore eye.

David stands up and turns toward the bedroom door. "I'm not going to say no, but let's save it for our third or fourth date. It'll give at least one of us something to look forward to. Let's have that date after I get out of the hospital. If you promise to be gentle, we can maybe celebrate like true rebels."

Chris stands up and goes to kiss David. As their lips get close, she takes his lower lip between her teeth and bites. Not hard enough to make him bleed, but enough to let him feel some pain. She lets go and her lips smile, but her eyes bore into his with what looks like cruelty. "Fine. When you get out and the checks come in, you can bring me my cut, and I'll teach you how to have sex like an adult."

As David leaves, he turns to her. "You'll know when I'm coming in. You'll recognize the name."

David can't wait to tell this story to his spiritual advisor—his mother.

CHAPTER 37

ANOTHER con, another identity. David secures a new California driver's license for himself. He finds an answering service with a terminating line that he can use as his personal phone number and an address that he can pretend is his residence. He opens a checking account under the identity to hold the expected insurance checks.

The next two weeks involve purchasing policies from six insurance companies that sell private health insurance coverage in California. One check to go to the hospital, five checks to go into their pockets.

Like cops searching a crime scene for clues, David and Sunny walk around the neighborhood near Cedars of Lebanon. If David has a talent for inventing cons, Sunny is a genius in implementing them. They scope out several places to stage the mugging. They narrow it down to three, then two, then, after some debate, one secluded spot near the Church of Scientology, where the darkness will give refuge to their conspiracy.

Once David receives all the policies at the answering service address, he and Sunny know they're ready to go forward. He, Sunny, and Sal convene again over the plan. Sunny spreads out a local map of the hospital area and, like assembling a complex puzzle, she takes the lead using a marker to emphasize each location.

"We'll have dinner near the hospital. Here's the diner…" Sunny circles a location on the map. "After dinner, we'll take a walk away from the business district and any witnesses but close enough to quickly find a phone." She follows the marked streets with her pen and circles the area where they'll stage the mugging.

She looks at David. "Sal will hit you in the head, not hard enough to really hurt you, but hard enough to leave a bruise or an abrasion. Some proof that you were hit."

She looks at Sal. "After you hit David, we wait a few minutes. I'll act like I'm overcome with panic and grief. You'll find a phone and call for an ambulance. I'll stay with David. We'll give a police report under our regular California identities. David will carry identification under his new identity. We claim we can't describe who attacked David. He's the victim, so there shouldn't be any suspicion."

Sal breathes in deeply. His arms are crossed in front of his chest, and he only briefly makes eye contact with Sunny. He can't even look at David. "I'm really not comfortable involving the police."

"We don't have a choice. You can't have a mugging without a police report. Just let me do the talking." Sunny looks at Sal in a mock pout with her lower lip distended. "Don't worry, baby. You'll be too upset to talk. When the ambulance brings David to Emergency, we follow in the car and make sure they get him admitted. That's where the big money is. Does that cover it?"

"That covers it," David says.

That night, they have dinner at the designated diner on Sunset, not far from the Church of Scientology's new Celebrity Centre International. Sunny and Sal are so on edge they barely touch their food. In hushed tones, they repeatedly review the plan.

David appears to be calm as a monk. He eats like it's his last meal because he's seen hospital food, and it's an understatement to say he's not impressed.

Soon after David finishes eating, Sunny announces, "Dinner is over. Come on, let's get this over with."

Sal pays the check, and they head down Sunset to Catalina. They turn to the spot that Sunny and David previously chose. It's a parking lot off Catalina not far from several stores and restaurants. The night is between twilight and darkness. No one is around. The spot is desolate. The air is moist, and the tension is like an electric current charging both the air and each of them.

Sunny gives David a hug and kiss and asks, "Are you sure you're ready for this?"

David looks at Sal. "Are you ready?"

Sal cracks his knuckles. "As I'll ever be." He looks around to make sure they're alone. "Close your eyes."

David closes his eyes.

In all fairness, nobody anticipates how difficult it is to hit someone with just the right amount of force to bruise but not hurt. And maybe they should have experimented with some other body part or a soft board or Styrofoam, or something.

But it also can't be overlooked that Sal has been frustrated. No, make that infuriated, with the life that David has dragged him into. He has been trying to break away with Sunny from David for two years. He spent time in jail because of David. He lost his business because of David. He's a fugitive… because… of… David.

Sal makes a fist and hits David in the head. There is a sickening thud as his fist connects with David's forehead, and David drops like he was clubbed with an axe handle. Sunny goes pale. Suddenly, the *faux* injury is all too real. Sunny screams as tears pour from her eyes. She's in shocked disbelief and disassociates with, well, everything.

While Sunny, in a semi-fetal position, cradles David on the cold concrete, Sal takes the lead. He runs to a nearby record store. He bursts in and yells, "Someone call 911. There's been a mugging across the street!" Several customers follow Sal back to the parking lot.

Sunny checks to make sure David is breathing. He is. She uses her purse as a surrogate pillow for him. Even with the small crowd gathering behind her, all she can focus on is David. Within minutes, red-and-white flashing lights are streaking over the walls like shooting stars in every direction as emergency vehicles arrive.

As Sal implements the plan, Sunny watches like a mirror. She sees what's happening but can't focus to engage.

Over and over, Sal gives the police a credible report. He repeats it to the paramedics. He explains that they were just going for a walk after dinner, and a couple of guys in masks dressed in black came out of nowhere and attacked. No, it happened so fast that he couldn't describe them. They were average height and weight. It was dark. He couldn't make out details.

Sunny watches as the paramedics check David's pulse and check the purple bulge growing on his head where he was hit. They look into David's eyes. The pupils are dilated. As they place David on a board and fasten a brace around his neck, David throws up his last meal from the diner. Sunny feels some relief as David seems to partially regain consciousness and moans in pain.

The paramedics check David's other vitals and carry him into the ambulance. One paramedic looks at Sunny. "Do you want to ride along?"

Sal waves her into the ambulance. "You go. I'll follow in the car."

The Celebrity Centre for the Church of Scientology was established to cater to celebrities with a unique environment that would accommodate their unique schedules and where recruitment could be enhanced by peer reinforcement of their choice to use Scientology to further their spiritual growth.

Chris has been waiting months for a punk rock celebrity to be admitted. Now she takes the call that... John (Johnny?) Ramone is in the emergency room. She races to the emergency room like a startled deer with her clipboard and an inappropriately hopeful look in her eyes.

When she enters the small room where Johnny Ramone is supposed to be, she sees David surrounded by a grieving woman and the guy who delivered coffee at Equitable. There are no nurses. Chris closes the curtain behind her and, with raised eyebrows and her trademark smirk, talks to David without realizing he's in and out of consciousness. "Dude, you're such a dick. Why would you let me think that Johnny Ramone was here?"

David says nothing. Chris notices the knot on his head and realizes that he's drifting in and out of awareness. She turns to Sunny. "What happened?"

Sunny waves her hand at Sal, who takes Chris out into the hallway. "Nothing has changed. Things just got out of hand. Let me give you whatever information I can. His mother will give you whatever else you need as soon as Da—I mean John—is a little better." Sal hands Chris an insurance identification card. "Here. This will get you started."

Chris sets the clipboard on a counter and throws her arms over her head. "Who are you? Aren't you the guy who ran coffee and pastries at the office building?"

Sal closes his eyes in exasperation. He takes a long breath in and a longer exhalation. "I'm his stepfather. Please, someone will be up shortly to give you whatever you need."

A doctor comes in and examines David. "We need to take John for a cat scan. Once those results are in, we'll be in a better position to let you know what damage he has from the mugging. We're certain that he has a concussion."

Sal asks, "Are you going to admit him?"

The doctor closes the curtain. "Of course. We'll keep him for at least a few days for observation."

The doctor leaves and soon, a nurse takes David to Imaging. It's just Sal and Sunny in the room. Sunny glares at Sal with a look beyond hatred. It's closer to a look of loathing. She gets up. As she leaves the room, she turns back to Sal and says in a chillingly composed voice, "I'll be back. I have something to do."

Sunny's name describes her personality. She has infinite patience, and her optimism is like a ray of sunshine piercing through the clouds. But she's a mother. And like mothers the world over, she's as protective as a fortress to her children.

And Sunny has a secret. She has a dark side that very few people have seen.

Sunny goes to see Chris, but not just to give her information about David.

CHAPTER 38

DAVID is released ten days after he was admitted for a concussion and observation. Sunny gets copies of the medical bills for the insurance companies. The hospital bills, including tests, ambulance, doctors, and room rate come in at just over twelve thousand dollars. The claims are sent, and the insurance drafts dribble in over the following weeks. They total sixty thousand dollars—more than six times the average annual salary.

Once the insurance drafts clear, Sunny withdraws most of the cash and keeps it in a safe deposit box in a different bank. Some of the cash is kept hidden in Sunny and Sal's apartment, where David stays until he fully recovers.

Chris takes David to lunch at Big Boy. It's the Christmas season and, even though there's no snow or chill in the air, Los Angeles has plenty of Christmas spirit. There are Christmas trees—some real, but most fake—festooned with lights of all colors and patterns. Stars, bells, and snowmen are strung across busy streets. People flock to holiday markets and, of course, there are Hollywood holiday shows. Both Chris and David love the season.

Chris finishes her burger, blots her mouth with a paper napkin, and demurely says, "So, tell me." She smiles and looks around as if someone is eavesdropping. "Do you want to go back to my place?"

David stifles a laugh and says with a tease, "Yeah, but my doctors don't know if I'm well enough to be tied up and tortured yet."

Chris laughs so hard that tears fall down her cheeks. "You're such a shit. Besides, you'd like it the way I do it. No, I mean, maybe we can be more… vanilla this time with your head and all."

David eats a fry to buy time. Two fries later, he turns to face Chris in the booth. He takes her soft hand and gazes intently into her eyes. His own blue eyes are filled with regret. With hesitation, he says in a grave tone, "I've wanted that for a long time. But I want to be in shape for the first time. Last thing I want is to have a splitting headache just as you're on the verge of the longest, deepest, most mind-blowing orgasm of your life."

Chris pulls her hand away from his and breaks off the gaze. She tries not to, but she starts laughing hysterically. She sticks her finger down her throat like she's going to vomit. "Dude, you're such an idiot. At least no one can say you lack confidence." She reaches into her purse and produces a small, gift-wrapped box. "I got something for you."

David looks at the paper. It's black velveteen with little snowmen. "Can I open it? Or do I have to wait for Christmas?"

"No. Open it now."

David rips into the paper and opens the top of the box. There is a small, ring-sized jewelry box inside. He opens the jewelry box. It contains a golden medallion of some kind.

Chris takes it from him and holds it by the chain for him to view. "It's a Saint Dismas medal."

David examines the medal and chain.

"I'm not religious, and I don't know what faith you are. But you'll like this. Saint Dismas is known as the Good Thief. He was one of two thieves crucified next to Jesus and he stood up for Jesus, telling the other thief that, 'We're getting what we deserve, but he, Jesus, has done nothing wrong.' Saint Dismas represents the power of redemption."

David takes the medallion and holds it tightly in his fist. "I don't know what to say."

Chris takes a sip of Diet Coke and laughs. "Well, that's a first." Then she pulls a chain out from around her own neck and shows David that she has an identical medallion. "I bought one for myself since I also seem to need redemption."

David snickers quietly as he fondles her medallion and looks at his own. With a smirk, he asks, "Does this mean we're going steady?"

Chris laughs as she tucks her medallion into her blouse. "You wish. More like we're members of the same secret club."

David rubs the medallion in his hand. "I really like that." He puts his medallion around his own neck.

They finish lunch, and Chris brings David back to Sunny and Sal's apartment.

Sunny meets her at the door within earshot of Sal. "Your share is twenty-one thousand five hundred dollars. I can show you the numbers. I'll bring your cash later."

"No problem. In the meantime, take care of 'Mr. Ramone.'"

They both laugh conspiratorially as Sunny closes the door.

Sal sees Chris leave and visibly relaxes. The plan really worked. He feels like things with Sunny have maybe settled down since he concussed David. Like, maybe Sunny has resolved some of the anger that she originally had. After all, Sal reasons, he did step up at the mugging and the hospital when no one else could. The con was successful, in large part, because of him.

He didn't even argue when Sunny suggested that David stay with them after he left the hospital. Sal turned his charm dial up to ten and warmly agreed to let David stay. And Sal just knew for a fact that nobody could resist him when he turned on the charm.

* * *

December seventh. Pearl Harbor Day. A day that President Roosevelt said, "…will live in infamy." It's also Sunny and Sal's fifth wedding anniversary. David felt well enough to go back to his place the day before and give them some alone time.

Sunny makes scrambled eggs, bacon, sausage, and toast for breakfast. Sal packs it in like a wolf. Sunny coos across the table, "Happy anniversary. I've got something special planned for us tonight."

Sal has a broad smile, and he moves to embrace Sunny. "I don't even know what it is, but I can't wait. What is it?"

Sunny leans in and kisses Sal. "It's a surprise."

Sal's voice gets higher. He bounces in anticipation. He looks at Sunny with large, wide, dark brown eyes and a pouty expression. "I hate surprises. Tell me."

"Hmm. Let's just say that it's going to be an adventure for you and an anniversary that you'll never forget."

Sal grips Sunny in a tight embrace. His brows knit, resembling a "V" shape. "Come on, now you have to tell me!"

"When we go out tonight, just dress casually, but not like a bum." Sunny mimes locking her lips closed with her fingers and goes into the bedroom to get dressed. She comes out looking amazing. She wears a tight gold lamé jumpsuit with a large, gold belt that cinches her waist and gives her a perfect hourglass figure.

Sal quickly puts on his best dress shirt and slacks, just a blue button down and khakis. He briskly escorts Sunny to the car. "Where are we going?"

Sunny raises her eyebrows and repeats the lip lock mime. "You'll see when we get there."

For once, Sunny drives. As twilight approaches, the sunset turns a brilliant orange. The sun looks like a new penny dropped into the pocket of night. Sunny drives toward the ocean, and Sal can smell the briny tang of the sea air. She pulls into a small parking area outside of Chris's apartment. She pulls out a thick envelope. "We need to give Chris her share of the take. I hope you don't mind."

Sal is in too good a mood to mind. He isn't about to say or do anything to ruin his surprise. They get to the door, and Sunny gently knocks. Sal notices that her movements are hesitant and cautious.

Chris opens the door. She's in a black dress with gold piping from Frederick's of Hollywood. She has long legs, and the dress displays almost every inch of them. The gold jumpsuit Sunny wears and the black dress Chris has on make their blond hair look like genuine gold.

In the living room, near the floor-to-ceiling windows is a Christmas tree with the kind of white lights that look like Tiffany diamonds if Tiffany diamonds were incandescent. Chris doesn't have any other lights on in the room, but she has several Christmas-scented candles scattered around. It gives the room a romantic glow with a holiday subtext.

Chris motions Sal and Sunny to sit on a sofa next to a coffee table on which stand an open bottle of Crown Royal and three glasses. She picks up the bottle. "You like Crown Royal, right?"

Sunny and Sal love Crown Royal.

"Do you want ice or any mixer?"

Sunny takes ice. Sal takes his neat. Chris pours the drinks and holds out her hand for the envelope. She takes it from Sunny and counts the hundred-dollar bills. When she finishes, she says, "Please make yourselves comfortable while I put this away."

She leaves, and Sal turns to Sunny in disbelief. "Is this your surprise?"

Sunny smiles reassuringly. "Yes. Surprised?"

"Flabbergasted. But aren't she and David—"

"It's just business between them."

Chris comes back into the room. They have another drink. And another. When the full bottle is half drained and Sal is half in the bag, they sit on each side of him. They're seductive, charming, and magnetic: Susan Anton and Goldie Hawn chewing up the scenery in a sensual film. Sal can't believe his good fortune. This really will be a night to remember.

Achilles has his heel. Superman has kryptonite. And Sal has a bad back. Sunny unexpectedly puts her arms around Sal's neck when he stands up, and she jumps into his arms. Sal catches her out of pride. And then his back feels like someone lit a campfire in it.

He gently lets Sunny go and stumbles back to the couch. Chris and Sunny feign surprise. Sunny looks pleadingly at Chris. "Do you have a heating pad or something?"

"Yes, of course." Chris looks at Sal. "Maybe you'll be more comfortable on my bed. I have a firm mattress." She leads the way. She turns the flat lights on in her bedroom, which makes it look far less ominous than when David was there. Sunny leads Sal to the bed and helps him lie down on his back. Chris gets the heating pad and brings it over to Sal. Sunny is on Sal's left and Chris is on Sal's right.

It takes seconds, and it's over before Sal can even react, especially fighting the pain in his back. One handcuff manacle is attached to Sal's left wrist by Sunny and one handcuff manacle is attached to the right wrist by Chris. The other ends of the chains are already firmly attached to the bedposts behind Sal's head. Sal pulls but he has no leverage, and his back won't let him use his full strength.

It takes Sal a precious minute to figure out what's happening. He pulls vainly at the chains and turns to Sunny with a wane smile. "Honey, what is this?"

Sunny ignores him. Chris comes around the bed, and they turn away from Sal while they whisper secret plans.

Sal raises his voice, not in anger but in concern. "Look, babe, I don't know what this is, but it's not my scene."

The women don't acknowledge Sal. They continue whispering. Now Sal goes from concerned to angry. "Look! Enough! I don't like this bondage shit!"

They look at Sal. Their gaze is patronizing, as if he were a pathetic child. Sal thrashes and pulls at the chains. He tries to lift his legs to get better leverage, but his back refuses to cooperate. Now he yells. No, he howls with rage as his anger becomes volcanic. His face is stop sign red, and his hands are white with strain. "Let! Me! Go! Now!"

Sunny opens the bedroom door to let herself out. "Make sure he has cab fare, will you? I'm taking the car."

Chris sits on the bed next to Sal. He literally snarls like an animal. Chris puts her index finger to his lips and quietly says, "Shh."

Sal quiets down. He wants to get whatever this is over with.

"You know, I really like Robert. Of course, not as much as Sunny. If you haven't figured it out, she's not very happy with you either. You didn't have to hit him that hard."

Sal says nothing.

"I don't like hurting anyone who doesn't want to be hurt. But I'm protective of people I care about. So, for you, I'm going to make an exception." Chris cooly stands up and walks to a nightstand next to the bed. "So, here's what's going to happen, tough guy: On behalf of myself and your wife, I'm going to beat the shit out of you, and there's nothing you can do about it. Nothing sexual is going to happen. Your clothes will stay on. But you're going to look like you went ten rounds with Ali."

Sal's eyes widen. His face is frozen. His heart is pounding out of his chest. He pulls again at the chains, but he knows they won't give. He wonders whether he can talk Chris out of it, but he knows that no amount of charm will change her mind.

Chris takes two pairs of brass knuckles out of her nightstand. "The only thing you do have control over is how you're going to take your beating. You going to scream and cry like a pussy? Or are you going to take it like a man?"

"Fuck you."

Chris glares at him, and in a calm voice she whispers. "No, fuck you." She straddles Sal. Now he's completely helpless. She slides the metallic knuckles onto both hands. She goes to work on Sal's face and head for ten full minutes that Sal feels will never end. His face and head are a mass of welts and bruises. He thinks his nose might be broken. Both his eyes are swollen practically shut. Sal doesn't say a word. He doesn't complain, whimper, or even grunt in pain.

Chris doesn't break a sweat. She pauses and says with derision, "Do you see? It's possible to mess someone up without giving them a concussion."

She gets off Sal and sits on the chair next to the bed. "In case you're thinking of retaliation, clear that shit from your head. With your activities, you don't want to bring in the cops. But if you did, I would simply say that you and your wife came in wanting this. And you know what?" Chris stands up and leans menacingly over Sal. "Sunny will agree with me. You really pissed her off."

Chris goes back to the nightstand and returns the brass knuckles. From the next drawer, she withdraws a thirty-eight-caliber pistol. She checks to make sure it's loaded. She uses the phone on her nightstand and calls for a taxi to be there in twenty minutes. She presses a hundred-dollar bill into Sal's left hand and unlocks the handcuffs. "I'll admit one thing. You took your trimming like a man. I'm impressed." She points the gun at his center mass. "A taxi is coming to take you home or wherever you're going. Sunny wanted me to make sure you have cab fare. That's what the hundred is for. It should take you wherever you want to go. Now get the fuck out of my house."

Sal slowly gets out of bed. He staggers out of the room and leaves the apartment. His face hurts like hell, but the real pain is in his heart. Ten minutes later, the taxi picks him up, and he heads back to his place.

It's just past midnight. Sunny is sitting on the couch. The sexy jumpsuit has been replaced by a gray sweatsuit. A suitcase stands near the door. It's packed with Sal's personal things. Sal aches to his very soul. He has been betrayed, beaten physically and emotionally, and now he knows he'll be alone. He fights tears of anger. "I want my share of the money from the hospital scam."

Sunny shakes her head. "You don't deserve any of it. You put my son in the hospital. David invented the con, and David and I put it together. What did you do?"

"I was the only one who handled things when the shit went down."

"You caused the shit to go down!" Sunny screams.

"I want ten thousand dollars, or I go to the police. I'll take all of us down."

Sunny goes into a shoebox in the closet and takes out cash. "All I have here is nine thousand. Take it or leave it."

Sal takes it. He goes into the bedroom and takes a card case out of a hidden pocket in a pair of pants. It has his original Salvatore Rossi driver's license. He takes his license, the cash, and his suitcase and leaves. And he goes to the police.

CHAPTER 39

OKAY, Sal doesn't go directly to the police. First, he catches a redeye from LAX to Fort Lauderdale Airport. When he lands, he pays cash and spends the first night at the Pier 66 Hotel, a luxury hotel designed by legendary architect Frank Lloyd Wright where when they were dating, Sal and Sunny used to go when their shifts ended. That night, Sal sits alone at a table in the rotating rooftop lounge enjoying the view and thinking about their time together and the consequences of what he has finally decided to do.

The next morning, Sal enjoys an expensive breakfast and follows it with a taxi trip to the Pompano Beach National Bank, where he deposits the remainder of his cash in a savings account.

Sal does something then that he hasn't done in three years. He visits his mother and sister, still living in Pompano Beach, Florida.

Sal's mother, a rotund woman with more salt than pepper in her hair and a permanent forward slouch has a heart as big as the bowls of spaghetti alla carbonara that she serves to her family on Sunday nights. She greets Sal like he has just returned on a surprise leave from Vietnam.

His older sister, Theresa, is equally joyous but more cautious. "Sal, you shouldn't be here. FBI have been sniffing around, and it's just not safe for anyone if you're caught." Then she notices his bruised face. "And what the hell happened to you?"

Sal melts into a puddle of tears. He hasn't cried like this since he was a child and his dog died. His mother cradles him in her arms. "What did they do to you, *me neonate?*"

"I can't talk about it. Sunny and I are no longer together. And I'm turning myself in." His hands trembling, Sal takes the savings passbook and signature cards out of his pants pocket and hands them to his sister. "Theresa, there's about eight grand in the account. Sign these and bring them to the bank, and you'll have access to the money. After I turn myself in, hire a lawyer for me. It shouldn't be a lot of money because I'm just going to plead guilty to whatever charges are out there. I'll do my time and move on with my life when I get out."

Now Sal's mother is crying.

Theresa says, "You should see a doctor first. Get those bruises and cuts looked at."

Sal looks at Theresa with weary eyes. "What's the point? Why spend whatever money I have on doctors? They have doctors in jail. I'll be fine."

Theresa and Sal's mother drive Sal to the Fort Lauderdale Police Department, where Sal confesses to everything he did. Aiding a fugitive, fraudulently transacting traveler's checks, jumping bond, and kicking the shit out of his scumbag son-in-law in Arizona. But he only confesses to his own crimes. He doesn't—actually, he can't—bring himself to talk about Sunny, David, or anything that he thinks implicates them.

* * *

Back in Los Angeles, Chris meets with David and Sunny in Sunny's apartment. David is amazed at how close Sunny and Chris have gotten—and it unnerves him a little. They explain to David that Sal left with his share of the money. Sunny tells David that they had a fight over Sal's treatment of David during the mugging.

David scrunches his face. "What if he goes to the police?"

Sunny shakes her head from side to side. "He would only be implicating himself. He won't do that."

He shakes his head in disbelief. "It was your anniversary. It must have been some fight."

Chris and Sunny look at each other in a way that sends shivers down David's spine. "Yeah, it was some fight," they say in unison.

David wonders whether the odd feelings he's getting from Chris are a residue of the concussion or something else.

Sunny gestures everyone to the round table. "So, now we have to find someone else to go to the hospital."

Chris absently spins a pen on the table. "I can get someone to play the patient."

David sighs and tilts his head from side to side. "No. It's not safe to take on another partner."

Sunny stands up and pours coffee for Chris and herself. She brings Chris her cup and sits down again. "I'll be the patient."

David bites his lip while still shaking his head. "No. I won't let you get hurt like that. We've got to think of something else."

They sit in silence for a long minute as they ponder the dilemma. Sunny and Chris sip black coffee and David sips a Coke. Suddenly, David interrupts the reverie. Sunny can tell from experience that he has an inspiration.

"Maybe we're thinking about this all wrong. We tried to make the damages severe so that the hospital bill will be larger and the payoff bigger." David pauses.

Sunny and Chris fix gazes on him. Chris can't take the silence. "Yeah, go on."

"But we might be able to build the payoff instead by simply having more insurance policies. Even a modest hospital bill is a lot of money." David looks at Chris. "With you keeping the insurance companies separated, we can make a four-thousand-dollar bill forty thousand dollars by having ten insurance policies."

Chris and Sunny stay silent. They continue to stare at David.

David pushes his chair back slightly and props his feet on a free chair. "Last time, we had five policies and a twelve-thousand-dollar bill. Sixty thousand dollars. Let's say that we get sixty policies with a one-thousand-dollar hospital bill. We get the same payoff; we just pay more in premiums to get the policies. But the premiums are small for a month or two of coverage."

Sunny straightens in her chair. She squeezes David's hand, her eyes wide with understanding. "So, if we get a hundred policies with a thousand-dollar bill, we'd make a hundred thousand dollars."

David stands up and gently squeezes Chris's shoulders. "And a thousand-dollar bill is low. Between x-rays, ambulance, emergency room, and doctors, we can run up at least five thousand dollars easily even if you aren't admitted for several days. You don't need a serious injury."

Sunny glances at Chris. "I can be a pretty good actress."

Chris ignores her. She rubs her chin and stares at the ceiling. "I don't know. That seems like a lot of paperwork to juggle."

David gets more excited as his idea unfolds. "We only need to do it once. That kind of money can be enough to simply move on with. We'll split it as equal partners."

Now Sunny also looks at the ceiling, questioning the premise. "Where would we ever find all of those policies?"

David smiles. "Where we find anything we need: at the Hollywood Library. We can get the policies anywhere in the country. We'll come back here to Los Angeles to stage the accident so Chris can do her thing with the paperwork."

The next day, Sunny and David check out the reference area of the library. There are Yellow Pages for every major

American city dangling from wire racks like upside down birds on a wire. Everything they need is in one place. Sunny and David skim the spines of the books to pick out cities. They're limiting their search to major cities in the California vicinity when Sunny has a thought and goes to the reference librarian. "By any chance, do you know what state has the most insurance companies?" She really doesn't expect a quick answer.

Like a talking encyclopedia, the reference librarian surprises her. "Texas. Their insurance laws are very liberal, they have a business-friendly environment, a large population, and a long border with Mexico."

Sunny grabs Austin, Houston, Dallas, and Ft. Worth Yellow Pages. There are well over a hundred companies that sell some form of health insurance. The Yellow Pages are fastened to the wire, so she calls David over. They pour through the pages, writing down company names and numbers as they go.

David can't believe their good fortune. He calculates in his head the money they can make from just a fraction of all these companies. "It looks like we're going to Texas."

When they return, he sits in his apartment at the table holding the phone. He anxiously taps his fingers on the wooden tabletop. Finally, he calls Chris. She answers on the third ring. "Hey, trouble, we figured it out. My mother and I are going to Texas tomorrow to buy policies. Wanna come to my place tonight before we leave?"

Any response but an immediate "yes" would make David nervous. There is a delay as Chris says, "Hold on," and puts the phone receiver down on a hard surface. When she returns, she seems in good spirits, even lively. "Hey, trouble." She copies David, not having a better nickname. "Yes, I can come over tonight. Be there in an hour?"

David didn't expect her to be there that soon, but he doesn't want to jinx it. "Sure. See you then." He makes sure that she has his address and hangs up—and immediately struggles to clean up his place.

Chris comes over and looks around his apartment for the first time. Her place is a haven of cleanliness where even the ocean air smells sanitized. David's place isn't. "This place isn't exactly a temple to Comet cleanser, is it?"

David laughs uncomfortably. "You want to go to a hotel?"

Chris shakes her head. "Do you have any beer in that fridge?"

"Yeah. For guests."

Chris goes into the fridge and gets a beer. Landfills have less spoiled food. "I think something in there tried to bite me."

"Did it draw blood?"

"It better not have." Chris finds a bottle opener buried in a drawer, pops the cap, and drains a third of the bottle in one gulp. She sets the bottle down and starts looking around the apartment. "Where is your bedroom?"

David leads Chris to the one bedroom. He picked up the dirty clothes that were lying around, but his sheets haven't been changed in a while, and he makes a bed like a teenager, with the fitted sheet barely tucked in and a zebra print blanket with no bedspread. His two pillows have pillowcases that don't match and a freaking Superman insignia on one of them.

Chris looks at David with disdain. "How old did you say you are? Have you ever been laid before?"

A strained laugh escapes David's throat. "Of course."

Chris paces the room rolling her eyes. "In this room? What did it cost you?"

This isn't going as David had hoped.

Chris sits on the bed and pats the mattress for David to join her. "Look. I really wanted to hook up with you tonight, but… I just can't here."

David takes her face in his hands and kisses her. The kiss is delicious. Their mouths move in perfect intimate harmony as they meld into an intense union. He opens his eyes for a moment and stops. "You kiss with your eyes open."

Chris crinkles her nose and pulls her face back a little. "You do too, or you wouldn't have known."

David's narrow eyes get a little wider. "I just opened my eyes for a second."

Chris pulls away from David and stands up. "Let's go into the living room and talk about something." She walks to the living room and sits down on the sofa. David follows. She tells him about what happened to Sal. "I just don't want to have any secrets from you."

In that moment, David knows two things: First, he can never look at Chris without thinking about her beating the shit out of one of the toughest guys he knows. Second, that his relationship with Chris is as much an illusion as his own identity. She doesn't even know his true name. And he has so many more secrets than she has. Hell, he has more secrets than anyone. And the fact is that he could never come clean to her. Maybe someday, but... well, maybe someday. "Thank you for sharing that with me, Chris. I appreciate it. I'll tell you what; let me call you when we get back from Texas. Maybe we'll fly to Hawaii or someplace and spend some of the money. We'll find a nice clean paradise."

David walks Chris to her car. He kisses her one last time and watches her drive away. He wistfully watches his relationship go from friends to partners in crime to lovers, to nothing. His heart splinters like delicate glass, and tears uncontrollably roll down his cheeks.

David immerses himself with the health insurance plans. He looks at the list of companies and imagines the potential windfall they could collect. He feels more confident than ever, maybe to compensate for his acknowledged loss over Chris. He begins to consider himself invincible. A criminal mastermind. He becomes more certain than ever that he could get away with anything.

As he brags to Sunny, she cautiously listens and gently tells him to not be overconfident. But David is barely an adult, and sometimes a child's mistakes can crush all of their plans and dreams. If David's check kiting to save his bakery in Hollywood, Florida was his original sin, Texas is his penance.

PART V: GALENA, TEXAS

CHAPTER 40

DAVID and Sunny settle in the Fort Worth area of Texas. Instead of an answering service, they check into a trailer park named the Cedar Grand and rent a trailer, not only to keep costs down but to supply an address and legitimacy for the identity that David creates for Sunny.

With another baptismal certificate, well respected as identification in Texas, Sunny's new identity becomes Susan Wilder. Once a phone is installed in the trailer, the identity is as complete as if she'd been born into it. Sunny even adopts a bit of a Texas drawl to blend in.

Texas is as different from any of the cities that David has visited as a cemetery at night is to Mardi Gras in New Orleans. For one thing, everywhere seems so freaking far from everywhere else.

The insects are literally monstrous. There are scorpions and spiders the size of small birds. On a walk around the trailer park, David encounters an ant hill visible from forty feet away spewing venomous, inch-long red ants that envelop the vicinity. He thinks that if the government could draft those ants and get them to the Viet Cong, they could win the Vietnam conflict in a year.

People are friendly, but friendly without authenticity. Like a door-to-door salesperson trying to win a steak knife set. David hears more "bless your hearts" in a week than he has in his entire life. He thinks that "bless your heart" is the Texas way of saying "fuck you."

He guesses it may have something to do with the Christian churches that seem to stand on more corners than fast food joints and gas stations combined. Not that David has problems with any religion or philosophical bent. But if it wasn't Christianity, David would swear that a cult had taken over the entire state.

He expects the men to be cowboy rugged, but not so... rugged. Men seem to travel in packs of at least five floating on a river of testosterone and always ready to throw down. One cowboy with a belt buckle the size of a collector plate tries to impress Sunny by telling her, "Baby, everything is larger in Texas. The biggest state in the union." The not-so-hidden innuendo demonstrated by his fingers locked around his massive belt buckle is that "everything" includes a prodigious member of his that would be more impressive if it weren't obstructed by the buckle.

When David says, "Did you know that if Alaska ever cut their state in half, Texas would be the third largest state in the union?" Mr. Buckle and his friends want to take David outside for a Texas beat down. David can fight if he must, but he doesn't like fighting because, well, it's stupid and, oh yes, because people get hurt. He can't wait to leave and get back to Los Angeles.

Once Sunny has her new driver's license, they get to work. Health insurance companies are called. Applications are collected, filled out, and returned with the initial premiums. And this all takes time.

As they wait, David and Sunny check out the area. They go to restaurants. They go line dancing. And they go to nearby communities. One of those communities is Galena, about fourteen miles due east of the trailer park. Galena identifies as a third of the self-proclaimed Golden Triangle, which includes Galena, Bedford, and Arlington. Galena consists of vast empty lots mixed with homes and businesses.

David and Sunny stop at a diner next door to one of those vacant lots. The diner—no name, just Diner—is classic Americana. Lots of windows and metal on the outside with a big red neon *DINER* sign in front above the entrance. Step inside and there is one room with a tin roof and a red-and-white counter in front of a kitchen, partially hidden in the back, where plates are set onto a stainless-steel shelf to be picked up by servers and brought to the counter and tables. Booths and tables are lined up along the windowed walls. Booth, table, booth, and repeat.

The vacant lot next door has a hand painted "For Sale by Owner" sign prominently displayed in the center of the land. David and Sunny sit at a booth near a window where David has a view of the vacant lot. He stares at the vacant lot like he wants to buy it.

They order lunch. The menu shows five kinds of burgers, and David orders the classic. It would never make the menu of Hamburger Hamlet. Between bites of his burger, he asks Sunny, "How are we doing on money?"

"Not bad, but not great. The insurance premiums will really drain our cash."

David downs a couple of fries. "How many insurance companies are out there?"

Sunny chuckles. "So many."

David stares out the window. "Every insurance company we get is worth a fortune. Will we get them all?"

Sunny drizzles dressing on her chef salad. "I doubt it, David. We only have so much money."

David studies the vacant land. He also looks at the owner of the diner drinking coffee and chain smoking in a booth toward the back. David guesses that he's about forty, but he can be off maybe five years in either direction. His brown eyes are narrow, reptilian, and they dart around the place like those of a nervous bird. The owner wears an untucked button-down shirt. He's thin for his six-foot frame. He wears a Texas baseball cap festooned with a single star over the bill.

Every ten minutes or so the owner tours the diner. He sticks his head in the kitchen at the two Black cooks. "Come on, Boy!" (not "boy" but "Boy!"), shouting the word like a verbal attack. The cooks sling food in the kitchen and clean floors and counters. Pretty teenage white girls hustle tables as they try to stay out of the owner's reach to avoid getting groped.

Sunny looks at the waitresses and shakes her head in sympathy. "Been there, done that, got the tee-shirt."

David also notices the place is busy for an after-lunch crowd on a weekday. "I have an idea. What was that Chicago restaurant you used to bring me to as a kid?"

Sunny thinks about it for a few seconds. "You're thinking of White Castle."

David explains his latest brainstorm to Sunny, who doesn't like it. "We agreed not to do any con that would hurt an individual."

David points his chin at the owner. "Look at that guy. He's a dick. He's everything I hate about this state and maybe more."

Sunny breathes in deeply and exhales slowly. "I have a bad feeling, and we agreed that any bad juju allows either of us to veto any con."

David takes a bite of his burger and talks with his mouth full. "I think you're being paranoid. It'll either work or it won't. If it doesn't, I've done nothing wrong. If it does, we'll be long gone. Besides, having the extra money can be the difference between a fifty-thousand-dollar payoff or a hundred-thousand-dollar payoff."

Sunny grits her teeth, then relaxes her jaw. "All right. If you're sure. But we must be especially careful about this one."

"Let's do it." David clinks his plastic Coke glass to her coffee cup.

The next day, David purchases a light blue button-down dress shirt and a rep tie. He purchases a briefcase. He purchases a piece of plywood, a wooden stake, a hammer and nails, cans of white and black spray paint, and large stencils.

The day after his purchases, after sundown, David drives to the vacant lot and replaces the "For Sale by Owner" sign with a new white sign that reads:

COMING SOON

NEW HOME OF WHITE CASTLE RESTAURANT

FEATURING TWENTY-CENT HAMBURGERS

For a week, everyday David and Sunny drive by the lot without stopping to make sure the owner of the vacant land hasn't noticed and taken down the sign. After a week, David comes into the diner wearing his shirt and tie and carrying his briefcase. He sits at the counter and orders a Texas burger made with chili, cheddar cheese, and barbecue sauce and takes almost the whole dispenser of napkins.

When the waitress brings his food, he points to the crowd. "It's pretty busy in here today. Is this typical?"

The waitress wipes the counter around David. "Yeah. The weekend crowd is usually big. Especially after football games at the high school. Friday and Saturday nights are really something else."

David grabs even more napkins. "Glad to hear that. I'm a field agent for White Castle, and we have an option on the property next door. I want to make sure that once I give approval, the place works out."

The waitress leans in close enough to whisper. "Do you really have twenty-cent hamburgers?"

"Oh, yes," David says, glad that the sign has been noticed. "They're little hamburgers and cheeseburgers. You can eat them by the stack. I've seen people order forty or fifty at a time."

The waitress drops the check and turns to David. "I can't even imagine eating that many sandwiches."

David picks up his check and looks it over. "Just wait. You'll love them."

As he hopes, the waitress finds and talks to the owner, and the owner sits down next to him before he gets halfway through his burger. "You're enjoying your meal?"

David glances at the owner like he doesn't want to be disturbed. "Yeah, it's pretty good."

The owner puts a toothpick in his mouth. "Best in town. Did I hear right that you're with this White Castle restaurant?"

"You heard right. I can get you some coupons if you want."

The toothpick travels from one side of the owner's mouth to the other. "No, no. Look, I don't know if you realize it, but there ain't enough people in this town to support two restaurants right next to each other. You sure you want to locate here?"

David looks around and waves his hand at the room. "Looks to me like a good crowd."

The owner plucks out the toothpick. "For one restaurant. Not for two. Besides, how do you sell a hamburger for twenty cents? You'd lose money on that."

David smiles and leans back on his stool like a teacher explaining math to a first grader. "First, everything is mass purchased. We have operations all over the country. Second, they're little burgers. Cute little burgers made with onions, pickles, and, if you want, ketchup and special mustard. They're tasty. Addictive."

The owner drops the wet toothpick in an ashtray. "Look, I'm sure you wouldn't want to look bad in front of your bosses. I've been here my whole life. My customers love me. If you open here and fall flat, you'd really look bad, wouldn't you?"

"Well, yeah. But I'm not usually wrong about these things. I think we'll both make a living. Besides, we've already put a non-refundable deposit on the property."

The owner's reptilian eyes narrow. He smiles at David, showing gold teeth where his incisors used to be. He leans in, suggesting that David do the same. "How much of a deposit?"

"Ten thousand dollars."

"How about if I can get that back to you?" The owner looks around as if afraid that someone else is listening. Then he whispers in David's ear, "And an extra thousand for your trouble."

David subtly shakes his head "no" while he stares at his meal. Then he looks up at the owner and says, "Let me finish my burger and think about it. I'll see you before I leave."

A new toothpick finds its way to the owner's mouth, balanced between his front teeth. "Yeah. And by the way, your lunch is on me."

David takes his time finishing his meal. He leaves the waitress a very generous tip and walks over to the owner's usual booth in the back. "All right. There's another spot in Dallas I've been checking out instead. When can you get the money?"

"Give me a week. Call me at this number." The owner pulls a napkin from the dispenser on his table and writes his name and phone number on it. He hands it to David.

David takes the napkin and says, "Make it cash. I don't want my bosses to know I made a deal with the competition. I'll tell them that the owner of the lot changed their mind and returned the deposit." He and the owner shake hands, and the owner covers the back of David's hand with his other hand like a preacher's handshake. The owner stands up without letting go of David's hand. He looks David in the eye with mock appreciation and as David leaves, he says, "Bless your heart."

CHAPTER 41

FRIDAY, a week to the day after David's deal with the owner of the diner, David calls the owner on the napkin phone number. "Hello. This is—"

"I know who this is. I have your money. It took a while to get it, but it's here. In cash. How do I know you'll keep your end of the deal?"

David expects this question and has an answer ready. "I'll bring a signed quit claim deed giving you White Castle's rights in the property next door."

There is a pause for several seconds. "Well, now, that sounds perfect. Meet me at the diner in an hour."

David hangs up. Sunny has been listening to his end of the conversation. Now she bites her nails and pulls on her hair in frustration. "Are you sure about this, baby?"

David grabs the car keys off a table. "Mom, you know I can't be a hundred percent sure of anything. But he sure seemed ready to pay the money and move on."

Sunny looks anguished for ten minutes while David waits expectantly for her approval. Then she says, "You drive over and pick up the money. I'll wait here. Find a phone booth and call me as soon as you're on the way back. If I don't hear from you, I'll take off and we'll connect through your sister."

They hug. They kiss. Sunny wishes David luck, and he heads to the diner.

When David pulls into the parking lot, he can't believe that he feels his own heartbeat playing "Wipeout" in his chest. He sits in the car and calms himself. He thinks, *My mother's paranoia is really rubbing off on me, but that's all it is. Paranoia. I'm good at this, and these hicks are easy marks.* He puts on his best innocent face and goes inside. He sees the owner in the usual booth and walks over, briefcase in hand.

The owner asks with a snarl, "Do you have the deed?"

David hands the owner the quit claim deed unsigned. "Do you have the cash?"

The owner hands David an envelope filled with hundred-dollar bills. David counts them. There are one hundred ten. Eleven thousand dollars. David squares the bills, puts them back into the envelope, and takes the deed from the owner. He takes a pen from his briefcase as he places the envelope inside and locks the combination latch. He signs his name individually and as a representative of White Castle and hands the useless, executed quit claim deed to the owner.

David slides out of the booth and extends his hand. "Pleasure doing business with you." The owner doesn't move to shake his hand. David walks out to his car. He places the briefcase on the passenger seat, exhales in relief, puts the car in reverse, and drives out of the parking lot and onto the access road headed to the highway. He never makes it.

After less than five minutes, in his rearview mirror, David sees the flashing red-and-white lights that bring fear to every driver, but horror to someone who has just committed a crime. David knows one thing: Never, ever run from the police. It's the quickest way to get shot. Especially if you're running on foot from a fat redneck cop.

He pulls over and rolls down the window. He pulls out his Robert Marino California driver's license. Three officers approach the car. Each of them has flat-top haircuts so big you could iron on them. None of them are in uniform, but they have badges attached to their belts. Two stand next to the rear passenger windows with their hands on their service weapons.

The cop who comes to David's window is tall. His flat top is reddish, and he has a green polo shirt paired with khaki pants. The gleaming badge is right next to his fly. He has an overbite that reminds David of Rocky the flying squirrel. David can tell just by the way he carries himself that he's in charge. He can also tell that if this is more than a simple traffic stop, this guy will be real trouble.

The cop's voice is confident, even friendly. But what really unnerves David is the smile. It's sinister. It reminds David of the smile kids get when torturing ants with a magnifying glass. He remembers his theory that a happy cop is a bad cop. And this guy's happiness reeks of cruelty.

The cop extends his hand for David's license. "You're the representative for White Castle restaurant?"

At that moment, David knows Sunny was right. He hopes he gets to tell her so. He hands the cop his license. "I am, Officer. How can I help you?"

The cop looks at the license. "Marino? You sure ain't Mexican."

"No. Italian."

"You sure ain't Italian either. Not dark enough. And your hair is too light."

David feels his heart race. "You ever hear of Frank Sinatra?"

"Yeah. Of course."

David feels his breathing get harder. "Blondish. Italian."

"Hmm. Didn't realize he was a wop. My name is Lieutenant Justice."

For a moment, David thinks this may be a setup. The owner's way to con the con. "Seriously?"

Justice puts David's license into the breast pocket of his polo. When he doesn't bother calling it in, David knows for certain that it's not a hoax; he's in trouble.

Justice leans in through the window and takes the keys out of the ignition. "The owner of the diner happens to be my cousin. Did you know that?"

David says nothing.

Justice's smile gets bigger. "I think you better come with us."

He opens the door, and David steps out onto the blacktop. "Turn around. Hands against the hood."

David has a better look at the other two cops. These three cops could be the Three Stooges if the stooges were conceived by their father and sister. The last time David was arrested, he feared going to jail. He felt his life was ending. This time, he knows for certain that he's on a knife's edge of really getting killed if things go any more wrong. He tries to hide the shaking in his hands and the tremble in his voice.

Justice pats David down. "You got anything in your pockets that I can hurt myself on?"

"No."

Justice turns David's pockets inside out—fifty in cash, keys, a wallet, a cotton handkerchief. Justice hands the contents to one of the other cops, who places the contents into a clear plastic bag. "What do you do with the handkerchief? Blow your nose and put the snot in your pocket?"

David says nothing while the other stooges laugh at the slight.

Justice cuffs David's hands behind his back. The cuffs cut into David's wrists. Justice guides him into the back of his unmarked car before he slides in to drive.

David turns to Justice. "What about my car?"

Justice doesn't even turn around. "Don't worry. We'll bring it in."

Riding shotgun with Justice is Daryl. Daryl is big. He's built like a heavyweight boxer but not lithe like Ali. More like George Foreman if George Foreman didn't hit the gym for a couple of months. It turns out, Daryl does like to box and work out—just not with opponents who can hit back. He has large ears which, along with his omnipresent sunglasses, make his face look like an owl.

The police station is small. It's a common space with three open offices, each office with cluttered desks facing a wall and chairs. One chair for the guy working at the desk, and a side chair for guests—either the voluntary or involuntary kind. The rooms are ruled by metal and cheap veneer and lit by even cheaper fluorescents.

Justice motions David, still handcuffed, to the chair next to his desk. "Now. First. My cousin says that there was a woman with you when you first came in."

"Your cousin's mistaken."

"Look, we can do this the easy way or the hard way. If you're really with White Castle, just show me a business card. Give me a number to call. If you're smart, you'll cooperate, and we can get you back on the road."

Justice's sneer leaves no doubt in David's mind that he's nothing but prey to these guys. In his head, he hears Justice saying, *"Bless your heart."*

"How about instead you let me call a lawyer?"

Justice leans into David. "You don't need to call a lawyer if you haven't done anything wrong, do you?"

Just then the third cop comes in and approaches Justice with David's briefcase in one hand and some other loose papers from David's car in his other hand. He has sad cop eyes and a perpetual pout. David doesn't know for sure, but he imagines this cop is the guy who does the scutwork around the station. Cop Three hands the suitcase and other papers to Justice.

Justice examines the briefcase in his hand. "Thanks, Clint. What do we have here?"

Clint puts the briefcase on Justice's desk. "This here is where your cousin's money is." He holds up the papers. A receipt from a trailer park. "I reckon this is where Mr. Marino is staying while he's in town."

Justice looks at the receipt. "Bring Mr. Marino to a cell."

Clint brings David to a row of three dark cells behind the offices. He unlocks David's cuffs and motions for David to walk into the middle cell and then locks the door behind him.

What seems like a half hour later, Clint returns and unlocks the cell door. He motions for David to turn around and pulls David's hands back behind his back while he re-applies the handcuffs, although not as tightly as Justice had them. Clint guides David back to Justice's desk and motions for David to sit down. Daryl the hooty owl cop stands to the side like a gargoyle. David's briefcase is still on Justice's desk. It's still closed. Justice is no longer smiling or friendly.

"Open it."

"No."

"Open it or we'll break the lock."

"Do you have a search warrant?"

"We don't need a search warrant."

"Then you don't need me to open it."

Justice's sinister smile returns. He tells the room, "I'm going to go get a cup of coffee. Keep an eye on our wop guest, will you?"

Justice leaves the room with Clint following like a Labrador. After Justice and his pet leave the area, Daryl moves to stand in front of David. "Stand up."

David stands up. It isn't easy with his hands cuffed behind his back.

Daryl slams a straight punch into David's solar plexus. David folds like a cafeteria napkin. He feels bile rising in his chest. He's a nausea bomb ready to explode, but not quite.

Daryl pulls David upright by the hair. "You better not puke in my house. Turn around."

David turns around, and Daryl takes off the cuffs.

"Take off your clothes."

"What?"

Daryl slaps David hard in the back of the head. David is taken by surprise and falls forward. "Get up and take off your fuckin' clothes."

David is helpless and terrified. He removes his pants down to the tighty whities. He folds the pants with the pockets on the outside and says a prayer. If he has any chance, this is the make-or-break moment.

Daryl starts to go through David's pockets again as he says, "Take off the shirt."

David takes off the shirt, and Daryl sees the Saint Dismas medal dangling around David's neck. He forgets about the pants. His eyes blaze with fury as he gets within inches of David's face. "What is this?" He pushes two fingers into the medallion so hard David feels like the medallion is going to penetrate his breastbone. "Good thief?" Daryl pushes the medallion a second time as he says these words like they're part of a total assault. The second two-finger poke hurts worse than the first. "Good thief, huh?" He pokes the medallion a third time, a needle trying to penetrate a concrete wall.

David doesn't dare block the attacks, so he retreats into the wall next to Justice's desk. "Yeah, it's the patron saint."

"I know who the fuck Saint Dismas is, you prick. It offends me to see his medal around your lying piece of shit neck."

Daryl goes into Justice's top desk drawer and pulls out a piece of paper, freshly typed. He hands it to David, who carefully reads it.

I give permission to the Galena Police Department to search my premises at the Cedar Grand Trailer Park. I further give permission to the Galena Police Department to confiscate any evidence that they consider relevant to any investigation against me. I grant this permission freely of my own free will and hold harmless the Galena Police Department and any of their personnel from any liability as a result of this search.

"You're going to sign this and open the briefcase before Lieutenant Justice comes back from his coffee break."

David can't be sure that Sunny has followed the plan and left the trailer, so he plays for time. "I have the right to a phone call."

Daryl unzips his fly. "You have the right to suck my dick."

David's fear has made him numb. "You must know I'm not going to do any of that. Including the dick invite."

Daryl turns David around and hits him in the kidneys. David barely remains standing. Daryl then points to the chair next to Justice's desk. "Sit down." As David sits down, Daryl takes two pairs of handcuffs out of a desk and cuffs each of David's wrists to an arm of the chair.

David uses humor to cope. "I had a girlfriend that wanted to do this."

"Spread your legs."

"What?"

"You heard me. I said, spread your legs!"

David spreads his legs. Only the tighty whities cover his private appendages. He estimates that Daryl wears a size twelve cowboy boot because Daryl puts that boot between David's legs mere inches from his groin. David quickly closes his legs around the boot.

"Did I tell you to close your legs? Open them... now!"

David opens his legs, and the point of Daryl's boot wedges into David's scrotum, trapping his testicles between the toe of his boot and the seat of the metal chair. Daryl slowly presses down his toes. David calls for help. Nothing. Daryl presses harder. Nobody comes in.

David thinks of Sunny. *Keep this going as long as you can to make sure she's gone.* He grits his teeth with the pain. Somewhere, he remembers a doctor telling him, after getting hit in the balls, that testicles are very resilient. He hopes that's true because this is like getting kicked in the balls in slow motion. And the pain comes and goes at this owlish cop's discretion as he alternately squishes down and eases the pressure. David's helplessness is as bad as the pain.

Daryl puts his face inches from David's. David can practically taste his bad breath and nicotine-stained teeth. "Look, moron, why are you making this so hard on yourself? Open the case and sign the paper. Then I'll put you back in your nice comfy cell."

"I want a lawyer. I want a phone call."

"We all want shit, don't we? Oh well, I tried."

Daryl goes to his desk drawer and takes out a cigar. He cuts it with what appears to be a cigar guillotine. The end of the cigar snaps off neatly. He opens and closes the blade a couple of times, holding it in front of David's face. Then he grabs David's left pinky and puts the pinky into the cigar cutter. David feels the sharp metal touch his skin and wonders about two things. One, how bad will it hurt getting his finger cut off, and two, will he ever get laid again with a deformed hand? "How about I just open the case?"

Daryl pulls the cigar cutter away from David's pinky and puts it away. He lights the cigar, savoring the flavor, and blows clouds of smoke in David's face. Then he draws deeply on the cigar and holds David's right arm in place. David jerks helplessly against the cuffs and Daryl's grip as the cigar slowly gets closer to his skin. Daryl raises his eyebrows in delight as he burns about three inches of flesh on the inside of David's forearm near the elbow.

"You really want to negotiate?" The palm of Daryl's big hand grabs David by the forehead. His index finger on the same hand pulls David's eyelid back. He holds the cigar precariously over David's open eye like a flaming dagger.

"No. You win."

Daryl lets go of David's eye. He takes his time and finishes the cigar while gazing at David, naked and shaking with both fear and the cold air conditioning against his bare skin. Then he takes the cuffs off and hands David a pen. David signs the release.

"Open the case."

David opens the case.

Daryl uncuffs David and puts the handcuffs back into the desk drawer. He tells David to get dressed. When David is dressed, Daryl goes into the other room. He comes back a minute later with Justice and Clint.

"Robert here has decided to cooperate." Daryl removes the envelope from the case and hands it to Justice. "I'm pretty sure this here's your cousin's money." He hands Justice the release. "Robert also signed this release so we can go search his trailer."

Justice is pleased and not surprised. "Well, good job, Officer. Let's put Mr. Marino here back in his cell and go check out his place."

Clint brings David uncuffed into his cell and locks the door. When he's gone, David stands on the piss-soaked concrete floor in front of the grimy metal sink. He fills his hands with water and splashes it onto his face. He pushes the sink water plunger faucet several times and runs cold water over his arm burn. Then he looks over at the thin foam mattress on the metal bunk. It has footprints like someone stood on it to reach something. David doesn't care. He lies down on his back and breathes in and out and immediately falls asleep.

CHAPTER 42

DAVID is gone as effectively as if he were abducted by aliens. No call. No clue as to what happened. Sunny knows that something has gone wrong with David's plan, but she doesn't know what. Was he arrested? Was he killed? Was he in a car accident on the way back to the trailer park? All these horrible thoughts cross her mind and tear at her soul along with an overwhelming loneliness. One thing she knows: when you're a thief, you can't call the cops.

Another thing Sunny knows: if David is alive, she must keep herself safe to help him. She takes the cash, clothes, and personal items, and anything else she thinks she'll need. She calls a taxi and has the driver take her to a hotel in Fort Worth. She checks in as Susan Wilder and immediately starts calling attorneys from the Yellow Pages. She makes the earliest appointment she can for the next day.

Early the next morning, on Saturday, Sunny meets with Travis Cassidy, attorney at law, in his office. After assurances of confidentiality, Sunny tells him how they tried to con money from the diner and that David has disappeared.

Travis sits at his desk and takes it all in. "I've never met anyone like you and your son before. I usually do traffic violations and domestic stuff. I don't know if I can defend him, but if he has been arrested, I should be able to file a writ and get him a bond hearing."

Sunny's face is both stoic and desperate. Her voice is the frantic rhythm of a mother seeking her child. "Is he even alive? I just need to know where he is. If he's all right."

"Let me make some calls." Travis calls the Galena Police Department. The call goes unanswered, so he leaves a message. "No answer. I don't know what we can do before Monday."

Sunny stands up and leans across his desk. "Can you go over to the police department and ask in person?"

Travis turns in the executive chair behind his desk. "I don't think it will help."

Sunny goes into her purse and takes out cash. "Will you do it for two hundred dollars?"

Travis thinks this over. "Look, it's your money. If you want to pay me to make a fool's trip to the Galena Police Station, sure, I'll do it for you."

Sunny gives Travis two hundred-dollar bills. Travis makes some other calls and drives to the Galena Police Station. Clint is on desk duty.

Travis comes in wearing his Stetson hat and lizard-skin boots. He sees Clint at the front desk. "How are you doing? Travis Cassidy. I'm an attorney out of Fort Worth." He hands Clint a business card. Scales of justice are on the front above his name. "I'm looking for a young man that you might have detained yesterday. Robert Marino. Do you have him in custody?"

Clint studies the card for several long seconds. "No, we didn't arrest anyone yesterday. It was quiet." Travis notices that Clint can't hold eye contact with him. Clint has a forced smile that drips insincerity.

"Are you sure? Maybe he was arrested while you were off duty. The kid is missing. Were there any accidents in town?"

Clint covers his mouth with the business card as he talks. "No, counselor. Not that I know of. Maybe you can check back Monday when we have a full staff."

Travis narrows his eyes and glares at Clint for several seconds. Finally, he thanks him and heads back to his office. Clint immediately calls Justice.

CHAPTER 43

JUSTICE shows up fifteen minutes later with a file folder of papers confiscated from David's trailer. He spreads them out on his desk. He looks at Clint with blood in his eyes. "How the fuck did that asshat get a lawyer?"

Clint meekly shrugs. He cowers at Justice's anger. "I don't know. The guy just showed up. I didn't say anything."

Ten minutes later, Daryl shows up with several coffees. Ten minutes after that, the Galena Assistant State Attorney shows up with his own coffee and a pissed-off expression. He wears cut off blue jeans and a "disco sucks" tee-shirt. "Why am I here on a Saturday?"

Justice takes one of the coffees from Daryl. "Because we got ourselves a serial con man. From what I can tell, this Robert Marino, or whatever the hell his real name is, has been all over the country pulling cons. I guess he has an attorney, but we have him dead to rights."

Justice proudly hands the assistant state attorney an American Express check receipt from the stacks of papers on the desk. "It looks like he has been forging traveler's checks." Then he hands the ASA some partially filled-out property deeds. He displays them between his hands like a court exhibit. "I think he's been forging property deeds and somehow collecting money on them." He grabs a stack of papers and slides them across the desk to the ASA. "Thirty health insurance applications under different names. "Who knows what he plans to do with these?"

The assistant state attorney takes the paperwork from Justice. "Has he done anything here in Galena?"

"Fuck, yeah. He tried to scam my cousin out of eleven grand. He would have succeeded, too, if my cousin didn't have a cop in the family who could put a stop to it. Here is a quit claim deed to the vacant property next door."

The assistant state attorney scans the paperwork. "How did you find all of this incriminating evidence?"

"At his trailer."

The ASA drops the papers on the desk like they caught fire. "How and when did you get a search warrant?"

Justice scoops up the dropped papers off the desk and holds them out for the assistant state attorney to take from him. "I didn't need one. He voluntarily let us search his place." He triumphantly hands the signed release to the ASA.

The assistant state attorney examines the release and the signature portion. He frowns at the signature line. "What is this? It looks like U.D."

Justice looks more carefully at the signature. A not-so-well-known fact about David is that he uses the same undecipherable scrawl to sign every name he uses. No one can tell if it's the right name. Justice sees the U.D. and gives the document to Clint. He points to the U.D. "Go back to the cell and find out what this means."

Clint goes back to the cell where David is lying on the bunk.

David hasn't eaten in over eighteen hours. "Hey, don't you guys have to bring me some food?"

"Yeah, sure." Clint holds up the paper and points to the signature. "What does U.D. mean?"

David smiles. "Under duress."

Clint comes back with the document. "It means 'under duress.' "

The assistant state attorney slams his hand down on Justice's desk. Papers fall off in protest. "What... did... you... do?"

No one says anything.

"I need to know now. What did you do?" Justice looks at Daryl, who stammers an answer.

"I might have smacked him around a little."

The ASA glares at Daryl without a blink. "How little?"

No one answers.

Justice nonchalantly holds his hands up. "Look, we didn't leave any marks. It's the word of a piece of shit con man against three cops."

Daryl stares at his size twelve boots.

"What?" The assistant state attorney growls at Daryl.

Daryl is still looking at his boots. "He wasn't going to sign the form. I might've pushed a little too hard."

The ASA stands in front of Daryl. "What the fuck does that mean?"

Daryl can't take his eyes off the floor. "I... burned him. But just a little bit."

"You burned him? With what?"

Daryl doesn't say anything. Justice looks at Daryl. Eyes blazing like, well, justice. "What did you do, Daryl?"

Daryl looks up, pleading at Justice. "I used a cigar and burned him a little on his arm."

The assistant district attorney stands up and sweeps his arms over Justice's desk, scattering the papers to the floor. "Fruit of the poisonous tree."

Justice motions for Clint to pick the paperwork up off the floor. "What is that?"

"Fruit of the poisonous tree? It means none of this is worth shit. And I should prosecute y'all for at least a half dozen felonies, including being ignorant redneck assholes. You want to play cops and robbers? You need to learn the rules. Tell me something. Is this kid a nigger?"

The cops stare at each other with guilt and fear in their eyes.

Justice answers for them all. "No. He's a white boy."

"So, you got a white boy in lockup," the assistant state attorney's voice roars, "with an attorney!" He takes a breath to control himself. "You tortured him like you were the Viet Cong to get a worthless search release. Then you broke in and searched his house." The ASA stands up from his chair. "Did I get all this right? Am I missing something? Come Monday, maybe Tuesday, I wouldn't be surprised if his attorney calls the FBI and makes a civil rights complaint. Are you ready for that?"

To a man, they look like they've eaten a big salad and found hairy worms at the bottom of the bowl. The assistant state attorney stands and waits for someone to say something.

Justice obliges. "What about my cousin?"

"This is a quit claim deed. It conveys whatever interest that this kid had in the property. He has no interest, so he gave no interest. It promises nothing. What else you got?" The assistant state attorney leans on the desk with his closed fists, glaring at each of the cops.

Justice doesn't return his gaze. "What can we do?"

The ASA stops leaning and runs his hands through his hair. "Let him go with an apology?" He turns his gaze out the window. "Maybe. Just maybe, if you can get him to confess—legally, not with your redneck abuse—you can swap that evidence and still make a case. Did you read him his Miranda rights?"

"Technically, we never formally arrested him for anything. He's never been booked."

The assistant state attorney picks up his half empty cup of coffee and heads to the door. He opens the door, throws the dregs onto the sidewalk, and puts the empty cup onto a windowsill. "This gets better and better. Cut him loose. And pray to Jesus that this blows over."

The ASA then stares at Justice. "One more thing. I was never here. It's Saturday, and I'm out with my kids. Got it? Not here!" He leaves and slams the door on the way out, cursing under his breath.

They sit silently for a long time. Clint's face is a knot of torment. He whines at Justice, "I can't go to jail."

"No one's going to jail except the asshole we got locked up. Invite him to join us and follow my lead."

Clint goes to the cells and opens David's door. He motions David into the offices. David hesitantly enters and sees Justice and Daryl both have friendly smiles pasted on their faces.

Justice stands up and greets David like an old friend. "Come in. We need to talk. We've been to your place, and we want to talk to you about some of the brilliant cons you've managed to pull off."

Daryl says to Clint, "You know, if this guy was at Watergate, Nixon would still be in the White House. Some of this stuff is amazing."

Justice says to Clint, "Can you believe that this guy got a deed from a piece of property and sold it to a third party?" He looks at David. "For… what was it? Five grand? Fifteen grand?" David says nothing.

Justice offers him a chair. "David. Have you eaten anything?"

David cautiously sits down. "No."

"Clint. Get David a burger from the diner. And French fries. Me too. David, do you want a shake?"

David looks around the room like he's somewhere other than the Galena Police Department. His eyes settle back on Justice. "Sure."

"What flavor?"

"Any flavor is good."

Clint heads to the diner. Justice notices the burn on David's arm and asks if he can see it. "Daryl, get the first aid kit. I'm sure we have some burn salve in there."

Daryl reluctantly gets the first aid kit, and Justice puts salve on the burn. The relief is immediate.

David has no clue what is happening. He wants to keep the goodwill going as long as possible, and he doesn't want to give them more reasons to torture him. They talk about where David's been. How he likes Texas. David's family. And occasionally, they fish for crimes that David has committed. David tries to go right to the edge without implicating himself.

After Clint gets back with the food and they eat, Justice tells David, "I'm sorry, but I'm afraid you've got to stay here through Monday. Clint, take our guest back to his cell."

As David gets up, he palms a nail clipper off Justice's desk. He doesn't know why, but he reasons that anything they don't know he has will give him an advantage.

Justice's smile stretches across his face like a Welcome to Texas billboard. "We'll talk again Monday and see if we'll prosecute you or not for stealing from my cousin. We'll know something soon."

Clint brings David back to the cell and locks the door.

CHAPTER 44

DAVID spends Sunday morning and afternoon alone in his dark, grimy cell. He stares at the bars and catwalk and tries to make sense of the changes in attitude. His normal rule is that a happy cop is a bad cop. What does it mean when these guys have made a hundred-and-eighty-degree shift?

With absolutely nothing to do, David has plenty of time to analyze the situation. He doesn't pray much, but he does now. And he doesn't like to break promises, especially to the Lord. He doesn't pray for redemption or promise to reform. Instead, he prays, *Lord, if you guide me back to freedom, I swear I will never return to Texas.* And he knows he never will.

He sizes up the situation. *They tortured me for permission to search my place. If they found my mother, they would be gloating about it. Which means they didn't. Did they find anything? Probably. Maybe they simply have everything they need to send me away, and they no longer have a reason to act like the assholes they are.* There are too many questions with too few answers. David stops speculating.

That afternoon, they bring in another prisoner. They put him in the cell to the left of David. David hears the door clang closed and the heavy lock snap. There's a thin metal wall between the cells.

The new guy rustles around his cell and mumbles curses to himself. He kicks the door bars and shouts in frustration. "Ey. What you in for, homey?"

David moves toward the adjoining wall between the cells. "Mistaken identity."

"Yeah. Right. They busted me with a joint. You been here long?"

David sits with his back to the wall. "Since Friday."

"Man, you must be buggin'. What's your name?"

"Robert. Yours?"

"I'm Moe."

Moe and David hear a distant police radio. Moe gives it another five minutes until the radio stops, and he hears the cops leave the station. He tells David in a softer voice, "You in trouble, man."

"Yeah, I know."

There is a pause and Moe's voice is softer. "No, you don't. Why they so scared of you?"

"I have no clue what you're talking about."

"All I know is that they busted me with a joint. A lousy joint! They told me they'd let me go if I could get you to talk about some sort of game you been runnin'."

David frowns and puts his ear closer to the wall. "So why tell me?"

Moe is silent for fifteen long seconds. "These fuckers crippled my brother. They came out by our crib. We didn't know it was po-po. We thought it was KKK or some shit. Anyway, my brother comes out with his heater and fires it to scare them away."

"Who did he hit?"

"He didn't hit shit. After he fires, the po-po come out with their po-po broomstick. They yell 'Police!' And my brother drops his rod."

"And he was arrested?"

"Yeah, but after he drops his rod, he holds up his hands and yells, 'I surrender!' I was there. I saw him do it."

Moe is silent for several more seconds. "He gave up. He put up his hands and dropped his rod. And after he surrendered, the fuckin' po-po said, 'No you don't.' They aimed low and blew his legs off. They crippled my brother for not a damn thing."

"I'm sorry."

"Point is, I ain't never seen them talk about no one like they talked about you. They want you bad. And I swear to Jesus H. Christ that if they don't get something, they gonna take you into some woods out of town and put one in the back of yo head. You dig it?"

They hear voices past the cells and shut up. Clint comes in with sandwiches in cardboard containers for each of them. He brings the sandwiches to each door, looks carefully at each cell, and silently leaves.

David has been feeling pending doom since he was arrested. This confirms his fear. He gets as close to the cell as he can and speaks very softly. "Maybe you can help me."

"What you mean?"

"If I get out, I'm going to need a ride. You got a car?"

"Yeah. I drive my brother's car. But you ain't gettin' out. And even if you did, why should I help you and get myself in deep shit?"

David unboxes his sandwich. "First, I'll give you information to give them to get out of here now. Second, I'll get you three hundred dollars."

"You ain't got no three hundred dollars."

"You'll get it as soon as I get picked up."

"Five hundred dollars."

"Four hundred dollars. And three, it will really stick it to the Galena po-po for your brother. If they're afraid of me, it will make them insane to lose me. It's a small revenge, but still revenge."

"Okay. Sure. How you gonna reach me?"

"You got a phone?"

Moe laughs. "Yeah, you got a pen to write down my number?"

David laughs. "Yeah, I kind of do. Give me your digits slowly."

Moe tells David his phone number, and David uses the file end of the nail clippers to carve the number onto the cardboard that the burger came in. He tucks it into the ass of his tighty whities.

Moe says, "So, here's the thing. Find a payphone. Call the operator and tell her you want to call my number collect. When she starts to put the call through, just say 'Help.' Say it clearly. I'll hear it and know it's you and you need help. I live close, and I've been here all my life. Stay hid for ten minutes and I'll come and find you."

"How will you find me?"

"For four hundred dollars, I'll find you. I know every hole around in this place."

David looks at the plain bologna sandwich on white bread and takes a bite. "Tell the po-po I bragged about passing fifty grand in bad checks from the Wells Fargo Bank in Dallas under the name John Silverman. The Jewish name should make them salivate."

They spend the next few hours talking about music, TV shows, and Moe's family. Soon, Clint comes for Moe, and David doesn't see him again.

The next morning, Monday, Clint comes for David. "Come on, you have court."

David is thrilled. He can plead his case to a real judge. Maybe he'll get a bond.

The court is in the same building on a higher level. The halls are filled with attorneys, cops, and Galenians who have business with the court. David is the only one handcuffed. They bring him before the bench along with the assistant state attorney and Justice.

The judge addresses David. "I see here that you are being charged with check fraud. How do you plead?"

David, still handcuffed, stands up from his chair pushing it back. "Your Honor, I haven't been charged. I've been kidnapped by these police. I've been tortured, held for days without a phone call, and not allowed an attorney."

The judge isn't moved. "I'll enter a plea of not guilty. Make sure he gets a phone call." It's over in less than a minute.

Justice escorts David to the hall and half drags, half throws David onto a bench bolted into the wall.

David looks up, his face a mask of anger. "What about my phone call?"

Justice's sinister smile returns. "You've already had it."

The assistant state attorney comes out and taps Justice on the shoulder. "The judge wants to see us."

Justice takes the handcuffs and chains David to the bench. "He'll be fine there. Let's go."

Justice and the assistant state attorney disappear into the courtroom. David waits five minutes. No one is paying attention to him. He knows it's now or never. He reaches with his free hand to the nylon thread around the belt loop and removes the handcuff key that he picked up in New Orleans, that Sal made fun of him for.

David takes the cuffs off completely from both ends and puts them in his pocket. He sees a pay phone at the end of the hall. He takes out the cardboard with Moe's number from his underwear. He casually walks to the phone and dials zero. The phone rings. And rings. And rings. David can barely stand the wait.

Finally, he hears, "Operator."

David moves close to the phone and covers the speaker and his mouth with his hand. "I need to make a collect call." He gives her the number and the name Robert. The moment the phone answers David clearly says, "Help."

The operator says, "I have a collect call from Robert."

David again says, "Help."

The operator, understanding this is a secret message, disconnects the call.

David hangs up the phone, walks to the exit, and takes the stairs to the street level. He takes the stairs two at a time and fast walks out of the lobby and through the parking lot to the vacant wooded areas on the other side of the street. He hides by the outbuildings, scanning for any pursuers. There are none.

There are scorpions and spiders the size of frogs. David recalls the venomous red ants. He's the exact opposite of a survivalist. He hates the woods, the desert, or any place where there isn't air conditioning and room service.

Now he's hiding amid vile insect predators. He waits and looks for Moe. Nothing. *How long has it been? Five minutes? Five hours? Did Moe get the message? Was he just bullshitting me? A jailhouse promise he didn't intend to keep?*

David has no other plan except hope that the insects don't do too much damage while he thinks of an escape plan. He swats. He slaps. He scans the ground and skies for predatory bugs. His mind turns off. He has no plans. He just wants to survive. And then he's no longer worried about the insects. Because he hears a clear... rattle. David had forgotten about snakes. He hears a rattler, and he has no idea what direction it's in.

He freezes in place. A move in any direction could bring him closer to a rattlesnake bite that would get him caught or, more likely, dead. He stays in one place for what seems like a month. Suddenly, he sees a long branch come from behind him. The branch has a fork at the end and moves under the snake. In one quick motion, the branch flicks the snake ten feet away from David.

Moe grabs David by the arm. "Let's go."

They run to the other side of the outbuilding, where Moe's car is parked. Moe unlocks his door and reaches inside to get the front passenger's lock for David. "How'd you get out?"

David holds up the handcuff key and handcuffs. He throws them into Moe's back seat. "Here. A bonus present. Thanks for saving my life."

"Yeah. About that. I think that brings the cost back to five hundred dollars."

David touches Moe's shoulder as Moe floors the gas. "Yeah. It does."

Moe drives David to a pay phone between Galena and Bedford. David calls his sister Ava.

"Hello?"

"It's David."

"Oh. Thank the Lord."

"Can you reach Mom?"

"Yeah. She has an attorney for you."

David gives her the location of the pay phone. "Tell her to come pick me up and bring five hundred dollars."

* * *

Justice finishes with the assistant state attorney and comes back to the empty bench.

He turns to one of the deputies on duty. "Did you see anyone escort my prisoner somewhere?"

The deputy just shrugs. Justice goes downstairs to the jail and, finding no David, he frantically goes back to the court. He sees the ASA talking with the judge. He snarls at him. "He escaped."

The judge looks down from the bench. "The kid you just brought in?"

"Yeah. I had him cuffed to the bench, and he escaped. I'm going to canvass the area."

The assistant state attorney tugs on Justice's wrist to stop him. "No. You're not. He just gave you a gift."

Justice shrugs off his hand. "He's an escapee."

"You never booked him. You tortured him. He has a lawyer. Believe me, this is a gift. Leave it alone. With luck, no one finds him. He leaves Texas and never comes back, and you're home free."

* * *

When Sunny arrives in a taxi, she holds David so close that he can't breathe.

"Mom, this is Moe. He saved my life."

Sunny hugs Moe. "How can I thank you?"

Moe and David say in unison, "Five hundred dollars."

Sunny counts out five one-hundred-dollar bills and pays Moe. She pushes David into the open taxi door. "Let's get out of here."

They drive to Sunny's hotel room, where David gives her his news.

PART VI: JOLIET, ILLINOIS

CHAPTER 45

DAVID and Sunny are finally in her hotel room. Thick traces of tears streak their faces after David tells Sunny what happened. David sits on the bed. Sunny sits next to him on an ugly orange desk chair and squeezes his hand in hers to show she feels his pain.

"I'm out," David says to Sunny like Jesus addressing Peter. "Yeah, it's all fun and games until Sheriff Andy Taylor's psychotic cousin and his demonic deputies in Cow Shit, Texas, who think that civil rights are an etiquette column, decide it's fine to torture suspects and Black folks. Did I ever tell you I hate Texas?"

Sunny lets go of David's hand and wipes her eyes. "Every day that we've been here."

David looks out the window and snarls. "I don't think that it's any coincidence Kennedy was assassinated one town over." He fingers his Saint Dismas medal. "Chris told me this represents redemption. It's time I get over myself and my ambition and focus on getting life back to what it used to be."

Sunny moves and sits on the bed next to David. She squeezes his leg in a gesture of understanding. "Whatever you want to do, you know I'm here for you." She goes to the bathroom for the sixth time for a Kleenex and comes back. "What about the problem in Florida? We've still got to make that go away for you to have a normal life."

David stands up and heads for the door. "Yeah, I know. I'm going to take a walk and grab some pop. You want anything?"

Sunny stands up and shakes her head. "No, you go ahead. I want to check something out."

When David leaves, Sunny calls Information for Lex Haller, the attorney from Florida whose demand for ten thousand dollars sent them on the road to this fugitive life.

The phone rings and rings. Finally, someone answers. "Abraham and Haller."

"Is Lex Haller in?"

"Who may I say is calling?"

"Tell him it's Sunny Rossi."

"One moment please." A brief pause. "Please hold for Mr. Haller." Another, longer pause.

"Lex Haller."

"Mr. Haller, this is Sunny Rossi. I don't know if you remember me."

Sunny hears papers shuffling. Haller is searching for a file. "I do remember you, Mrs. Rossi. Your son jumped bond at the arraignment. The court issued a warrant."

Sunny tries to control her breathing to keep her cool. "Yes. I remember it well. What will it take to clear it up?"

"Ms. Rossi, a warrant is like a heat-seeking missile. It flies around in the system until it finds its target—in this case your son—and it explodes on his body as he's being arrested. Nothing can stop it."

Sunny breathes in for a count of two and out for a count of four. "We only ran because you told us we needed ten thousand dollars to keep him from going to prison."

There are several moments of silence. Sunny hears Haller place the phone on the desk. She hears footsteps and a door close. She hears Haller pick up the phone. "Ms. Rossi, I probably shouldn't have said that to you. The fact is there is a lot of drug money floating around South Florida. Hell, make that all of Florida. Attorneys are expected to get results for the generous fees we receive. Hold on." Sunny hears Haller tell his receptionist to hold his calls. "Because of this, judges are willing to settle cases quickly if they get their beaks wet."

"Beaks wet?"

Haller's voice turns gruff. "Don't play naïve. You know what I'm saying."

Sunny quickly exhales. No more breath control. "Yeah, I get it. Ten grand buys David out of this jam."

"It would have. Back then, but not today. He didn't show up. I'd need to convince the judge to quash the warrant. It's more exposure for the judge. Plus, David would have to get the hospital to drop the charges on the check. He'd have to pay it."

"So how much are we talking about?"

"The judge would require twenty thousand dollars. Cash, of course. I would require a thousand dollars to prepare the motion. I don't need cash. And, of course, the check to the hospital would have to be settled."

Sunny scribbles all of this down on a hotel notepad. "Thank you, Mr. Haller, I'll be in touch."

"No problem. And call me Lex."

In his tone, Sunny hears Lex flirt. She uses her most honeyed voice back. "Thank you, Lex. I'll be in touch."

When David returns, Sunny shares her conversation with Haller.

David's blood boils. "Let me get this straight: I was placed in this situation because of a greedy lawyer and a corrupt judge?"

Sunny punches a table and scowls. "Looks like."

David feels a plan forming like a tickle in the back of his head. "Mom, neither of us is in any shape to get out of here tonight. Let's get a good night's sleep and talk about it in the morning."

The next morning, David's plan is formed. Sunny takes him out to a large breakfast of scrambled eggs with cheese, hash browns, sausage, and pancakes at the hotel restaurant. It's too early to serve burgers.

Between bites and sips of Coke, David talks solemnly. "Mom, much as I don't want to, I think it's best if we split up. I'm kind of nostalgic for Chicago. I'll go there and take care of Florida. You go back to Los Angeles. Deal with whatever stuff we have there. Tell Chris what happened and that I'll be in touch when I'm able."

Sunny stares in silence at David. "What's your plan? I know you have one."

For the first time, David hesitates to share his plan with Sunny. "I don't want you to worry."

"Now I'm definitely worried." Sunny's and David's pale blue eyes fix each other's gaze. David cracks first. He tells Sunny his plans.

Sunny notices her hands shaking and presses them on the table to stop them. "That's insane! Do you really think you can do it?"

"Yeah. It's a challenge, but I think I can pull it off."

CHAPTER 46

THEY don't have anywhere near twenty thousand dollars left. Sunny and David drive silently in a rental car to Oklahoma's Will Rogers World Airport.

All the while, David stares out the passenger window at the cursed flat land of Texas and watches the street signs incessantly. He audibly exhales when they cross the Oklahoma border.

"I expect that the plan will take two months to execute. Hopefully, we'll be done at the same time."

Sunny looks away from the road to David. "You'll keep in touch?"

"Every day. I won't be distracted and won't stop until the job is done. Then we can see each other again."

Sunny drops David at Departures. He has no bag. Sunny climbs out of the car with him to give him one final long embrace. She came so close to losing him. Now, after just a couple of days, it feels like she's losing him again. They've been through so much in the past couple of years. Sunny's heart breaks, but she manages to muster a smile. She won't cry until long after she leaves the state of Oklahoma.

David flies to O'Hare Airport in Chicago. He takes a taxi from the airport to Rent a Wreck, a car rental service that needs no credit and has cheap daily rates. He rents a 1969 baby blue Ford Fairlane with large rust spots on the fenders and doors where the blue paint is scraped off. The air conditioning doesn't work, and the windows stick. But the engine runs, and it has everything David needs.

He spends the first night in the car and the next day, he heads to Joliet, where he rents a cheap, furnished walkup studio apartment. The neighborhood reminds him of where he and Lester used to chase the deadbeats in Florida. The walls of the apartment are puke green and the gray porch railings are missing half their iron. Security and one small month's rent. It's perfect for his base of operations. Time to get to work.

After a visit to an art store, David settles into his mission. He left his ID equipment and baptismal certificates in Los Angeles, so he goes to lower tech. He creates a realistic traffic ticket under another false identity. He drives to Indiana and uses the traffic ticket to purchase American Express traveler's checks. He doesn't have a lot of money to start, but it doesn't take long before he gets enough money for a stake to get the job done.

David studies a hundred-dollar bill like monks study an ancient scroll. He evaluates the quality and color of the paper and the colors of the inks. He spends a week contemplating the intricacies of the bill. He notices all the patterns. He notices how the numbers in the four corners of the bill correspond to the first letter of the serial number. He studies the various messages hidden in the intricate designs. He scrutinizes the watermarks and the raised quality of the ink.

He mounts two pieces of posterboard to his wall. In the middle of one, he tapes the front of a hundred-dollar bill. In the middle of the other, he tapes the back of a hundred-dollar bill. All around each of the bills, David scribbles notes on what he must do to reproduce those bills himself.

United States currency is one of the most intricate engravings in the country. Expert artists create master dies that are used to create perfect engraving plates. The ink used is thicker than commercially available ink. The printing process is intaglio. The ink flows into the recesses of the engraving plates and leaves a tactile impression on the bills. And the paper is impossible to replicate exactly. It's a combination of cotton and linen that resists wear and tear. It has an unmistakable feel, and the color is an odd green with barely perceptible red and blue filaments.

But the hardest thing to duplicate is the US Treasury seal. It's printed under the denomination of the bill so that the seal is always obscured by the word. Unless you happen to be an artist of the highest order, it's almost impossible to recreate the seal.

David takes each challenge in order. He tests hundreds of paper samples until he finds one close enough to pass muster. He blends various inks for color and thickness until he finds the combinations he needs. He goes to the library, checks out everything he can find on intaglio printing, and replicates that process.

But he doesn't have the skill to replicate the Treasury seal. He's so close, but it doesn't mean anything. He tries to freehand it, but he isn't that talented. He tries to copy it, but it can't really be copied under the "100" printed over it. David begins to feel that, not for the first time, he has failed. And with that failure, he remains a fugitive.

Defeated, since he can't complete such an essential part of the counterfeit, David heads to the library to return the books on printing. On a hunch, he looks up US Treasury Department in the *Encyclopedia Britannica* and finds, to his astonishment, that under the entry is the US Treasury seal. Problem solved.

Like a painter creating a masterpiece on a blank canvas, David starts the process. He needs two hundred passable one-hundred-dollar bills. He spends a month staying in and eating quick frozen meals, sleeping four hours a night, and churning out hundred-dollar bills on a hand-crank portable printing press with random serial numbers. Each is separated with a standard paper slicer.

David hangs bills everywhere in his apartment to dry. Bills hang on long pieces of rope on the shower curtain rod. Bills hang from curtain rods behind blackout curtains. Bills hang all over the kitchen. The more he makes, the better he gets at it. He burns the first bills and replaces them with better replicas. He pays no attention to anything but making money.

At eight in the evening, to the hour, once David has completed the two hundred bills, there's a knock on his door that echoes through the apartment. It's insistent and demands immediate attention. His blood freezes. He starts to pull bills off clips. Then he hears pleading in Spanish from the other side of the door.

"*Ayuda. Por favor ayuda.*" Help. Please help! David cracks the door. He speaks the only full Spanish sentence he knows. "*No hablo Espanol.*"

The boy at the door is maybe fifteen years old. He's thin and wears a ratty white tee-shirt, jeans, and no shoes. He struggles with his words.

"Please... use... phone."

The last thing David can do is let anyone use his phone. "What is it? *Que pasa?*"

All the boy can say is, "*Nina.* Baby. Please help."

David steps out into the hall and locks his door behind him. The kid leads him down the hall where there is a half-open door. David steps inside the door. The first thing he sees are three children of various ages sitting on a sofa watching television. The second thing he sees is an older man holding his hands in front of him like they have second-degree burns. The older man repeats over and over, "I have turpentine on my hands. I can't help."

The third thing that David sees is a woman. Maybe in her thirties. Short, black hair. Big pregnant belly. She's wearing a short-sleeved, button-down blouse with a butterfly pattern. That is paired with green polyester pants that are now pooled at her feet along with her panties as she lies writhing on a soiled carpet.

David is stunned. Of course, he's heard about women delivering babies outside of a hospital, but always with someone who knows what they're doing. He has no freakin' clue what to do. And he has an apartment full of counterfeit bills to conceal.

He runs back to his apartment and gets a pair of new disposable gloves that he uses for mixing inks. He tells the older man who seems to understand some English to, "First, get me a clean towel. Then find a payphone, call the operator, and get an ambulance. *Ahora!*"

The man brings David a yellow cotton bath towel with fringed edges. David lays it under the pregnant woman's rapidly expanding vulva. He uses it to cover the grimy carpet.

"Help is coming. Can you, maybe, not push?" David has no idea what that means. He thinks he saw it in an episode of *Marcus Welby, MD*.

As soon as he says the words, a mass comes out of the woman. David can tell it must be the head and, sure enough, it's with the rest of the baby right behind, covered in slime.

David catches the baby in the towel. The baby is tangled in a cord like a spider caught in its own web. Slowly, carefully, David unties the cord from the baby's neck and frees it from the baby's body. He wraps the baby in the towel and places it on the mother's chest.

His first instinct is to go back to his apartment and lock the door behind him. But he knows someone will come looking for him. He stays until the ambulance arrives and lets the ambulance driver cut the cord and take the mother and baby to the hospital.

But David knows as sure as the Lord made little green apples that this apartment is now done. He doesn't have time to indulge the satisfaction or the humility he feels at helping to bring a new life into the world. It's time to move on to the next part of the plan.

CHAPTER 47

AFTER weeks of near-constant printing, David has two hundred passable counterfeit hundred-dollar bills in a Marshal Fields shopping bag that he found in a dumpster. He's no master counterfeiter, but he reasons that bills to bribe a judge won't see a bank until his verdict is decided. He stashes the cash under a blanket on the floor well of his car's passenger seat.

He loads all the remaining ink, paper, printing plates, and equipment into black garbage bags and stashes the bags in the car trunk. Then he carefully drives to a dump in the next county and carries it all to the biggest garbage pile he can find. David handles everything with disposable plastic gloves, so he has no fear of prints should anything ever be discovered.

He then calls Sunny in Los Angeles from a pay phone and gives her a progress report. She's astonished as he tells her about the baby's delivery.

"Did you talk to the hospital about the check?" he finally asks.

Sunny writes on a legal pad with notes for her to-do list. "They took twenty-five cents on the dollar for the check. I sent them twelve hundred fifty dollars, and they agreed to send me the original check by overnight mail."

David pumps his fist that it's settled. "Good. I'm done here. Make the call to Haller."

Sunny dials the number. "Mr. Haller, please."

"May I say who's calling?"

"Tell him it's Sunny Rossi."

A pause. A click. "Sunny, it's Lex. What can I do for you?"

Sunny forces a smile so that enmity doesn't come through in her voice. "I told you I'm ready to get David's problem resolved. I have everything you asked for. What's next?"

There is a long pause as Haller considers his next words very carefully.

"When and where can you deliver the money?"

"It will be in overnight mail. Return receipt."

"That's not necessary. This isn't going to happen overnight. I still need to draft the motion and serve it to the State. They'll respond. I'll reply, and then a hearing date will be set. I would say at least ninety days."

"I'll send your fee for the motions and the original check from the hospital right away so you can get started. When will you need the rest of it?"

Haller pauses to sign a brief. "Between my reply brief and the time of trial."

In a voice that is as smooth as velvet to Haller's ears, Sunny says, "Lex, I don't want to be duped, here. I need to know. Will this work?"

Haller confidently says, "No guarantees, but it always has."

"And the judge won't get the money until we know that David is out of trouble?"

"The judge will get the money first, but don't worry. The ruling is assured."

"All right. I trust you, Lex. I'll keep an eye on the court record. After you file your reply, I'll send you the rest."

"I'll get to work after I receive the bad check to the hospital and the payment."

Sunny says nothing for a few seconds. Then in a shy, playful voice she says, "After everything is settled, maybe we can go out and celebrate."

Haller's voice seems to rise a half-octave in anticipation. "That would be great. I'd really like that."

"Goodbye, Lex." Sunny hangs up the phone and detaches the device from the Radio Shack microphone that recorded the entire conversation to a nearby cassette recorder.

The next day, Sunny receives the hospital check at Ava's apartment. She copies the check and sends it with Haller's thousand-dollar payment, in American Express traveler's checks, to Haller's office with Ava's apartment as her return address.

Three months later, after Florida's reply brief is filed, David purchases a used car and drives thirteen hundred miles from Chicago to Memphis, Tennessee. In the car trunk is an expensive Hartman brown ultra suede briefcase. Inside the briefcase is the counterfeit currency.

David drives the speed limit and does nothing to attract attention. His destination is a brand new delivery company called Federal Express. Inside an office that seems as sanitary as an operating room, he fills out the label. He uses a Memphis general delivery return address.

Lex Haller receives the Federal Express box the next day.

His assistant carries the large, white-and-blue box in and drops it on his desk. "This is addressed to you, Mr. Haller."

Haller is on the phone. "Thank you. Just leave it there." He picks up the box by a corner and is surprised at the weight. He carries the box to his car, places it into his trunk, and uses a letter opener to cut the tape. He opens the box.

Inside is a gorgeous briefcase and a note: *Thank you in advance. The case is a little extra gift for the judge. I look forward to seeing you when this is over.* The note is signed by Sunny. Haller smiles with satisfaction and closes the trunk.

That evening, Haller goes to Bachelor's Three, a nightclub and restaurant owned by New York Jets quarterback Joe Namath. It's early enough that the crowd is thin. He carries the briefcase to the bar and approaches a man who appears to be in his mid-forties. The man is dressed discreetly in a gray suit, white shirt, and rep blue tie. His hair, once dark brown, now has hints of gray at the temples. He wears unassuming glasses that may or may not be prescription but make him look scholarly. His face exudes all the warmth of a chemistry textbook. It reveals no emotion whatsoever.

Without a word of conversation, the two men take a table. Haller places the briefcase at his feet. "Hello, Hector. How is the Honorable Judge Diaz?"

"He's good. *Bien.* I read your briefs. It's going to be a coin toss. With all the depraved acts these days, why did this *pendejo* run?"

The server comes by. Haller orders Jack on the rocks. Hector orders a slow gin fizz. Haller gives the server his card for the tab. They both fondle their drinks.

"He's a kid. He didn't know any better."

Hector sips his reddish drink. "I'm sure the judge will take that into consideration."

Haller knows that's code for him to expect a favorable verdict.

They sip their drinks and talk Miami Dolphins. Haller gossips about his conquests with other cases, but Hector is too discreet to contribute. He listens and smiles appropriately.

Just before he finishes his drink, Haller leans onto the table. "Hey, Hector. Do me a favor. I kind of have a thing for the kid's mother. Try to make sure that there aren't any continuances on this. Okay?"

Hector finishes his drink. "There shouldn't be any problem." He lifts the briefcase out from under the table. "This is a beautiful case."

"It's a gift for Judge Diaz."

"It may be a gift for me." Hector downs the remainder of his drink in a gulp and leaves with the case.

David reasons that fake money in an expensive briefcase will give the bills more gravitas. It's like cheap cologne in a fancy bottle. The packaging will help impute the value of the bills and cause the judge to resist placing the bills into another container. And he's right. Hector carries the ultra-suede briefcase like a precious chalice. The bills are neatly stacked in thousand-dollar bundles. Hector takes one of the bills out of each stack and snaps it. It sounds genuine. He's satisfied.

* * *

Oral arguments on Haller's motion are a week later.

The Broward County attorney stands between the prosecutor's table and the judge's bench "Your Honor, this motion should clearly be denied!" She screams her anger at the incredulity of the motion while her hand slashes in accusation at the defendant's table, empty except for Mr. Haller. "The defendant fled the jurisdiction years ago. He has never been caught. Hollywood police describe him as a threat to society. The bondsman lost twenty thousand dollars in bond because he fled. It's against public policy to just quash the warrant. Let him surrender and be brought to trial. If there is no case against him, then let them prove it. At trial!" She glides back to her seat and settles into her chair.

Judge Diaz writes feverishly on a legal pad behind the bench. Haller waits for the judge to signal his turn to speak.

Haller rises confidently. He glides to the front of his table with his notes and fixes his gaze on the judge. "Your Honor, I don't know where Mr. Adler is, but this case should never have been brought by the State of Florida. They have no evidence. They have no original check. The hospital doesn't want to prosecute. There is no victim. Mr. Adler was barely of legal age when he allegedly wrote the check..." He pauses. He turns from the bench, tosses the papers in his hand on his table, and turns back to the judge while he says with indignation, "To help his mother get emergency medical care!"

"Objection!"

Judge Diaz pauses a beat and considers the objection. "Overruled."

"Mr. Adler has no criminal record. None. He was an exemplary student at Miami Beach Senior High. And though, technically, the check amount rises to a felony, it's one bad check. Not a spree. The kid made a mistake. Let him come in from the cold and restart his young life."

Diaz takes a recess to consider the facts and reconvene with a verdict. When he returns, it's clear from his smile toward Haller that David is free from the warrant.

A week after the hearing, an angry Haller stalks, scowling, into Bachelor's Three. Hector doesn't meet him at the bar. Haller searches the room and sees Hector in a far corner of the room, brooding while sipping a whiskey sour. Haller stands over the seated man. "Hector. You better have a damn good reason for dragging me here during a deposition. I had half a dozen people in my office and suddenly you expect me to drop everything?"

Hector calmly extends a hand that motions for Haller to take a seat at the table. With his other hand, he places a hundred-dollar bill on the table between them. "It's fake."

Haller picks up and examines it. "The bill?"

Hector nonchalantly shakes his head. "All twenty grand. Fake. Counterfeit."

Haller looks like he got kicked in the balls with a steel-toed boot. "The Adler money?"

Hector coolly gazes at Haller. "Judge Diaz took a couple of hundred dollars to the Coral Ridge Country Club. He used one to tip his caddy. Even his caddy could tell it was fake. It was very embarrassing for His Honor to be caught tipping his caddy with a counterfeit bill."

Haller drops the bill like it's on fire. He realizes his fingerprints are on it, and he picks it up and wipes it with his napkin. "I'll make it up. I'll get the cash. I'll buy it back."

"There is nothing to buy back. It's gone. Do you think Judge Diaz wants the Secret Service involved in this *mierda*? I took care of the money. It's ash. What you will do is forget you ever heard of me. Forget any interest we have or have had in each other. You're dead to me, and to anyone I represent. You got that?"

Haller's face turns ashen. "Hecter... I have a lot of big cases out there. Drug cases from Mexico and Columbia. They take it very badly when they don't get results from their retainers. They don't pay me for plea bargains. Please, Hector."

Hector motions for the server and pays the tab. "Then get them results. You'll just have to be as good an attorney as you advertise. *Buenas suerte*, Lex. We won't meet again."

Haller is angry. No, he's enraged. He breaks every speed limit as he drives to his office and scours his files for contacts on David or Sunny. He finds Ava's phone number. He closes his office door and dials.

Ava answers. "Hello?"

"This is your brother David's attorney. I need to talk to him or your mother immediately. David is in even bigger trouble than he was before. Please, tell him to call."

"I'll see what I can do."

Ten minutes later, Sunny calls Haller's office.

"Haller and Associates."

"Mr. Haller, please."

"May I say who's calling?" asks his assistant.

"Tell him it's Sunny Rossi."

Haller snatches the phone. "Sunny."

"Yes, Lex."

"Your son gave me counterfeit money."

"I know."

Haller lies. "The Treasury Department is looking for him."

"I don't think so."

Haller squeezes the phone and clenches his teeth. "Listen, you must make this right. You can't do this and get away with it. Counterfeiting is a federal offense."

There is a brief pause. "No, you listen, Lex. If anyone gets the Secret Service involved, we all go down." Sunny plays the tape: *"And the judge won't get the money until we know that David is out of trouble. The judge will get the money first, but don't worry. The ruling is assured."*

"You bitch! You can't use that tape. In Florida, you need two parties to consent to a taped conversation. You just committed a felony yourself!"

Sunny chuckles, amused. She wonders if David has rubbed off on her, or if the apple really didn't fall far from the tree. "In Arizona, where I called you from, you only need one party to consent. I'm not worried, and... thank you for the excellent job with David. Goodbye."

PART VII - SCHAUMBURG, ILLINOIS

CHAPTER 48

1981

DAVID and his wife, Tina, rush to get dressed in semi-formal wear for probably the fifth wedding this year. David wears a vested, brown polyester suit with a tan button-down shirt and a gold tie from Joseph A. Banks. Tina wears her trademark black-and-white palazzo pants paired with a white, pleated satin blouse. Tina's Greek family has more weddings than Chicago theater has opening nights. Tina's two kids, a boy and a girl, ages eleven and nine, from Tina's previous marriage, argue over another mundane thing. Well, mundane to David and Tina. Not to them.

"Fat ass!"

"Kmart Face!"

"Mom! He called me Kmart Face!"

Tina rolls her eyes while Sunny laughs. "Do you want me to take care of them?"

"I would so like that. What does 'Kmart Face' even mean?" Tina is a black-haired beauty who met David at a disco in Melrose Park. A divorced mother of two, she's the hardest worker David ever met. After the Florida verdict, David stayed in the Chicago area and made it permanent when he met Tina.

After dating for a year, David shared everything with Tina. Even before they were married, they felt like soulmates. Please excuse the cliché. Like David, Tina was a rebel. She was oppressed by her father and after that by her first husband. She broke free and found that she and David had a profound connection. To protect her kids, she would never participate with David in any cons, but she certainly wasn't David's Jiminy Cricket. She accepted that his felonious personality was part of his past and a part of his present.

After David married Tina, they moved from her clean but small two-bedroom walkup to a hip, modern apartment complex in Schaumburg with indoor and outdoor swimming pools, tennis courts, a recreation center, and everything that newlyweds could ask for. All courtesy of David's extracurricular activities.

Tina has worked in restaurants all her life. She now works at Arthur Treacher's Fish & Chips for slightly more than minimum wage. David works at a large computer company doing data entry and customer service. Neither job pays well. In the age of yuppies, they're not.

Sunny has kept the name Susan Wilder. She has even managed to get a social security number under that name. She works in credit collections and is very good at it. But she's still a fugitive from justice due to the World's Fair con, and that limits her ability to see her children and grandchildren, even after all these years. And it hurts.

Now, Sunny giggles and teases her way into the kids' bedroom. "Hey, some of my best friends shop at Kmart, and they would kick your butts if you called them that. How about you guys cool it for a while, and I'll let you stay up and watch Benny Hill? Now, who wants to go to the arcade?"

The kids cheer, forgetting their differences.

"Okay. Let me get my coat, and we'll leave after your mom and David leave. Wait here. I'll get my coat."

The coat closet is behind the entrance to the apartment such that when the door to the apartment opens, it blocks the coat closet. Sunny goes to the closet and reaches for her coat.

The pounding at the front door cascades through the apartment.

"FBI! Open the door!"

Tina sprints to the front door before Sunny can react. In one fluid move, with her left hand, she shoves Sunny into the coat closet and closes the door behind her. With her right hand, she opens the front door, blocking the coat closet. "Can I help you?"

Agent Dianne Symmons fills the open door, holding her cred pack. "Where's David?"

David emerges from the living room. "What can I do for you?"

Symmons has done this dance with David at least a dozen times in the past year. "I'm looking for your mother. Do you know where she is?"

Tina slips away to tell the kids to stay in the bedroom.

David says, "You keep asking me the same question, and I keep giving you the same answer. I haven't seen her in years."

Tina comes back. "I'm sorry, but we can't help you. I think she's in California."

Symmons glares angrily at David and Tina. She has no more patience with either of them. "You do know that it's illegal to lie to the FBI. If we find out you're lying, you'll be joining her in prison. Believe it."

David glares back. "And you think that I wouldn't rather go to jail than turn in my own mother? I'm sorry; you must have had a horrible childhood."

Symmons moves toward David with blood in her eyes. "When I put you away, I'll make sure the judge fucks you so hard that you'll already be the bitch of your cell block."

David steps forward. Symmons's partner emerges from behind her and puts his hands on her shoulders to guide her back. He releases his gentle hold on Symmons, reaches into his breast pocket, and retrieves a card. He gives it to Tina. "If you hear anything, please let us know."

Without expression, Tina takes the card. "Yeah, right."

Symmons stalks down the apartment hall and says to her partner, "Let's stake the place out for a night. I have a feeling that she's going to be here. Did you see how dressed up they were?"

Her partner holds the exit door. When they hit the evening air, he stops. Symmons also stops and turns to face him. He lights a cigarette and offers one to her. They light up off of one match. "I did, but I have plans, Dianne. And I just don't have time to keep going down this same rabbit hole."

Symmons clenches her jaw and stares at her partner with narrow eyes. "Screw you too. These guys must be brought to justice." She steps ahead and stalks to the car before they drive off.

David and Tina let Sunny out of the closet. Tina flashes a warm smile at Sunny and helps her off the closet floor. "Sorry, Sunny."

"Don't apologize. You saved my bacon again."

Tina turns to face David. Her voice is tight with exasperation. "David, we need to do something. We can't keep going on like this. Sunny, you should stay the night. No going out with the kids. Order pizza or something for dinner."

Sunny extends her lower lip in a pout. "Of course. I'll tell the kids we'll do the arcade another time. Time to break out the Nintendo."

It's a fundamental law of electricity and electrical circuits that electrons take the path of least resistance in a circuit. That law also applies to the criminal mind. Whether a bank robber, a drug dealer, a hitman, or a con man, the more a criminal succeeds at crime, the easier it is to go back to it. It becomes the criminal's path of least resistance and the path he or she falls back on.

So it is with David. Before the beginning of his journey, rules and laws felt like they were etched into his DNA.

He was as tight as a new pair of dress shoes. Now, laws and rules are more like suggestions, and not even strong ones. He tries to be responsible, but only if it's convenient. Unless there is a cop following him, even a speed limit is nonexistent.

And David wants to make his family happy. He spent a long time off the grid without training in any career option. Tina's ex has a lucrative business. It seems like Tina's every relation and friend own a successful restaurant. Even with both David and Tina working, they can't afford the monthly bills that are mounting up. What's a con man to do?

David's solution is to target various personal finance companies, like the one he used to work for. Every other month, he sets up an identity and phony credit file in a midwestern state, applies for the maximum twenty-five-hundred-dollar signature loan, and clears about two grand after all expenses. He uses random locations and random identities. It pays for the apartment and keeps their heads above water, but that's about it.

When David and Tina return from the wedding, Sunny is asleep on the couch. David walks over and gently wakes her. "Mom, can I talk with you?"

Sunny opens her eyes, stretches, and sits up, instantly alert. "Sure, baby. What's up?"

Tina checks that the children are asleep and comes in with a glass of wine to join them. "Is this a private conversation, or can anyone join?"

"Not private at all. I have a plan, and I want your opinions."

Tina and Sunny go to the small dining room and take seats at the table. David goes into the master bedroom and comes out with the tiny credit application from the Riviera Casino. He hands it to Sunny. "Remember this?"

Sunny takes the paper and half smiles. "Yeah, if we wanted a credit line at the casino, we just needed to fill this out." She hands the form to Tina.

David looks at Tina, who sips her glass and places it on the table.

He picks up the form and hands it back to Tina. "Right. What information do they want, honey?"

Tina reads the form: "Occupation, income, and bank account information."

"And what information doesn't it call for?

Sunny and Tina look blankly at David.

"No credit checks. No references."

David lays out the new plan to go back after the Vegas casinos.

PART VIII - ATLANTIC CITY, NEW JERSEY

CHAPTER 49

SUNNY remembers Sammy D at the Riviera. Even the memory of him makes her shudder. "David, we already took our run at Las Vegas. I don't know if it's smart to go back there. Frankly, it terrifies me."

"This is a completely different plan. We get in and get out. No shows, no meals, just take the money and run."

"I get that, but still…."

David gently touches Sunny's leg to stop her. "How about this? We go to Las Vegas and collect credit applications for the casinos we want to hit. We won't do anything wrong. Just stay as tourists and get the applications. No danger there. Right?"

Sunny stares blankly out the window. "I guess."

Tina smiles. "A Vegas vacation. I like that."

"Before we go to Las Vegas, we set up two casinos in Atlantic City. Those casinos just opened about a year ago. We don't even know if there is mob influence there. You would think that new casinos would want to avoid that reputation, with the government regulators scrutinizing every interaction."

David catches Sunny's eye and offers her a comforting smile. His face shows total confidence. "We let Tina fly home from Las Vegas with the credit applications. We fly directly to someplace near Atlantic City and try the plan as proof of concept. Afterward, we can talk about going back to Las Vegas. If we decide to go back to Las Vegas, we'll already have the credit applications to get started, and we'll know that the plan works."

Tina takes another sip of wine. "That sounds like a good compromise."

Sunny nods. "Yes. I like that idea better. We won't go back to Las Vegas unless the plan works in Atlantic City." She then frowns and touches her chin. "Why so much money? Won't that simply make us bigger targets?"

David nods in agreement, but not quite. "I would agree with you given all that we've been through. But I think one big score is safer. We hit them once and we're out." He goes into the bedroom and comes out with classified advertisements from the *Arizona Republic* that he copied from the library. "Check out these businesses for sale. We can start or buy a business that you and Tina know, like a restaurant. It will be larger than the bakery we lost. And we'll have enough capital to make sure we can run the business right this time. And we'll all be together."

Sunny and Tina look at the ads and start to dream of a large family-owned business in Arizona near Ava and David. All the family together.

Sunny looks at David. "What about the FBI?"

"Eventually, the statute of limitations will expire. If we wait long enough, we can bring the whole family under one umbrella and live out the rest of our lives together."

The dream is larger than the perceived risk.

CHAPTER 50

DAVID sets his next personal finance con in Northfield, New Jersey. The twenty-five hundred dollars he gets is staked into the larger casino con. He rents a car, drives to Atlantic City, and casually walks the boardwalk to various casinos. The energy is magnetic. The sea breeze is refreshing and intoxicates him. He buys some original saltwater taffy from a vendor and chews the sweet morsels while he visits the casinos.

As with Las Vegas, the casinos are a kaleidoscope of colors. The crowd is even thicker and more vibrant than in Las Vegas. David blends in and plays low stakes blackjack or roulette.

Soon a hundred dollars drops down to ten. He asks the dealer to call the pit boss over. "Excuse me. Any chance that I can get a credit line?"

The pit boss gets a credit application. "Here, fill this out and bring it to the cashier."

David takes the credit application. It's nearly identical to the one from the Riviera. He puts the application in his pocket and moves on to the next casino. Before the evening ends, he has nine casino credit applications.

Tina picks David up at O'Hare Airport. David puts his overnight bag in the trunk and slides into the passenger seat. No seatbelt. He holds the credit applications in his hand like a winning hand of poker.

"They're the same. We're good to go."

Tina high fives David while she navigates airport traffic looking for the exit.

CHAPTER 51

THE next week, Sunny and David tour office spaces in Barrington, Illinois. They come to a three-story building on a main road. Inside they see offices for consultants, construction companies, and suppliers. They pay the manager a three-hundred-and-fifty-dollar deposit and get the key to a small, empty space with phone access.

They drive down the same road until they find the First National Bank of Barrington. They pull into the parking lot facing the bank. David leans over the steering wheel and peers out the front window at the sign. "I think we can work with that."

Sunny nods in agreement. "Let's go. They probably have cameras on us right now."

The next day, they find an answering service in Barrington that has a residential-sounding address to take direct mail. They pay fifty dollars for two months' service.

The day after that, David uses a pay phone at Dunkin Donuts to order a phone for the office. He calls the Illinois Bell business number. "I need to order a business line, please."

"Certainly. Can I get the address?"

David gives her the address of the office they rented.

"And the name of the business?"

He pauses a beat before answering. "First Bank of Barrington."

"And the nature of the business?"

"Banking and finance."

"I can have the phone installed this week. What type of equipment do you need?"

David gives a thumbs up to Sunny, who returns the salute. "At least two stations with the ability to put callers on hold."

As an afterthought, he adds, "I also need a personal telephone line at the address. Unlisted."

The operator puts David on hold. When she returns, she says, "The rental price of the equipment will be thirty-five dollars a month with a one-month security deposit."

"Agreed. We'll pay with the first invoice."

The phone equipment is delivered in two days. Sunny and David are there to accept the delivery of the phone equipment. David plugs the phones into the wall connections and gets dial tones. Sunny goes to a local department store and purchases two folding chairs and two folding tables, and they set up their stations.

For the next part of the plan, David calls the First National Bank of Barrington.

"First National Bank of Barrington, can I help you?"

In his most professional voice, he says, "Yes. Can I get your routing number?"

The operator complies. David writes it down on an index card and tapes it to one of the folding tables for future reference.

David and Sunny sit at another card table with the credit applications spread out on top like a deck of cards waiting to be scuffed. David picks through the papers. "Which ones should we use?"

Sunny slides a couple in front of her side of the table to read. They're identical except for the names of the casinos. "This is a proof of concept, so let's keep it short. You pick one, and I'll pick one. We'll each apply at each casino."

It doesn't take David long. "Okay. I choose the Playboy Club and Casino."

Sunny rolls her eyes at David's obvious choice. She quickly follows. "I choose Harrah's Casino."

They fill out the credit applications in less than five minutes. The name is their alias du jour. David's occupation is a chemical engineer. Sunny is a public relations manager. Their home address is the answering service. Their home phone number is the personal unlisted line. Their bank is the First Bank of Barrington. The bank's address and phone number are the office with the directory listing of First Bank of Barrington. If anyone calls directory assistance, they'll find the bank listed; therefore, it's legitimate.

The bank balance on the applications is one hundred thousand dollars. They each seek a fifty-thousand-dollar line of credit at each casino. They mail the applications directly from the Barrington post office and wait. They spend every banking hour at the office and plan for the eventual trip to Atlantic City. They only wait a few days for the fish to bite.

The bank phone rings. Sunny answers, "First Bank of Barrington."

A pleasant male voice says, "This is the Playboy Club and Casino in Atlantic City. I need to do a balance check."

"One moment please." Sunny presses the hold button.

David waits for ten to twenty seconds and picks up the line. He drops the tone of his voice an octave. "May I help you?"

The casino voice is rapid, like a teenager waiting for their special someone to call. "This is the Playboy Club and Casino in Atlantic City. I need a balance check on..." He gives the alias.

"One moment please." David presses the Pause button. It's a short pause before he reconnects. "It looks like he has a mid-six-figure balance."

The casino voice pauses for a few seconds. "Thank you. And what is your routing number?"

David reads from the card with the routing number for the First National Bank of Barrington. The name is close enough to the fake First Bank of Barrington that it's never distinguished.

"Thanks. I appreciate the help."

Within an hour, the personal phone in the office rings. David uses his regular voice. "Hello?"

The casino voice is a perky female. David pictures the Playboy ears and bunny tail on the caller. "Hello. This is the Playboy Club and Casino in Atlantic City. How are you today?"

David chuckles softly. "Fine."

"You applied for a credit line of fifty thousand dollars."

"Yes. I plan to vacation there soon, and I wanted to make sure I have a backup line in case I don't bring enough money to gamble."

"I'm pleased to inform you that your credit line has been approved. Just show your identification to the cashier, and she'll make the chips available to you."

"Thank you. I look forward to the visit."

And so it goes. Each application is approved for fifty thousand dollars: two for David and two for Sunny. Two hundred thousand dollars on the line.

CHAPTER 52

LESS than two weeks later, Sunny, David, and Tina pack their bags and fly out to Las Vegas. They stay at Bally's Hotel on the strip and visit downtown where the casinos are bunched together like eggs in a carton. David and Sunny pick up a credit application at every casino cashier. On the strip, they visit five casinos a day for five days. On Friday, David counts the credit applications. He tells Tina and Sunny, "I have thirty."

Sunny says, "I have thirty-two."

David does the calculations in his head. "Round yours to thirty, Mom. We know we can get approved easily for fifty thousand dollars. If we even ask for a thirty-thousand-dollar line, we're looking at a one-million-eight-hundred-thousand-dollar payoff."

In the silence, they can practically hear Tina's jaw drop open.

Sunny stares out the window at the Las Vegas strip view. "Let's make it fifteen thousand per application. Nine hundred thousand dollars. If it works out in Atlantic City, why not?" She stares at the strip skyline. "It's beautiful here. You realize if we succeed, we can never come back?"

David also looks out at the lights of the strip. "Of course, we can. Only we'll be legitimate high rollers. Okay, fifteen thousand dollars per application. Almost a million dollars in cash."

The following day, they take a taxi to McCarran International Airport. Tina flies back to O'Hare and goes home. David and Sunny fly directly to the Philadelphia International Airport. The flight takes hours. They try to sleep on the plane, but they can't.

Once they land, David pulls their bags out of the overhead bin. He peers blearily at Sunny. "Where do you want to stay?"

Sunny yawns and stretches as best she can in the airplane aisle. "I don't care. Somewhere generic."

At the Arrivals gate, David flags down a taxi. He carries the bags into the back seat behind the driver. Sunny slides in next to him.

The taxi driver hits the meter. "Where to?"

Sunny rolls down her window and sniffs the fresh air. "Holiday Inn. Whichever one is closest."

A half hour later, David and Sunny are unpacking and freshening up in a generic Holiday Inn room. They've been on a plane or in an airport since early morning. They can barely keep their eyes open.

Sunny looks at David. His eyes are bloodshot. "It's about sixty miles to Atlantic City. How do you think we should travel?"

David calls the front desk.

A pleasant female voice answers, "Front desk."

"Hello. Do you have transportation to Atlantic City?"

"Not directly. If you want, a bus will be by in thirty minutes with an Atlantic City destination."

David tells Sunny, "Maybe we should take a nap first."

Sunny goes into the bathroom and splashes cold water on her face. She comes out holding a hotel towel. "Could you sleep on the bus?"

David slaps his own face. "Yeah. I probably could."

They put on their disguises. David wears a black blazer and Jordache jeans over a white button-down shirt and black-frame glasses. It's the outfit he expects a straight chemical engineering nerd would wear. Sunny wears a tomato-red linen suit jacket over a white silk crepe blouse and beige soft leather pants. It's what she imagines a public relations guru would wear. They head to the lobby and just make the bus before the driver closes the door. They take a seat right behind the driver.

In the seat, they put their heads together and close their eyes, but despite the soothing vibration of the road, sleep still eludes them. People come and go. The driver tells passengers what stops on which to get off. After twenty minutes, they just stop trying.

The bus gets to Atlantic City close to midnight. They arrive near the boardwalk, and their adrenaline surge chases away the drowsiness like a morning mist.

David practically springs out of the bus. "Are you ready to get rich?"

Sunny steps cautiously onto the driveway. "Don't get cocky. We do this just as we planned."

They walk down the boardwalk to the Playboy Club and Casino and split up. Sunny posts herself near some easily recognized slot machines.

David goes to the cashier. "Hello. I have a credit line that I'd like to draw down on."

It's a weekend, and the crowd is thick. The cashier goes through the motions. "Do you have your driver's license?"

Of course. David has more driver's licenses than the casino has slot machines. He takes out the appropriate identification and hands it to the cashier, who disappears into the back. Chills go up David's spine and goosebumps form on his forearms until the cashier returns with a form.

"Please sign here."

David signs the form.

The cashier addresses David like he ordered a to-go burger at McDonald's. "How much do you want in chips?"

"Five thousand."

"Denomination?"

"Twenty-fives and hundreds."

David takes the green and black stacks of chips in a tray and settles in at a roulette table. He loses five hundred dollars in less than twenty minutes. He looks at his remaining chips and shakes his head, feigning dissatisfaction. He casually wanders as if he wants a better table and goes to the slot machines where Sunny stands by. He gives the remaining chips to Sunny, and she cashes them at another window.

David repeats the process ten times in five-thousand-dollar increments. After adjusting for gambling losses, he clears forty-two thousand dollars in cash. He goes to a crowded blackjack table.

The dealer finishes her round and looks up. "Place your bet, sir?"

"Actually, where can I get an authentic cheesesteak sandwich?"

The dealer takes no time to answer. "The best cheesesteaks are at the White House."

David looks puzzled. "The White House? Like in Washington, DC?"

The croupier chuckles. She's seen that confusion before. "No. Just tell any cab driver you want to go to the White House. They'll take care of you."

With that excuse, David cashes out what's left of his chips and heads out. Sunny meets him in front of the casino. They do go to the White House, and the cheesesteaks are as scrumptious as advertised. Then they flag down a taxi and have it take them to Harrah's.

At Harrah's, they switch roles. David hangs out by a gift shop, and Sunny plays the tables with her credit line. She meets David, and David cashes the chips. Out of boredom, he starts playing low stakes blackjack. He feels a hand on his shoulder.

"Let's go." Sunny tugs at him as gently as a Madonna.

Bleary-eyed, David turns. "Are we done?"

"You are. You're too tired. I'm tired too."

David shakes the sleep from his head. "I'll be fine. Let's finish up."

Sunny's face is solemn and stone-like. "You're too tired."

"I am not."

"I just watched you take a hit on a pair of queens against the dealer's five."

David picks up his chips. "Okay. You win."

Out of the corner of her eye, Sunny sees the pit boss talking to the dealers near her. "I'm getting a bad vibe. Let's go now."

They get to the front of the casino. The bus that they came in on won't be back for at least forty-five minutes. Sunny is wearing a trench pacing on the gaudy rug. Every sight and sound is a threat. David suspects that he isn't the only one who needs rest.

Then he sees the solution: a sign near the front desk for a limousine service with a ten-minute pickup. He calls the number and fifteen minutes later, he and Sunny are both sound asleep in a stretch limo traveling the sixty-five miles back to the Holiday Inn in Philadelphia.

The next day, they sleep ten hours and wake up refreshed and excited that they're ninety thousand dollars richer. They even enjoy a free buffet breakfast before they head to the airport.

At O'Hare, they split up. Sunny insists that David keep sixty thousand dollars. Six hundred one-hundred-dollar bills. David takes a taxi home and when Tina meets him at the door, he throws the bills into the air and makes it rain. He wonders how much larger the paper rain cloud will be when they come back from Las Vegas.

CHAPTER 53

IT isn't fair to say that Dianne Symmons is obsessed with Sunny or David personally. She's simply fixated on justice. It's how she's wired. But these two have eluded her justice for too long. They're like splinters that she can't extract. After her partner pissed on her plans for a stakeout, Symmons periodically drives solo around David's apartment complex.

At about one in the morning, a week after David and Sunny arrive back from Atlantic City, Symmons takes a flashlight and approaches David's car in the dark parking lot. Its bright beam pierces the smudged car windows and illuminates the interior. Symmons feasts her eyes on stained seats, a grimy dashboard, and fast-food containers all over the passenger and rear floors. The rear bench seat resembles her own chaotic desk except covered with garbage, receipts, crumpled papers, and more fast-food containers.

But Symmons is focused. She's looking for something. Anything out of the ordinary. Some clue as to where Sunny might be. Her light flashes on a shiny black object on the floor between a crumpled Filet-O-Fish wrapper and a discarded White Castle box. Symmons squints and after fifteen or twenty seconds, she recognizes it: a black one-hundred-dollar casino chip. She focuses even harder to make out the center of the chip. The identity of the casino? A Playboy bunny.

Symmons can't sleep that night. Her first call of the day is to the Playboy Casino in Atlantic City. She calls over and over and sucks on her cigarette like a hungry baby sucks on a bottle while she waits for someone to talk with.

"Hello, Playboy Hotel and Casino Atlantic City."

"This is Dianne Symmons with the FBI. Can I talk to one of your loss prevention specialists?"

There is a long pause. "Hold on please."

A shorter pause, and a low male voice sounds in the receiver. "Ms. Symmons, this is the casino manager. What can I do for you?"

Symmons crosses her fingers. "Have you had any recent thefts?"

"I don't know how to answer that. We're a casino. Everyone tries to steal from us. Cheaters, card counters, embezzlers, boyfriends of bunnies... You need to be more specific."

"I have it on good authority that you were visited by a couple of con artists. I don't know what their game was or when exactly they were there. It was probably recently. Have there been any unusual activities? Any unusual losses?"

The casino manager puts the phone down to sign some vouchers. When he returns, he says, "No unusual activities. The only unusual loss was a guy who hasn't yet paid a substantial gambling debt."

Symmons lights a new cigarette off the one in her mouth and crunches the old one in a black metal ashtray buried on her desk. "Was this a regular customer?"

"Hold on a minute." The casino manager puts Symmons on hold and calls for the credit application. "Ms. Symmons, I think you might be onto something. This was the customer's first time here. He used a fifty-thousand-dollar line of credit and skipped. Do you know where we can find him?"

Symmons jumps out of her chair with excitement. "Maybe. Can you fax me a copy of that credit application?"

"Of course. Please keep me informed."

Symmons calls the other Atlantic City casinos and finds out that Harrah's was also hit for the same amount, on the same night, by a woman. The investigation turns up the two unused credit lines. Questions plague Symmons's thoughts. *Why didn't they take the rest of the money? David could have gone to Harrah's and Sunny to Playboy. Did something spook them? Where did they stay in Atlantic City?*

Symmons goes into brainstorming mode. She stands at a whiteboard and scribbles her theories with multicolored markers. Will they hit other casinos in Atlantic City? Definitely not. Will they repeat the con? Maybe. If so, where?

The where is pretty much a gimme. When it comes to gambling, there are several places to go, but the all-time champion is—may I have the envelope please—Las Vegas. If they're going to repeat the con, that's where it will be.

Symmons knows what must be done, but she needs to involve her supervisor, Bruce Aaron. Symmons waits twenty minutes outside Aaron's office. She paces. She drums her fingers on the side table next to the chair. She crosses and uncrosses her legs and chain smokes to her last cigarette. Aaron opens the door, and two agents spill out of the office.

Aaron beckons Symmons to come in and sit down. He takes his seat behind the desk and leans forward on his elbows. "What case are we discussing, Dianne?"

"The Rossi matter. The case that originated from the governor of New Orleans."

"Yes." Aaron sits back in his chair with a disgusted expression, as if Symmons farted and left shit on his carpet. "The one that the Honorable Governor Edwards wanted handled right away. Isn't that case cold now? Don't you have more important cases to pursue? How many cases are on your current load?"

"Over fifty. But Aaron, these guys have been all over the country ripping off businesses, and now they have their sights set on Las Vegas casinos."

Aaron leans back in his chair. "Do you have proof?"

Symmons looks down at her shoes and takes a long pause. She looks back up and meets Aaron's gaze. "They stole a hundred grand from Atlantic City. I think we can catch them in the act in Las Vegas. I just know they're going to hit there."

Aaron shuffles some papers to show her that the conversation is over. "Vegas can take care of itself. They have security everywhere."

Symmons stays seated. She leans in and covers half the desk with her torso. "If my hunch is right, they won't have security against this." She lays out her understanding of what she has not so affectionately named the Casino Credit Heist. "I want permission for a warrant to obtain copies of all credit applications over five thousand dollars received by Las Vegas casinos in the past month and going forward for sixty days. And I want FBI presence at all those casinos when and where we suspect they'll show up."

Aaron peers at Symmons over his reading glasses. "Damn it, Symmons, do you know how many hours of work that will take? How many credit applications will that include? Hundreds? Thousands? And a presence at potentially every casino? Are you insane? I can't afford those resources. And frankly, we're still getting over the stigma of this Unabomber prick. And the Tylenol Killer."

Symmons holds her hands folded in supplication. Her voice is urgent. "Aaron. Do you know how much money they can get away with if they succeed? As much as a million dollars. Please have my back on this. Do me this favor. I promise, you won't be sorry."

Aaron's face softens. Symmons has never once in all the years she has worked for him asked for a favor. "I'll have to convene a meeting."

Dianne stands up, heads for the door, and turns around. "Will you recommend it?"

Aaron stands up and makes a shooing motion toward the door. "Yes, Dianne, I will recommend it. Put together your plan. Now get the hell out of my office."

CHAPTER 54

SUNNY pulls into the parking lot of David's new burger fixation, the Schaumburg Fuddruckers Restaurant. As she passes through the double doors, she sees David already at the condiment counter. She watches him dress his half-pound burger in ketchup, mustard, diced onions, lettuce, and tomato. Then she saunters up beside him and catches his eye.

David feels her presence and doesn't even turn around. "Hi, Mom."

Sunny's face lights up. "Hi, son." She gives him a half-hug because his hands are full.

David goes to a table in the back of the dining area. Sunny goes to the front and orders a chicken sandwich.

Sunny feels fortunate that she can drive directly to meet David. For David, driving to meet Sunny is like going on a scavenger hunt because he never knows when the FBI is following. It's drive here, stop there, go to every indirect destination to make sure he's not followed. Sunny settles at David's table.

David sets down his plate of food. He picks up his messy burger and talks before taking his first leaky bite. "Mom, have you given more thought to Las Vegas?"

Sunny's eyes glance nervously around the room. "I have, and it's tempting. It's so tempting. But it's so much money at once. You're talking about a million dollars."

"So, it's the amount that bothers you? You get in the same trouble for ten thousand or a million. I'd rather we make a million for our troubles. It went well in Atlantic City, right?"

The counter calls Sunny's alias. "Susan, please pick up your chicken sandwich."

Sunny excuses herself and picks up her sandwich. She dresses it in lettuce, onion, and mayonnaise, grabs a cup of black coffee, and balances her tray back to the table.

David takes a sloppy bite out of his burger. "I asked about Atlantic City."

Sunny takes a bite of her sandwich. "It did go well. This just seems, I don't know; too good to be true, I guess."

She grabs some paper towels from a roll on the table and gives them to David to blot orangish mustard from his shirt. "How about this? We set the foundation for Las Vegas. Get the office and the phones, send in the credit applications, and only then do we talk about it further. How does that sound?"

"Like a step in the right direction." David knows that once the work is done, the decision to do the Las Vegas con will be easier for her.

* * *

David takes vacation time the following week, and they travel to Milwaukee, Wisconsin and repeat what they did in Barrington. They open a small office. The First National Bank of Wisconsin occupies the largest building in the state. They order phones and acquire a listing under a similar name, the National Bank of Wisconsin. They set up their phone stations and send in sixty credit applications, each with a credit limit request of seventeen thousand dollars, a total of one million dollars plus an extra twenty thousand for gambling and expenses.

Soon the calls come in from casino representatives chasing after gamblers like paparazzi chase after celebrities. Sunny and David spend forty-eight hours playing phone theater with the casino credit departments. They sleep at the office eating cold pizza to make sure they're present if the credit departments decide to call their personal phone line in the evening.

When the dust settles, Sunny drives David back to Illinois. "It sure seems to me like they want us to take their money. Every credit application is approved."

David puts the passenger seat back and closes his eyes for a well-deserved rest. "You feel more comfortable with the decision to go in?"

Sunny checks her speed. The last thing she wants is a ticket driving away from a soon-to-be crime scene. "Yeah. I guess I do. When do you want to go?"

"Let's give it a few weeks. I'll make sure it works for Tina."

Sunny says nothing for several minutes. "Let's tentatively get tickets and reservations for the last Saturday of the month."

David opens his eyes and imagines his schedule. "I should be able to take another couple of days' vacation. Sure, that sounds good."

Sunny laughs into the steering wheel. "Honey, after that trip, it won't matter. Every day will be a vacation."

* * *

The next week, David gets a call from an old high school friend he hasn't seen since he left Florida. "David Adler?"

David doesn't know the voice and doesn't like surprises. He answers with suspicion. "Yes?"

"Been a long time. It's Jason Cohen. Remember me?"

David's smile beams in sudden recognition. "Yeah, Jase. Long time, what's happening?"

"What's happening is our ten-year reunion. I had a hell of a time finding you. I'm on the reunion committee, and I wanted to invite you to come party with us." The date Jason gives is the last Saturday of the month.

David's smile collapses. "I'd love to come, but I have plans."

"Don't say that. Everyone wants to spend time with you. Please try to be there."

David takes a deep breath. "I'll let you know. Give me a good number to reach you."

He goes to a pay phone and calls Sunny. He tells her about the call and that he would love to go to the reunion party. "I'd love to bring Tina and introduce her to some of my old friends. Should we put off the Vegas trip?"

Sunny lowers her gaze. Through pursed lips, she says, "How about this? We're scheduled to be in Las Vegas at two in the afternoon. You go to your reunion party and catch a redeye out of Miami International Airport. We'll start bright and early the next morning."

David's eyes brighten back up with his mother's compromise. "Yeah, that works. Tina can fly back to Illinois, and I'll fly straight to Las Vegas. But promise you won't start without me?"

Sunny crosses her fingers. "I promise. You only get one ten-year reunion. Enjoy it."

The last Saturday of the month, Sunny posts herself at the Circus Circus Hotel and Casino. As much as any Las Vegas resort can be called a family place, that is what Circus Circus seems to pride itself on. Circus acts perform constantly to the delight of children, and they maintain a video game room to take children's minds off the fact that they can't play the ubiquitous multi-colored games in the casino. It's far from the fanciest hotel on the strip, but for Sunny and David, it's reasonably central to the strip and downtown. They can strike out either north or south and start collecting chips.

David is at the Dunes Hotel just north of Miami Beach. The night before his reunion, he and Tina take in the hilarious *Tubby Boots* show before a terrific dinner at the Newport Beach Hotel next door. At a prearranged time, right before his reunion party, he calls Sunny from his hotel room to hers.

"How are you doing, Mom?"

Sunny is breathing harder than normal. She tries to keep her voice steady. "More important is, how are you doing? How's your party?

David holds the phone in one hand and his name badge in the other. "I feel like I'm on top of the world. Yesterday was perfect. Tonight, I'll introduce my beautiful wife to some of my best friends, and tomorrow, we'll collect enough money to put all our problems behind us. What could be better?"

Sunny says nothing for several seconds. "Honey, I'm going to get started tonight."

David collapses onto a chair. His voice is a shout. "No! Mom, you promised not to start without me! We need to watch each other's backs."

A single tear escapes Sunny's right eye. "You just told me what a great time you're having. Don't worry. Let me get started and when you get here, we can finish up and go home. You just enjoy yourself."

David knows it's useless to argue. "I'll call you in three hours. Will you make sure to get back by then, so I know you're all right?"

Sunny draws a huge breath and shakes the anxiety out of her body. "Of course, son. Just enjoy yourself."

David thinks, *I would enjoy myself more if I knew she was safe in her hotel room.* But he goes to the reunion party. His old friends share stories about him with Tina. They dance to music from the sixties and disco. He introduces

Tina to girls he dated and some he wishes he'd dated. It turns out to be a fantastic time.

Three hours into the party, David excuses himself, finds a pay phone, and pays five dollars in quarters for a call to the Circus Circus. The hotel operator connects him to Sunny's room.

A man answers. David swallows hard. "Who is this?"

"This is FBI Agent Johnson."

David hangs up. He knows his mother is in custody. The evening, the past years, his whole life is deflated. All he can do is sob while Tina holds him. He knows his journey is over. He never returns to the party. The next morning, he goes back to Illinois with Tina. He won't talk. He sits up every sleepless night staring out a window, his eyes filled with tears. If he listens hard enough, he can swear he hears a pack of wolves outside circling in for the kill.

The following Monday, David takes the remaining Atlantic City money and hires a lawyer for his mother and one for himself. He knows that it's only a matter of time before he'll also be arrested.

The next day, he goes to work. He doesn't make it past the lobby. The receptionist can barely look at him. Her voice cracks as she says, "Human Resources wants to see you in the conference room."

David leans into her desk and lowers his voice. "What's going on?"

"I don't know," the receptionist lies.

He enters the conference room. At the table are his supervisor, a balding man in his late thirties with a face that perpetually looks like he's sucking on a pickle, who wears a black Izod polo shirt, the Human Resources director, cuffs rolled up to his elbows on his blue button-down dress shirt with no tie and, surprisingly, a court reporter typing on a strange-looking device.

The court reporter speaks first. "Can I get everyone's names for the record?"

David automatically responds, "David Adler."

"Cliff Gunderson, Human Resources."

"Frank Savalas, Customer Services supervisor."

The court reporter stops typing. "Thank you."

Cliff Gunderson picks up a file folder. The court reporter resumes typing. "Mr. Adler, I regret to inform you that your employment here is terminated." He slides papers to David. "You are entitled to two weeks of severance and your accumulated unused vacation time. Here is a check for that amount."

Gunderson waits for David to look at the papers he has just received. Then he pulls out a document from his stack and points to David's paperwork. "If you wish to continue our health insurance, this is the paperwork you will need to fill out. Do you have any questions?"

David glares at each of them across the table. "Yeah. Why am I being terminated without any notice? What did I do?"

The two men exchange uneasy glances. Gunderson speaks up while Savalas looks everywhere but at David. "We can't go into anything at length. We have government contracts and can't afford to go out on a limb for you or anyone."

David stands up and snarls at the group. "Where are my personal things?"

Savalas's pickle-pucker mouth opens. "I gave all your property to the FBI. They requested it. It was on our property, and I complied." He slides a card across the table. "You can call this agent if you have any questions."

The card is from Agent Dianne Symmons.

CHAPTER 55

A phone rings at Symmons's cubical. "FBI Agent Symmons."

"FBI Agent Platt."

Symmons smiles. She always has time to share her day, her job, and her life with her first partner, friend, and mentor. No one is closer to her.

"I just wanted to congratulate you on saving Las Vegas," Dale says.

Symmons leans back in her chair. Her smug smile betrays her satisfaction. "You heard about that?"

"Everyone on the inside heard about that. I hear that the only reason it didn't make the news was to protect the casinos from other would-be con artists who might do the same thing."

Symmons takes out a cigarette and puts it unlit between her lips. "That's okay. I don't do this for publicity."

"Well, I want you to know that I'm proud of you."

She lights the cigarette, puffs, and blows a stream of smoke. "Thanks, Dale. I'm just glad I have you around." Her voice trails off for a few seconds.

"Hey, what's wrong, kid?"

"It's just that the job isn't done. We got the mother, but the son is still out there doing fuck knows what. I won't be satisfied until he joins her behind bars. Then this case will finally be done."

"Don't you have his signature on the credit applications?"

Symmons pulls out a credit application from the middle of a seemingly random pile. "Yeah, and it's the same signature that he uses in all his crimes. But they're in different names, and no one at the casinos can pick him out of a photo array. I think he was wearing some disguise."

"Can't you get a court order for handwriting samples? Like we did in Utah? If a handwriting expert identifies the credit application signature to the handwriting exemplars, you might have a case right there."

Symmons sits forward on her rolling chair. One hand slaps the desk and the other drops her half-smoked cigarette in the ashtray. "Dale, that... is... brilliant. I have hundreds of his signatures tied to different crimes over the past few years. All of them have been dead ends, but with an expert witness, I may be able to get Legal interested. When are you going to be in town?"

"Soon. We need to extradite a bank embezzler from Illinois to Ohio. Maybe we can get together either before or after."

Symmons taps her pack of Lucky Strikes and pulls a new one out with her lips. She lights it up and breathes in hard. "Count on it, Dale. We'll spend the evening together."

She writes up a request for the legal liaison to get a court order for handwriting exemplars from David.

If David seemed unresponsive and depressed when Sunny was arrested, he's absolutely robotic when he loses his job. He sleeps nonstop. Nothing matters anymore. He barely eats. Tina wishes he drank or smoked pot or something, thinking maybe that would help.

The knock at the door, mercifully, comes while Tina is at work and the kids are at school. David answers. A tall, very thin man wearing a Brooks Brothers suit stands at the entrance. "Are you Mr. Adler?"

David stands at the door like he's on Thorazine. "Yes."

He hands David an envelope. "You've been served."

David opens the envelope and looks at the document. He calls his lawyer. They meet the next day at the lawyer's downtown Chicago office.

The room is all oak and legal texts, the binders of which are festooned in a cryptic code of indexing that only the learned can decipher. Joseph Sallinger is very learned. In his late fifties with a shock of silver hair, he wears a silver silk tailored suit that looks like it was made for his coif. His skin is as rough and tanned as his well-worn briefcase. He carefully reads the documents served to David.

"This is a court order that requires you to show up at the FBI office in the Dirkson Federal Building to give them samples of your handwriting. This could be a problem. They must have your signature at least on the casino credit applications."

David listens patiently. "Can you get rid of it?"

Sallinger shakes his head. "No. They already have the order. If you don't show up, the judge will probably hold you in contempt. You'll be arrested and held until you comply."

"So, you're saying—"

"I'm saying there's nothing we can do. If the handwriting samples match, as they most likely will, you'll probably be arrested later. We'll have to deal with the consequences. Try to get your bond as low as possible. Attack their evidence."

On the date of the demand, with a heavy heart, David drags himself to the FBI headquarters in Chicago. He waits in a room outside a heavy steel door secured by a numbered keypad from the inner sanctum. As he anxiously walks from one end of the room to the other, he notices, behind a window of bullet proof glass, the receptionist blotting tears from her eyes as she and others watch a news program.

David goes to the window and extends his linen handkerchief to blot her tears. "What's happening? Why is everyone so upset?"

The receptionist waves off the handkerchief offer. With tears streaming down her cheeks, she points to the television screen. "We lost five agents today. They were killed in a plane crash this morning bringing a prisoner to Ohio."

David cranes his head to see the television through the thick glass. He furrows his brow. "That's awful. I'm sorry to hear that." But he has an idea based on his theory that an angry cop is a good cop when you're an outlaw. He just doesn't know if he has the balls to pull it off.

Eventually, he's led through a labyrinth of cube dividers into Dianne Symmons's cluttered workspace. She's sitting behind her desk with a space cleared between piles of papers in front of the guest chair for David to work.

Symmons's face is stoic. She has never been much of a crier, but David can see that this tragedy weighs on her soul. She motions for him to take a seat in front of the only space devoid of paper piles.

David sits down at the desk. Symmons gives him a pen and a blank piece of lined paper. He takes the pen in his left, nondominant hand, in case he has to write.

He forces a big smile. "So, Agent, you guys lost some men today, huh?"

Symmons glares at David. Her expression is granite. "Sign your name three times on these lines."

David doesn't write. "You know what that is, right?"

Symmons says nothing.

He leans in. "A very good start."

Symmons growls. "Shut up."

Once started, David knows he's all in with this angle. "Who'd you guys hire to fly the plane? Captain Kangaroo?"

Symmons leans forward. Her face is now crimson with anger. "I said, just sign the paper and shut the fuck up."

David sees the rage seething. There's no turning back. "Yeah, sure. Now, if some of those agents' whores were on the plane and died, that would be a real tragedy."

Symmons grabs David by the collar of his button-down shirt. Buttons fly off like shrapnel. She drags David to her side of the desk, a whirlwind of papers fluttering to the ground. She spins, and her grip pins him hard to a nearby filing cabinet. She screams, inches from his face, "I said shut your fuckin' mouth!"

David leans his head forward and with a smug smile he hisses in Symmons's ear, "Don't look now, but I think you just did a Bozo no-no. And your mood ring has gone black."

Dianne pulls David toward her and slams him back into the filing cabinet.

He cries out with everything he has. "Help! Someone help!" He turns to Symmons with a tear in his voice. "Don't be mad. I didn't know you hated Jews!"

It takes seconds before people show up, but no one wants to interfere. Was she attacked? Is there a security breach? Does he have a gun? What is going on?

Symmons has too much rage to even talk, much less explain, until Bruce Aaron comes racing around the corner so fast, he slips on the scattered papers. "Symmons! Explain yourself! Let go of him! What the hell is going on?"

Symmons starts to calm. She lets go of David. "What... he... said."

David jumps in. "I just mentioned I was a Jew, and she went crazy." He massages the back of his neck. "I think I have whiplash." He stands up, slumped over like a wilted flower. "I'm leaving to see a doctor unless I'm under arrest or something."

Aaron looks at the cubical. Papers are scattered as if a mini tornado tore through the department. There's a dent in the filing cabinet. David's shirt looks like he suddenly became the Incredible Hulk. And David himself, whether truly or by design, looks helpless and fragile.

"No. You can go." When David passes Aaron, he holds David's arm and says softly, yet with conviction, "I think you're a terrible person. There will be a reckoning for this."

Aaron turns to Symmons. "First, you're going to come into my office and explain yourself. Next, you're going to take the rest of the day off. Don't come back in until I call you. At the very least, I expect you'll be suspended pending an investigation."

Symmons's face is still a mask of rage. "That jagoff said—"

"I don't care what Mr. Adler said. You are the professional. You failed at that, and there will be consequences for those actions."

David leaves and doesn't straighten himself up until he crosses Adams Street headed directly for his attorney's office. His attorney's receptionist takes one look at David and sends him in. David tells his attorney what happened. He leaves out his taunts to Symmons.

Sallinger walks around his desk and helps David into a chair. "Mr. Adler, this is certainly a blessing in disguise for you. I'll file a motion to quash the judge's order based on the FBI's insane treatment of you and what, I will argue, is their continuous harassment. I doubt that the judge will make you go through that again. I may also file a lawsuit in the Court of Claims on your behalf. You might have a civil suit."

David smiles for the first time since his mother was arrested. "Wouldn't that be nice?"

The lawyer calls his secretary in to take photographs of David. He takes the torn shirt from David and sends his secretary to purchase a new one.

CHAPTER 56

SYMMONS goes to all the funerals. She doesn't cry. Some say that sadness and anger are two sides of the same coin. It's the same emotion, but one focused inside and the other focused outside, on others. She saves her anger like a hidden cache of ammunition, and her only target is David Adler.

Aaron suspends Symmons while they investigate what Aaron charitably calls "the incident." Symmons is confident that when she formally explains what pushed her to such rage, she'll be exonerated. But she's humiliated that this prick—this asshole—could get over on her. Worse, because she couldn't keep it in her pants, he just might skate on his crimes.

Dale's funeral was the worst, of course. Symmons knew his wife. They weren't best friends, but she would occasionally join Dale and her for dinner. She spent a holiday or three with them and their kids. Their kids. Two of them. A boy and a girl. All of their worlds ended with Dale's death. And Symmons knows, with frustration, that there are no bad guys to blame for this tragedy. No one to drag to justice or even to civil court.

Through the grief, all she can think of is David's vicious attack. How he used this tragedy to his advantage. And his words. "A good start. Captain Kangaroo. Whores." There are no bad guys to blame. But she vows to Dale that David Adler will not fuckin' get away with it.

Like a stalker, Symmons has kept tabs on Vito Pasquale ever since he had his henchman threaten to ground broken glass in her face. He single-handedly was responsible for her fall as a singer and her career as an FBI agent. He's her boogeyman. He's the tormenting figure in her recurring nightmares Now, she's about to offer him her soul.

* * *

The first thing Symmons thinks as she walks into the lounge is, *This isn't like in the movies. Where's the classy Italian restaurant with pasta, wine, and goons all over the room?* The lounge is a dive bar in a strip shopping mall in Westchester, New York. Symmons scans the dodgy drinkers and sketchy staff until she finds him. Vito Pasquale is sitting at the end of the bar where he can easily see the door. Next to him is a giant of a man in a black suit and skinny red tie who can't fit on the bar stool. He stands to Vito's right; literally his right-hand man. Vito is dressed in a multi-colored sweater and khaki pants. He has grown a full beard and mustache since they last met. The beard is black with gray streaks and makes Vito look even more of a menace.

Symmons approaches Vito and without a word, the giant moves and stands maybe ten feet behind them. Symmons sits next to Vito in the space vacated by the giant. They turn so their conversation is toward the bar.

A customer tries to sit down on a stool next to Symmons.

In one stride, the giant leans over the newcomer and says to him, "I think you'll be more comfortable at the other side of the bar."

The newcomer is about thirty. His black muscle shirt reveals that he gets in plenty of time pumping iron at the gym. He tilts his head upward to look into the giant's eyes. "I just sat down."

The giant calls the bartender over. He turns to the newcomer. "What are you drinking?"

The newcomer takes his eyes off the giant and turns to the bartender. "Rum and Coke."

The bartender delivers the drink. The giant tells the bartender, "It's on the house." The bartender walks away. The giant takes the drink off the bar and holds it out of the newcomer's reach. "We'll play *Let's Make a Deal.* I'm Monte Hall. Door number one, you take this free rum and Coke and enjoy it in peace at the other end of the bar. Door number two, you enjoy this free drink here, without any teeth. You have two seconds to choose."

The newcomer chooses door number one.

Meanwhile, Vito is eyeing Symmons like an alley cat eyes a canary. He sips his own drink. "I know you."

"You used to." Symmons sets her FBI cred pack on the bar between them.

Vito takes a pair of readers from his pocket and reads the identification without touching it. "Dianne Symmons. Yeah, you used to play the piano. Yes?"

Symmons snatches away the cred pack and puts it into her back pocket. "You know damn well I did."

Vito curls his upper lip, unimpressed. "And now you're a federal agent? I know a lot of FBI agents. You aren't here to arrest me. No backup. You aren't here looking to play piano. Although, as I recall, you were pretty good at it. What is it that you want, FBI Agent Dianne Symmons?"

Symmons tries to fix Vito in her gaze, but her eyes wander around the room out of her control. She feels like the floor is moving under her. She knows her next words will seal her fate. "You owe me. I need a favor."

Vito stares at Symmons in smug disbelief. "I don't owe you shit, FBI Agent Dianne Symmons." His voice hits FBI hard. "So, you come to me for a favor?"

Symmons swallows hard. In her fantasies, she pictured domination of this meeting. Now she feels like the frightened eighteen-year-old pinned to the wall with a handful of broken glass mere inches from her face. "Yes. I need a favor. There's a perp. A con man. I need you to help me with him." Vito motions to the giant, who instinctively goes to the bartender and brings Vito a shot of Jack on the rocks. Vito doesn't offer anything to Symmons. "You maybe want him to disappear? Like a ghost?"

Symmons leaps off her barstool. "No! Nothing illegal! At least not like that. No bodily harm. I just need you to lean on him."

Vito smiles, amused. "FBI Agent Dianne Symmons? Why are you here? What do you want from Vito Pasquale?"

Symmons tells Vito the story of David and his crimes. She tells him about David's theft at the New Jersey casinos. She tells him how David pushed her buttons and got out of signing the handwriting exemplars needed to convict him.

Vito listens intently. He makes Symmons wait a full minute before he answers. "And you want me to what? Persuade him to sign?"

Symmons finally meets his gaze. "Exactly."

"And how am I supposed to do that without bodily harm?"

Symmons tells Vito how.

Vito suddenly laughs like he has just won a high-stakes hand of poker. "Ha. Maybe instead, I should offer this David Adler a job. He sounds like a rainmaker."

Symmons smolders in her uncharacteristic vulnerability. "Not funny."

Vito finishes his drink. "Not meant to be. And what's in this for me? You know what my last name, Pasquale, means?"

"No."

"Pasquale means 'friend.' Right now, I'm not your friend. If I do this for you, I'll be your friend, FBI Agent Dianne Symmons. I'll be your friend and you'll owe me a favor. That favor will be in the bank for me to use later. Is that agreed?"

Symmons breathes hard for several moments before she sells her soul. "Agreed."

Vito gets up and motions the giant over. As he leaves, he turns to Simmons. "Stay out of the office. I'll take care of everything. Leave both your and this David Adler's personal number and address with my associate."

The giant takes out a notebook and a pen. They look tiny in his hands. The giant takes Symmons's information and escorts her out of the bar.

CHAPTER 57

THE next morning, David's phone rings. Before he can say hello, a voice tells him, "This is David Adler." The caller knows it his him. It leaves no room for questions. The male voice has some sort of European accent. The tone of voice sounds professional. It has a velvet softness but with an underlying strength that can cut steel.

David sits down. His hand squeezes the phone. "It is."

"We haven't met yet. I represent interests in the casino industry. Specifically, the Playboy Club and Casino. First, congratulations on finding a weakness in our credit security."

"Okay."

"Second, you'll immediately repay every dime you stole in Atlantic City."

Every part of David stiffens. But he knows better than to admit he stole the money. "I don't know what you're talking about. Who is this?"

"You did not file phony credit applications at various Atlantic City casinos?"

David's breath is ragged. "That's right."

"Then you have no reason to be afraid of providing handwriting samples to the FBI."

Now David relaxes a little. He goes to his Rolodex and looks for Sallinger's number. "Who is this?"

"Look, stupid, let me be clear. You have a wife. You have two children. Your mother is in jail. I wish all of them safe, comfortable lives." There is a very long pause while that statement hangs in the air. "I heard from... a friend... how you used a real bitch move to avoid giving the handwriting samples."

David finds the number and growls into the phone. "And just who is your friend?"

"David, shut the fuck up when I'm talking to you."

David shuts the fuck up.

"You have a week to give the FBI the handwriting samples that they need. Capice?"

David says nothing.

"Tell me you understand. I want to hear it."

David understands. "I understand."

"If I hear from my friend in a week that she's still unhappy with you, well, she's not the only one who will be unhappy with you. Your wife, your kids, and your mother will not be happy with you. In fact, you won't be happy with yourself. Goodbye, David Adler. Do the right thing. There won't be a second call."

The phone clicks off, but David can't bring himself to put his handset down. The call seems like a bad dream. He tries to convince himself that it never actually happened. But it did happen, and he knows what he must do. He calls Sallinger and, over his protests, he arranges to voluntarily provide the handwriting samples.

The next day, David goes to the federal courthouse and gives the FBI all the handwriting samples that they requested. He doesn't even try to hide his signature. He won't take any chance that his family or his mother will be placed in jeopardy.

When he's finished, David drives back to his apartment. He eats the burgers and pizza that he knows he'll miss after he gets arrested. He tells his family how much he loves them and hopes that they'll wait for him to get out. He visits his mother and sends money to her commissary account. And he waits.

David thinks this may even be for the best, a chance to truly move on with his life and put the past behind him. Doing his time gets him a clean slate unless, of course, the courts shop him around like an infomercial blender. Then he'll be in prison for the rest of his life.

* * *

In less than a week, while David walks to his car, two men approach him and hold up their cred packs. "FBI. You're under arrest for mail fraud and wire fraud."

Dianne Symmons emerges from the car and tells him to turn around. She puts the cuffs on very tight. As David's hands squirm, she tells him, "You have the right to remain silent…" She finishes reading him his rights as she opens the back door and holds his head while he gets inside.

Symmons enters the other back door and sits next to David, glaring and smiling at him while the two male agents sit in front. David won't give her the satisfaction of complaining about the cuffs or anything else. They drive into Chicago and deposit David at the Metropolitan Correctional Center, where he eventually stands trial and is convicted and sentenced to five years in prison.

EPILOGUE

THE prisoner on the aisle, chained to David's right, looks over David's shoulder at the view out the window. He's older, maybe fifty. His black hair recedes from his hairline like a distant horizon. "Can you believe these fuckers drove to Atlanta to take us from Chicago to Kentucky?"

David doesn't take his eyes off the scenery while he answers. "I just hope they stop somewhere so I can take a piss."

"Yeah, and maybe get some water. How long did you get?"

David turns to face his shackled seatmate. "A nickel. You?"

"A dime. So, you'll be out in—"

"With luck and good behavior? Three to Four."

The older man smiles sympathetically. "Short timer. Do your time, don't get hooked on anything, get in shape, and you'll come out better than you went in."

David looks back out the window. "The hardest part was not knowing whether the sentence would be five years or fifty. Now that I know, I can take it one day at a time."

The older man looks again over David's shoulder at the scenery in silence for several more minutes. Then he asks, not really expecting an answer, "What are you going to do when you get out?"

David looks to his right at the older man and smiles broadly. "Nothing to worry about, my friend, I have a plan."

ACKNOWLEDGEMENTS

WRITING a memoir like this is a gut wrenching endeavor. It could not have been done without the support of my family, and you may not have had the opportunity to read it without the trust and patience of the team at Wild Blue Press. They really have found a better way to help authors publish.

Thank you to Steve Jackson, Michael Cordova, Jazzminn Morecraft, Stephanie Johnson Lawson, Elijah Toten, and Donna Marie West for the opportunity to get this book out.

And a special thank you to Eve Porinchak for her early work and belief that it would succeed, and for the Midwest Writer's Conference in Muncie, Indiana for giving me the confidence to persevere.

For more news about DJ Adler, subscribe to our newsletter at *wbp.bz/newsletter*.

Word-of-mouth is critical to an author's long-term success. If you appreciated this book, please leave a review on the Amazon sales page at *wbp.bz/Adler*.

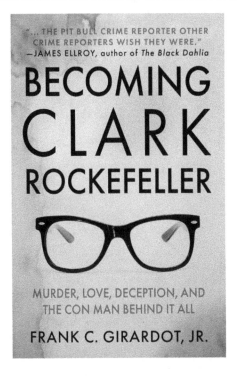

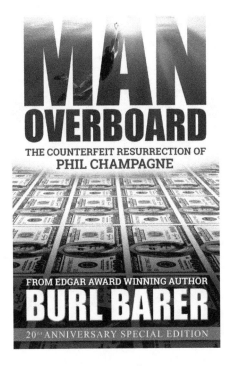

ALSO AVAILABLE FROM WILDBLUE PRESS

https://wbp.bz/manhattan

The true crime story of a family of altruistic jewel thieves and four decades of daring capers and sweet escapes, including a 1992 New York mega-heist.

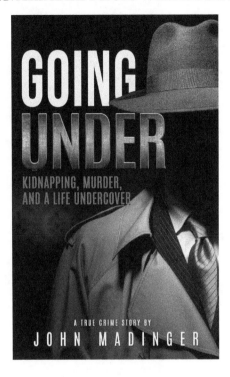